"I'm sorry," Elise whispered. "What must you think of me?"

"That you're the most intriguing woman I've ever known," Drake said as he reached for her hand. "I don't think you're silly. Tell me why you're afraid."

Elise pulled away, a lonely ache forming in her chest at that moment.

"What is it, sweet?" Drake reached for her hand again. "Come back to me. Don't go."

Elise fought the temptation to lean on a person other than herself or her sister. She wanted to open up to Drake, share a deeper bond, but what could she say that wouldn't spur more questions and the revelation of her darkest secrets? She wanted to trust him, but in reality he was little more than a stranger…

Carla Capshaw
and
Louise M. Gouge

The Duke's Redemption
&
The Captain's Lady

HARLEQUIN® LOVE INSPIRED®CLASSICS

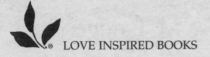

LOVE INSPIRED BOOKS

Recycling programs
for this product may
not exist in your area.

ISBN-13: 978-1-335-45468-3

The Duke's Redemption & The Captain's Lady

Copyright © 2020 by Harlequin Books S.A.

The Duke's Redemption
First published in 2010. This edition published in 2020.
Copyright © 2010 by Carla Hughes

The Captain's Lady
First published in 2010. This edition published in 2020.
Copyright © 2010 by Louise M. Gouge

www.Harlequin.com

Printed in U.S.A.

CONTENTS

Florida native **Carla Capshaw** is a preacher's kid who grew up grateful for her Christian home and loving family. A two-time RWA Golden Heart® Award winner and double RITA® Award finalist, Carla loves passionate stories with compelling, nearly impossible conflicts. She's found inspirational historical romance is the perfect vehicle to combine lush settings, vivid characters and a Christian worldview.

Carla loves to hear from readers. To contact her, visit carlacapshaw.com or write to carla@carlacapshaw.com.

Books by Carla Capshaw

Love Inspired Historical

The Gladiator
The Duke's Redemption
The Protector
The Champion
Second Chance Cinderella

Visit the Author Profile page at Harlequin.com.

THE DUKE'S REDEMPTION

Carla Capshaw

God is our refuge and strength, always ready to help
in times of trouble.
—*Psalms* 46:1

Dedicated to:

My wonderful family. I love each one of you!

My first critique partners—
Carole McPhee, Lydia Hawke and Mary Veelle—who
read and *re*read this book without ever complaining.
Also, Sheila Raye, Paisley Kirkpatrick, Stacey Kayne
and Jean Mason. I appreciate you more than I can say.

As always, thank You, Lord!

Prologue

Charles Towne, South Carolina
December 1780

The cold muzzle of a pistol scraped her temple. The hammer cocked a warning beside her ear. A familiar voice rasped, "Don't move, Fox, or I'll be forced to relieve you of your thinking power."

Elise Cooper froze in the middle of her escape through the tavern's second-story window. Her hands gripped either side of the narrow frame, one booted foot on the floor, one planted on the sill. A chilly, smoke-tinged breeze swept through the open space, ruffling her long cloak and loose black breeches.

Hawk had startled her, but she wasn't concerned about the weapon. The real danger lurked outside. Her gaze never left the moonlit alley that cut behind the tavern. More redcoats crept from the darkness.

"Hawk," she said, thankful her mask helped disguise not only her face, but her voice, "we have no time for your nonsense tonight. Blow out the candle and hurry your pace. Redcoats are infesting the room downstairs and may suspect we're here."

"Of a certainty, they do," he replied. "You've finally been bagged. Your days as a spy have come to an end."

Elise released an exasperated sigh. Hawk, the alias by which she knew him, possessed a fiendish sense of humor. To protect her identity as a woman, she always wore a mask when disguised as the Fox. Though he'd refused to tell her why, Hawk wore one, too. Neither had ever seen the face of the other, but she'd been privy to his games on more than one occasion. She fully expected him to lower the pistol and howl with laughter. He thought himself astoundingly clever, but under the circumstances, she found him most trying. "Cease this, Hawk. We have no time to linger. The English—"

"Are coming," he interrupted gleefully. "Yes, I know. I arranged this meeting. The soldiers are awaiting my signal to make your arrest. I'll be rewarded quite handsomely once I deliver you to my superiors."

Surprised to hear the pride in his voice, she tried to turn and look him in the eye. He jammed the muzzle harder against her temple. "I said don't move."

The menace in his tone convinced her he was serious. Her stomach lurched with fear. Anger blazed through her. "Why hand me over now when you've had the opportunity to do so for well over a year?"

He chuckled. "And give up my play? I think not. Posing as the Hawk has been quite amusing. Sadly, my superiors have ordered your arrest. Since we work so often together, they chose me to do the deed."

Elise bristled at how easily he betrayed her. "And the ransom being offered didn't hurt, I suppose. If I may ask, when did you become a turncoat?"

He stiffened in response. "Turncoat? Not I. My loyalty has always been to my king and England."

Her eyes searched the back alley in hope of seeing a loyal fellow who might aid in her escape. No one appeared save another pair of redcoats. There were eight of them now. Their freshly polished Hessian boots gleamed in the moonlight.

As the gravity of her situation compounded, her thoughts raced in time to her quickening heart. The enemy soldiers moved closer, their indistinct voices carried on the breeze.

"If you're no traitor, explain the many secrets that have passed from your hand to mine?"

"I've shared only what my superiors wanted you rebel scum to know. Remember last month, when I sent you the message about supply wagons leaving Charles Towne for Savannah?"

"Of course." She tried to ease away from the pistol. The Colonial army never ceased being desperate for supplies. At the time, the information she'd carried from Hawk to her spymaster had been considered a boon. "Then the attack *was* a trap. It seemed too coincidental. Did you assist in the murder of those men yourself?"

He laughed. "What do you think?"

She broke into a clammy sweat. If Hawk succeeded in turning her in, she doubted even her gender would save her from hanging.

Dear Lord, please help me.

Four of the redcoats made for the tavern's back door. Her pulse throbbed in her ears as her thoughts shifted frantically. So much began to make sense. How many times had she rendezvoused with Hawk, only to find his information had become mysteriously inaccessible?

Yet, many of his leads had been first-rate. Hawk had earned a glowing reputation within the Patriot ranks. Now she understood why. He'd kept her and her contacts hooked with promises of important information, providing just enough to earn their trust.

"This is ridiculous." She stalled in an effort to reason with him. "There must be a bargain we can strike."

She had to flee, but how? Hawk held a pistol to her head. Soldiers waited below, both inside and out. She could no longer make use of the ladder Josiah had propped outside the window. She'd be shot, either by Hawk or his lobsterback friends before she ever touched the ground.

"Ridiculous?" Hawk's hot, menacing breath fanned the back of her neck. "I disagree. If anything, I find the situation most unfortunate. More than once I wished we weren't on opposing sides in this war. Under different circumstances, you're a man I could respect."

"Then kill me if you plan to. I've no wish to meet my captors, and you know I'll tell them nothing."

"Most likely not. All the same, keep your hands against the panes. 'Tis safer when I can make out where they are."

While she considered her options, she allowed him the liberty of searching her, careful not to give him an impatient trigger finger. His hand dipped beneath her cloak and inside her loose wool coat, feeling for weapons. Waiting for the right moment to strike, she held her breath. She'd bound her breasts with strips of cloth under her billowy black shirt and vest, but failed to flatten them completely. When his hand passed over her chest, she heard his sharp intake of breath. "No! You can't be a woman!"

In one quick movement, she swung her arm and knocked the pistol away from her temple. The foot she had poised on the windowsill slammed downward. Her heel found its mark, crushing his toes. Hawk bellowed in pain. His hold slackened enough for her to face him.

The candle's small flame sputtered in the draft, providing meager light to see the masked man she stood with eye to eye. She rammed her fist into his stomach, winding him. He recovered quickly, raising the pistol an inch from her face. She swiped the barrel away, then tried to wrench it from his grasp.

Hawk released her waist and lashed out with the back of his hand. The blow to her jaw stunned her. She stumbled back in pain, loosening her grip on the weapon as she hit the wall behind her.

"Hold your ground!" Hawk snarled. "I'd hate to shoot a woman, but I will if you force me to."

Staring down the barrel of the pistol, Elise stilled. She could turn and run, making her back a perfect target, or she could stand and fight. Hawk was bigger, stronger, but she was fighting for her life. The redcoats considered a captured spy fair game for hanging. She had no wish to die in so shameful a manner.

Better to take a bullet than dangle in the breeze.

She ducked and threw herself forward, scrambling to reach him before he fired. Leading with her shoulder, Elise plowed into him with the full force of her weight, driving him back several paces until he slammed against a table. Hawk fumbled the weapon and dropped it to the floor, where it landed with a solid thump on the wood planks.

Their eyes locked for an instant. They both lunged for the pistol. Hawk reached it first.

Elise rallied before he took aim and fought with all her might. Her ribs ached. Her jaw throbbed. Fear coursed through her blood. Her arms and legs burned from the exertion of fighting her stronger opponent. Finally, she succeeded in twisting his wrist until the pistol's barrel pointed at his belly.

"Stop this wretched business," she demanded, panting for breath. "Let me go!"

"Ha! Think again, you rebel wench."

He grabbed for her once more, but she sidestepped his advance. With one last effort to disarm him, she aimed her knee and made contact with his groin. He groaned in agony and doubled over. She dug her nails deep into his hand, praying he'd drop the weapon.

A blinding flash of light and a loud explosion jolted Elise. Hawk jerked and groaned in pain. Acrid smoke stung her eyes and nostrils.

"Hawk?" Frozen with shock, Elise stared into his horrified and slowly dimming eyes. The scrap of black silk he wore concealed the rest of his expression.

The firearm slipped from his fingers and thumped on the floor. A bone-chilling gurgle escaped his throat and gapping mouth. He reached for her, his fingers clawing weakly at her upper arms. Another frigid breeze whipped through the small room. The candle flickered out the same moment his body went slack.

In the darkness, he fell toward her. She braced against the wall, her body absorbing his heavy weight as he slid down the front of her and fell to his knees.

"Please Lord, no…." She covered his nose and mouth, searching for breath, but found none. Hawk… dead? The prospect was unimaginable.

As gently as she could, she lowered him to the floor.

Shouting drew her to the window. More redcoats ran
toward the tavern. The shot had warned them to investigate without waiting for his signal. Her cloak swirled
around her as she raced to the dead spy and knelt beside him.

Frantic, Elise reached for his jacket. Moonlight exposed the growing stain of blood on the floor. She'd
never killed anyone. Bile and remorse clogged her
throat. Her hand trembled as it slipped inside the gar-
ment, searching for anything to aid her. Hawk had
planned to deliver her to the English. He must have
some kind of identification to offer them.

His warm blood oozed through her fingers. A sheen
of tears blinded her before she blinked them away. The
bullet had blown a hole in his belly. For him to die so
quickly, it must have also found a vital organ to rup-
ture. She shuddered, fighting nausea when lack of time
denied her the luxury of turning squeamish.

Heavy footsteps pounded on the stairs leading from
the tavern below. Outside her door, she heard multiple
voices, a rattle of keys, the shuffle of boots on wood.

A key scraped in the lock just as her fingers made
contact with a sheet of folded parchment. She pulled it
free of Hawk's inner pocket a moment before the redcoats stormed through the door.

Chapter One

Hawk Haven Manor, England
February 1781

The moment the coach rolled to a stop, Drake Amberly, Fifth Duke of Hawk Haven, shoved open the door and leapt to the cobblestone drive. Icy rain struck his face, ran off the brim of his hat and slid down his neck, under the collar of his greatcoat. He marched up the wide front steps of his family's palatial home, his mood fouler than the weather.

Chaney, his wizened butler, opened the ornately carved front door in perfect time, allowing him to enter the manor's grandiose hall without slowing his pace.

"Good day, Your Grace."

"I've yet to find the good in it." Drake shed his hat and coat before passing them to the efficient servant. He raked his fingers through his black hair and turned in the direction of the sweeping staircase. Changing his mind, he headed for his study. His mud-splashed boots clapped on the marble floor, echoing in the domed space as he passed gilded mirrors and a display of fine porcelain. "I'm not available for the rest of this miserable day."

"Yes, Your Grace."

Drake crossed the threshold of his mahogany-paneled study, the sound of his steps muffled by the room's thick red carpet. The welcoming crackle of a roaring fire in the hearth and the familiar smell of leather-bound books did little to soothe his irritation.

He took his place behind the massive antique desk and without pause snatched up a quill. Dabbing the tip in ink, he flipped open one of his journals and began ciphering the figures from his latest shipping venture. Trade was an unpopular activity for the nobility, but Drake gave little credence to convention. Convention had caused him nothing but grief. Besides, he enjoyed dabbling in business to relieve his boredom, or annoyance, as was the case today.

Drake slammed the quill down on the desk, sneering as flecks of ink splashed across his accounts. Shoving the book away in disgust, he leaned back in his chair, his thoughts turning toward his former fiancée.

Were all women deceivers? He'd heard the rumors about Penelope, but finding her in the arms of another man was not something he could tolerate. He'd broken their engagement this morning and would speak with her father tomorrow. No strip of land was worth having a wife who couldn't be trusted.

A knock sounded at the door. Chaney peered into the room. "Pardon, Your Grace, but a Lieutenant Kirby is here. I explained you're unavailable, but he claims to have news of Lord Anthony. I thought you might wish to see him straightaway."

Drake frowned. "Show him in. If they've sent someone, it must be urgent."

The butler departed. Drake closed his journal. An image of his brash younger brother came to mind. From childhood, Anthony had longed for adventure. When the revolt began in the Colonies six years ago, he'd booked passage on the first ship bound for New York. Determined to join their distant cousin's regiment, Anthony had been blinded by his ambition and lust for glory.

"Your Grace?" Chaney spoke from the doorway. "Please allow me to present Lieutenant John Kirby."

Drake studied the new arrival as he walked into the room and stopped several feet away. The man was short, wiry thin. Dirt marred his craggy face and sodden wig. His bulging eyes held respect and a hint of fear.

Kirby bowed low. His uneasy gaze flicked down at his less-than-spotless uniform. "Please forgive my appearance, Your Grace. The ghastly weather—"

"No matter, Lieutenant." Drake remembered his own battle with the soggy roads earlier in the day. Impatient, he motioned toward one of the chairs in front of his desk. "It would appear none of us is at his best this afternoon. Have a seat and tell me what news have you of my brother? I've received no word from him since before the new year."

Kirby sat on the edge of one of the leather chairs. Fidgeting, the soldier cleared his throat. His nervous gaze fell to the floor. "The news I have is ill indeed, Your Grace. I regret to say I've been sent here on the worst sort of errand. There's no delicate way to put this. Your brother, Lord Anthony, is...dead."

"Dead?" Drake choked, inwardly absorbing the news

like a blow to his gut. He'd anticipated something dire, an injury perhaps, but dead…? Not Anthony.

"Yes, Your Grace. I'm sorry to be the bearer of such tragic tidings."

Drake stood and faced the windows that framed the gray winter sky and constant drizzle. Though it was just after one o'clock, the dreary weather made it dark as early evening.

He took a deep breath, desperate to relieve the sudden painful tightening of his chest.

Anthony will never come home.

The thought went round and round in his head. If only he'd insisted Anthony remain in England. He should have found a way to curb his brother's tempestuous nature. Now he'd lost the opportunity forever. "Are you certain? There's been no mistake?"

"I'm positive, Your Grace."

"How? Which battle?"

Kirby cleared his throat as though he had more news he was reluctant to convey. "No battle, Your Grace. A notorious spy known as the Fox murdered him."

Drake clamped his jaw. Fury mingled with his initial shock and raged through him. His brother wasn't the casualty of an honorable fight on the field of battle. A traitor had killed him in cold blood. "When?"

"The last week of December. In Charles Towne, South Carolina colony."

"Was this 'Fox' apprehended?" Drake swung around to face the messenger. "If so, I want his neck in a noose posthaste."

Kirby squirmed in his chair. "That's the rub, Your Grace. The Fox escaped. The soldiers who caught him—"

"I thought you said the spy eluded capture. Make up your mind, man. Did he or did he not?"

After an uncomfortable pause, Lieutenant Kirby explained. "He…he *was* caught, but the soldiers let him go without realizing who they'd bagged."

Drake seethed. "What ineptitude! 'Tis a wonder the rebels haven't won the war with lackwits such as those to fight."

"Yes, Your Grace, but you see, Lord Anthony arranged the Fox's capture with Captain Beaufort, my superior officer. As a cousin to your family, Captain Beaufort knew your brother on sight, but the men he sent to meet him did not.

"When our men arrived, Lord Anthony was dead. The Fox remained, or so I heard, refusing to remove his mask. Apparently, the spy had rummaged Lord Anthony's clothing and found his identification after he shot him. The Fox then used the papers to switch his true identity with that of your brother. Our men believed the Fox was dead until they took the body to camp. Once there, Captain Beaufort immediately realized the deception. By then, the Fox had flown, reward and all."

"Reward?"

"Aye, there's a price on the brigand's head. Your brother, also known as Hawk, was to collect it from the soldiers sent by Captain Beaufort."

Drake's brow furrowed in disbelief. "You're suggesting my brother was involved in espionage?"

Kirby gulped. "Yes, Your Grace. Lord Anthony spied for His Majesty. The traitors believed he worked for them, but I assure you, his loyalty to England never wavered."

Drake considered the information. Truthfully, he

couldn't imagine Anthony being self-disciplined enough to make a successful spy. That his brother had chosen such a reviled occupation surprised him. Its need for secrecy conflicted with his brother's demand for attention. "How long did he work in that capacity?"

"I don't know, Your Grace, but I suspect for some time. From what I understand, the rebels thought highly of him, too."

"The rebels," Drake said scornfully.

"They're tenacious and unpredictable," the soldier added. "None is so bold as the Fox."

Drake's jaw worked as he struggled to conquer his temper. "So, the scum got away with murder and the reward. Very clever."

"Aye, Your Grace. Your cousin, Captain Beaufort, thought you might prefer to keep this matter secret until the Fox is found and punished. Because of that, he dispatched me to deliver the news, rather than someone from Whitehall. I secured passage from Charles Towne the day after your brother's shooting and arrived in London yesterday morn."

Drake returned to his place behind the desk. "Who is leading the hunt for this Fox?"

"As far as I know, Captain Beaufort remains in charge. However, he did say he would post further information to Hawk Haven by way of special courier if any became available."

The muted sound of rain outside filtered through the lead glass windows. Grim resolve filled Drake's mind. No one could be allowed to kill an Amberly and escape unpunished. "Tell me everything you know about this rebel spy."

Kirby tugged at his ear, and his brow pleated with

concentration. "I don't know much. No one does. The Fox is the most elusive spy in the Colonies, Your Grace. So little is known about the sly dog, stories boast he's a phantom."

Drake snorted in contempt. "Phantoms do not murder people."

"No, of course not, Your Grace. In truth, the only certain information is the Fox resides in Charles Towne or the nearby environs. Most likely he's a man of wealth, perhaps a planter."

Frustrated, Drake rubbed his angular chin. His pain and fury grew with each tick of the clock. "There must be a suspect or two. Anthony must have known something of the person with whom he dealt. Why didn't he tell Beaufort the traitor's whereabouts, and simply have the man arrested?"

Kirby shook his head. "He couldn't, not without compromising his position in the enemy spy ring."

Drake had heard enough for one sitting. He stood, barely controlling the need to smash something. He snapped his fingers, and Chaney entered from where he'd been waiting in the hall. "That will be all, Lieutenant. My butler will show you to a room. Prepare for a possible journey. Should I hear no word from Beaufort by week's end, you and I shall return to the Colonies to root out this slippery vermin ourselves."

"Yes, Your Grace. With God's help we'll find him soon." Kirby stood, clicked his heels and bowed as he backed out the door.

With God's help, indeed.

Drake stared through the window at the mournful weather. In his youth, he'd trusted in God, but no longer. Years of grief and disappointment had hardened his heart until he'd been able to forget God as effectively as God had forgotten him. Now, there was no room in his life for forgiveness or faith. It was vengeance he needed to set things right.

His fingers drumming steadily on the desktop, his mind quickly formed a plan. He'd wait two days to hear from Beaufort. Then he'd hunt down the unsuspecting Fox. When he located him, and he had no doubt of his success, he'd make certain the fellow danced at the end of a noose posthaste.

Chapter Two

Charles Towne, South Carolina
July 1781

Elise patted her powdered wig into place, smoothed the green silk gown over her hips and took a deep, relaxing breath as she prepared to leave the safety of her bedchamber.

Dear Lord, You've promised You'll never leave me. Please help me through tonight.

Taking a deep breath, she stepped into the dimly lit hall and closed the heavy door behind her. A moment later, Christian Sayer departed his own chamber two doors down. A handsome young man, Christian looked the picture of a wealthy planter's son in a finely woven white shirt, honey-toned breeches and matching embroidered waistcoat. A well-cropped wig disguised his dark brown hair. His blue eyes sparkled with their usual mischief. Like her, he possessed unquestioning loyalty to the American cause, and worked under the directive of his father, spymaster Zechariah Sayer.

Christian greeted her with an appreciative glance

and bowed gallantly. "You look sublime, dearest. That bright shade of green you're wearing matches your eyes precisely." He sighed as though put upon. "I can see tonight's ball will offer me little enjoyment. I'll be far too busy fending off the sea of gents bent on wooing you."

Elise rolled her eyes and restrained her laughter. She wasn't the plainest of women, but there was nothing spectacular about her brown hair, and her lips were too full for her oval face. Christian loved to tease. More oft than not, she was his favorite target. Other than her half sister, Princess, he was the only person she held dear. She loved him like a brother.

"I can take care of myself, thank you. If one of us must defend the other this night, it will be I protecting you. Alice Harris has marriage on her mind, or so I hear."

"Alice Harris, you say? She's fetching enough. Since you won't have me, I suppose she'll do. Tell me of her plans, will you? With a woman like Alice, I'll need to be prepared."

"What makes you think I know her full intentions? Alice and I are hardly confidants."

Christian flashed a wicked grin. "I'm aware that you know everything, my dear Fox."

Elise swatted him with her folded fan. "Shh, you silly dolt. Don't bandy that name about. Do you wish to see me dangling from the nearest hangman's tree?"

"Rest easy. There's no one here. Do you think I'd be that foolhardy?"

"I suppose not, *Wolf,*" she agreed, using his own alias. "But we can't be too careful. Charles Towne is crawling with redcoats. So many will be in attendance tonight, one would think King George himself planned to call."

"Aye, you know father has little choice but to include them if he hopes to maintain control of Brixton Hall. Thank God they believe he's a Loyalist or we'd all be out on our ear."

Elise said nothing as they meandered toward the top of the stairs. What she wouldn't do to be released and away from the Hall. But then where would Prin go? Surely the war would end soon, and she and her sister would be free. "There's no doubt Zechariah is convincing in all that he does."

"Do I detect a note of bitterness, Elise?"

"What would I have to be bitter about?"

"I can think of a good many things," Christian said with sympathy.

"It's just that I'm so tired of this life, of always playing the role of someone other than myself," she said, sorry the conversation had taken a personal turn.

"We all wear masks of one kind or another to protect ourselves, m'dear. You play the scatterbrain, Zechariah the Tory and I—"

"The soulless rake," she interjected sweetly.

He grinned, unrepentant. "I do my part. Innocent girl that you are, it might surprise you to know that the wives and mistresses of British officers are more forthcoming with their secrets once they've been exposed to my charm. It's delicate and dangerous work."

"Dangerous? Ha!"

"Of course it's dangerous. Have you not heard? There is no fury like a woman scorned. Once I've gleaned my information I'm required to move on to the next fair dove—"

"Sitting duck, you mean."

"Ah, but it is the least I can do for our cause."

They stopped at the top of the stairs. Once again Elise suffered a twinge of unease. Christian squeezed her hand in commiseration. "We all do what we must. Seven months have passed since Hawk's betrayal. Father is growing impatient with you. If you don't join the ranks again soon, he'll send you back to Roger."

At the mention of her stepfather, she grimaced. Roger was akin to a viper in her mind. He lived for profit no matter the pain he caused others. Her voice dipped to a whisper. "No one is more aware of my precarious position than I. I'll act my part, and no one will ever guess I'm a murderess."

Christian frowned. "Shush, don't speak nonsense. You did what you had to do and defended yourself against the traitor. Should you have died or allowed your capture in order to line our enemy's pockets with silver?"

She sighed. T'was a familiar argument. "I know I had no choice. Still, the nightmare plagues me. I've prayed and I know the Lord has forgiven me, but I can still feel Hawk's blood on my hands."

In the flickering candlelight of the stairwell, her friend's expression changed to one of concern as he displayed a rare moment of seriousness. "I know, but you should put your mind at ease. You didn't pull the trigger or intend to see him dead. In my estimation, the world is a far better place without a turncoat among us."

"Perhaps, but I wish I'd not been the one involved."

"Trust me, the memory will fade in time." Christian pulled her close for a brief hug. "Now, tell me of your new orders."

They continued down the stairs, and she grew more reluctant with each step. "His name is Drake Amberly. He claims to be a ship owner interested in reestablishing trade with colonies under British control. Zechariah wants to know if he can be persuaded to join our cause."

Christian frowned. "I met Amberly yesterday in Charles Towne. He's a disturbing gent, not one to tangle with, I'd wager. He conveys an easy temper, but there's a menace about him, a danger he fails to conceal completely. Be careful of the man."

Elise took his advice to heart. "It's time we changed our conversation. This close to our destination even the walls are listening."

They finished their descent in silence. Elise used the time to compose herself like an actress preparing for opening night. The chatter of their guests' conversation wafted through the house, growing louder until it became a roar as she and Christian reached the mansion's first floor. House slaves hustled past carrying silver trays laden with food. The scents of roast pork, fowl and spiced fruit blended to create an appealing combination.

"So, the pair of you has finally decided to join us." They turned in unison to see Zechariah walking toward them, a scowl pinching his shiny brow.

A short, rotund man, the elder Sayer possessed a massive belly that separated his crimson waistcoat from the top of his fuchsia trousers. His stock appeared as though he'd tied it without benefit of a looking glass and his skin shone more ruddy than usual thanks to the chalked wig that sat askew atop his head.

In the eighteen months since she'd arrived at Brixton Hall, it never ceased to amaze Elise that a man unable to harmonize his own clothing could effectively coordinate one of the Patriots' most successful assemblies of espionage.

"Of course, Father," Christian said. "I'd never miss so grand a gathering, especially one given in my honor. A man turns five and twenty but once in his life. Nothing could keep me away."

Known for his sour disposition, Zechariah grunted, obviously not amused by his son's facetious manner. "I don't appreciate being left to greet our guests alone."

Before Christian could reply, the straining of a harpsichord and stringed quartet shifted tempo, announcing the commencement of dancing. Merry laughter drifted into the foyer from several nearby rooms.

"Our guests seem happy enough," Elise commented in an effort to change the subject. Now was not the time for the two men to quarrel, as they were wont to do far too often.

The spymaster took her hand, but continued to eye his son. "Yes, and we should join them. As usual, the ladies are eager for this young buck's attentions. The gentlemen have already begun to ask after you, Elise. In fact, there's one in particular I want you to meet."

Drake leaned against the mantel, watching the festivities with sharp eyes. The merriment of the party might have cheered him under different circumstances, but frustration flayed his nerves and wore his patience thin. Kirby hadn't exaggerated the Fox's elusiveness. Drake had spent a fortune in bribes, yet learned little concerning the rebel spy. Only a nearly nonexistent trail had led him here to Brixton Hall, one of the largest plantations in the Carolinas.

His contacts had assured him the Fox would be in attendance tonight. A ball such as this provided the perfect opportunity for spies and their web of associates to carry out their business unnoticed and unhindered.

Drake raised his glass and sampled the sweet punch. He suffered no illusions the Fox would give himself away. He planned to keep a watchful eye, search for clues that might reveal the man's identity at a later date.

He perused the room, absorbing each detail. Compared to the drawing rooms he frequented in England, this one was small and plain, though artfully decorated in bright shades of yellow and blue. An abundance of Chippendale furniture lined three walls. The rugs had been rolled back to reveal a polished, wood-planked floor where a group of laughing dancers performed a reel.

Since his arrival in the Colonies three months prior, Drake had done his best to change his manner, dress and speech to match that of a man of trade. Lieutenant Kirby assured him he'd succeeded in his deception though they hadn't stayed anywhere long enough to put his disguise to a serious test.

Drake located Lieutenant Kirby near the refreshment table. The soldier had been contributing to the hunt by eavesdropping as he moved from place to place about the room.

The music faded. All eyes turned toward the doorway as Zechariah, his son, Christian, and a stunning young woman entered the room. The guests clapped for long moments, quieting for Zechariah when he raised his hands to plead for silence. The planter welcomed his friends and neighbors before offering a joyous toast in honor of his son.

It was the woman, however, who arrested Drake's attention. He watched her, his interest keen. Like the other women in attendance, she wore an elaborately arranged wig. Quite inexplicably he felt a prick of irritation at being denied a view of her hair's true color. Her face was pure beauty, with large wide eyes, a slender nose and full luscious lips that begged to be savored.

His eyes roamed over her tall, gently curved frame. The green gown she wore shimmered against her luminous skin. Diamonds around her neck and dangling from her delicate ears sparkled in the luster light, but it was her bright smile that lit up her face, and for him, the room.

He straightened into a more attentive posture, unable to divert his eyes from the girl as she allowed Christian Sayer to lead her to the dance floor, where the other guests followed them in a minuet.

Drake's fingers clenched the glass in his hand. He didn't care for the scene before him. The girl gazed into her escort's eyes too often for Drake's liking, flashing Christian a beautiful smile that Drake began to covet for himself.

Kirby joined him. "She's fair to look upon, is she not, sir?"

With his eyes riveted on the couple, Drake nodded. "Indeed. Who is she?"

"Her name is Elise Cooper. I heard the wallflowers discussing her while I enjoyed the refreshments. According to them she's an orphan and Zechariah's ward. They also mentioned she's as dimwitted as she is pretty."

"Jealous harpies, I'd wager. What of her relationship

with the son? 'Tis clear the puppy's besotted with her. Are they affianced?"

"I don't believe so, sir. I've heard no word. Perhaps they will be."

Not if I win her first. Startled by the thought, Drake rejected it immediately. He had no time nor inclination to court her, no matter how beautiful she was. Still, he breathed a sigh of relief when the girl relinquished Christian to another partner and went to stand with Zechariah at the edge of the dance floor.

Across the room, the fine hairs on Elise's arms and the back of her neck stood to attention, alerting her to the odd sensation of being watched.

She looked around, trying to appear nonchalant. Her breath caught in her throat when she noticed the man observing her. He was dark, handsome in a fierce sort of way. His sculpted lips turned in a seductive half smile, but it was the long scar along his jaw that intrigued her.

Tall and broad-shouldered, he cut a fine figure in a black waistcoat and breeches. His stark white shirt and elegant but simple stock stood in sharp contrast with his golden skin. He wore his black hair tied at the nape, one of only a few men in the room bold enough to refuse a wig.

His gaze captured hers, and his magnetic eyes seemed to discern her darkest secrets. His stare rattled her nerves and made her instantly more aware of herself in a manner that was most disconcerting.

To a woman used to being in the midst of trouble, he seemed the essence of it. She decided then to steer clear of him, for in one glance she knew his ilk: pure danger in masculine form.

Zechariah patted her hand. "Elise? Are you ill?"

She blinked and looked down into his round face. "I'm fine. Why do you ask?"

"You've nearly drawn blood."

Her gaze fell to where her fingernails dug into his linen-clad arm. She released him immediately.

Her spymaster fiddled with the froth of lace at his wrist. "Get hold of yourself, girl. You'll never accomplish what you must if you're more skittish than a colt."

Elise narrowed her eyes and bit back a sharp retort. She kept her expression cheerful so as not to give away the game to onlookers, but she resented his tone.

She despised Zechariah's hold on her life. But he'd offered the escape she'd prayed for as part of the bargain she'd made to free her sister. For now, she could do little but accept his sharp ways. Others believed she was his ward, when in actuality he was her warden.

"I'm neither skittish nor incapable of performing my task. The man by the mantel, the dark one, he startled me is all. I turned to see him staring a hole in my back."

Zechariah observed the man covertly. "That, my dear, is Drake Amberly, the man you're to investigate. You'd do well to encourage his interest. If he were to become besotted with you, it would make your task that much easier."

Elise bit back a sharp retort. Her instincts warned that Amberly was the one man in the Colonies she should avoid at all costs. "I have a troublesome feeling about him."

"Perhaps meeting him will alleviate the sensation." His amiable tone cloaked a rod of iron. "Allow me to introduce you."

She took a deep breath and released it slowly. The un-

ease she'd labored under for much of the day increased.
Her palms grew moist. The closer she walked toward
Amberly, the faster her heart raced.

When they came abreast of the man, Zechariah extended his beefy paw in greeting. He spoke loudly,
competing with the party's din of music, dancers and
conversation. "Amberly, I'm pleased to see you've
joined us. I hope the journey from Charles Towne was
not too taxing."

"Not in the least. The river was smooth, the boat
swift. I arrived in no time at all."

"Excellent, I'm glad to hear it." Zechariah rocked on
his heels, his hands clamped behind his back. "I trust
the maid saw you settled?"

"Most comfortably, thank you. Your hospitality is
much appreciated."

Even as he spoke with Zechariah, Amberly's eyes
returned to her face again and again. Heat rose to her
cheeks. She hoped the powder and rouge she'd applied
before the party disguised her reaction.

"We're pleased to have you here." Zechariah turned
to her. "Amberly, I'd like you to meet my ward, Miss
Elise Cooper. Elise, this is Mr. Drake Amberly, direct
from London. He'll be staying with us for the next few
weeks while he convinces me to contract his shipping
line."

No one told her he'd be a long-term guest. She offered her hand politely, schooling her features to prevent her dismay from reflecting on her face.

His large, tanned hand engulfed her much smaller
one. He bowed and kissed the back of her knuckles.
His scent of spice and soap teased her senses. She shivered, aware her response to him was profoundly pecu-

liar. Every nerve in her body warned her to make an excuse and run away. Only the force of her will kept her planted before him.

Intense, lushly lashed eyes caught and held hers. "The pleasure is all mine, Miss Cooper. I am most fortunate to make your acquaintance."

His voice was deep and smooth except for a few clipped words that reminded her of the English upper class. The observation brought her halfway back to her senses. She had to remember her orders and not allow herself to be waylaid by a handsome face.

She giggled, resorting to her role as a featherbrain. Experience had taught her a man let his guard down around a woman he considered a simpleton. "I'm charmed, Mr. Amberly. A girl could lose her head with a man as handsome as you in the room."

"Why thank you, Miss Cooper. I'm flattered."

He seemed more amused than complimented. She tapped him playfully with her fan and gifted him with a flirtatious grin. "Surely not. I've seen the other ladies swarming you tonight. Most likely you've grown weary of praise." She motioned toward the dancers behind her. "Forgive my boldness, but would you be so kind, sir? I truly love to dance. Since my escort is the guest of honor, he's obliged to take a turn with the other ladies tonight. I fear I'll be left to sit with the matrons if one of you fine gentlemen doesn't take pity on me."

"It would be my honor, Miss Cooper. However, I never acquired the skill of dancing. May I interest you in some refreshment instead?"

"You never learned to dance? How unusual," she remarked, her eyes as wide and innocent as a babe's.

"Dancing isn't a sport in large demand on a ship."

She smiled coyly. His refusal to dance might work to her advantage. Perhaps she could get him alone, away from the crowd and music that would disrupt conversation and her ability to uncover more about him. "I so wanted to dance, but I suppose a glass of refreshment will do. Why don't you fetch us a drink? I'll gather my shawl and meet you in the garden. It's such a pretty night. I see no reason to waste it indoors."

Amberly grinned. "A superb idea, Miss Cooper. To the garden it is."

Drake enjoyed the view of Elise's slim back as she departed. What an intriguing female. He wondered how many men swallowed her act. She played the part of an empty-headed chit, but intelligence shone from her startling green eyes. He wondered what game she played at. In his experience, all women had something to hide. Despite his earlier decision not to pursue her, he found uncovering her secrets might provide an interesting diversion during his stay in South Carolina.

Zechariah cleared his throat, reclaiming Drake's attention. "I apologize, Amberly. Our Elise possesses a double portion of boldness. I hope you weren't offended."

"No, indeed I find her delightful."

"Excellent. She's a wonderful girl, if not the smartest one. Now, if you'll excuse me, I must see to my other guests."

With a nod, Zechariah left and entered conversation with a nearby couple. Drake made his way to the refreshment table and accepted two glasses of punch from a servant before heading to the garden.

Not far from the open French doors, Christian Sayer

intercepted him. "Evening, Amberly. I trust you're enjoying our hospitality."

"Very much. I just spoke with your father and his ward—"

"That's why I'm here. Is one of those glasses for Miss Cooper?"

Drake nodded.

"Then I'll tell you this as a friend," Christian's smile held an edge of warning. "Miss Cooper requires the greatest respect. Should you harm her, I'd be gravely disappointed. Treat her well. I'd hate to have to shoot you."

Drake cocked an eyebrow in mild disbelief. The puppy was actually warning him off—an unusual event to be sure for a man used to being hounded by every flesh-peddling mama in England. His sister would howl with laughter if she were here to witness Sayer's threat.

Drake suppressed his amusement and considered Christian with new eyes. The younger man possessed the demeanor of an open, friendly individual, yet it was clear he had darker, hidden depths. Could *he* be the Fox?

Making a mental note to watch Christian more closely, Drake tipped his head. "Save your threats for someone who will be impressed by them, puppy. Now, if you'll excuse me, Miss Cooper is waiting for her drink."

Chapter Three

Drake shouldered his way past the unyielding younger man and followed the sparsely furnished hall to the front of the red-brick mansion.

A servant in a white-and-scarlet uniform opened the door for him to cross into the balmy night. A full moon shone from the velvety black sky. Strategically placed lanterns lit the English garden spread out before him. Beyond its hedges and curved walkways, a wide, well-tended lawn sloped into the inky ribbon of the Ashley River.

He searched for Elise among the strolling guests partaking of the floral-scented air, but it seemed she'd disappeared. His fingers clenched round the glasses he held as disappointment assailed him. He found himself quite put out at the idea of not being able to speak with her. She was by far the most captivating woman he'd met in the whole of his twenty-eight years.

His eyes lit with pleasure when he finally located her across the expansive lawn, near the water's edge. She stood half turned toward him, a lace shawl draped around her slender shoulders. She appeared to be speaking with someone, but he saw no one in the shadows cast by a towering oak. He hoped it wasn't another man because he pitied the chap who tried to snatch her from him.

Drake shook his head to clear it. The fervor of his response to Elise surprised him. He brushed away the sensation, refusing to ponder the speed, the intensity of his reaction to the woman, for he'd never experienced a like emotion to compare with it.

Surely he'd learned his lesson, he thought in self-disgust. Women weren't to be trusted. His wife had ended their union with betrayal, and the recent episode with his faithless fiancée had surely soured him on marriage for good.

So why did sighting Elise bring him such relief? Was it simply her beauty? Or perhaps it was the light of mystery in her eyes? Whatever it was, she was the first thing to please him since he'd learned of Anthony's death. The long winter voyage across the Atlantic had put him in a fouler mood than when he'd left England, and the added frustration of finding so little information about the Fox proved infuriating. For the first time in months he looked forward to concentrating on a subject other than his brother's murderer.

Elise lifted her head and caught him watching her. She tossed him a jaunty smile and beckoned him with a wave of her hand. He descended the steps at a leisurely pace, not wanting to seem overeager in his haste to reach her. His boots crunched the gravel as he followed the garden path to her side.

From her place beside the tree, Elise watched, transfixed by the predatory confidence Drake exuded and the warm manner in which he studied her. She was relieved to see he wasn't offended by her bold request to meet her in the garden. He was by far the most intriguing man she'd ever met. Pity she had no wish to fall in love. If she did, he would be a mighty temptation indeed.

Princess whistled low and quiet from the shadows. "The man carrying the glasses is him, isn't it? I can't tell rightly in the moonlight, but he seems awful dark to be an Englishman."

Without taking her eyes from Drake, Elise nodded. "From what I understand, he spends most of his time on a ship."

"What's his name again?"

"Drake Amberly."

"He reminds me of a loaded pistol that's primed and cocked. Maybe even more dangerous."

"My thought precisely, Prin."

Elise focused on her sister, hoping Amberly thought a view of the river interested her. Her sister's large eyes, straight nose and high cheekbones were similar to her own and their shared father's, but the night hid the mocha-brown skin and simple muslin gown that proclaimed her position as a house slave.

Prin's mother, Abigail, had been their father's property for a handful of years before Samuel decided he needed to marry and produce the legitimate son he longed for. Another girl, Elise had been a bitter disappointment for him.

Prin had been raised among the other slaves, but she'd done her best to protect Elise from their father's drunken rages. An airtight bond of love had been forged between the two girls. Now their situations were reversed. Elise protected Prin. As long as she did what Zechariah dictated, she'd be given ownership of Prin once the war ended. From there, Elise planned to use the funds she collected from spying to create a new life for them both somewhere free from the hated chains of slavery.

"You can't be too careful round a man like that," Prin warned. "He walks like he owns the whole earth."

"True," Elise whispered. "He's arrogant, but not meanly so, I think. I suppose it comes naturally to him. Men like him seem to acquire that particular trait at birth."

Elise glanced back over her shoulder. Amberly had traversed half the lawn, but remained too far away to hear their conversation. She watched him, disliking the way her heart fluttered in anticipation of his arrival. He carried himself like a nobleman, as though he were well aware of and comfortable with his position in life. With purpose and a complete disregard for others' opinions of him.

"Jus' be careful," Prin warned.

"You know I will be." Her sister never ceased to play the part of mother hen. "You should go before he gets here. Tell Zechariah you delivered his message and I've learned no news as yet. I'll meet with him after I've had a chance to speak with Amberly."

"That old dragon wants a miracle," Prin reminded her, speaking of Zechariah. "Your past work has spoiled him. You're usually so quick to give him the information he wants, he thinks you can read minds and don't need to talk or listen none."

"Well, then, he's deceived. I—"

"My, that man looks dangerous," her sister interrupted.

Elise frowned and continued to focus on the river.

"Prin, please go back to the house and deliver my message. Then wait in our room, all right? I want you safe. You know how the soldiers like to make free with their hands."

"Maybe I'll just hide over there in the bushes. When you get ready to head back to the house, I'll go up with you."

"No. What if Amberly sees you? There's enough lantern light to expose you, and how would I explain your presence in the shrubs?"

"I'm your chaperone?"

Elise shook her head at her sister's persistence. "I don't need one with all the other guests strolling about."

"Fine," Prin grouched. "I'm going. Just remember the trick I taught you. A knee to—"

"'If he tries to touch what he shouldn't.' Yes, I know. Now *go*," she whispered.

A snapping twig announced Amberly's arrival. Elise spun to face him just as he joined her. He offered her one of the crystal glasses he held. "Miss Cooper, the drink you requested."

Smiling brightly, she accepted the glass. Her fingertips brushed his, and a pleasant sensation danced up her arm. Surprised by the contact, she forgot the clever quip she'd devised to begin the conversation and gain the upper hand.

She took a sip of fruity punch while gathering her wits. Amberly's intense gaze flustered her, making it difficult to concentrate when questioning him should have been foremost in her mind. Forcing her thoughts to regroup, she flashed him a flirtatious grin, and slipped back into her least favorite role. "Why, thank you, Mr.

Amberly. I do believe you've saved me from disgracing myself in a faint. I'm as parched as a hot summer day."

"My pleasure, Miss Cooper. I'm pleased to be of service." He peered into the darkness behind her. "You seem to be alone, but I thought I saw you speaking with someone. I trust I didn't interrupt?"

"No. My maid brought a message from Mr. Sayer. I sent her back to the house."

Drake's brow furrowed. "I spoke with him moments ago. He warned me off you."

Perplexed that Zechariah would do such a thing, she lowered her lashes to hide her confusion. "He did?"

Drake stepped closer, dried leaves crunching beneath his boots. His dark presence engulfed her, made her feel tiny. Nervous excitement shimmied in her belly. She had to crane her neck to look into his eyes.

"It's obvious he's smitten with you, but I hope you don't feel the same way about him."

Realization dawned. Christian must have been the one to warn him off. The tension tightening her muscles suddenly released. Laughter bubbled to her lips. "Christian isn't smitten—"

"He is. I've no doubt." He paused. "But, I fear I'm more so."

Elise's heart beat out of control. She flipped open her fan and fluttered it rapidly, hoping to cool the blush that warmed her cheeks. "You must be jesting. We've just met. Perhaps you were out to sea too long, and the sun has addled your brain?"

He grinned. "No, I simply know beauty when I see it."

His comment sent a gush of relief through her. Her nervousness receded, though her disappointment increased. He was just another shallow man interested in a woman's outward appearance. She'd dealt with such nonsense before.

She dropped her fan, letting it dangle from the silk cord about her wrist, and batted her lashes. "Thank you, Mr. Amberly. I feared with all the other lovely ladies here tonight, I'd be the least noticed among them."

"You needn't have worried, sweet. You outshine all the other ladies of my acquaintance—here and in England."

Determined not to be taken in by his flattery, she took another sip of punch. "You're a prince to say so, sir."

"I'm not a prince, Miss Cooper." His white teeth flashed in a grin. "Perhaps something slightly less grand. Perhaps a duke?"

She knew he jested, but something in his words suggested a double meaning, one she had yet to grasp. Another couple walked close by, admiring the river. She nodded to them as they passed but didn't speak until they were out of earshot. "Hardly, sir. It's just an expression. You needn't worry I'd mistake you for a genuine member of royalty. You've not the bearing for it."

His smile faltered imperceptibly. One dark brow rose in question. "Is that so? How many royals have you known?"

"Few to none," she admitted, glancing out over the river where moon and lantern light shimmered on the calm surface. "Although, I did have the pleasure of meeting Lord Cornwallis and his entourage at a ball I attended last summer."

Amberly gave no reaction when she expected him to be impressed by the announcement. Whenever she mentioned the general's name, most English men and women expressed a keen interest in the details of the man leading Britain's southern campaign.

She changed the subject, searching for a topic that would encourage him to speak of himself. "Still, I suppose no ball competes with plying the open sea. I envy you, Mr. Amberly. Shipping must be a fascinating occupation."

His thick eyelashes dipped to shield his eyes. If she hadn't been watching him so closely, she wouldn't have noticed. "To be sure, Miss Cooper. 'Tis quite fascinating if one enjoys endless days of bobbing along like a cork, going mad from boredom and smelling of fish. One can only scan the horizon so often. Two weeks into an Atlantic crossing, a ship, no matter how large, becomes excessively small indeed."

"You surprise me, sir. The few sailors I've met love their lot in life more than they love their own mothers. You speak as though you can't bear it."

"On the contrary. I enjoy the sea and all its wonders, but I'm a practical and truthful man. Sailors who have naught but good to say about it are lying or victims of brain rot."

She laughed. "I doubt I'd make a good sailor. I hate the feeling of being penned in. Yet, I must admit the sense of freedom one must feel holds great appeal for me."

Drake moved closer and leaned against the tree. He crossed his arms over his broad chest and gave her a lazy smile.

This close to him she could smell his spicy cologne. Prin was right, he was dark for an Englishman, almost as dark as the Indians who lived near her father's Virginia farm, and so mysterious she found it impossible to drag her eyes away from him.

Somewhere behind Elise a woman laughed, drawing her back to the task at hand. She had to focus. Prin's future freedom, as well as her own, depended upon her being in control and sober of mind. She took her thoughts in hand and continued her quest with renewed purpose. "I'm curious about you, Mr. Amberly. I'd wager you have more than a few secrets."

He shrugged in casual affirmation. "A few perhaps. No more than most men, a lot less than most women."

She glanced away. Her entire existence was a blend of shadow and light. She possessed so many secrets even she had trouble remembering them all.

He reached out and ran his fingertip down her cheek. Startled by the caress, she caught her breath. She wasn't used to being touched with such gentleness, and the feather-soft brush of his finger was a pleasurable sensation she loathed to end.

Straining her willpower to the seams, she pulled away. Her hand trembled as she tugged the edges of her shawl tighter around her shoulders. "I… I must go."

"Don't," he said.

"I must."

"Why?"

Matters had gotten out of hand. She'd lost her concentration. She needed to regroup her thoughts and felt sure she'd swim in confusion as long as she stayed in his company. "We have other guests. Mr. Amberly and I must see to them."

She turned in the direction of the well-lit brick mansion. "Fare thee well. Goodnight."

He reached for her wrist, but she pretended not to

notice as she moved beyond his grasp. He followed her. She heard his pursuit and stepped up her pace.

"I shall see you again soon, Miss Cooper."

His tone was sincere enough, but to her flustered senses the statement sounded like a threat. "Not if I see you first, sir."

His rich laughter stretched across the velvety night. "My heart is broken, dear girl, but thank you for the warning. I'll be sure to sneak up on you the next time we meet."

"Well," Zechariah demanded a few hours later in the study. "What news have you, girl? You and Amberly seemed cozy enough."

Elise shifted on her feet. She stood before the study's waning fire, summoned to the old man like a disobedient servant. "*Cozy* isn't the word I'd use."

Her spymaster kept his back to her as he poured a drink and replaced the bottle's crystal stop. Christian sat in the corner, hidden in shadow. The ball had ended several hours prior, and their guests had gone or sought out a bed for the night.

The old man faced her, took off his flowing powdered wig and tossed it to a nearby chair, where it landed in a cloud of chalk. Candlelight reflected on his bald head. He scratched his scaly crown and sighed before eyeing her with what she thought was suspicion. "I care not about the word, girl. I only wish to know if you discovered something useful."

"No—"

"Then what am I to do with you? If you've forever lost your ability to aid our cause, I'll ship you back to Williamsburg in the blink of an eye."

Her jaw tightened. He'd used the same threat on many occasions. Before Hawk's death she would have paid it no mind, but since that fateful night her guilt made her nearly useless as a spy. His irate expression signaled a real cause for concern. If he sent her back to Williamsburg, she'd be under Roger's thumb once more. All hope of freeing Prin would be lost. "You didn't allow me to fin—"

"We're all risking our lives in this business. Some of us more than that," Zechariah continued with an angry slash of his hand. "We have to stay sharp and spare no opportunity to locate the information we must acquire."

Elise listened to the lecture, biding her time with a prayer for patience. Zechariah would run out of steam soon. Then she'd have her say.

Sayer's tirade came to an abrupt stop. His countenance softened imperceptibly. "You're not the first of our number to have a part in killing a man, you know. Hawk was our enemy. You did right to lay him low. I'll have no more of this pouting. You must move on."

He forestalled her when she began to protest. "Elise, I'd hate to lose you. In the past, you've proven your worth, but the war situation is grim. I cannot coddle you a moment longer."

"You've no need to coddle me," she said between clenched teeth. "I learned no information to support Amberly's claims, but I observed something you may wish to consider."

Sayer's eyes gleamed. "Ah, I knew you'd not disappoint."

Elise bit her tongue and refrained from reminding him of the diatribe he'd cast her way a moment ago. "I believe he's more than he says he is. A minor aristocrat, perhaps."

Christian stood and entered the candlelight. "What makes you think so?"

"His manner and his story conflict. He told Zechariah he operates in trade, that he's come to America to reestablish shipping lines between Carolina planters and England. But Amberly proclaims his finer breeding with each word he speaks."

"I didn't notice anything out of the ordinary," Zechariah said.

"I'd wager he's changed his accent as best he can, but if you listen closely, you can hear his cultured tones."

"It's possible he's putting on airs," Christian offered.

Elise nodded in agreement. "Yes, but I've spoken with sea captains and sailors before. I know many men of trade. None have his confidence or air of command. It's as though he owns the world and accepts it as his due. I've only seen that sort of bearing in the lords and ladies I met in Williamsburg, or more recently, in the entourage of General Cornwallis."

The spymaster rubbed his whiskered chin. "The maid who unpacked for him saw nothing out of the ordinary. His clothing and trinkets are of good quality, but nothing is especially grand—"

"Of course it isn't," Elise said with a touch of impatience. "If a man wishes to hide his identity, what does he do? He pretends to be the opposite of who he really is."

Zechariah gave her a sharp look. "Don't sass me, girl. I know what a man does to hide his identity. I've been doing it for a good many years."

Chastised, she nodded, but didn't apologize.

"Still," he said, "you've said nothing to convince me he's a spy."

"No, but if I'm right, there's trouble afoot. Everything he's told us regarding himself would be a lie. He'd have to be here for some other purpose...."

The room fell into silence as each of its occupants considered the situation.

"The man *is* hiding something," Zechariah conceded. "I can smell it. If he's a spy, then you must find him out."

Elise nodded. Christian frowned.

"Spend every possible moment with him until the truth is discovered." The spymaster's gaze pinned to her face. "He's taken with you, girl. And you need to reestablish your worth. This is the perfect opportunity to do so."

Elise thought of her strange reaction to Amberly. The oddly delicious, frightening way he'd made her feel. "Zechariah, I... I'm not the best choice for this errand."

"Nonsense, there's no one better. Prove yourself once more or I'll be forced to replace you with someone willing to face the noose if necessary. I'm sure your mother and your weasel of a stepfather will accept you back in Williamsburg, but I might have to sell your sister."

Like a foul stench, his words hung in the air.

"You've no need for concern. I'll do your bidding, as you well know."

"Excellent. Within a week, I want more information on Amberly than even his parents possess of him. Do we understand one another?"

Christian interrupted from beside her. "I'll help, Elise. The two of us might enjoy more success if we work together. However, there is one small problem."

"What?" Zechariah asked irritably.

"I warned him off before he followed Elise into the garden."

"Aye, he told me," she said.

"And why, pray tell, did you do that?" Zechariah slapped the top of the tidy desk. To Elise, "Did Amberly listen? Did the man keep his distance?"

Elise hesitated, recalling Drake's vibrant presence, the way he'd affected her. Yet, to tell Zechariah of her reaction would make her weak in his eyes. He might think she'd grown unable to separate her feelings from her work. "He must have, for none of his actions were untoward."

Zechariah frowned in Christian's direction, but spoke to her. "Pity. Now you'll have to convince him his attentions are welcome."

She doubted that would pose a serious challenge. "I understand."

Zechariah passed her a small packet tied with string. "Good. Now that's settled, here are the letters I want you to deliver to Tabby tomorrow. She'll need to pass them near a flame's heat for the message to appear."

Elise accepted the envelopes. The recent invention of invisible ink amazed her. "If I'm to take these to Tabby, how am I to spend time with Amberly?"

"He has business in Charles Towne. You'll have time on the ferry to charm him."

Never more unsure of herself, she nodded and made for the door.

Chapter Four

Sleep refused to visit Elise. Despite the cool breeze ruffling the white lace curtains of her bedchamber, she was hot and sticky with perspiration. Moonlight illuminated the far side of the room, but barely reached the mosquito-netted bed where she tossed and turned.

More and more of late, her prayers seemed to go unanswered. Without the Lord's guidance she felt adrift and abandoned. With her future and the future of her sister in ever-increasing peril, she clung to the scripture that promised the Lord would never leave her.

But, she had to admit, her faith had begun to bow under the weight of His silence in the midst of her endless concerns.

Prin released a long-suffering breath. "Who you wrestlin' over there?"

"I can't sleep," Elise mumbled. The ropes holding the feather mattress creaked as she flipped to her back. "I believe I'd find more comfort on a stone slab."

"It's a mite better than the mats and cold musty ground of the slave cabins."

"I know," she whispered. "I have no right to complain."

"What's ailing you, then? The truth, if you please."

"Nothing." She couldn't talk about Zechariah's threats with her sister. Prin would protest by way of silent mutiny and hot cups of tea in the spymaster's lap at breakfast. In all likelihood, Zechariah would use the excuse to relegate Prin to the slave cabins instead of turning a blind eye to her presence in his home as he did now.

"So you've taken to lying? I thought my mother taught you better."

Prin was like a hound with a strong scent in her nose. If she ran true to form, Prin wouldn't leave her sister alone until she was fed a satisfactory tale.

"Nothing in particular, I should have said." Elise sighed. "In truth I have much on my mind, none of which I wish to trouble you with."

"I'll wager you do have much on your mind. My name may be Princess but you're the *queen* of frettin'." Her sister turned smug. "Good thing I'm here. I knew you'd come to me for the truth."

"You know I'm always glad you're here with me, but in this case, I wouldn't know what truth you speak of."

Prin rolled her eyes. "Of course you do, Lisie, you're not the brainless girl you play so well. You're not blind either. Your problem's a simple one—man trouble. Did you find out whether Amberly's married or not?"

Truth to tell, she'd forgotten to inquire about such basic information. In retrospect, she felt quite inept. If her reaction to the man hadn't distracted her so, she would have had him volunteering those simple facts without him realizing. "No, but then you're the one de-termined to see me wed."

"I want to see you settled and protected."

"But I have no wish to marry."

"You're nineteen," Prin pointed out. "Fast becomin' an old maid."

Elise groaned. "And any man within five colonies is an acceptable candidate?"

"I just want you safe and happy."

Elise crossed her arms behind her head and closed her eyes. Her sister's concern tugged at her heart. Still. "I can't see how being shackled to a man can provide any woman with happiness."

"Why are you being such a mulehead?" Prin huffed. "Marriage and misfortune don't have to mean the same thing."

Elise turned her head and strained to see her sis-ter's face. The fat candle she'd lit while preparing for bed no longer burned. In the faint moonlight, she could make out little except the outline of Prin's cheek and the brightness of her eyes. "Just because you've found happiness with Kane doesn't mean we're all destined for an equally joyful end."

"But findin' a husband would solve all your prob-lems."

Aghast, Elise sat up in the bed and twisted toward her sister. "I believe it's finally happened."

"What?"

"You've gone daft."

"Have not."

Elise scrunched the bedsheets in her fists. It was illegal for slaves to wed, but ever since she'd found a minister willing to officiate a secret marriage between

Prin and Kane, her sister had become convinced Elise needed to marry as well. "In all seriousness, how can you be foolish enough to believe marriage would solve my difficulties? It's more likely a husband would multiply them. Recall, if you will, how our father treated both our mothers."

"Aye, Pa was a bad seed, but not all men are such fiends."

"Then let's consider Roger."

"Why? The man's a goat's bottom, nothing more. Just 'cause your ma believed his sweet talk and found misery in matrimony, don't mean all church aisles lead in the same direction."

Elise wasn't so certain. Without care for her reputation, her own mother had abandoned her in favor of a handsome man's honey-coated promises. Once she and her new lover were free to wed, Roger showed his true colors, and in the end, her mother found herself tied to a second wicked husband.

Her voice husky with remembered pain, she whispered, "Zechariah is another fine example of male selfishness gone awry."

Prin clucked her tongue and shook her head on the pillow. "You're just bein' a goose. Zechariah has principals even if he's *far* from perfect. And before you mention some other poor fool, what about Kane? Or how 'bout Christian? They're as good and fine men as there ever was born."

"True enough."

"Then why not your friend? You both have this spy business in common. He won't keep you from carryin' out your stubborn convictions. You could chase around the countryside together, bring down all the redcoats.... 'Sides, he fancies you."

Elise rolled her eyes. "Christian is a gentleman and a dear, but he fancies *many* women. Besides, how could I think to marry a man who stirs nothing in me but feelings of the brotherly sort?"

Prin took a deep breath and let it out slowly. "You're just too hard to please."

"Can we cease this?" Elise lay down, her back to her sister. "I'm tired and must get some rest. I'm off to Charles Towne in the morning, and the ferry leaves at half past seven. Amberly will be on it, so I must sparkle."

Prin laughed at her sarcasm. "I'm right for sure. That Englishman must have got under your skin like a hungry tick. You only desert subjects and get all huffy when you know I'm right and you're feelin' hooked."

Elise pulled up the sheet and punched her pillow. "Enough, Prin, truly. You couldn't be more wrong about my interest in that man. Beyond finding out his background for Zechariah, he doesn't concern me in the least. Now go to sleep."

"I wasn't the one tossin' and turnin'. That was you in a tumble."

"Do be quiet, will you?"

"It *is* that man." Prin leaned over her. A giggle in her voice, she whispered, "That tall, mysterious and darkly handsome *English* man."

Elise gritted her teeth. An unsolicited image of Amberly invaded her mind. She saw again his golden eyes and knowing smile. Heard his smooth, rich voice in her head. She squeezed her eyes closed tight, desperate to ward off the warmth that suffused her heart when she thought of him. "Believe what you will. You always do, no matter what I say."

"It's your own fault, you know. You prove me right so often I'd be silly to doubt myself."

A rooster's crowing startled Drake from a deep sleep. The creature sounded as though it were right outside his window. He pushed back the mosquito net and swung his legs over the side of the bed. His bare feet hit the smooth wood, and he took a moment to clear the grogginess from his mind.

Last night he'd declined Zechariah's offer to have a servant wake him. Normally an early riser, he hadn't anticipated the image of Elise occupying his thoughts or disturbing his rest enough to make him oversleep.

Wearing the same clothes from the previous night, he stood and stretched his knotted muscles. He crossed to the open window, hoping for a breeze that was, unfortunately, not to be. The sun had barely risen, but the heat was high and the air steamy with humidity.

He looked out across the lush green lawn to the dock. The ferry to Charles Towne had yet to arrive, though a few people waited along the bank of the smooth-flowing river.

Abandoning the window, he made use of the pitcher of cool water and ornate basin on top of the bureau. He changed into fresh clothes, pausing to tie his hair back with a leather string before heading to the first floor.

Downstairs, the clatter of cutlery lead him to the dining room. Zechariah Sayer sat at the head of a long, polished pine table, a plate of bacon, eggs and fresh rolls arranged before him. An array of foods filled the silver trays along the sideboard, scenting the room with the aroma of cinnamon and fried bacon. A handful of servants stood along the bright green walls, obviously waiting for Sayer's other guests to arrive and break their fast.

Zechariah picked up his steaming cup of coffee and gestured toward one of the chairs. "I'm afraid most everyone else is still abed. I'm an early riser myself. Can't abide the idea of frittering away half the day in idleness."

Drake pulled out the chair and made himself comfortable. He snapped his napkin from its neat fold and spread it across his lap. One of the female servants placed a plate of breakfast in front of him. He noted how attractive the girl looked with her lovely brown eyes and full lips. She reminded him of Elise, which was nonsense. He must be going round the bend. The chit was invading his dreams and now he was starting to see her in every pretty face he came across.

He took a drink of his coffee and added a teaspoon of sugar to mute its bitterness. "I, too, prefer an early start. At home I enjoy exercising my horses in the cool of the day."

"We have a full stable here. Make use of it if you wish." The older man took a bite of egg and chewed with greedy enjoyment. He poked his fork in Drake's direction. "Just stay clear of Elise's gelding, Freedom. She's in love with the mount. I'd hate to have to rescue you from her ire if you borrow him."

A half smile curved Drake's lips. He accepted a roll from the pretty, light-skinned slave. "Thank you for the offer—and the warning. I shall look forward to riding tomorrow. I believe you said the ferry leaves for Charles Towne this morn at half past seven?"

"Aye," Sayer said, motioning toward the mantel clock with his knife. "It should be here by now. You'd best hurry if you hope to be aboard."

Ten minutes later, Drake joined the other passengers waiting on the riverbank near the garden house. Birds chirped, hidden in the towering oaks. The musty smell of moss hung in the steamy air. Kirby had stayed behind to continue the hunt for clues to the Fox's identity. Drake had yet to see Ellse, and his disappointment was acute. With the ferry leaving soon, he'd have no chance to see her for the rest of the day.

Waving, the ginger-haired ferry captain jumped onto the dock, his freckled face split in a huge, snaggletoothed grin. "Miss Cooper!"

Drake pivoted on his heel to find Elise rushing up the path. His chest tightened in appreciation. She was exceptional. The daylight allowed him to see details of her face previously concealed. Her smooth skin and startling green eyes were no mistake of the candlelight. She'd forgone a wig and a cap, allowing him to indulge his curiosity about her hair. Dark brown with thick strands of red and gold that glinted in the morning sun. Tied at the nape, the long tresses hung over her shoulder and swayed below her waist as she walked.

With a smile and a wave to the captain, Elise joined Drake at the back of the queue. All bright smiles and vivacious energy, she reminded him of a perfect spring morning.

"Hello, Mr. Amberly. Fine day for a sail."

"Fine day, indeed, Miss Cooper. Most fine, now that I'm aware you're following me."

"Following you, sir? You're mad if you think so." She

lifted the leather satchel she held. "If not for a friend in need, I'd still be asleep."

He smiled. "Then thank heaven you're a friend willing to help."

Elise ignored the sudden racing of her heart. With the letters for Tabby hidden in her satchel, an emergency stop at Riverwood Plantation to rescue muskets and Drake Amberly to dissect for information, she had too much to do to be taken in by his charm.

The bell rang, announcing their imminent departure. The other dozen or so passengers, some carrying chickens or leading goats on leashes, moved en masse onto the ferry's deck.

Drake helped her onboard, but the captain was there to meet her. He doffed his tricorn. "Good mornin', Miss Cooper."

"Good morning, Captain Travis. How's your mother since her illness last week? Did the honey and lemons I sent make a difference?"

The young man beamed. "She's back up to snuff, ma'am, and told me to thank you. The toddy she made did the trick. Her lung rattle's gone."

"I'm glad to hear it. Let me know if she needs anything else."

The captain nodded his appreciation and reluctantly went back to his work. Elise moved starboard. She placed the satchel between her feet and beneath the hem of her yellow skirt before taking hold of the ferry's rail. Drake joined her, his height and broad shoulders casting a long shadow over the deck.

"I dare say our young captain is another of your smitten conquests."

"Don't be silly, Mr. Amberly. Travis isn't smitten,

he's my friend." In truth, he was her partner in espionage. Over the past year she'd taken this particular journey more times than she could count. Beyond her regularly scheduled trips, Travis aided her often when an unexpected need to travel presented itself. Zechariah paid him well for his inconvenience, but his loyalty was free.

"Like Christian?"

The ferry wobbled as it launched. She gave him a saucy grin. "Careful, Mr. Amberly. We haven't known each other long enough for you to be jealous."

He frowned. "Perhaps not, but I do believe I am."

He sounded as surprised by his confession as she was to hear it. Facing him, she was struck by how dangerous he was to her peace of mind. Something rare and beyond her experience had snuck up and bloomed between them. Other men had been as blunt, but they'd left her cold. With Drake, she felt as if she were being bathed with the sun.

He brushed her cheek with his fingertips and slipped a tendril of her hair behind her ear. "It's my fondest hope we'll grow our acquaintance."

Breathless, she stared into his golden eyes, wishing she was the carefree young miss she pretended to be. She forced her gaze out across the river. *Focus, focus,* she warned herself. *Prin is depending on you. The patriots need you. Dear Lord, please help me!* Determined to carry out her task, she straightened her shoulders and lifted her chin. "I agree, Mr. Amberly, we *should* grow our acquaintance. By all means, let's chat."

Chapter Five

"Shall I begin, Mr. Amberly?" Elise prayed their discussion would go well. What a blessing it would be if she were able to uncover all the information Zechariah required before they reached Charles Towne. With her orders fulfilled, she would be free to avoid the man and no longer have to worry about the disturbing emotions he stirred in her.

"If you like. But first, please call me Drake?"

"It wouldn't be proper."

His golden eyes danced with mirth. "Last night I was given to understand you care little for propriety."

"What of your family and background?" she asked, determined to keep the conversation focused on him. "Are your parents living? Have you any siblings?"

His expression sobered. "My mother was of Roman extraction. My parents and older brother perished on a return voyage from Rome ten years past. I was left with the care of my two younger siblings. A sister, Eva, and brother, Anthony. Anthony passed away a few months ago."

Her heart twisted with pity. "I'm so sorry. There's nothing worse than losing a loved one."

"I agree. Especially when he died by means of foul play."

"My goodness! That's doubly distressing."

"I've come to terms with his death, but I won't rest until his murderer is punished."

She leaned forward and touched his hand in commiseration. "I'd want to do the same if it were my brother, but I hope you won't allow your vengeance to rule you."

"Anthony has no one else to avenge his honor."

The fire in Amberly's eyes frightened her. "I believe vengeance is best left to God."

"Are you a religious woman, Miss Cooper?"

"Religious? Not terribly," she admitted. "However, I am a Christian and do my best to follow God's word."

Drake glanced across the river to the passing shore. "I gave up on God ages ago. A man can only endure so many disappointments before he realizes his faith has been misplaced."

Elise noticed his white-knuckled grip on the ferry's rail. Her heart went out to him. "I don't believe the Lord abandoned you. Not when His word promises He'll never leave or forsake us."

His mouth tightened into a hard line. "I hope you're right."

She recognized the bitterness and grief churning beneath his matter-of-fact tone. She understood loss. In the past two years, her home, freedom and many of her loved ones had all been taken from her, yet she couldn't imagine how empty her life would be without her faith to sustain her.

A flock of birds landed on the river's calm surface. Elise used the distraction to gather her thoughts. "What of your sister? I'm certain you must miss her."

His expression softened and she could tell he and the girl were close.

"Eva is fifteen. She's a hoyden despite my best efforts. She's still in the schoolroom and loathes every moment of it. I've no doubt the servants have their hands full while I'm away."

"I'm sure she'd prefer sailing the seven seas with you."

"Most doubtful. She prefers horses to anything or anyone else. I understand you also have a horse you're quite fond of. Zechariah warned me of your ire should I borrow him."

"Zechariah exaggerates."

"He said you'd take a horsewhip to me. That he'd have to scrape me from the stable walls if I dared to touch the beast."

An indignant retort bubbled to her lips until she noticed the teasing gleam in his eyes. She laughed at her own quick temper. "I see that you jest at my expense, but Freedom is dear to me."

"No doubt."

"Zechariah loaned him to me when I first arrived to stay at Brixton Hall."

"And when was that?"

"Eighteen months ago."

"I'm sorry."

"Why? The Sayers are amicable people."

He nodded in agreement. "I, too, have found them as such. But the circumstances that brought you to Zechariah's wardship must have been tragic for you."

She bowed her head and her fingers fiddled with the end of the silk tie joining her bodice. She knew he must think her an orphan. Most people assumed she needed a protector because they believed the history Zechariah had created for her when she came to work for him at Brixton Hall. "Aye, most tragic."

She looked beyond him to the calm river and marshy green banks that stretched as far as the eye could see. In truth, her situation was grim for entirely different reasons. She'd come to work for Zechariah because of her stepfather's greed. After Roger wed her mother, Anne, he'd claimed the Virginia land and slaves as Anne's property, then sold everything off for a tidy sum.

When Roger sold Prin to Zechariah, Elise did all she could to see her set free. Sayer refused to sell her, but had offered Prin's freedom as the prize in exchange for Elise's loyalty and work as a spy until the war's end.

At the time, she'd been praying for a way to escape Roger and thought the Lord had made a way. For half her spy's pay, she and Prin received room and board. In exchange for his silence, Roger gleaned another quarter of her profits though he never let her forget he could make just as much or more by turning her over to the British if she refused to compensate him for his silence.

Up until the night of Hawk's death, she'd been convinced the Lord would see her through. That her success as a spy had been God's reward for serving a just cause. Now, racked by guilt for her part in a man's death, she wasn't so certain.

"Have you been in shipping long?" she asked in an effort to draw the conversation back to Drake.

"Twelve years, counting my stint in the Royal Navy."

"The navy?" Elise asked with interest.

"Aye, I left home at sixteen and went to sea. Over the next two years, I learned to love all things nautical and decided to make my fortune in shipping. When my father and older brother passed away unexpectedly, I took on the responsibilities of family matters, though I never forgot my own aspirations. I bought my first ship at twenty. Since then, I'm happy to say, I've steadily added to the line and hope to see its continued growth and prosperity."

"From the moment I saw you last evening, I knew you were a determined man."

He shrugged. "I suppose so. However, I must confess my determination is born from a fear of being idle. My family has farmed for years. Unfortunately, it bores me senseless."

"How coincidental. My father farmed near the western border of Virginia."

"Virginia? I've heard the land is rich and untamed, but that living there is nearly impossible with the savages roaming hither and yon."

"It can be," she acknowledged. "We did well enough in our dealings with the natives. My father made treaties with their leaders, and we respected one another. It was beautiful there. Untouched country with trees so high the mist settled in their branches and an abundance of game that would feed an army for a score of years."

"The place sounds like Eden." His expression turned thoughtful. "I was under the impression land grants were given by the king for service rendered. Did your father begin as a military man?"

She lowered her eyes. "No, I'm ashamed to say he didn't believe in the king's sovereignty."

His eyes darkened. "He spoke treason."

"Yes, but it doesn't matter now. He died two years ago."

"I apologize," he said and quickly changed the subject. "What did you like best about living in Virginia?"

"More than anything else, I enjoyed the solitude and freedom. A blessing I've had to relinquish since I came to live at Brixton Hall."

"Little wonder you named your horse as a reminder."

The ferry's bell rang and the craft lurched as it shifted course. Drake looked over his shoulder. "Obviously we're not to Charles Towne. Where are we?"

"We're docking at Riverwood Plantation. Its owner, Robert Gray, is a friend of the Sayers. Did you happen to make his acquaintance at the ball last night?"

"I don't believe so."

"He's a pleasant man. Last fall a storm struck and ruined many of the Grays' fields right before the harvest. Zechariah is exchanging rice for other supplies to aid him."

"Is Gray one of the rebels or is he Tory?"

Elise thought of the gunpowder and muskets being traded for rice. "I believe his politics match those of Zechariah. I don't usually pay attention to such things. Men are always preaching to us women that we shouldn't bother with politics. They say our minds are too simple and can't grasp the intricacies required to understand. They're probably right. I have enough trouble counting my cross stitch."

Elise almost choked on her words. She expected Amberly to agree with her in typical male fashion, but he surprised her.

"I don't believe it," he said. "I find that women, given the right encouragement, have no difficulty understanding any given subject. Some are even more clever than men, while the majority are more cunning."

The ferry jarred against the dock. Watching the deckhands rush to tie the mooring lines, Elise noted the cynicism in Drake's voice. She wondered what foolish woman had hurt him.

A loud crash drew Elise's attention to a crate being hauled aboard. She drew in a sharp breath. The box contained weapons and ammunition sorely needed by the patriots. French and American privateers smuggled the weapons as far as Riverwood. From there, she or Christian supervised their removal to Brixton Hall, then saw them farther upriver, and that much closer to the swamps that provided protection for the war-ravaged militia.

It was dangerous to transport munitions to Charles Towne, especially in broad daylight. Under normal circumstances she would have collected them under the cover of night. She didn't have that option today. At the ball last night, a loyal agent had warned Zechariah that the British had gotten wind of Riverwood's stash and planned to raid this afternoon. Now when the Brits arrived on Gray's doorstep, they'd find nothing stored but indigo and cotton, the very crops English merchants demanded of their Colonial brethren.

Seeing the box was safe, she released a sigh of relief, which quickly disappeared when she noticed Amberly's interest in the crate. Hoping to distract him, she entwined her arm with his and acted as though she might faint. "I declare the sun is blinding me. It's strong enough to set my skin afire."

"Would you care for a drink?" he said with concern.

"No, thank you. I just need to sit down." She hated to play the roll of insipid female, but she wanted him as far from the crate as possible. After all, he *was* English and subject to suspicion.

The ferry rocked again, announcing its departure

from Riverwood. She heard the slap of water on the sides of the ferry and felt safe for the time being. The crate would be hidden away from notice. All would be well as long as they avoided the British patrolling the river.

They arrived in Charles Towne a short time later. The British-held city provided the main port for English supplies entering the Southern colonies. From the ferry's deck, Elise watched as ship after ship filled every available berth, their tall masts rising high like a forest of leafless, swaying trees. Seagulls squawked as they dipped and dived in the cloudless blue sky.

With no berth available, the ferry captain anchored in the harbor. He signaled a pair of skiffs to transport his passengers ashore. Grateful for the development, Elise viewed the situation as a blessing. With the ferry anchored away from shore, enemy soldiers would be less tempted to search the nondescript craft. Evidently the Lord had taken pity on her after all.

Elise stepped aboard the second of the smaller boats. Amberly followed and sat beside her on one of the rough-hewn benches that ran horizontally within the skiff. Seven other passengers joined them. The craft moved at speed once the oars were put to water.

The closer they came to the pier, the greater the odor. The stink of rotting fish, unwashed bodies and over-ripe produce infested the wind. Elise removed a scented handkerchief from the satchel she held secure in her lap and covered her nose and mouth.

Drake leaned close. "As I said, Miss Cooper, women are often more clever than men. If not, I'd be the one with something to spare my nose from this stench."

Elise handed him the cloth, but he declined. "I'd think you'd be familiar with the putrid scents of a wharf, Mr. Amberly."

"Aye," he commented drily. "The same as a grave-digger grows used to decay."

The wharf teemed with life. British regulars lined the pier, their black knee-high boots gleaming as they paced in the sun. The racket of hollering sailors, hawking merchants and bustling pedestrians vied with the pummel of waves against the seawall.

Elise waited while a sailor tied the skiff. Drake jumped to the dock and helped her alight from the swaying craft. She moved aside and watched with admiration while he handed up the other women who'd accompanied them.

Finished with the task, he offered to carry her satchel but she refused. They walked along the pier, occasionally stepping over piles of refuse and other debris. Rough-looking sailors pushed and shoved through the crowd, their crude speech booming in her ear.

Drake slipped his arm around her shoulders, pulling her closer to his side as though to protect her from the ruffians. The action startled her. He had no way of knowing her duty to discover information for Zechariah had made her familiar with these harsh surroundings. Drake's care touched a deep chord of gratefulness within her. Other than Christian's brotherly concern, no man had ever shown her such consideration.

At the end of the pier, a congested street stretched before them. Drake asked her for the address she wished to visit, then approached a carriage for hire. He spoke to the driver for several moments before motioning for her to join him. She followed, and when he opened the door for her, stepped into the less-than-grand interior.

"Shall I put your satchel topside?" Drake asked.

"No." She sounded sterner than she meant to, but she had the letters to protect. "No, thank you. Seems everyone is in need of something these days. Luggage has a tendency to walk off on its own."

Drake finished with the driver and removed his tricorn before climbing into the coach. "'Tis the same in London. Thieves delight in robbing a body blind."

Elise tucked the satchel under the seat behind her feet. She swept back the folds of her skirt, making room for him on the worn cowhide seat across from her. The space was so small Drake's head brushed the roof. The ill-sprung hack bounced into motion, eliciting a grunt from him when he bumped his head.

She sat forward in concern. "Are you all right?"

Drake rubbed the abused spot. "Quite so, but I believe I'll be ordering a new coach built before the day is out."

Within a few blocks, the coach rolled to a stop in front of a two-story brick dwelling with a painted black door and shutters. In the side yard, a clothesline hung between Tabby's house and the one next door. A bright green dress and half a dozen white petticoats flapped in the breeze.

"It seems we're already here." He sounded disappointed. "I hope you won't miss me too much while I'm gone."

She would, for he was stimulating company. "Don't be silly, Mr. Amberly. I shall forget you the moment I leave this coach."

Hand to his heart, he said, "You wound me sorely."

She rolled her eyes, trying not to laugh. "Just don't bleed on the cushions. The driver will charge you an even greater fare, and you've already been swindled."

"How so?"

"I heard the outrageous price you settled on when we left the wharf."

"I hired the driver for the whole day."

"But you're paying him for a week."

He shrugged. "I'll not worry about the price and consider it charity. The poor man has twenty-two children and six grandchildren to feed."

"Impossible. He can't be a day over twenty."

"Chasing his grandchildren keeps him young. He turned five and seventy just last week."

Elise shook her head as she recalled the driver's boyish face. Chuckling, "You're mad, Drake Amberly."

"Aha! You called me by my name. Since you've relented, I'll expect you to use it all the more."

The driver thumped on the roof. Elise glanced up. "I believe he thinks we're too obtuse to notice we've stopped. It's no wonder considering how easily he took you for a fortune."

"A pittance, merely."

"If you're not concerned about your funds, I'm certainly not. It's my reputation I'm worried about."

He chuckled. "I should have known."

"I don't want him thinking I'm a simpleton just because of the company I keep."

He picked up her hand and kissed her knuckles. With a wink, he added, "Finally, Miss Cooper, a kind word from your sweet lips. I shall carry it with me all day." He opened the coach door and leapt out. Offering his hand, he helped her down. "I understand the ferry leaves at half past three. I'll send the driver to meet you here an hour prior."

"I can make my own way."

He waved away her protest. "I've no doubt, but why when I've already hired the coach?"

"What about you? How will you return to the wharf?"

"I have business near the waterfront. I'll walk. If you should need me, I'm meeting an associate at a tavern called The Rolling Tide."

Elise glanced away. The shock of his announcement twisted her stomach. How was it possible Amberly chose the very tavern where Hawk had died?

"The Rolling Tide, you say? May I ask what possessed you to choose that despicable place? I hear the food they prepare is nothing short of hog slop."

Thick lashes screened his golden eyes, but the black door of the house flung wide before he could answer.

"Elise, you're here! I was beginning to think you would never arrive." Tabby Smith picked her way down the house's three front steps. With a bright smile on her face and a bloom in her cheeks, she made the picture of contentment. Heavily pregnant, she looked due to give birth any minute.

"Tabby, it's so *good* to see you." The two women embraced, and Elise turned and introduced her friend to Drake.

"It's a pleasure to meet you, Mr. Amberly." Tabby gave him a considering look. "Have we met before?"

Drake bowed respectfully and kissed the back of Tabby's hand. "I don't believe so, Mrs. Smith. I've no doubt I would remember your lovely face."

"I can see you're a charmer, sir." She winked at Elise.

"You'd best watch this one or you'll be married before the summer is out."

"Tabby, please!" Elise felt her cheeks heat. She faced Drake, who didn't bother to disguise his mirth. "Don't you have business down by the wharf, Mr. Amberly?"

"The wharf?" Tabby asked with interest. "If you find yourself hungry, visit a tavern called The Rolling Tide. I hear the food there is delicious."

To his credit, Drake didn't contradict her friend. "I've heard mixed reviews, but since you recommend it, I'll partake of lunch there." To Elise, "You're quite correct, Miss Cooper. I must be on my way." He propped his elbow on the door's inset window. "I hope to meet you again, Mrs. Smith. I shall see you at the ferry, Miss Cooper. Good day to you both."

Elise waved, bereft to see him go. "Good day, Mr. Amberly."

She watched the carriage ramble down the road until it turned out of sight. A wistful sigh broke from her lips as Tabby placed her arm around her shoulders and walked her to the house. "You have the look of a woman falling in love, my friend."

Elise lifted her chin. "Ridiculous. I only met the man last night. Besides, he's English. Other than spying on them, I have no interest in the enemy."

"Prudent, but the heart doesn't always follow the will of the mind. I was engaged to a wealthy planter when I met and eloped with Josiah. Now look at me."

Elise patted her friend's huge belly. "Yes, you're what…thirteen months pregnant?"

Tabby giggled, "Feels like twenty. What do you think your Mr. Amberly meant when he said he'd heard mixed reviews for the Tide?"

"Oh, Tabby, that's my fault." Tabby and Josiah owned The Rolling Tide. The inn had been the favored spot for her and Hawk to meet because Josiah provided a lookout and did anything else he could to help her. He'd been the one to prop the ladder by the window the night Hawk planned to turn her in. Her face scrunched with guilt. "I told him the food was terrible."

Tabby stopped in her tracks and slowly turned her head in disbelief. "You did what? How could you? I prepared the roast leg of lamb myself this very morn. My dumplings are the talk of Charles Towne."

"I know, but it startled me to learn he had business there."

Tabby patted her shoulder in commiseration. "Now I understand. But once he tries my greens and ham, he'll think you have no taste at all. Did you bring the letters?"

Elise nodded. "They're in my satchel. I wrapped them in the blankets I knitted…."

She spun in the middle of the walk and ran to the dirt road, looking in the direction Drake had traveled. "Of all the witless… How could I have been so careless, Tabby? I've forgotten my satchel in Amberly's coach!"

Without any comment, her friend waddled up the steps as fast as her rounded body would take her. Elise ran past just in time to pull the door open wide.

"Henry!" Tabby called her servant. "Fetch the wagon. We have an Englishman and my blankets to catch."

Chapter Six

Drake jumped down from the coach. Disgust raged through him as his gaze swept over the vine-covered windows and red front door of The Rolling Tide. He'd visited the tavern once before, upon his arrival in Charles Towne. Captain Beaufort, his distant cousin and Lieutenant Kirby's superior officer, had brought him here to see the room where Anthony had breathed his last.

The thought stoked his anger until a red haze filled his vision. Perhaps he should have arranged to meet Beaufort elsewhere and saved himself from more bad temper, but in a strange way the place helped him feel closer to Anthony. Somehow it was less painful to cling to his fury than to think of his brother as gone forever.

Except for the short time Elise distracted him, he'd refused to quit his hunt for the Fox. Perhaps the girl's ability to soothe his hatred, if only for a little while, was another reason she appealed to him so much.

The carriage driver, one of Beaufort's spies, jumped down beside him.

"Your name is Goss, correct?" Drake asked.

The driver chewed the twig he'd been using to pick his buckteeth. "Aye, Your Grace, Robin Goss."

Hearing the rube use his title, Drake arched a brow in annoyance. "Captain Beaufort must have informed you of my station. However, kindly remember not to bandy that information about. For the time being I'm simply Mr. Amberly. You may address me as such, or a simple 'sir' will do. Now, I understand I'm paying you a week's wage to await me today."

A cocky grin split the driver's face and his calculating eyes lit with amusement.

Irritated by the man's shifty demeanor, Drake wondered if Goss was as trustworthy as Beaufort believed. "I have instructions for you. At half past two, you're to go to the house we departed on Church Street. Wait for the young woman I accompanied there and return her to the wharf before half past three. Wait with her until I find you. Do you understand?"

"Yup, sir, I understand. I'll follow your instructions to the letter."

Drake bristled at Goss's thinly veiled sarcasm. "You do have a watch?"

"Nope, do I look like I'm made of money?" The clodhopper jabbed the air over his shoulder with his thumb. "I'll listen for the church bells."

"Don't be late."

"Never am." The driver climbed up to his seat and positioned his foot on the brake.

Drake glanced into the coach one last time. The corner of Elise's satchel peeked out from under the bench. He opened the door, intending to collect it, then reconsidered.

"I have a change of plans for you, Mr. Goss." With

an easy shove, Drake closed the coach's door. "Miss Cooper has forgotten her satchel. Rather than await me here, return to the house on Church Street and deliver her belongings."

"Do I come back here once I'm done, or do I wait for her there?"

"Leave yourself available for her. Perhaps she and her friend will have need of you this afternoon."

The driver took up the reins. The church bells announced the noon hour. A steady flow of coaches and wagons clattered past, kicking up the thin layer of dust that covered the street's worn bricks. Robin glanced back over his shoulder. "If she don't choose to make use of my carriage, just deliver her to the wharf like you wanted?"

"Yes," Drake said. "And should you do as I've instructed without fault, I'll double your wage once you return Miss Cooper to me safely."

The spy's eyes bugged in his head. "Real pounds, none of them worthless Continentals?"

Drake took a coin from his pocket and tossed it to the driver. "Genuine sterling."

Robin chucked his twig into the street and a grin spread from one large ear to the other. "You'll have no reason for complaint. I swear it on my mother's grave."

"Brilliant." Drake watched with satisfaction as the coach leapt forward into traffic.

Turning back to the hated tavern, he gritted his teeth. A pair of drunken redcoats threw open the heavy door and stumbled out, laughing boisterously as they passed. Drake shook his head in disgust as he watched them weave their way down the boardwalk. Foxed before noon. With gadabouts like those soldiers, it was little wonder the war had yet to be won.

He caught the door before it closed and entered The Rolling Tide. The heavy portal banged closed behind him, casting the cavernous room into near darkness. He paused a moment for his eyes to adjust. A thin cloud of smoke and the aroma of roasted lamb met him before anything else.

To his right, a fire glowed in the wide, blackened hearth where a leg of lamb turned slowly on a spit. In a far corner, a man reclined with his feet atop a table, his chin to his chest as he snored into his mug. The other patrons, mostly soldiers, raised their cups for refills as two tavern wenches flitted about with pitchers of ale.

His heart ached. Anthony had bled to death in this Spartan place. Helpless fury reared its ugly head like a dragon inside him needing to release fire. The place should be razed to the ground, its every stone smashed into dust.

Forcing himself forward, he took the steps to the second floor two at a time and knocked on the door marked with a number 3, the very room where his brother died. He'd been there before, knew the coffin of a space was hardly bigger than a closet at Hawk Haven. Loosening his collar, he longed to leave, yet his duty to Anthony nailed his boots to the floorboards.

Captain Beaufort, a tall, rigid-backed military man with sandy brown hair and deep-set dark eyes, opened the door. The captain bowed low the moment the door closed. "Good day, Your Grace. It's an honor to serve you once more, cousin."

"Enough with my title, Charles. I thought you understood my request for secrecy. Imagine my surprise when even your spy addressed me as 'Your Grace.'"

"I do apologize, Your...sir. It won't happen again. It's just such an honor..."

Drake scanned the shabby room with its meager furniture and barren walls. Despite his show of deference, his cousin was the same dandy he'd always been. His undeserved air of self-importance grated on Drake's nerves. He pulled out a chair, took a seat and motioned for the captain to do likewise. "I trust you have pertinent news for me this morn?"

Beaufort puffed out his chest, obviously delighted with himself. "I believe so, Your Grace. One of my spies, a frequent contact of your brother's, met with me last night. As you know, I only suspected the Fox had connections to Brixton Hall. He confirmed the brigand frequents the plantation and may even have been at the party last evening."

"We're finally making progress." Drake began an immediate mental inventory of the faces he'd seen at Brixton Hall. "It's doubtful the Fox is Zechariah—"

"Indeed not," Beaufort scoffed. "He's staunchly loyal to His Majesty. Zechariah left his position in the colony's legislature rather than cast his vote for war against the Crown. He sells his crops to British troops instead of feeding the rebels and he allows his townhouse here in Charles Towne to be used as barracks for many of my officers."

Deep in thought, Drake rejected several other candidates. All of them were older, keen of mind but soft around the middle, hardly fit to traipse about the city in disguise. He considered the free servants, deciding on a few to watch, but rejected the slaves as prospects, since he doubted the Africans would have the necessary freedom to roam the countryside without Sayer's knowledge.

Elise came to mind, not because she might be the Fox, but because his thoughts seemed to wander in her direction with a will of their own. He savored her image, then frowned when he remembered Christian. "Perhaps it's the son."

"Again, most doubtful," said Beaufort. "Christian Sayer has a sterling reputation. He served in the Tory brigade before he fell from a horse and injured his leg last summer. I'd stake my life on the whole family's loyalty. There must be someone else. One of the freeman on the estate, a frequent visitor or another relative we haven't yet met."

"Perhaps you're right," Drake agreed, still suspicious of Christian. The puppy had looked hale and hearty to him the previous night. "Zechariah invited me to stay a fortnight. I may have to prevail upon him for the whole of it."

"Perhaps we should be honest with the Sayers," Beaufort suggested. "Tell them what we suspect and glean from them what we can."

"No." Drake moved to the window. "Before going to Zechariah, I think it best to watch Christian for a time. You may trust him, but I do not. There's something about him that seems peculiar. He displays an open personality, but there's a dark quality beneath his sunny facade."

Drake looked out over the busy street and the pair of frayed horses tethered in front of the tavern. "We'll leave this matter between the two of us for the time being."

"But sir…"

Beaufort's argument droned on, but Drake heard no more once he saw Elise and Tabby Smith arrive in a mule-drawn wagon.

Elise handed the reins to Tabby while her friend set the brake. Drake admired Elise's graceful movements as she climbed down from the wagon. Her glorious dark hair hung in a thick rope to below her trim waist and glowed in the bright daylight. He was certain she grew lovelier each time he saw her.

She seemed to be in a hurry, agitated. He didn't see her satchel and he suspected she and Goss had passed each other on the road. She started round the front of the building, as though she meant to go to the side alley, then stopped, retraced her steps, and helped her pregnant friend down from the wagon.

Drake undid the latch and pressed opened the lead glass window. "Miss Cooper," he called, just loud enough to be heard over the clatter of traffic.

Elise froze as though his voice were a gunshot. Her gaze flew to the upper story of the tavern. "Drake!"

She raised her hand to block the sun from her eyes. It surprised her to realize how much happiness lurked beneath the initial alarm of Drake catching her there. Was it possible to actually miss someone she'd seen such a short time ago? "Did you happen upon my satchel, Mr. Amberly? I believe I left it in the coach."

He raised his hand to his ear as though he hadn't been able to hear her, but she was sure she'd spoken loud enough. "One moment, I'll meet you below downstairs."

"There's no need," she assured him, but he'd already gone.

In front of the tavern, Elise balked at the door. She'd

hoped to find the coach waiting outside, enabling her to retrieve her belongings and leave without Amberly ever being the wiser. She should have known better; her luck of late had been spotty at best. "You know I vowed I'd never step foot in The Tide again, Tabby. Just being here is a nightmare."

Tabby took her elbow and dragged Elise a few steps forward. "I know this is difficult for you, but you have to—"

"Do what I must. Yes, I know Tabby, but…" Her stomach rolled in rebellion. "But, I don't think I can."

"Of course you can." Tabby reached for the door's large brass knob. "How will you explain to your Englishman if you run off like a ninny?"

Tabby pulled the door halfway open. Hearty conversation spilled from inside. Elise stepped back, skittish as a calf on market day. "First of all, he's not *my* Englishman. Second, he believes I'm a proper young lady. I… I'll tell him I have Puritan beliefs. That I'd be ashamed to step foot in a tavern."

Tabby bit back a giggle. "A good Christian girl you may be, but a Puritan? He'll not believe it."

Without further ado, Tabby yanked the door open wide and, with a push, sent Elise reeling into the tavern's main room. "See? You're in."

Elise straightened. Her eyes narrowed on Tabby. "You're an evil woman, Tabby Smith. To think I thought you were my friend."

Tabby laughed. "Discounting Prin and Christian, you know I'm the best friend you've got."

Disgruntled, Elise said nothing, since Tabby spoke the truth.

A bright smile lit her friend's face. "There's my sweet husband."

Elise turned to see Josiah Smith approaching them. "Goodness, Tabby, what shall I say if Amberly realizes you're Josiah's wife? I told him the place was terrible and you claimed no knowledge of it beyond the food. Surely, he'll question our silence."

Tabby patted her arm. "I'll say nothing and I'll warn Josiah. He won't give away the game."

"There's my beautiful girl," Josiah said as he ambled forward, his leather apron stretched across his belly. After a quick greeting to Elise, he gave his wife a hearty embrace and led her toward the kitchen.

Elise envied their close bond, and wished a similar one for herself, but felt sadly convinced she'd never find that kind of love and mutual admiration.

Her heart leapt with excitement when she saw Drake at the base of the stairs. Her gaze traveled leisurely over his face, admiring his straight nose, the rakish scar along his jaw, the darkness of his sun-drenched skin.

His mouth turned in the cool half smile she'd begun to find endearing. Their eyes met and locked. Seeing the laughter in his eyes, she realized she'd been staring like a goose and he'd caught her at it. There was nothing else for her to do but hope he wouldn't mention it.

Ha! He'll probably crow all day long.

Elise tore her gaze away and brushed her damp palms in a smoothing motion down the front of her skirt. The man was driving her mad. Despite her best efforts to cover the fact, he seemed to understand how much she favored him. Against her will, her eyes slid back to his face.

As he crossed the room, she admired his inborn confidence. His piercing gaze held her as if he owned her. She felt caught but lacked the will to escape. Begrudgingly, her admiration for him grew.

Tabby returned to her. "Wake up. Do you want your Englishman to think your body has mutinied against your brain?"

"Don't be addled." Elise dug her fingernails into her palm to regain her composure. She noticed Josiah had stayed in the kitchen.

Drake reached her and enveloped her hands in his. "What a pleasant surprise. I thought I'd be deprived of your company for most of the day."

The warmth in his eyes made her feel more light-hearted than she had in years, an odd sensation to be sure, given the severity of her circumstances. "I left my belongings in the coach. I wished to fetch them back."

He reached out as though he couldn't contain the action, and brushed a lock of hair from her brow. "I assumed you would need the contents and returned the carriage to Mrs. Smith's. You must have passed it on the road."

She glanced at her friend. "I didn't see it on our way here, did you?"

"I doubt I'd have recognized it if I had," her friend admitted. "To me, one hired carriage looks the same as all the others."

"When did you send it?" Elise asked Drake.

"The church bells rang twelve just as he left."

"Was the driver to return here?"

"No, I told him to wait for you in case you needed him this afternoon. I also instructed him to deliver you to the dock in time for the ferry."

Elise felt herself soften toward him. "That was very thoughtful of you, Mr. Am—"

"Drake," he insisted.

She gave in against her better judgment. "Drake. I appreciate your kindness."

Tabby cleared her throat. "I hate to interrupt the two of you when you're so intent on one another, but we're drawing strange looks standing here in the center of the room."

At that bold reminder, Elise pulled away until Drake had to release her hand. "Then perhaps we should leave. We need to find the coach."

"That won't do," Drake protested. "I'm certain the driver will return here once he realizes you're no longer in residence. If you leave now, it's more than likely you'll miss him again."

"If he doesn't run off with the satchel instead," Tabby said as Drake pulled out a chair and shuffled Elise into it.

"Miss Cooper assures me I'm paying him well to await me today." He rounded the table and helped Tabby settle before taking a seat for himself. "I've paid him half of what we agreed. I have no doubt he'll return for the balance. It's only a matter of time before he revisits with your things."

Josiah hovered a foot away. "You there," Tabby spoke up, drawing her husband's attention. "What are you serving today? I've always found the fare you serve pleasant enough, but my good companions here have heard mixed reviews." She grinned at Elise. "However, good food or not, I'm eating for two and I suppose I'll have to take my chances."

Josiah looked affronted but played along. Obviously

Tabby had taken the chance to warn him. "A pox on the liar that slandered my tavern, ma'am. It just so happens you're in the finest eating establishment in all Charles Towne. Let me fetch Louise. She'll serve you some dumplings while I prepare a platter of lamb."

Tabby shooed him away with the wave of her hand. "Be quick about it then. I'd hate to have this babe before I get to eat, no matter how bad the food may prove to be."

Elise ducked her head and covered her laughter by coughing into her hand. Josiah headed in the direction of the kitchen, muttering under his breath about the unfortunate man who'd married such a harpy.

"Well," Tabby huffed. "The service leaves much to be desired. I hope I *was* misled about the food or this place will have nothing to recommend it."

Louise, a buxom blonde, approached the table from the direction of the kitchen. She balanced the heavy tray she carried on the edge of the table and plunked a pewter mug in front of each of them.

"I'll have water to drink," Tabby said when Louise poured cider for Drake.

"Aye, mum," Louise replied, her cockney accent as thick as a loaf of bread. Elise knew the woman had arrived fresh from London less than six months earlier. Josiah must have warned Louise not to acknowledge Tabby as anyone but a common customer and not his wife. The woman ignored Elise and Tabby completely but favored Drake with a sultry promise in her wide blue eyes. She made a show of bending close so that her billowy blouse gapped open just so.

Elise narrowed her eyes and nearly gave in to the urge to pinch the flirt. To Drake's credit, she noted he did his best to ignore the eye-popping display. His restraint impressed her and her respect for him raised another notch.

"I believe I have enough," he said drily, reaching up to tip the pitcher away before his mug overflowed. "Any more and the table will enjoy quite a dousing."

"Oi!" the blonde exclaimed. "Ye're jus so 'andsome I lost ev'ry thought in me poor little 'ead."

The barmaid sloshed cider into Tabby's mug, but nearly missed Elise's altogether. "Wait right 'ere. I be bringing yer dumplin's sooner an ye can blink."

The blonde backed away from the table and rushed in the direction of the kitchen, looking over her shoulder at Drake until she ploughed into a redcoat and got a hearty shove for her trouble.

"Serves her right," Tabby muttered. "She gave me cider when I asked for water. That girl needs a good comeuppance."

Josiah returned with the platter of roasted lamb. Fresh herbs adorned the top and added to the mouthwatering aroma. "Where are your dumplings? I sent Louise to fetch them. She should have brought them out by now."

"She got…distracted," Elise answered. "I fear we'd best hurry and feed my friend. We've waited so long she's going to faint from starvation."

Josiah's eyes filled with concern as he focused on his wife. Elise felt guilty for teasing him. "Are you truly ill, missus? If so, I'll—"

"I'm fine," Tabby assured him. "Just hungry."

He nodded. "My wife is expecting and she complains of the same without ceasing. She used to be such a tiny little thing. Now she rivals my horse in size and my arms have ceased to fit around her."

Elise stifled another giggle. Tabby's look promised retribution.

"I'll go help Louise with the rest of your meal," Josiah said. "I promise I'll hurry."

"Don't forget the greens," Tabby called after him. She settled back in her chair once he waved that he'd heard her over the rumble of the other patrons. "So, Mr. Amberly, what brings you to this part of the Colonies? Are you an adventure seeker out to make a name for yourself in the war?"

Drake set down his mug. He smiled politely, but his eyes were inscrutable. "I'm here on business, Mrs. Smith. I wish to reestablish shipping contracts now that Charles Towne is free of the rebels' hold."

"Really?" Tabby replied wide-eyed. "I understood the rebels are everywhere." She leaned forward and lowered her voice. "Why, I'm as loyal as can be, but I admit I've got a soft spot in my heart for the Fox."

Elise's stomach twisted sickly.

Drake leaned forward, his interest palpable. "What do you know of him, Mrs. Smith? I've heard he's a cheeky fellow. Some inept farmer who survives on luck alone."

Elise took exception to that. "No doubt you heard such from the redcoats who've failed to catch him."

"No doubt," he said. "Do you know otherwise?"

"Goodness, no. Why would I know anything about the man?"

Tabby giggled. "Elise know anything about the Fox? How very funny."

Louise delivered a large steaming pot of dumplings

and a smaller one of greens topped with ham. "There you be, sir. I 'ope it's to yer liking."

"I'm sure it will be," Elise cut in deliberately. She gave the girl a hard, meaningful look and pointed across the room. "I believe the soldiers at yonder table need their mugs refilled."

The girl pouted as she left. Elise picked up her spoon to sample Tabby's light, fluffy specialty when Josiah lumbered over to the edge of the table. He motioned toward the door, where a man stood in the shadows. "There's a hired man waiting by the door. Says he knows you, miss. Claims he has some of your belongings."

"My satchel!" Elise jumped up, causing her chair to grate on the wood floor. "I'll be right back." She shot across the room, anxious to lay hold on the important letters.

She recognized the hack driver once she got close enough to see his face. The man's buckteeth flashed into prominence as he shifted the leather case, angling it behind his back. She held out her hand. "Thank you for returning my things."

He retreated a step. "I'm thinking I deserve more than your thanks, Miss."

Her brow furrowed in confusion. "Really? How so? What is it you think you deserve?"

His suggestive glance made her skin crawl. Annoyed, she bit back a scathing retort and held out her hand. "I suggest, sir, that you keep your mind out of the gutter and give me my satchel…unless you'd rather I call my friend."

The yokel peered over her shoulder. She was certain he could see Amberly's formidable presence. The driver's leer faded into sour resignation. "I'm thinking I deserve a reward."

"How so?" Elise inquired. "You're being paid to wait the day. By rights I should be able to leave my belongings in the coach if I like."

"Your friend seemed to think this here satchel was important to you."

"Of course it's important," she snapped. "For interest's sake, how much reward do you require?"

The driver studied the tips of his fingers. His eyes narrowed to sly slits. "A hundred pounds."

She gasped. "Are you crazed?"

"Crazed? Nah. I'm thinking it's a fair sum considering how much I could get for your letters if I took 'em to the Redcoats."

Her heart picked up speed. "What on earth do you mean?"

"Just that I can read between the lines, so to speak."

"Then you must be a soothsayer, for there's nothing between the lines but parchment."

The man regained some of his boldness. "Aye, unless there's a flame nearby."

Anxiety cut through her. This shifty, obnoxious hack driver had somehow discovered the letters' invisible ink. "I don't know what you're talking about."

He shook his head, his upper lip twisted in a sneer. "Don't make the mistake of thinking I'm a lackwit just because I'm hired help. Seems we're both more than we appear. Why don't we step outside?"

"I can't." Elise sent a covert glance toward Drake, who studied them with keen regard. Tabby chatted cheerfully in an unsuccessful ploy to sway his interest from her and the driver. "My companions will question why I've gone."

The driver tugged on his earlobe and scowled. "I'm thinking I'll keep this here satchel till you can lay hold of the funds. You can tell your fancy gent I'm holding it for safe keeping."

"That won't do."

Drake stood and started toward them. Her nerves jangled in alarm. If he interrupted, would the driver call on the redcoats in the tavern and give her away? "Take the satchel to the back alley. I'll meet you there as soon as I'm able."

"You're not going to try anything smart, are you? If you do, I'll take it up with the Brits."

"I'll not try anything smart," she assured him. "I just want my case and *all* its contents. Now go!"

With a sharp nod, he left, causing her to squint when he opened the door and a bright ray of light stabbed the darker interior.

Elise headed back to her companions, dodging various patrons as they stood abruptly from their seats. Drake waited for her a few feet from their table, his expression lined with concern.

Once she reached him, Drake pulled out her chair. She remained standing, offering a shrug when Tabby sent her a glance rife with questions. "I'm sorry, but I must excuse myself for a few moments more."

Drake reached for her hand. A surge of warmth shot up her arm and traveled straight to her heart. She held her breath as his dark eyes searched her face.

"Is all well with you?" he asked quietly. His thumb brushed her knuckles in a soothing manner. "I notice you have yet to retrieve your satchel."

"Every…everything's fine. I—"

"I believe," said Tabby, pointing toward the back of the tavern, "the privies are that way. You'll have to leave by the front door since the only other passage to the back is through the kitchen."

Elise sighed with relief, grateful for Tabby's quick thinking, even if her suggestion was a trifle embarrassing. She excused herself without further comment, and wove her way back through the maze of chairs, tables and customers to the front door.

Stepping into the heat and sunshine, she exchanged the raucous laughter inside for the noise of passing wagons and carriages. The wind caught her hair as she hurried around the corner into the side alley. She wrinkled her nose at the rancid smell. Ants covered rotting food and a picked-over ham bone while rats scurried away, abandoning their decayed feasts of fruit when she stepped too near.

Rounding the back of the tavern, she remembered the large group of redcoats waiting for her the night of Hawk's death. Bile rose in her throat.

A few feet ahead, her newest adversary leaned against the brick wall, one leg bent at the knee while he chewed his thumbnail. He noticed her arrival and straightened, his insolent sneer firmly in place.

Elise stopped just out of his reach. "I've only now excused myself from my friends. I need a few moments more to collect the sum you've demanded."

He picked at his large front teeth while he mulled things over. "You happen to be in luck. I've got just a few more minutes to spare. You best hurry though, else I'll start thinking you're playing me for a fool."

"I assure you I'm not. I'll return shortly."

Without waiting for his reply, she rushed through the tavern's back door. Bright light shone through the open windows, but even the breeze couldn't dispel the room's odor of stale ale and wood smoke. Pewter dishes and a cast iron skillet sat staked on a rough-hewn table near a large bucket of soapy water. Nearby a straw broom leaned against the wall, a small hill of crumbs and dust beside it.

The other serving girl, Alice, hoisted a large platter filled with steaming bowls of dumplings to her shoulder. "Miss Cooper? What are you doing back here in the kitchen? I thought I saw you with Mrs. Smith in the tavern room."

"You did, Alice. Tell me, where is Josiah? I need to speak with him. It's urgent."

The other girl returned her tray to the counter. "I'll get him for you. Be back in a rush."

Elise watched her go, willing her to hurry. She ran to the window, her nerves carrying her there to see if the hack driver still waited.

Josiah burst through the door several moments later. "What is it, Elise? Alice says you're mighty distressed."

"We must keep our voices low," she said, accepting his outstretched hands. "I fear I'm in one of the most prickly spots I've ever tripped into."

"Tell me," he whispered. "You know I'll do everything I can to help."

She quickly related the details of the situation. "Now the weasel is demanding one hundred pounds for my letters, or he'll seek out the authorities."

Josiah looked thunderous. "The dirty scoundrel! A hundred pounds is a fortune, Elise. The Tide is prosperous to be sure, but I don't have a sum like that just lying about. If I had it, you know I'd give it to you without a qualm, but I haven't."

She chewed on her lower lip and noticed the agony in his expression. She hated drawing him into her problems at all. "Don't trouble yourself, Josiah, truly. I have no doubts you'd help me if you could."

Josiah's face lit up in sudden realization. "Perhaps I *can* help."

"How?"

"I'll have Matthew and John fetch your belongings for you."

She shook her head. "They're liable to kill him. I know he's a thief and a scoundrel, but…"

"Such an outcome would solve your problems."

She frowned, remembering Hawk. "No, I want no more blood on my hands."

"You'll have no blood at all if he goes to the Brits. Corpses don't need it."

"Josiah, please stop. I must figure a way out of this pickle with no one dying in the process."

He crossed his arms, rubbing his chin as he thought through a plan. "Does this driver know your name or anything concerning you except your appearance?"

"I don't believe so," she replied. "Even the letters bear a false signature."

"Good," he said, nodding his satisfaction. "John and Matthew will collect him—"

"But—"

He held up his hand, halting her argument. "Let me finish. I'll have the two of them collect the scum. He'll be hurt no more than a good thump on the head. We'll keep him in a warehouse near the wharf until we know you're safe. Even if he goes to the Brits once we release him, he'll have no evidence. The letters will be gone. With the lads dragging him off, he won't be able to point a finger to any involvement here. He doesn't know your name. Without conclusive proof, he has nothing."

The back door swung open. Elise jerked in surprise. Her nemesis popped his head inside. "There you are. I thought I'd have to hunt you down."

She faced him, hoping she blocked his view of Josiah. The fewer people he could identify as helping her, the better. "As you can see, I'm here. I need a few minutes more."

He stretched his neck, trying to see who stood behind her. "You've had all the time I'm willing to give you."

"You can't be serious," she argued. "You're demanding a fortune. Do you believe I carry that sum on my person? I have to be given some time."

The driver's mouth tightened into a straight line, but the tips of his buckteeth overlapped his bottom lip, giving him the appearance of a rodent. "I'll give you until the church bells sound two, but not a moment longer." As he turned to leave, his eyes assaulted her with lecherous intent. "If you don't have it by then, we'll discuss what else you've got to buy my silence. Either way, I'll be waiting in my carriage."

"Just one more question," Elise said, squelching the desire to spit in his face. He glanced at her from over his bony shoulder. "How did you learn to read between the lines?"

"That's my secret."

"Very well, but why did you suspect me and my letters?" She wanted to shake the information out of him.

"I didn't suspect you. Who would, you being such a pretty wench and all? I was looking for coin when I found them in those knitted blankets. You don't need to know any more 'an that."

He left, whistling a merry tune. Once he'd gone, Josiah growled, "I'll send the lads to meet him. The ferret'll never know what hit him."

Elise waited as long as she dared before leaving the kitchen. She offered a prayer Drake wouldn't question why she'd been gone so long. She hurried along the back of the tavern, slipping once on a mildew-covered rock. When she arrived at the front door, she inhaled a deep breath and steadied her nerves. Brushing her moist palms down the front of her skirt, she combed her fingers through her hair and adopted a serene air.

Inside the tavern, a group of men played darts. As she neared the table, she saw Louise hovering behind Drake, pitcher in hand to refill his cup if he took even the smallest sip. He seemed unaware of the blonde's attentions as he spoke with Tabby.

He smiled when he saw her, a flash of white teeth that lit up his lean face. Elise brightened in return, surprised by the sense of safety he provided.

He stood when she drew near, his conversation forgotten. "I feared Mrs. Smith and I might need to form a search party."

She forced a giggle as she took her seat, trying and failing to hide behind her usual mask of frivolity. "Oh, I'm sorry to be gone so long, but I met up with an acquaintance and we had much to discuss." At least that wasn't a lie.

Tabby tsked her disapproval. "A sillier girl I've yet to meet. Didn't you think it rude to abandon one group of friends for another?"

"I didn't abandon you," Elise protested, thankful for

Tabby's attempt to divert Drake from asking deeper questions. "What would you have me do, ignore my friend?"

"You did well enough ignoring us."

Elise smiled sweetly. "Tabby, please do remind me to push you off a pier some day."

"Ladies, 'tis a pity to see the likes of such good friends quarreling. Mrs. Smith, surely we waited no longer than a quarter of an hour. Who among us hasn't been waylaid from time to time by an inopportune acquaintance?"

Elise made a face at her friend. "Yes, who among us hasn't?"

Tabby snorted. "I should have known you'd come to her aid, Mr. Amberly. If you're anything like other men, you've already been overpowered by her charms."

"Tabby!" Elise reddened with mortification. "Please, do be quiet. Mr. Amberly's no more enamored of me than I am with him."

Tabby grinned at Drake. "I wouldn't take a wager on that, my friend."

"Nor would I," Drake said, his deep voice as stimulating as a caress. His dark eyes bored into hers and for a moment Elise sat transfixed. "But if you'd like to lose your coin, my girl, I'm game."

Tabby's laughter broke the spell. "You'd best close your mouth, Elise. Hanging open as it is, you'll draw in flies."

Elise snapped her mouth shut, her face as hot as fire. "Are the two of you quite tired of poking fun at me? Is this some sort of punishment for my taking too long at the privy?"

Tabby giggled harder, her pregnant belly shaking

with mirth. Elise sighed and handed her friend a napkin. "Do stop, Tabby. It wasn't that funny."

Her friend dabbed at her eyes. "I'm so sorry. It's just… Elise…your face." She fell into another fit of laughter. "Goodness, now I'm the one who has to visit the privy."

Elise helped Tabby lever herself out of the chair in spite of her teasing. When her friend was out of earshot, Elise's gaze slunk back to Drake. "I'm sorry about that. My friend has an odd sense of humor."

He eased her hand into his larger one. "I'm sorry if you were embarrassed, but your friend is right. I'm captivated by you."

Speech deserted her. His sincerity rang true and yet her instincts assured her Drake Amberly wasn't a man given to shallow feelings or light declarations. Never in her life had she wanted to believe a man so much.

Yet she couldn't afford romantic attachments. No matter how fascinating she found him, she would have to deny the attraction. She'd learned that those she loved became pawns in Zechariah's game to bend her to his will. She removed her hand from his grasp, regretting the loss that same instant. A cheer from the soldiers playing darts erupted behind her. Drake leaned back in his chair. The tip of his finger circled the edge of his mug as he watched her from under lush downcast lashes. "I see I've spoken too soon, but I'm not a man easily dissuaded once I find something I want."

The faint sound of church bells jolted her with a reminder of her satchel. "What time is it?"

Drake extracted his watch from the pocket of his waistcoat. "Two o'clock."

She scanned the smoky tavern. Josiah was nowhere

to be seen. The bell tolled a second time. Her agitation increased. Her hands balled into fists in her lap. Where was he? Had Matthew and John failed to retrieve her belongings…or was the driver on his way to the Brits with the evidence that could hang her?

Chapter Seven

"Then what happened?" Prin gasped.

Elise glanced into the mirror where she sat in front of her dressing table. Never had she felt so much relief in retiring to her bedchamber, the cloak of night putting an end to her horrid day.

In the candlelight, her sister's reflection looked back at her, beautiful dark eyes wide and anxious. Elise took a dollop of lavender-scented cream and rubbed it into her throat and hands. "Josiah came in smiling. At that point, I knew Matthew and John must have met with success. Later, Josiah confirmed it when we had a moment to speak. Amberly seemed unfazed by the need to hire another coach."

Prin sat on the windowsill. Distracted by something outside, she waved an ivory-handled fan in hopes of encouraging a breeze. "Your Englishman is plum spoiled. I thought it the first time I saw him."

Elise joined Prin at the window. Far beyond the lawn, the orange glow of a bonfire betrayed the location of slave row. Her heart ached for Prin. She knew her sister longed to be with her husband, but it wasn't possible for Prin to stay with Kane in one of the men's cabins.

"I thought you said he was dangerous?" she said, trying to distract Prin from the woeful song that carried across the darkness.

"Aye, that too."

"Well, whatever he is, he dealt with his disappointment rather well considering the sum he paid that ferret of a driver." Elise caught Prin's attention in the mirror. "Will you finish braiding my hair?"

Prin set her fan aside and began finger-combing the mass of Elise's dark tresses. "Why would your man worry what he paid? Judgin' by those fancy togs of his, he doesn't seem short of money."

"True," Elise said in contemplation. "But surely a tradesman would grumble when losing such a large sum over a hired coach. Still, he's English. They're an enigma at the best of times."

Later, Prin tucked in comfortably beside her, Elise finished her prayers and watched the flickering shadows on the plastered ceiling. The mantel clock chimed midnight. She left the bed, picking up her fan from the side table as she went. At the window, she leaned against the sill and looked out into the night, idly tapping the fan in her palm. A mosquito bit her arm. She swatted the pest and rubbed the sting.

Stars winked in the velvety sky, and the slightest whiff of smoke laced the sultry air. The nearby outbuildings stood as darkened apparitions in the yard. Farther afield, the fires no longer burned on slave row. The singing had stopped, casting the night into an eerie, silent clam. Even the trees stood motionless, not enough breeze to sway their limbs or rustle the leaves.

Elise lit another candle and glanced at the bed, where Prin's thin form made little more than a bump on the feather mattress. If only they'd been left alone in Virginia, she thought for the thousandth time. Their father's farm had burned after a bolt of lightning struck during a violent storm, but they could have rebuilt, gone on just as they had, and enjoyed a life of peace and freedom with their father's hateful presence buried in the ground.

This whole mess was her fault, Elise thought. If only she hadn't written her mother, unwisely mentioning her father's death in the tornado, Roger would never have had a chance to enter their lives and muck them up so cruelly.

"Oh, do stop, Elise," she whispered to herself. It helped nothing to fret about the past. She needed to concentrate on the present, for that was all she had. Her future was too precarious to contemplate and best left in God's hands.

Drake leaned back against the wooden bench, his arm propped along the narrow back as he chewed a sprig of mint. He'd quit the stifling confines of his room over an hour ago, hoping the fresh night air might clear his head, but he and a hooting owl remained wide-awake.

Here in the garden, the fresh scent of herbs and the sweet smell of flowers combined with the mustiness of damp earth. The gentle lap of the river should have been relaxing, but it wasn't. Thoughts of Elise kept him from sleep. Even the knowledge that he'd managed to track the Fox to his den didn't ensnare him as much as she did.

Usually a man of single-minded determination, he knew he should be devising some form of trap for his enemy, not mooning after a young woman he knew so little about. Yet today he'd admitted his attraction to Elise like an untried lad. Little wonder she hadn't taken him seriously.

Truth be told, he didn't understand his rash behavior. Past relationships had taught him to be wary in his dealings with women. He'd never had trouble attracting females, but he felt his title and fortune were his biggest draw. His wife had certainly let him know she thought so and his recent fiancée's unfaithfulness solidified the belief.

The owl hooted, and insects filled the night with chatter. Perhaps Miss Cooper had managed to dodge his every defense and capture his attention because her interest in him seemed genuine though she knew nothing of his true identity?

Whether or not that was the case, he couldn't deny he found her beautiful, witty and charming. Her mix of strength and vulnerability made him admire her and wish to protect her. He tensed remembering how every nerve in his body had jumped to attention the moment Beaufort's spy entered the tavern with Elise's satchel.

Something was amiss between her and Goss. The odd little man had disappeared after he left The Rolling Tide, and Elise seemed agitated when he queried her about the situation on the return trip to Brixton Hall.

Clearly, she doesn't trust me. He rubbed his eyes with the palm of his hand. He would just have to give her time.

He frowned. Time was a precious commodity, and he had far too little to squander. He had a few weeks at best before he wore out the Sayers' welcome, and once he found the Fox and saw the brigand hanged, he'd need to sail for home.

He clawed his fingers through his hair. The wisest course would be to leave Elise alone and put neither of them at risk of heartbreak...unless, of course, he could convince her to return to England with him.

Chapter Eight

Elise sat down for a breakfast of sausage and eggs the next morning, still tired from a restless night. Her few snatches of sleep had been filled with dreams of Drake's golden eyes. Today, she would have to be strong and establish a dividing line between them. It wasn't the wisest course of action when she considered the information she'd been ordered to obtain from him, but she had little choice if she hoped to keep her heart and emotions intact once the assignment ended.

Christian entered the dining room and locked the door behind him. "Hello," he grumbled, his level gaze making her uneasy. He broke eye contact and moved to the sideboard. "You're looking well this morning."

"And you're looking flat." Elise eyed her friend's mussed hair and rumpled clothes. His usual exuberance was muted by an obviously long night and overabundance of ale. "What happened? Were you trampled by a runaway horse?"

Christian grunted in response. He chose a plate from the sideboard and filled it with a pile of dry toast. Sitting across from her, he adjusted the candelabra and studied her with red-rimmed eyes. "How is Amberly?"

Elise lowered her lashes, shielding her gaze from Christian's scrutiny. She used her fork to push a bite of egg around her plate. "I suspect he's fine. He's out riding with Zechariah."

"Good, then we have time to talk. I can't put my finger on why, but I believe our guest is up to something quite rotten."

Elise shook her head in Drake's defense. "I don't believe so. Mr. Amberly and I have spoken on numerous subjects. He's neither said nor done anything to conflict with his claims. Why, if you could have seen the devotion in his eyes when he spoke of his family, you wouldn't question his honesty either."

He rolled his eyes. "Dearest, don't be a fool. He's aiming to gain your sympathy."

"Well, he has it. 'Tis a sad thing indeed, but his younger brother recently passed away."

"Passed away? How? Did he suffer from some malady or die in battle?"

Elise refolded the linen napkin in her lap and placed it next to her plate. "He died by means of foul play. Whether it was here or in England, I know not."

After a moment's contemplation, Christian shrugged. "Most intriguing."

"What?"

"How easily he's played you."

She scowled.

"I believe your emotions may be involved. It's made you vulnerable."

"I think you're in league with Prin to drive me mad. Ever since the ball she's been making sly innuendoes and harping on the fact she thinks I'm in love. You're both ridiculous. I've known the man less than three days, and besides, emotional…entanglement doesn't interest me in the least."

"I know." His eyes bore into hers for a moment. "However, I might be less doubtful if you sounded more convincing. At any rate, I believe Amberly means to have you. That he's not above using you for his own satisfaction, then abandoning you whenever he returns to England."

Elise wanted to believe better of Drake, to trust her instincts concerning his intentions toward her, but her mother's similar situation with Roger and Christian's emphatic warning chipped away at her hopes for the Englishman.

"I saw the two of you at dinner last night," he said.

"We didn't speak three words to each other."

"True, but neither of you could stop looking at the other." Christian paused again and his voice became earnest. "I saw the interest in Amberly's eyes the instant he noticed you at the ball and again last night. That kind of emotion will grow and grow until someone gets burned in the end. And it won't be him."

Elise looked away.

"As someone who cares for you, as someone I believe you know you can trust, I think it's only right to mention in all likelihood the man's intentions are far from honorable. Put simply, he's not going to be here long, and I don't want to see you hurt."

Elise's heart fell. Of course, Christian was right. How could she have so easily forgotten the lessons of a lifetime? Didn't men always find a way to get what they wanted? Some, like her father, used abuse and pounding fists to force their will. Others, like her stepfather, made promise after false promise to manipulate their prey.

"You're not saying anything I don't already know."

"For shame, I hate being redundant." He finished his last slice of toast. "At the risk of repeating myself *again*—be careful."

"I assure you I will be." She picked up her cup. "Both with Amberly and Beaufort. Zechariah mentioned he'd invited the captain for a visit today."

"Not today. He's been delayed in Charles Towne. Seems one of his spies has gone missing. You don't happen to know about that, do you?"

"Why would I?"

"Oh, I don't know. From what I can piece together, the man is a hired driver last seen at The Rolling Tide."

Elise blinked with genuine surprise and quickly told him what had transpired the previous day. "I can't believe that rodent-faced driver is one of Beaufort's spies! Though it does explain how he knew about the invisible ink. How did you learn the truth about him?"

"Beaufort and I spent the whole of last night with a couple of his cronies in a mean game of Whist."

"You must have been bored to tears." She laughed. "By the look of you, I thought you'd been charming one of your marks."

A cocky grin spread across Christian's mouth. "You like believing I'm no more than a handsome rake. I try not to disillusion you."

She took another sip of tea and regarded him over the rim of her cup. "I never said you were handsome."

He ignored her last comment and rubbed his chin, deep in thought. "When you arrived in Charles Towne yesterday afternoon, who chose the coach? You or Amberly?"

"He did. Why?"

"Because when I mentioned Amberly was our houseguest, Beaufort turned strangely quiet. I couldn't fish any more information out of him."

"That in itself is an oddity."

"Indeed. I'm thinking it's mighty convenient Amberly chose a driver who just happened to be one of Beaufort's spies."

Elise had to concur. She hoped Drake was incapable of anything sinister, but she was too seasoned a spy not to be wary.

"Where did you go once you left the wharf?"

"Tabby's." She hesitated. Her heart prompted her to protect Drake, but her responsibilities lay elsewhere. "Then Amberly left for The Rolling Tide."

"You can't be serious. When did you plan to tell me?"

Elise left her seat and approached the window. Gardeners with scythes in hand clipped the rolling green lawn, refreshing the humid air with the scent of cut grass. "Now. He said he had business."

"What kind of business?"

She wrung her hands, her heart and head at odds for the first time in her life. She had to admit the evidence cast a suspicious light in Drake's direction, but a part of her insisted she give him the benefit of a doubt. "Something concerning his shipping interests."

A knock sounded, preventing Christian from asking further questions. Elise crossed the Oriental rug, unlocked and opened the door. A house slave in a simple blue dress stood there, a nervous look marring her pretty face. Knowing the young girl frightened easily,

Elise smiled to put her at ease. "Good morning, Tess, what can I do for you?"

The girl's hands relaxed against the front of her dark cotton skirt. "Prin's not feelin' so well. She told me to find you and ask you to go up to your room."

"Of course, I'll go straight away." Thankful for a reprieve, Elise turned back to Christian. "I'll speak with you later."

She ran up the stairs, in a hurry to reach Prin. Her sister never complained of being ill unless she was near death's door. As far as three doors down, she heard the sound of someone retching. The upper floors of the house were nearly empty this time of morning. Only Prin remained as far as she knew. She burst into a run.

Entering the room, she gagged on the stench of vomit. Her eyes darted around the bedchamber, passing over the empty, rumpled bed and wide-open windows that provided enough breeze to rustle the sheer white curtains, but not enough to clear the smell.

"Prin?"

A slight moan drew her eyes to the corner where her sister sat on the floor, a chamber pot in her lap. Ashen beneath her mocha skin, her night rail had fallen from one shoulder and a sheen of perspiration dotted her upper lip.

Elise dashed across the room, kneeling by her sister and holding the pot as another heaving fit shook Prin's thin form. When the spasms subsided, Elise held her for a moment, soothing the dark curls from her sister's clammy forehead. "Are you feeling any better?"

"A little," Prin whispered. "I need some water to rinse my mouth."

Elise eased away to fetch the drink. "Here you are,

dearest. What's made you so ill? Was it something you ate?"

Prin rinsed her mouth and spat into the chamber pot. "I don't know. I've felt poorly for the last week or so. It's been worse and worse until this morning, when I couldn't keep anythin' down."

"Why didn't you tell me?"

"You've got so many things to worry about, I don't want to be more of a burden."

"You're never a burden." Elise kissed the top of Prin's head. "I love you more than anyone. One day soon we'll be free of these lives neither of us wants to lead. In the meantime, the Lord will help us through. He promises not to give us more than we can handle and I don't want you working yourself into the ground."

Elise dampened a cloth with the pitcher's remaining water and pressed it to Prin's brow. Crossing to the bedside, she pulled a cord and rang for one of the kitchen staff. "I'm going to order you some dry toast and tea."

Prin groaned. "I don't think I can eat at the moment."

"You will in a little while. You mustn't allow yourself to become too weak." Elise took the pot from Prin's shaky fingers and set it outside the door.

Returning to Prin, she helped her sister back to the four-poster bed. She covered her with the wrinkled white sheet, then opened another window in hopes of clearing the air.

"I'm so hot," Prin tugged off the sheet. "I miss the cooler air of home. It's only July, but if the heat keeps risin' I'll be a puddle by August."

When Tess returned, Elise ordered the food and hot tea with honey.

The maid nodded and collected the chamber pot

without being asked. "I'll get you a clean one of these too, Miss."

Elise returned to the bed, where she found Prin slumped against the pillows with her eyes closed. "She'll be back in a few minutes. Toast will help settle your stomach and the tea with honey will soothe your throat."

"I feel so weak, I think a wisp of smoke could carry me off."

Elise squeezed her sister's hand. "I'd catch you if it did."

Prin smiled weakly. "I know."

Another knock sounded at the door. Elise answered it, accepted the laden tray and carried it back to the bedside table. Tess deposited a clean chamber pot on the floor near the door and left.

Elise held Prin's head to help her with the tea. "Be careful, it's a little warm," she warned.

Prin took a sip, then turned her head away. "I can't drink any more."

"Try some toast."

"Not yet."

Elise settled her sister against the pillows. "You say you've been feeling this miserable for a week?"

"At least."

"Have you had a fever?"

"No."

"If I ask you a question will you be honest with me?"

Prin cracked open her eyes. "I've never lied to you in my life."

Taking a deep breath, Elise stood and leaned against the bedpost. "Could you...could you be with child?"

Prin nodded, her eyes welling with tears. "I think I jus' might be."

The muscles along Elise's neck and shoulders tightened into painful knots. Their problems were compounded. If the war didn't end before the baby's birth, Zechariah would be the lawful owner of the babe. She would be forced to buy her own niece or nephew. How she *hated* slavery! The meager funds she'd been saving to buy Kane when they left would never stretch to pay for a child as well.

Dear God, You have to help us.

"Does Kane know?" she asked, striving to sound calm.

"No. I feared admitting it even to myself."

Elise tried to offer a comforting smile. "Everything will be all right."

"How can it be?" Prin's beautiful dark eyes filled with tears, breaking Elise's heart. Prin rarely cried and always endeavored to be a pillar of strength and cheerfulness. Elise sat on the edge of the bed and gathered Prin in her arms. She rubbed her back, hoping to offer silent comfort.

Prin lifted her head and looked out the window in the direction of the slave cabins. "If not for you, I'd be out there with 'em, sleepin' in the bugs, and eatin' nothing but gruel. Much as I don't want to be there I sometimes feel guilty I'm not." She started to weep in earnest. "Oh, Lisie, Kane lives like that, and there's nothin' I can do for him. What am I gonna do when this war ends and we're free to go? How am I 'spose to take our babe and leave him here sufferin'?"

Elise wiped the tears from under her sister's large brown eyes, now red from misery. What could she say to ease her sister's pain? She could think of nothing. How could she make promises to take Kane with them? Even if Zechariah agreed to sell the burly slave, she knew it might take years to earn enough additional funds to buy his freedom. "I don't know, dearest. We'll have to pray the Lord provides a road to lead us all to liberty."

Prin's shoulders slumped with dejection. "And what if He doesn't?"

"He promises to make a way when there isn't one. We'll have to believe Him."

Prin nodded. "I know you're right. It's jus' so hard to believe sometimes."

"I know, dearest." She endeavored to sound more positive. "However, we *do* know a babe is a blessing. You'll need to tell Kane as soon as possible. He'll want to know. He loves you very much."

"Aye, he does," Prin said with a tremulous smile that returned some of the usual brightness to her cheeks.

Elise fetched a fresh sheet from the linen press and covered Prin. "Don't fret anymore, all right? For now, though, let's keep the child a secret from all but Kane."

A rap at the door startled Elise. "Who is it?"

"Christian," came the muffled reply. "Are you ladies decent?"

Elise glanced back to Prin, who'd pulled the sheet to her throat. "Yes, come in."

The door creaked open. Christian nodded to Prin. "You're still ill?"

"Aye, just a little."

"I hope you feel better soon." He looked to Elise. "Zechariah is back from his morning ride. He's looking for you."

"For heaven's sake, what now?" she groaned in exasperation.

"The post arrived earlier. Perhaps there's a letter for you."

Her glance slid to Prin, who appeared as though she might retch again. Elise fetched the clean chamber pot and handed it to her. "I'll be there in a bit, Christian."

"I'll tell him." Christian nodded to both of them and quietly left the room.

A few minutes later, Elise found herself standing before Zechariah's big pine desk in the library. The large room smelled of old leather books and a recent cleaning with lemon oil. A clock ticked on the mantel, the only sound in the room.

"Christian said you wished to see me."

The spymaster lifted his balding head and set his quill next to a small jar of ink before removing his spectacles. "Amberly's the one who wants to see you, Fox. What are you doing wasting half the day in bed while the man is practically frothing at the mouth for want of your presence?"

"I haven't been abed. I've… Did he ask after me?"

The old man's eyes took on a crafty gleam. She could almost see his ears perk to attention. She wasn't a fool. Her question had been too quick and betrayed her personal interest in the Englishman. Hopefully, Zechariah wouldn't guess just how fascinated she'd become.

The spymaster shrugged casually—too casually. "He spoke of little else."

Her brow furrowed. Intrigued and flattered, she wished she could scoff at his words, but thinking of Drake's interest in her warmed her heart. "How tiresome for you."

"No, indeed. Combined with Christian's report and other news I received earlier, 'twas most enlightening."

Elise brushed a nonexistent piece of lint from the skirt of her peach-colored gown. "Are you going to share the information, or am I to root it out on my own?"

"Don't sass me, girl." Zechariah's eyes bulged with the warning. "Sit down. You're giving me a crick in the neck."

Elise pulled up a Chippendale chair and sat on the blue silk seat. "Is that better?"

"Much." The old dragon looked at her with unreadable eyes. "I've no need to repeat Christian's information. I know you had breakfast with him, and he will have told you of Beaufort's missing spy himself. Amberly is the tricky one. On one hand, he's an aboveboard fellow, a man of trade with a verifiable story who's smitten with a lovely young woman. On the other hand, he's an Englishman, and a possible aristocrat-turned-spy if your suspicions are correct."

"I believe I was wrong," she said, giving in to an inexplicable need to protect Drake.

Zechariah shook his head. "On the contrary. I've spoken with Amberly and I think you may be right. Christian believes it, too. In fact, he thinks Amberly knows Beaufort well. If our guest *is* an aristocrat, he and Beaufort may even be related in some way. It's just a hunch, mind you, but I know the captain prides himself on his distant but lofty connections." Sayer glanced out the window. "Aha, there's Amberly now."

She moved to the window with deceptive calm. Her breath locked in her chest and her spirits lifted the moment she spied him leading his horse across the lawn.

The sun glinted on his black hair, and a disturbing emotion—part yearning, part panic—settled over her.

True, he was a handsome and powerful sight in his black breeches, boots and billowy white shirt, but Drake's appeal went deeper than simple good looks. It was his core of strength that drew her, his humor and gentle care.

"Why are you standing there gawking, girl?" Zechariah's knowing laughter made her cringe. "Go catch him."

He followed her rapid flight to the door. "Christian is on his way to check the muskets you smuggled yesterday. Amberly looks as though he's turning on that same path. It wouldn't do for him to discover them. I'll depend on you to provide a distraction."

Chapter Nine

Drake led his borrowed mount, Valiant, toward a sandy path that ran along the gently lapping river. A breeze blew from the east, ruffling his hair. Black clouds warned of a storm's rapid approach. He'd heard of the fast-moving rains that swept over this part of the South Carolina coast. With the humidity high and the temperature rising, he'd be grateful if a good soak brought respite from the heat.

He followed the trail into a copse of tall oaks dripping with musty Spanish moss and edged by a thick growth of spiky, fan-shaped shrubs.

Thunder rolled in the distance. Valiant neighed and stamped his hoof, spraying sand and sending a lizard skittering into the undergrowth. Drake stroked the horse's sleek gray muzzle while he studied the surrounding area. He meant to find a divergent path or hidden means of travel that might aid the covert operations of the Fox. Kirby had scouted much of the plantation's rice fields and outer acreage the previous day. To Drake's disgust, the lieutenant had found nothing suspicious.

Drake's brow furrowed with frustrated anger. The narrow trail seemed to stretch out before him into another dead end, but he was certain there had to be something to give the brigand away. He only had to find it.

Three days had passed since his arrival at Brixton Hall. Three *more* days the Fox had been allowed to live unpunished while Anthony lay in a grave. It galled him that neither he nor any of Beaufort's spies had made any headway in locating his prey. The trail grew colder by the hour.

Lost in his thoughts, he reached out and plucked a leaf from a nearby bush. Spring green, it reminded him of Elise's lovely eyes. A twig snapped behind him. He turned and saw her peering around an overgrown shrub. For a moment, he wondered if his will had conjured her up. Obviously caught staring at him, she blushed and lowered her lashes before flashing him a beguiling smile.

He tied Valiant's reins around a low branch and met her halfway as she walked toward him. Before either of them spoke, he drew her into his arms, as if it were the most natural thing in the world for him to hold her.

Elise didn't resist, though she knew she should. It felt wonderful to abandon herself to the bliss of simply being with him, to forget the troubles that plagued her life if only for a few moments.

Watching him as she had been for the last several minutes, she'd realized she might try to deny her feelings to Prin, the Sayers, or even herself, but this Englishman fascinated her. The awareness terrified her, waged an internal war that confused as much as stimulated. How could she have fallen into the trap of wishing to be with this man when every instinct she possessed warned freedom should be her ultimate goal?

Drake brushed a light kiss across the top of her head. "Good morn, sweet. Seeing you here has turned this already fine day into sheer perfection."

His words warmed her heart. "Sir, you're a shameless flirt."

"Hardly, love, I simply state the truth."

Thunder rumbled again and Valiant whinnied nervously in protest of the portentous sound. Elise had been intent on Drake and hadn't noticed the darkening sky. She suddenly wished she could hide. "I *hate* storms. You need to fetch Valiant. We're in for a downpour. We should head back to the main house before it hits full force."

The black, fast-moving clouds drew Drake's attention. "I don't think we'll make the house before the deluge begins."

A loud clap of thunder drowned out her reply. Her heart lurched with fear even as the first fat drops of rain hit the dusty path.

"Elise, don't fret. Come with me. I'll return you indoors."

He reached for her hand just as another deafening blast of thunder boomed like a cannon above them. In her mind, she saw her burning home. She heard the screams of loved ones, smelled the horrible stench of scorched flesh and bone. Pure fear propelled her into action. "No time! The slave cabins are around the next bend."

Drake rushed to collect Valiant. He leapt into the saddle, then leaned down to pluck her up and deposit her in front of him. Elise clamped her arms around

Drake's waist. She ducked her head and pressed her cheek to the center of his chest, drawing comfort from the steady beat of his heart. At Drake's command, the horse sprang forward in an agitated race for escape.

The storm intensified. Bright bolts of forked lightning split the raging sky. Wind whipped through the trees and the rain struck like cold, sharp needles on Elise's exposed skin. Desperate to calm her terror, she prayed for mercy, begging God to help them reach cover.

Drake reined Valiant to a halt outside the first structure in a long row of rustic cabins. He helped Elise dismount, jumped down beside her and set Valiant free to find his own shelter. Lightning flashed overhead and thunder crashed around them. A slave woman, her head wrapped in a kerchief, opened the door and bustled Elise inside as if she knew her well.

Inside the hovel, wind whistled through the parchment-thin walls, but at least the cabin provided a meager haven from the storm. Drake slammed and bolted the door against the wind. He ducked his head to keep from bumping it on the slated ceiling. In one quick glance he noted the dirt floor, simple table, bench and rolled mats along the wall. Disgusted by the rough treatment the slaves endured, he turned to find a dozen sets of large, wary coffee-colored eyes peering at him from the next room. Wanting to relieve the women's anxiety, he started to offer his thanks for their shelter, but the door closed abruptly, leaving him and Elise alone.

Violent thunder shook the cabin. Elise spun to face him, her soft lips curved in a wobbly frown.

Drake gathered her close. Her arms locked around

him as though she worried the wind might pick her up and steal her away.

When her trembling subsided, he lifted her chin. "Elise? How do you fare?"

"I'm so glad you're here with me," she whispered. "I never feel safe, but when I'm with you all the fear fades away."

"You can stay with me forever if you wish."

She pressed her cheek to his chest. Outside lightning flashed and the wind howled. Its cold fingers rattled the shutters. She shivered against him.

He held her tight, enjoying the way she fit against him. Never before had he felt as though a woman had been made just for him.

Outside, the storm continued to rage, but Elise no longer noticed. Her world had shrunk to include just the two of them, and her senses revolved solely around the man who held her with such protective care. The first man who'd made her feel secure. The first man she'd ever loved.

Ice spread through her veins. She didn't want to love Amberly. He'd said she could stay with him forever, but he couldn't truly be hers. Hadn't Christian warned mere hours ago that Drake would soon leave for England? If she didn't start using her head, she would be left with nothing but empty arms and a shattered heart.

She pulled away, a lonely ache forming in her chest that same moment.

"What is it, sweet?" Drake reached for her hand. "Come back to me. Don't go."

"I'm sorry," she whispered. "What must you think of me?"

"That you're the most intriguing woman I've ever known."

"Silly, you mean. I know it's childish to fear storms."

"I don't think you're silly. Tell me why you're afraid."

Elise clasped her arms around her middle and fought the temptation to lean on a person other than herself or Prin. She wanted to open up to him, to share a deeper bond, but what could she say that wouldn't spur more questions and the revelation of her darkest secrets? She wanted to trust him, but in reality he was little more than a stranger.

"Tell me, sweet."

Wind whistled through the shutters. The strength to fight him drained away. What would it hurt to tell him just one event in her past? She took a deep breath and related the story in a dull voice as if it had happened to someone else. "Two years ago my father's farm was hit by a terrible storm. Lightning struck our home and burned it to the ground. Most of our slaves, all people I held dear, died trying to escape or extinguish the flames."

Her throat constricted until her voice became a rough whisper. "That same night we suffered through all manner of violent weather. A tornado passed over and destroyed the outbuildings, including the slave cabins. Many of our people were found in the ensuing weeks, their bodies mangled as though the winds had carried them away and dropped them from a height."

He urged her to sit on the rough-hewn bench and took the seat next to her. His arm wrapped around her shoulders, he tucked her close against his side. "My darling girl, I can't imagine what you must have suffered. I'm glad you've found safety here with the Sayers."

She swallowed the bitter taste of denial. She could never tell him just how unsafe it was for her at Brixton Hall. Without examining her need to do so, she moved closer to him, like an orphan finding shelter on a bleak night. "You said you want to know my secrets. Few know this one. Indeed, I shouldn't tell you if the truth be known, but…once the war ends, I plan to leave Brixton Hall for good."

He frowned against her brow. "Why? Are you very unhappy here?"

The storm began to relent. Muted voices drifted in from the next room as she allowed her silence to speak for her.

He brushed his lips against her temple. "You're not planning to leave alone, are you? If so, 'tis foolish to entertain such dangerous notions."

"I'm not surprised you'd think so, but I don't believe it is foolish. I've relied on myself since that horrible night. If the Lord made a way, I'd leave Brixton Hall today, but I have nowhere else to go."

He stroked her hair and kissed the top of her head. "Why do you wish to leave? Are the Sayers cruel to you?"

"No."

Drake's tone turned chilly. "Is the puppy pestering you?"

"Puppy?" she asked, confused. "You mean Christian?"

"If he is, it will be my pleasure to persuade him otherwise."

"There's no need. Christian is my friend, not my dilemma." Bemused by Drake's unexpected display of irritation toward Christian, she wondered what her friend had done to encourage Drake's dislike.

"Sayer had the nerve to warn me off you the night of the ball. I didn't care for his presumption."

Aha. She smiled against his damp shirt. "No, I don't believe you would."

He grunted, then said seriously, "If you want to leave, come with me. I'll keep you safe."

Hope bloomed inside her...then wilted. "And be what, your mistress?" She laughed with ill-concealed contempt. "Never. I promise you, I won't ever be any man's strumpet."

"I'm glad to hear it." Long moments passed with only the rain dripping off the trees outside to mark the time. He'd meant to offer marriage. He realized the prospect was sudden, but why wait when he'd found a woman he could truly care for? He didn't care if she agreed because she wished to leave the Sayers; at least she wouldn't have chosen him for his wealth and title. He knew she was as drawn to him as he was to her. As far as he was concerned anything else could be dealt with and he would have a lifetime to convince her to love him.

"You said the Sayers are good to you."

"They're kind enough." She glanced to their linked fingers, and eased her hand from his grasp. "But I wish to be away from here, to have a home of my own."

"How do you plan to accomplish your goal? What of funds? If you refuse to be a mistress, how will you afford a home with no husband to secure one for you?"

"That's why I'm still here." Bitterness crept into her voice. "Brixton Hall is like quicksand. I'm up to my chin in it and no one cares."

"*I* do." Her face registered her distrust. He took both of her hands in his. "What can I do to make you realize I have only the best intentions toward you, Elise? What can I say to make you realize how quickly and completely I've come to care for you?"

She bit her lip. Her eloquent eyes spoke of her inner struggle to believe him.

"I don't want you for a mistress. I want you for my wife."

Elise couldn't mistake his sincerity. Her heart began to race. For one brief moment she allowed herself to forget the suddenness of their situation and to imagine spending a lifetime with him. The vision made her lightheaded. She wanted to throw her arms around his neck and shout, "Yes, yes, yes!" Instead, she willed her pulse back to normal and shook her head, determined to stay planted in reality. "You'd marry me because I'm unhappy at Brixton Hall? You...you can't just decide to wed a person on a whim."

"Who says it's a whim?" He shrugged as if they were discussing the most tepid topic, but his eyes were intense, expectant. "Can't you tell when a man has fallen madly in love with you?"

Her heart did a peculiar little flip, then almost stopped beating altogether. Blood rushed in her ears. She couldn't have heard him correctly. But no, she'd heard him quite distinctly. He loved her? Her own declaration of love sprang to her lips, but she bit her tongue. She couldn't leave with him. It would be cruel madness to encourage him when she was chained to Brixton Hall.

She swallowed the painful lump in her throat and reached up to brush a soft black curl off his brow. "I wish I *could* marry you, Drake, but I cannot." He started to speak, but she forestalled him by pulling away and placing her fingers over his lips. "Let's talk of it no longer."

"Don't change the subject, woman. You can't deliver the news you wish you could marry me, then forbid me to speak of it. I won't have it."

"Then we have nothing left to say. I won't discuss marriage any longer."

His expression proclaimed his displeasure. Clearly, he wasn't used to being rejected. "You're the most obstinate female imaginable."

"So I've been told." She traced his angular jaw and the long scar along his jaw. She hated the idea of him experiencing the least bit of pain. "What happened here? Did you fall?"

He released a frustrated breath and clawed his fingers through his damp hair. "No, if you must know, nothing so mundane. My younger brother, Anthony, had a ferocious temper. He was always trying to best me at fencing. I was seventeen at the time and refused to let him win. One day, unbeknownst to me, a young lady he fancied came to watch our practice. Naturally, I won."

"Naturally," she mocked, poking fun at his arrogance.

He laughed. "Cheeky girl. As you can imagine, Anthony's pride was on the line. He flew into a rage, deciding to take off my head in the process. Fortunately, he missed my jugular and nicked my jaw instead."

"He sounds like an animal." His mouth tightened and she realized her faux pas. She wouldn't like it if someone spoke ill of Prin. "I'm sorry. I shouldn't condemn a man I didn't know."

"No matter. Anthony's temper was his worst quality, but he had a sharp sense of humor as well. I wish you could have known him."

A horse whinnied outside and Elise jerked in surprise. She'd forgotten the world beyond the cabin, and she resented the reminder. "I don't want to go, but perhaps we should head back to the house. Zechariah and the others will soon notice our absence and wonder what's happened to us."

"I suppose you're right, although the idea of someone finding us here does hold some merit."

"How can you think so?"

"Simple, my girl. If I claimed I compromised you, it would put an end to this game of fox and hound we're playing. All I'd have to do is sit back and wait while *Zechariah* convinced you to wed me."

She tried to laugh, but his reference to her as a fox made her quail. "Sadie and the other fine women of this cabin would vouch for my good name. Besides, do you really want a wife who must be forced to wed you?"

His jaw clenched. A flash of some unnamable emotion crossed his face before he could bury it behind a glib facade. He stood, straightened to his full height and wrenched open the door. "Good heavens, no. I had such a wife and it's not a circumstance I'd care to repeat."

Stunned by his announcement, Elise stared at the cabin door he'd shut on his way out. A spasm of unreasonable hurt pierced her chest. She saw how much her thoughtless comment wounded him. Obviously he held deep emotions for the woman who'd been his wife.

His wife.

He'd had a wife. Why the knowledge stung, she didn't understand. He was a full-grown man. Of course he'd had a life before meeting her, but the thought of him in love with someone else cut to the quick.

A knock on the connecting door drew her attention.

Sadie peered around from the next room. "You be all right, Miss Lisie? I knows you afraid of them sto'ms."

"I'm fine," she assured the older woman, "Thank you for loaning us your room." With a hug and a wave to the other women, she left and hurried to find Drake.

The rain had stopped and the sky was blue again. Raindrops glistened on the leaves and pine nettles before dripping to the drenched earth. She breathed in the fresh, sweet air, hoping Drake hadn't wandered off too far without her.

When she found him checking Valiant's saddle, she heaved a sigh of relief. He didn't bother to look up from his task and she ended up addressing his back. "Drake, please forgive me. I had no idea I'd be reminding you of hurtful memories."

He paused in stroking the horse's satiny neck. Somewhere in the trees overhead, a bird chirped for its mate. "There's nothing to forgive, Elise. You didn't wound me. My wife died years ago. Her memory is no longer a cause for grief."

She wasn't convinced, but his manner shouted his unwillingness to discuss the topic further. Renewed tension stretched taut between them. If not for the singing birds and the croak of a bullfrog nearby, they would have been stranded in silence.

He grasped the reins. "We should be on our way."

"Yes, I suppose we must." As they walked along the path, she watched him from under her lashes. He'd retied his shoulder-length hair at the nape of his neck with a cord of black leather. In spots, the dampness of his thin cotton shirt stuck to his thickly muscled back and arms. Truly, he was splendid, exceptional to look upon, and the gentlest man she'd ever met. Forced or not, the woman he'd wed would have been an imbecile not to adore him.

He turned his head and winked at her. Caught staring at him yet again, she pretended not to see his smug expression, and lifted her chin. The sharp movement caused her loose hairpins to rebel and several of them slipped free, sending the damp mass of her hair in a tumble down her back.

She heard him chuckle and saw him stoop to retrieve the mutinous pins.

She tried to arrange her hair into some semblance of order, but the pins refused to hold. "I never could do much with my own hair." She brushed several thick strands back from her face. "Do I look presentable in the least?"

Elise caught her breath as Drake appraised her. His eyes were the color of molten gold in the sunlight and she wanted to bask in their warmth all day.

"You look stunning, love." He took her hand and entwined their fingers, golden-brown and creamy-white. "I could admire you forever."

She laughed nervously as they rejoined the path that led to the main house. "You must be addled."

"Hello there!" a voice called out. They turned to see Christian meandering up the shaded trail.

Her friend was perfectly dry except for his sodden riding boots. His dark brown hair ruffled in the light breeze. He must have passed the storm in the shed near the dock. She'd forgotten he was so close by, that she'd been sent to ensure Drake didn't discover him inspecting the weaponry she'd brought up from Charles Towne the previous day. She grimaced inwardly. Drake was making her lose her concentration as well as her heart.

"Hello, Sayer." Drake eyed Christian with a mix of impatience and irritation. "How did you happen to sneak up behind us and miss the downpour as well?"

Christian shrugged, though he glared at their entwined hands. "By having the wits to go inside, Amberly. There's a small shed near a dock upstream. Too bad neither of you had the same good sense. Why didn't you head back to the house when you heard the storm's approach?"

"We did start back." Elise stepped in to diffuse the male aggression. "But we didn't make it."

"Obviously, Elise. You look like a drowned rat."

"You must be blind," Drake said. "Miss Cooper couldn't help but look like a spring morning even on her worst day."

"If you say so, Amberly." Christian laughed. "So where did the two of you ride out the storm?"

"Sadie's cabin."

Christian smirked. "In a pinch, I suppose Sadie is an acceptable chaperone."

Elise narrowed her eyes and tamped down the urge to box her friend's ears. "Where's your mount, Christian? It's difficult to believe you *intended* to soil a fine pair of boots."

"Of course not. I had to let Apollo find his own shelter when the storm hit. The sorry beast didn't bother to return."

"Intelligent animal," Drake said cheerfully. "We had no such trouble with good Valiant here." With eyes only for Elise, he said to Christian, "Don't let us keep you, Sayer. We'll meet you later, up at the house."

Chapter Ten

Drake shut the door of his bedchamber, stripped off his shirt and removed his leather boots. A maid had straightened the room. The four-poster bed was neatly made and a vase of purple wildflowers graced the nightstand.

Reclining atop the covers, he crossed his arms behind his head and allowed his mind to wander. The thought of Elise made him smile. Was it possible God hadn't forgotten him after all? For the first time in years he offered up a prayer of gratitude.

"There you are." A feminine voice carried through the closed door from the hallway. "I was worried sick on account of the storm. I went huntin' for you, but Zechariah chased me back up here."

"I'm fine." He recognized Elise's voice. "I'm sorry I worried you."

"You don't look fine. You look like you took a tumble in a mud puddle."

"Why thank you, Prin."

Drake chuckled as the ladies moved out of earshot. When he'd left Elise in the garden, her hair in disarray, her cheeks flushed, he'd thought her the loveliest woman he'd ever seen.

Thinking about a lifetime with Elise, he realized he was happy about the institution of marriage for the first time in his life. Nay, he was ecstatic. Her shock when he'd proposed had matched his own, but once the words were out he had no wish to take them back. His first marriage had been by the king's command. Diana had never forgiven him for not being the man she loved, a French marquess she'd met at court.

At nineteen, he'd hoped for more than a lonely arranged marriage. He'd tried to warm to her, but Diana had wanted no part of him. Their union had been one of cool politeness underscored by her disdain for the whole affair. She'd insisted on living in London while he chose to remain at Hawk Haven. When she'd died of a fever in the fifth year of their marriage, he'd barely noticed her absence.

Older, wiser and far more jaded than any twenty-four-year-old ought to be, he'd refused additional attempts by the crown to shackle him a second time. He'd ceased tormenting himself with the hope of learning why God had taken most of his family and forgotten him, and his prayer life had dwindled to nil.

Only the need for an heir had spurred him to consider matrimony a second time. The fact that Penelope's dowry included a strip of borderland he'd long been interested in acquiring for his estate had added to her appeal. When he'd first met her, his former fiancée had seemed to have all the qualities a perfect duchess would need in abundance: impeccable breeding, outward beauty and a fine social standing. It wasn't until a month before their wedding that he'd begun to hear the rumors. Finding her in the arms of another man and discovering she'd only agreed to his proposal due to pressure from her family to wed a duke had been a blessing in the end. With his anger and embarrassment now cooled, he was grateful he'd learned the truth before the marriage. Had he wed Penelope as he'd planned, he never would have known love with Elise.

Thank You, Lord, for bringing Elise into my life.

Years had passed since he'd last spoken to God, but those few words acted as a ray of warm sunlight on his frostbitten soul. He realized just how much he'd missed the peace that came with daily prayer and a grateful heart. *Forgive me, Lord, for shutting You out of my life all these years.*

The clock on the mantel signaled he should dress for dinner. He leapt up, eager to return to Elise. For the first time in his life, he was certain he'd met a woman who was interested in him as a man and not a duke. She may have turned down his proposal, but he'd seen her regret in doing so.

Drake grinned. He wasn't a man who took no for answer once he'd made up his mind. He crossed to the wardrobe and removed the best set of clothes he'd brought with him. Tonight, he'd begin his campaign to win her in earnest.

He whistled a jaunty tune as he poured water in a basin and began to shave.

Once dressed, he left his chamber and headed for the dining room. Darkness had fallen. Crystal sconces along the hall and down the stairwell glowed with candlelight. The closer he came to the first floor, the stronger the aroma of fresh baked bread, spices and roasted meats became. His stomach growled with hunger.

When he entered the dining room, he found servants lighting the candles in the chandelier above a table set with fine bone china. A maid put the finishing touches on the flower centerpieces, bobbed a curtsy and scurried from the room.

Drake turned to go, deciding to wait for his dining companions on the veranda farther down the hall. Outside, the night was balmy, the stars and moon bright in the satiny black sky. Crickets chirped and an occasional lightning bug sparked in the distance.

He pressed his palms against the rail and enjoyed the tranquil quality of the place. It had been months since he'd felt relief from his grief. That he possessed any at present was due to Elise's influence. Simply looking at her made him jubilant, but the driving need to find Anthony's killer tempered his happiness. He couldn't come to terms with his brother's death until he found the Fox.

"Good evening, sir."

Drake whipped around to face his cousin, Captain Beaufort. "Charles, what do you mean by sneaking up on me?"

"I called to you, but you were lost in your thoughts, Your Grace."

"Quiet, man!" Drake lowered his voice to an annoyed whisper. "How many times must I remind you not to call me that. Do you want me to end up the bait for some colonial ransom-seeker?"

"My sincerest apologies, Your...er, sir. It's such a departure from propriety, so unnatural, I find it taxes my memory to call you aught but your title."

Drake ground his teeth in frustration. "I shan't remind you again, Charles. Another slip and I'll see you swabbing decks for the next twenty years."

Beaufort's eyes grew round as an owl's: "But, sir, I'm in His Majesty's army, not the navy."

"True, Captain, but I own a fleet of ships that I insist be kept spotless."

The captain gulped. "I understand, sir. I won't blunder again."

"See that you don't. Now, tell me why you're here. I thought you'd been delayed until tomorrow."

"I've sent Lieutenant Kirby to search for a man I've lost."

"Who?"

"The carriage driver who drove you yesterday. His name is—"

"Robin Goss."

"One and the same," Beaufort confirmed. "He disappeared after I spotted him outside The Rolling Tide yesterday afternoon. He didn't meet with me last evening as planned. I've ordered inquiries, but nothing's turned up. I'm hoping Kirby will have more success than I and learn something of his location."

Drake considered Beaufort's revelation. "I wondered what happened to the man when he didn't return to us. Elise chided me. She suggested I'd overpaid him and he'd run off with my coin to retire in Jamaica."

Beaufort gasped. "Miss Cooper dared to chide you, sir?"

Drake leaned against the rail and a fond smile quirked his lips. "Indeed, she did. Truth to tell, I find I enjoy being teased by her."

"I understand," the captain said with a sly grin and a wiggle of his bushy blond eyebrows. "Miss Cooper is a beauty even if she is a dunce. She'd make a fine mistress and provide you with a merry time while you're here in South Carolina."

"Actually, Captain, she's a stunning woman with a quick wit and sharp intelligence. I've no intention of making her a mere mistress. I hope to make her my wife."

Beaufort's eyes bugged. "Forgive me, sir, I mean no disrespect, but your *wife?* Isn't that a bit…sudden?"

"Perhaps, but I'll be leaving Charles Towne as soon as my business is concluded. I refuse to take a chance of losing her."

"But she's a colonial miss, sir. It's not right for someone of your…er…for someone like you to marry someone so common."

"On the contrary, Captain. There's nothing common about her." His gaze turned frigid. "She's perfect for me and I shall wed whomever I wish. I dare anyone to suggest otherwise."

Christian Sayer hastened into his father's study. He shut the door with a firm shove that set the candle flames to flickering. "I have news you're not going to care for."

Zechariah scrambled to his feet. "What is it, boy? Spit it out."

"I overheard Beaufort and Amberly just now. I thought to make introductions and engage them in conversation before dinner, but it seems they know each other well. The door leading to the veranda was ajar and I arrived just as the captain referred to Amberly as 'Your Grace'."

"I can't believe it!" Zechariah plopped back in his

chair, a look of stunned disbelief straining his round features. "Elise guessed rightly. He *is* an aristocrat."

"He's a duke," griped Christian. "We might as well have the Prince of Wales under our roof!"

Deep in thought, Zechariah rubbed his chins. "I'm sure we can produce results from this."

Christian held up a staying hand. "Wait, you haven't heard the rest."

"There's more?" Zechariah gasped.

"Aye, he has designs on our Elise as well."

The old man's eyes narrowed. "How so?"

"I heard him tell Beaufort he wants to wed her."

"You're jesting! If he's a high and mighty duke, you've got to be."

"No." Christian sat heavily in a leather chair near the fireplace. "I heard Amberly clear as a fire bell. He said he hoped to make Elise his wife."

"Well, I'll be," Zechariah said in amazement. "If she could be persuaded… Just think of the possibilities! Amberly may be privy to the most sensitive information. As his wife, Elise would be in an superb position to supply us with it."

Christian shook his head. "You've recovered fast enough. I thought you'd be reeling from shock."

"Nonsense, my boy." Zechariah tapped his temple with his index finger. "Shock forces the mind into action. Complacency makes it slow as molasses."

"She won't do it, you know. She's far too principled."

Zechariah's eyes burned with a crafty light. "I think she will. She's smitten with Amberly. You only have to see them together to know it."

"That may be," Christian conceded irritably, "but then you have the problem of persuading her to spy on her husband. If she cares for him enough to chance marriage, she'll be loyal to him. You'll lose her for us altogether."

"Elise is a girl of good sense. Her main goal is to see Prin free. If this business with Amberly comes to fruition, I'll simply concoct a new bargain with her. If she marries Amberly and agrees to give us information, I'll release Prin into her care."

Christian stood to leave. "You have it all worked out. I hope your plan doesn't ruin you or bring harm to Elise."

"How could it?" the spymaster said smugly. "Elise is too adept a spy to be caught. Besides, she'll be a duchess. Amberly will have the means to protect her if she's discovered."

"And when will you inform her of your plans?"

Zechariah blew out a candle and stood to leave with Christian. "I believe I'll have a word with Amberly after we sup. I need to see where he stands on the matter first. It would be foolish to put ideas in the girl's head before we know His Grace's true intentions."

Chapter Eleven

"Amberly, I'd like a word with you," Zechariah said as he snuffed his cheroot in a small pewter tray. A plume of smoke rose from the smoldering remains of rolled tobacco, adding to the haze and pungent odor that lingered in the parlor.

Drake stood as Zechariah heaved himself to his feet. Beaufort smoked a clay pipe near the open window. Curiously, Christian Sayer displayed none of his usual acerbic wit. He sat near the unlit fireplace, his feet on a stool, his eyes hooded as though he contemplated a matter of dire consequence.

"Not here." Zechariah waved Drake toward the open French doors. "In my study across the hall."

Drake followed the older man into the opposite room and waited for Sayer to light a candle before he took a seat in a padded wingback chair. "How may I be of service, sir?"

Zechariah sat behind his desk and lit an additional trio of candles. His chin dipped to his chest. Rolls of fat ringed his neck, giving him the look of a turtle peering from his shell. He studied his clasped hands for several ticks of the mantel clock, then eyed Drake with a shrewd gaze. "I trust you won't think me forward for saying so, Amberly, but I believe there's an attachment forming between you and my ward, Miss Cooper. I wish to know your intentions toward her."

Drake's brow arched in surprise. Had his admiration for Elise been so obvious? "I have the best intentions. I wish to marry her, in fact."

"You've asked her then?"

"I've broached the subject."

"What was her response?" Zechariah queried. "Yea or nay?"

Drake stomped down his irritation. He wasn't used to being questioned like a schoolboy, but Sayer was Elise's guardian. If—no—*when* she agreed to marry him, it would make life easier if he had the older man's consent. "As yet, nay. However, I plan to erode her defenses until she has no will but to answer in the affirmative."

"I see." Zechariah chuckled as he shifted a stack of papers. "You're a bold one, Amberly. I can't say you're the first suitor intent on wooing our fair Elise, but I believe you'll succeed where all the others have failed."

"Your words are encouraging, sir. May I ask why you believe so?"

Zechariah leaned back in his chair, his amusement apparent. "Because, my dear boy, you're the first man she's fancied in return."

Drake kept his face straight, but his pulse leapt within him. "I'm pleased to hear it."

"Yet, as her guardian," Zechariah inspected his fingertips, "I have to see to her well-being."

"Most certainly. Let me assure you I have her best interests at heart."

"Perhaps, but what of your circumstances, Amberly? Are you in a suitable situation to provide for Elise's needs, to ensure her happiness? Or do you plan to stow her away in one of your ships and subject her to the rigors of sea travel?"

"No, she'll not be floating about the high seas," Drake replied, a touch wary of his host's probing questions. "I'm quite capable of caring for my own. I guarantee that as my wife Miss Cooper will want for nothing."

"And what is your living situation in England?" Zechariah asked nonchalantly.

Drake lowered his eyes and brushed a wrinkle from his linen sleeve. His interest turned toward the window, where a breeze brought in the faint beat of drums. He hadn't noticed the pagan rhythm until now. He regarded Zechariah, who waited patiently for an answer. Why did he have the feeling there was an ulterior motive lurking beneath the old man's questions? "I am as well off as anyone, I suppose. Wealthier than some, less so than others."

"An ambiguous reply, Amberly. I'd wager you're better off than most."

Drake studied the man with a carefully blank expression. "I wouldn't know. I'm not privy to other people's financial affairs, sir."

Zechariah picked up a pipe and lit the tobacco. After several deep drags, he eyed Drake through the smoke. "And if this marriage were to take place, how quickly would you like to see it happen?"

"Once she agrees, I wish to marry as soon as it can be arranged. My business here is almost complete, I believe, and I would like to return to England the moment it's concluded."

Fleeting surprise rippled over Zechariah's plump face. "Your business is almost finished? Have you signed your shipping contracts then?"

"Not as yet, but I have leads and prospects." Drake stood and strolled to the window. He smelled a fire, but couldn't see one. Leaning against the frame, his eyes searched the darkness for the origin of the drums, but he saw nothing except a sky full of stars and the shadows of swaying trees.

"I'm glad to hear it. I've been giving your terms some thought." Zechariah set down the pipe and scratched his shiny pate. "I'd like to hire your fleet if we can come to a more reasonable price."

Drake's business instincts rushed to the fore. "And what is reasonable?" he queried suspiciously. "Half my original offer?"

Zechariah hooded his sharp gaze. "Would you take it?"

"Do you suppose me a fool, sir?" One of the candle flames flickered and died. "That's what I'd be if I let my services go for so paltry a sum."

"Paltry? You must be joking. Half your price is more than full for most other shipping ventures."

Drake shrugged as though it mattered not to him. In truth, it didn't. He had little use for the money. He'd lifted the price to discourage anyone from serious consideration of his offer. If his terms were accepted, he'd have no subterfuge in his hunt for the Fox.

"I couldn't possibly convince my captains to risk their lives for less than ninety-five percent. As you must know, English ships are the favorite prey for privateers and Frenchies."

"I know the risks, but you drive a hard bargain, Amberly. Suppose I used my influence to garner Elise's consent to wed you? Would you offer me a discount then?"

"You can't be serious," Drake said, his ire pricked. How dare the old man treat Elise as though she were nothing more than a head of cattle to barter? "I'll only accept Elise if she comes of her own accord. I was married before, you see, to a woman who wed me for numerous reasons other than myself. It was an unhappy union, not one I care to repeat."

"I see." Zechariah steepled his thick fingers and rested his chin on them. "What happened to your wife?"

"She died of a fever several years ago."

"And there's been no one since?"

Drake bristled at his host's audacity, but capped his annoyance. He usually asked the questions. It was a novel experience to be on the receiving end of someone else's interrogation. "No one serious. I told myself I'd never remarry. As the years passed, the sentiment faded. I engaged myself to another woman, a neighbor's daughter. I found her morals clashed with my own and broke off with her shortly before I left England."

"Seems right fickle of you, boy. What could she have done to deserve such coldness on your part? Am I to understand you'd discard Elise if you found she disagreed with you?"

Drake refused to explain the circumstances of his severed engagement. It was none of the old man's affair. "On the contrary. I don't believe Elise could do anything I wouldn't forgive and forget."

Sayer smiled coolly. "Hmm… I wonder."

At the slave cabins, a bonfire raged. Flames roared high into the night sky, filling the air with the smoky aroma of burning pine and dry leaves. Laughter flowed freely and the tempting scent of roasting boar made Elise's mouth water. Drums beat a frenzied pace, enticing a good number of Brixton's African population to dance with wild abandon.

Elise sat on a stump in the shadows, a child on each knee. An older girl, Mary, stood behind her, braiding her hair. Elise had volunteered to sit with the children while their parents enjoyed a rare hour of merriment.

Prin and Kane had walked into the woods to talk about the baby and share some privacy. Elise expected them back at any time. She'd have to return to the house soon. Zechariah wanted to speak with her at midnight.

She pushed the thought to the back of her mind. Her meetings with her spymaster had grown tense of late and she wanted to enjoy a few stolen moments before returning to face him.

Looking down at the little ones in her arms, she smiled at their sweetness. The youngest child, a baby girl of six months, gnawed on her little fist, while eighteen-month-old Jed clapped disjointedly to the pounding drumbeat. Elise bent her head and nibbled playfully on his neck, laughing when he squealed and giggled.

"Miss Lisie, I can't braid your hair if you bend your head like dat," Mary complained.

"I'm sorry, precious." She sat up straight. Mary was a solemn child and Elise knew the girl performed even the simplest tasks with the seriousness of a grave tender. "I won't move again until you're finished."

She closed her eyes and allowed the drumbeat to pulse through her. Little Jed smoothed his finger over her cheek, drawing her attention to his impish grin. She smiled back. She loved children, but somewhere along the way had given up hope of having her own. For one fanciful moment, she allowed herself to imagine being the mother of Drake's child. Would a child of theirs have his silky black hair and deep, golden eyes? She wished it could be so.

Elise blinked and kissed the top of the baby's head. She had no reason for this emptiness in her heart. She'd been content with her lot and clear in her purpose until Amberly had insinuated himself into her life. Soon, she would have a niece or nephew to spoil. She assured herself that when the time came any misplaced longing for a child of her own would disappear.

Mary dropped the completed braid against Elise's back and the tip brushed her tailbone. The little girl leaned forward and rested her chin on Elise's shoulder. "I'm all done, Miss Lisie. Who's dat man starin' at you over there?"

"What man?" Elise twisted in the direction Mary pointed. Drake stepped from the shadows a few feet away. The fire's orange glow shimmered on his skin. Her chest tightened, and it was all she could do not to smile like a simpleton.

His straight white teeth flashed in a charming grin as he strode toward her. "I'm surprised to find you here, my love."

Tenderness washed through her. "What are you doing here, Drake?"

"I heard the drums and came to investigate. I've been enjoying the view."

"Yes, the dancers are quite something, certainly different from what one usually sees in the sedate drawing room of Brixton Hall."

He crouched before her. His gaze slipped to where

Mary peeked over her shoulder. The child ducked behind Elise and whispered a hurried goodbye before she ran toward the row of cabins.

"I wasn't talking about the dancers," he said. "You with babes in arms is one of the most delightful views I've ever encountered."

A blush rose to her cheeks and she was grateful for the dark. "You have a knack for flattery, sir. Did you learn the art in school?"

He chuckled. "Of course. I made the highest marks of anyone."

Jed jumped off her lap before she could reply. She tightened her arm around the baby, who had fallen asleep, and watched as the little boy thrust himself at Drake. Drake accepted the child with ease and settled him on his hip. He found a nearby stump to sit on, and seemed not to notice when the child's busy fingers demolished his neatly tied cravat.

"Jed likes you," Elise said, pleasantly surprised he hadn't pushed the boy away.

Drake's long dark lashes lifted, exposing his magnetic gaze. "If only you liked me half as well."

She could drown in those eyes of his and be content. She sought a witty reply, but none came to her. Instead, she chose the truth. "I fancy you a great deal more than I should."

He grinned as if he'd guessed as much. "Then marry me. We're drawn to one another. There's nothing that stands between us to keep us apart. I can provide for you—you've nothing to fear."

His intensity sent a shiver down her back. His words threatened the future she'd planned for herself and Prin. How would he react if she told him of her sister? Would he be horrified like her neighbors would be if they knew she claimed a slave as kin?

She swallowed tightly, teetering on the brink of following her traitorous heart. She wanted to trust him, but didn't know how. "You don't miss a single opportunity to press your case, do you, Mr. Amberly? What is your rush?"

"I shall be leaving for England as soon as my business is complete. I refuse to consider returning without you."

The prospect of never seeing him again made her chest tighten with dread. "*Would* you leave without me?"

"Will you force me to?" In a driven tone he added, "How can I be more clear in my intentions, Elise? I want you for my wife, my love, the mother of my children. What say you? Will you have me or reject me?"

At the thought of saying no, a sharp, desperate pain sliced through her heart. Oh, how she wanted to say yes, but how could she? She had to stay out the war or lose the chance of ever freeing Prin.

A loud cheer rose from the dancers near the bonfire. Grateful for the distraction, she pretended great interest in the commotion. The roasted boar had been taken from the spit. She looked back to her would-be husband and noticed Jed chewing on a section of his shirt. "He's teething. You may want to stop him or you'll soon have a hole in your fine linen."

Drake glanced at the boy as though he'd forgotten Jed sat in his lap. Gently, he removed the cloth from the child, who immediately began to cry as if his life were ending. Elise stood, careful not to jostle the baby, and beckoned the little boy as he fled Drake's lap. She handed the baby to Drake and knelt to console the overly tired Jed.

Picking up the little boy, she cuddled him while he cried into the curve of her neck. "The children really should be abed. They've been awake all day," she whispered. Glancing up, she squelched the need to giggle at the sight before her. Drake, infant dangling from his large hands, reflected an expression of unvarnished panic.

"Do you need assistance?" she asked, holding out her free arm to relieve him of the baby. Drake complied in an instant, obviously eager to be rid of the squirming being. Tenderly, she cuddled the whimpering infant while trying not to laugh. "I take it you have little experience with babies?"

Drake dragged his fingers through his hair. The flames shimmered over his high cheekbones and those dark eyes of his shone with self-mockery. "You've found me out, sweet."

She smiled softly. "Are you averse to them, then?"

"My own or other people's?"

"Do you have your own?"

"None as yet." He grinned at her meaningfully. "However, to answer your question, I am fond of children."

Elise glanced at the baby girl she held and smiled. "Based on your smooth handling of this one, I would never have guessed."

"Go ahead and mock me, sweet. Once our own children arrive, I'll become an expert child-handler."

Surprise widened her eyes. He spoke as though they were already wed. Her lashes dipped to shield her study of his lean, sculpted face. She had no doubt he would be an ideal parent: strong, protective, dependable. The exact opposite of her own sire. "It's been my experience that men avoid child-rearing as though it were a disease."

He shrugged. "Some may, but I look forward to spending time with my offspring."

"Does that sentiment extend to changing their soiled diapers as well?" Elise teased.

"I said I plan to be with them, not change them. There will be plenty of nursemaids for that."

She chuckled and was about to reply when a rustling in the woods drew her attention behind her. Hand in hand, Prin and Kane picked their way through the brush. Kane, a giant of a man, was unmistakable. Black as pitch, his slick, bald head reflected the firelight that revealed his contemplative expression.

"Prin, I'm over here," Elise called out, relieved to see her sister in much better sorts than when they'd left the house an hour ago.

Prin waved in acknowledgment and gave Kane a quick kiss goodbye. She wove her way around stumps and fallen limbs to join her. "I didn't know you was still here, Lisie. I thought ol' man Sayer was of a mind to give you a talkin' to."

"Prin," Elise said with a slight nod in Drake's direction. "I told you I'd wait here for you. Did you forget?"

Leaning forward, Prin picked up Jed. The little boy sighed in his sleep, but didn't wake when she draped him over her shoulder. Her gaze darted toward Drake and her eyes flared when she saw him. Her manner instantly more servile, she tipped her head in greeting and curtsied before taking the baby from Elise's arms. "I'll take these little bundles to their kin and be waitin' for you to leave, Miss Elise. Jus' let me know when you're ready."

Choosing to ignore Prin's big grin and knowing laughter as she walked away, Elise turned to Drake. He stood and offered his hand to help her up. "Your maid, I presume?"

"Yes, Prin has been with me a long time and she's very dear to me. *If* I were to consent to wed you, she'd have to come along. I would never consider leaving her here at Brixton Hall."

He reached out and stroked her hair. "Whatever you wish, Elise. However, consider she won't be able to remain a slave if she returns with us to England. She'll receive a wage for her labors and the freedom to decide if she stays in our household or seeks out other employment."

"That's fine by me," she said, trying to contain her joy. "I have no doubt she'd wish to stay with us."

"Will Zechariah free her into our employ?"

Elise's thoughts raced. Would her spymaster allow her to end their agreement? Would he consider releasing Prin? For a moment, she allowed herself to hope and squashed the practical side of her nature that warned she dreamed for too much. "I don't know."

"Perhaps he might consider allowing me to purchase her. We can free her once we make for England."

She regarded him with amazement. His generosity astonished her. No one had ever been so kind to her. To spend the large sum it would take to purchase Prin, only to turn around and relinquish it was... "You would do that for me?"

His thumb caressed the back of her knuckles. He moved closer. His scent of leather mixed with spices filled her senses. She longed to wrap her arms around him and hug him tight.

He must have read her thoughts. With a gentle tug, he pulled her deeper into the shadows, farther away from the fire's shifting light and the revelry of the merrymakers nearby. He tucked a wisp of hair behind her ear and brushed her cheek with his fingers. His gentleness made her heart ache.

"Elise, I would do much more for you if you allow me to know your wishes. That you seem overcome by such a trifling thing makes me wonder ever more heartily of your situation here. What must I do to make you realize that *my* wishes include making you happy for the rest of your life?"

Without thought, Elise melted into his embrace. His arms banded about her, holding her close. How much time passed she didn't know and didn't care. She should return to the house, but even the shortest separation from the man she loved was becoming unbearable. Zechariah could wait a few more minutes. She rested her cheek against his chest. "I want to be your wife, Drake."

He leaned back, a look of hope etched on his handsome features. "Did I hear you correctly, sweet? Are you consenting to my proposal, or just toying with me?"

She laughed and nodded, suddenly alive with so much happiness, she thought she might take flight. "You heard me, sir. But there is a difficulty I must see to before we can announce our intentions."

His brow furrowed. "A difficulty? How so?"

"Trust me," she said. "Please, trust me."

He nodded. "I do, but—"

"Good." She pulled away before he could say more.

The separation wrenched like a physical pain. "Now I must go."

"Wait." He pulled her back for a soft kiss that left her grinning all the way back to the Hall.

Elise rapped on Zechariah's study door and waited for his command to enter. Once inside, she glanced at the French mantel clock. The tapered candles flanking the porcelain piece illuminated her tardy arrival.

"Where have you been?" Zechariah looked up from his work, his cheerfulness enough to rouse her suspicion.

"With Prin." She refused to elaborate and came to stand before his desk. "Why did you wish to see me?"

The spymaster waved her into a seat. "Tonight has been most fortuitous, m'dear."

"Truly, how so?" she asked, a bit wary. To her recollection, she'd never seen Zechariah so light of heart.

"Christian has uncovered some magnificent news on Amberly."

"Wonderful," Elise adopted a conspiratorial tone. She hoped her acting ability would stand her in good stead, though the protective instincts usually reserved for Prin rushed to the fore. "I'm very impressed. For my part, I find Amberly to be the most hard-shelled individual I've ever met."

Zechariah leaned back in his chair and folded his hands over his wide girth. "You were right, Elise."

"I was? How so?"

"He *is* an aristocrat." Zechariah beamed like a beacon. "In fact, he's even more. He's a high and mighty duke. Christian heard Beaufort refer to him as 'Your Grace.' Amberly rebuked the man and reminded him not to use his title. It all makes perfect sense, you know. The man's arrogance is a palpable thing. His wealth, his disinterest in negotiating for better shipping terms all point it out as truth. No real man of trade would be so unwilling to compromise his price."

"A duke? Why…he's practically royalty." Stunned, Elise thanked God she was sitting down. Otherwise, the sting of shock would have laid her low. As it was, she grew weak with dismay. Her stomach swirled in sickening waves of disappointment and heartbreak.

She couldn't possibly wed Drake now. Not when she'd spent years committing treason against the very crown he counted as family.

Humiliated, she bit her lip and pretended to swat a fly from her lap while she blinked back hot tears.

The old man startled her back to attention when he slapped his knee and chortled, "Imagine the funds we could winkle from the British if we offer a duke up for ransom."

She forced a smile. "Just think of it."

His mirth faded. "You don't seem as impressed as I thought you'd be, Elise. Perhaps my other plan will be more to your liking?"

"What other plan?"

He studied her until she squirmed. "My plan involves you more than anyone."

"Me?" She sat forward in her chair. "What am I to do now?"

Zechariah hauled himself from his chair and lumbered to the open window. One of his silk stockings sagged around his ankle, but he seemed not to notice. Easing himself onto the window seat, he sighed and leveled her with a thorough glance.

"You know, my dear, I love this land and hope with all my heart it will be a fine nation one day. 'Tis why I'm often so narrow of purpose and act in ways that may seem cruel when I force you to my will. In truth this war is only a game. As in chess, the craftiest player will rule. One move may make all the difference to which side wins or loses."

Elise nodded and worried at her lower lip. What he said was true. She knew he wasn't an evil man, just determined to aid the cause and see the Colonies set free of England's tyranny. She didn't begrudge him his sentiments because she shared them. It was his constant manipulation she detested, and the unnecessary way he used Prin as a weapon against her that she abhorred.

"To that end, I'm going to ask you to do something you may find objectionable in the extreme," the spymaster continued.

Fear crawled up her spine. "What is it?"

"I wish for you to wed Amberly."

She sucked in air and almost choked. "You what?"

"Let me finish." He held up his hand as if he expected a verbal comeuppance. "He's smitten with you. I confirmed it earlier when I spoke with him after we dined."

"You didn't!" She felt her cheeks heat with embarrassment.

"I know you're taken with him, so don't act affronted. Hear me out."

Elise couldn't deny his statement, yet seethed in silence. The high-handedness of her spymaster appalled her. So what if she wished to marry Drake? After years of his manipulation, Zechariah's plan rankled her to the marrow. He couldn't know for sure that she loved Amberly, yet Sayer had the nerve to ask her to sacrifice the rest of her life for his purposes.

"I ask that you espouse the man and convince him to remain in Charles Towne. The war situation is critical. The British have been routed from the Carolina interior, but their grip on Charles Towne grows ever tighter. Who can guess their next move? As Amberly's wife, you would be in the center of Charles Towne's British society. Think what beneficial information will be discussed in such close and exalted company."

"How can you imagine so? Have you forgotten that Amberly has gone to great pains to deceive us all, to make certain none of us learned his true station?"

Zechariah rested a hand on each of his knees and leaned forward. "Captain Beaufort knows his true identity. I must assume other important Brits do as well."

"And if I agree, you seriously expect me to spy on my husband? Surely, you know me better than that, Zechariah. My sense of loyalty would never allow it."

The spymaster rubbed his jaw in the palm of one beefy paw. "I feared you might say as much."

"Well, at least you give me some credit," she scoffed.

"Oh, I do, my dear. 'Tis the reason I'm willing to strike a bargain with you."

The craftiness in the old man's eyes made her heart twist with dread and fear.

Chapter Twelve

Elise stood before the mirror, admiring her wedding gown. The dress was the loveliest creation she'd ever seen. Cut in elegant lines, the pale green silk did wonderful things for her skin. The square lace-edged neckline suited her oval face and made her neck appear long and slender. She hoped Drake would be pleased when he saw her.

He'd returned to Charles Towne only this morning, so there had been no chance for them to speak in the week since she'd last seen him. She'd tried to keep busy in his absence. There'd been more than enough to do. She'd thrown herself into wedding preparations, visited friends and gone on long walks around Brixton Hall. Hours had been spent riding Freedom, praying she'd made the right decision.

Every time she remembered what she'd agreed to, her palms began to sweat and her lungs constricted until she couldn't breathe. She swallowed thickly, remembering the choice she'd made between principle and practicality. Her conscience rebelled at having to spy on Drake, but Zechariah's offer to free Prin now instead of waiting until the war's end had muted her protests. That, and the fact that if she declined his offer to report any unusual information, he promised to send Prin to an upriver plantation notorious for the mistreatment of its slaves.

How else was she to view the situation than as an answer to prayer? She'd spent long hours begging God for a way to see Prin, the baby *and* Kane set free. Her marriage insured Prin and the baby's safety. Now all she had to do was convince Zechariah to let her buy Kane.

She prayed Drake wasn't plagued by second thoughts concerning their marriage. She'd had none once she admitted he was her heart's choice for a husband. Even the distrust of men she'd learned from her father and stepfather's cruelty could not dim the hope she harbored for her future with Drake.

But Drake *was* a duke. As much as she loved him and wanted a life with him, she couldn't fathom his insistence to marry her, a colonial girl, when he could have any woman he chose. That he wanted her for his wife seemed incredible.

The soft strains of a violin filled the high ceilings and large open space of St. Michael's church. Anticipation raced through Drake as he waited in the wings to take his place at the altar. Today he would wed. He was as excited as a lad on Christmas day. He'd never been so nervous or so hopeful about his future.

The week he'd been parted from Elise had stretched like an empty eternity, but he'd had much to attend to. Besides paying Zechariah an outrageous sum for Elise's maid and horse, he'd secured the special marriage license, overseen the preparations for a rental house that would afford them the necessary privacy owed a newly wedded couple and written his solicitor in London announcing his nuptials. His primary concern revolved around safeguarding Elise's welfare. If anything happened to him she would be well provided for and free to do as she liked without the Sayers' charity.

He'd also doubled his efforts to hunt down the Fox. His informants inhabited every corner of the city, spreading the word that his reward for the spy had tripled. The Fox would eventually make a mistake and be caught, or someone greedy enough would turn him in.

If anything, Drake was more determined to avenge his brother and see the matter done. He looked forward to returning home with his bride and starting a family. Hawk Haven needed reviving, and Elise was just the woman to see it done.

The church's pipe organ boomed to life. The intricate notes throbbed, rattling the delicate stained-glass windows that cast colorful patterns on the polished wood floors. Footsteps sounded behind him. He turned to see John Kirby and Charles Beaufort rushing his way.

"Are you ready, sir?" the captain asked.

"I've never been more so, Charles. John, do you have the ring?"

The lieutenant patted the pocket of his new vest. His fingers delved into the brown wool and extracted the circle of gold. "Right here, sir. I'm honored you've given me the chance to serve as your best man."

"Yes, especially since Lord Anthony would have been your choice if not for his untimely demise," said Beaufort.

Drake lost some of his exuberance. "Yes, my brother's presence is missed today most of all."

Beaufort smoothed his blond wig. "You know it

would have been my honor to stand in his stead if it weren't necessary to keep our relationship a secret, sir. However, I'm happy to lend my presence here to ensure you have at least one family member to witness your union."

Drake straightened his navy waistcoat and slipped on the matching jacket. He clasped Beaufort on the shoulder, refusing to have his good mood marred by his cousin's awkward attempts to earn his favor. "Come, cousin, I'm to wed. I have no wish to wait a moment longer."

Taking his place at the front of the church, he held his breath as Elise floated down the center aisle, a vision in light green silk and creamy lace. Until he'd been separated from her, he hadn't been aware of how alone and empty he'd been. Just one look at her replaced his loneliness with joy.

As he took Elise's hand and spoke his vows, he thanked the Lord for the gift of her. Humbled by God's mercy and kind forgiveness, he marveled at how blessed he felt for the first time in years.

Chapter Thirteen

Pealing bells announced the wedding ceremony's conclusion. Outside the pristine white church, the sky was a clear watercolor-blue blemished only by a few inky clouds on the horizon. Elise purposely ignored them. Since the day she and Drake had spent trapped in Sadie's cabin, the threat of a storm no longer cast her into the throes of panic.

The bells stopped chiming. The wedding guests' laughter and conversation filled the churchyard. Elise regretfully left Drake's side and made it a point to speak with each of her friends and neighbors in attendance.

An hour later, she found Tabby chatting with Christian near a redbud tree. After hugging Tabby, she reached up to give Christian a peck on the cheek, but he wrapped his arm around her and turned his head just in time to plant his lips on hers.

She yanked free, a touch embarrassed by his gall. With a tight laugh, she thumped him in the ribs. "What are you about, you silly man?"

"I wanted to see Amberly's reaction." A mocking

smile turned his lips. "I believe I see smoke shooting from those ducal ears of his."

Elise heard the cold, sarcastic undertone that belied her friend's teasing manner. She turned her head sharply to scan the yard for Drake and found his gaze fixed on her. A scowl marred his brow. She offered him a smile, hoping to ease his displeasure.

When Drake smiled in return, she glared back at Christian. Until now, she hadn't realized her friend disliked Drake to such an extent, though she should have guessed.

Christian despised the English in a way that she had never completely understood. She loved liberty, embraced the hope America would one day govern herself, but she had never fully abhorred their mother country. Christian refused to tell her why he harbored such hostility, but she believed it had something to do with the untimely death of his mother. That Drake was both English and of noble birth made him a double target for Christian's antipathy.

She reached out and squeezed his hand in warning. "Be kind enough to remember that he's now my husband, Christian. I'll expect you to be civil, if not downright cordial."

Christian grunted. "You expect too much. The thought of you with that English popinjay makes me want to puke."

"Now there's a pretty sentiment on my *wedding* day," Elise said flatly. "Drake is not a popinjay. He's a wonderful, caring, loving man, who—"

Tabby hooted with laughter and clapped Christian on the back. "Listen to how protective she's become. You might as well keep your rancor to yourself. It's clear she's defected to the enemy."

"What are you implying, Tabby? I assure you I'm as a loyal as ever," Elise whispered, bristling with indignation.

"I didn't question your loyalty, my dear. I know you married for Prin's sake, not because you've turned Tory all of a sudden."

"The irony is rich, is it not?" Christian said mildly. He brushed a fly from his coat's honey-colored satin sleeve. "The rebel and the duke. I'm sure Amberly would love to know his wife is the mysterious—"

"Oh, do hush," Elise snapped. Her gaze darted to where her new husband spoke with Zechariah across the trimmed green lawn. Her eyes locked on Drake's handsome face. Her heart did a queer little flip of excitement and her breath faltered in her chest.

Tabby waved her palm in front of Elise's eyes. "I do believe she's been transported to another world."

Elise laughed self-consciously and turned back to her friends. "You're a terrible lot. Your baiting is most unfair."

"Hardly," Christian mocked, his tone as dry as a stone. "I can think of a great many things that are more unfair."

Tabby stepped in before Elise could rebut with a waspish reply. "What is wrong with you today, Christian? One would think you're a jilted suitor. Look at her face. You've wounded her, and for no reason. Elise has done nothing wrong. She's been true to her convictions, but she's a woman with limited choices. Like all of us, she wants to pursue a life of happiness and see her loved ones safe. In similar straights, I'm certain you'd act no differently."

Shamefaced, Christian nodded. Tabby entwined her arm with Elise's and led her away.

"Thank you, Tabby. At times, Christian can be such a mule."

"There's nothing to thank me for. Men usually forget they have more choices in this world. Sometimes they need a reminder, is all."

In deference to Tabby's delicate condition, they walked slowly, allowing Elise the chance to take in the scene surrounding her. Laughing children chased each other around the stately white church. One of them had brought a kite, and a handful of boisterous boys were busy tugging it free from an ill-placed pine.

"I wish Prin could have been here," Elise said quietly.

Tabby patted her hand. "It's to your credit that you care for the girl so well, for I know no other who would admit to such a relation. But your neighbors might have found it unseemly to have a slave present as a guest."

"I don't give a fig for their opinion on that score," Elise snorted.

"But you should," Tabby said sagely. "Consider how Prin would feel if she put in an appearance only to be shunned by others in attendance. As it is, she's safe and sound, tucked away at my house for the next few days. You need a day or two alone with your husband."

Elise bowed her head for a moment. "You're right, of course. People can be cruel. It's just…it's just that I'm nervous about…about tonight."

"Tonight?" Tabby exclaimed much too loudly for comfort.

"Lower your voice," Elise hurried to say. "Do you want me to die from mortification?"

Tabby flashed a wicked grin. "With a man such as your new husband, I doubt you'll die from mortification. More like you'll die from happiness. In fact, if I weren't as big as a Holstein and so in love with my darling Josiah, I just might be jealous."

Elise didn't have a chance to comment. A group of matrons stopped to chat and congratulate her on catching such a fine figure of a man. While the ladies shared sewing tips and recipes, Elise nodded and responded at the appropriate times, but Drake owned her attention. Each time she stole a glance in his direction, she caught him with his shimmering eyes alight and watching her. The magnitude of his love engulfed her from clear across the churchyard and her own tender feelings echoed in reply.

The church bells tolled five. Drake broke away from his conversation with Zechariah and headed her way.

She watched him stride across the lawn, a little stunned by the depth of her emotion for him. How he'd managed to consume her life so quickly confused her, but there she was, thankful to God, indeed grateful, that such a splendid man had been sent her way.

When Drake reached her, he kissed the back of her hand, sending a stream of warmth up her arm that didn't stop until it infused her heart.

"It's time to leave, my love." He didn't give her an opportunity to protest. Instead, he guided her to the church's wrought-iron front gates. Cheers and a shower of white rose petals and rice followed them into an awaiting coach.

The coach rocked as Drake stepped up and took his

place on the padded bench across from her. His lean, muscular frame dominated the rich interior. The scent of spice that clung to his skin mixed with the smell of the coach's new red leather seats.

Drake smiled, slow and smooth. His golden eyes roamed over her, reflecting the pride and pleasure he took in looking at her. "You're finally mine."

His voice reminded her of warm honey. Her mouth ran dry. With nerves stretched tighter than a sail in a blustery gale, she glanced out the window. She was Drake's wife now. By law, his possession to do with as he willed. She chewed her bottom lip and lowered her gaze to her clenched hands in her lap.

As eager as she was to be his wife, the situation filled her with fright, for she despised the idea of being owned—even by Drake. Ironically, her marriage had assured Prin's freedom while relieving her of her own.

Drake rapped on the coach's hardwood ceiling. Through the window she heard the driver cluck his tongue, spurring the team of matched grays into immediate motion. She leaned out the window, waving a last farewell to their guests.

The coach turned the corner. Her friends were out of sight. With nervous hands, she smoothed the front of her pale green gown. The well-sprung coach cruised along Meeting Street. She ran her hand over the smooth leather seat. Lifting her lashes, she flushed when she saw Drake studying her with an intense, unreadable expression.

"What's troubling you, Elise? You seem agitated. Are you having second thoughts about marrying me?"

"No, not really." The assurance stuck in her throat. "Are you?"

He seemed to relax, as though he'd been fighting a battle within himself and finally won. Why he should be uneasy, she couldn't fathom. It was she who faced the unknown. He'd been married before.

"On the contrary, our marriage pleases me to no end. The only thing that would make me happier is if you take off your wig."

"What?" She blinked in confusion. "Why?"

"I want to see your hair. I believe I've developed a most intoxicating fascination for it and I haven't seen it for a whole week."

His heated gaze singed her, released a flurry of nervous butterflies in her stomach. Instead of protesting, she reached for the pins that held her wig in place. One by one, she slipped them from the hairpiece and placed them in the pale silk purse dangling from her wrist.

The atmosphere hummed between them. Her hands trembled as they removed the wig and set it on the seat beside her. She removed the skullcap holding her wig in place and shook out her heavy tresses until they curled about her shoulders and flowed down her back. "Does that please you?"

"Everything about you pleases me," he murmured.

A deep rut in the road sent her lurching forward. His strong hands encircled her waist before she could slam back down on the padded seat. Before she knew what he was about, he tugged her onto the seat beside him. He wrapped his arm around her shoulders, anchoring her to him as equal currents of love and devotion swirled through her.

The coach slowed to a stop. With a low growl of irritation, Drake lifted his head, a dark frown marring his brow at the interruption. They couldn't have reached the house he'd rented already. He was about to query the driver when the sound of muted but insistent voices alerted him to something amiss.

"Where are we?" Elise asked.

"I don't know as yet. If we're not underway in a moment more, I shall have to inquire." He brushed the window curtain aside and leaned out to take in the scene. A duo of British regulars and their sergeant waited on horseback along the city street, while another regular held the horses' reins.

"I don't care if it's the king 'imself," the sergeant barked from his saddle. "A fancy coach doesn't mean you can pass this way without the proper identification. We don't allow you colonial dogs in this section of town if we can 'elp it."

"But, sir," the driver protested. "I—"

"Allow me, Artie," Drake reached into his jacket pocket and withdrew a packet of neatly folded papers before handing them in the direction of the offending officer.

The redcoat released the horses and snatched the papers from Drake's extended hand. He passed them to his superior, who untied the documents and started to read. After a few tense moments, the officer lifted his eyes, his face devoid of his former insolence and as pale as the parchment he held in his shaking grasp. "I… I do *sincerely* apologize, Your Grace!" He jumped down from his saddle and bowed, nearly losing his black helmet in the process.

The other three soldiers lost their bored expressions the moment they heard Drake's title announced. The two on horseback bounded to the ground. In unison, all three bowed so low they almost toppled over, then snapped to attention in a way that Drake would have found comical under different circumstances.

Keenly aware Elise was in hearing distance, Drake fixed the sergeant with a cutting stare and extended his palm. "My documents, if you please. I trust I'm English enough for your tastes to carry on into this part of the city?"

"Yes, yes, of course, Your Grace." The soldier thrust the documents back to Drake as if they'd suddenly caught fire. "I do apologize for interrupting your journey, sir."

Within moments the coach leapt forward. Drake scowled as he slid his identification back into his breast pocket. "I'm sorry you were subjected to that sort of odious behavior, sweet."

"I'm used to those types of remarks, Drake. Some of His Majesty's soldiers are quite courteous, but the greater number of them are overbearing as that little snipe." She pulled back the lace curtain and looked out to see they were turning toward the heart of British Charles Towne.

Sliding the cloth back into place, she cocked her head and studied her new husband. It had bothered her sorely that he'd kept the news of his title from her.

"Why did the sergeant call you 'Your Grace'?" The coach lurched over a particularly large rut in the road and Elise reached for a leather strap near the window to maintain her seat. "Drake? Is there something important you haven't shared with me?"

Chapter Fourteen

"Drake?" Elise prodded over the clatter of horses' hooves. She held her breath, waiting for him to admit the truth. What a relief it would be to no longer have to hide her knowledge of his aristocratic status. "*Is* there something you should tell me?"

Her fingers bit into the silk-tufted side panel as the coach bounced over another rough patch of road. She'd almost abandoned hope of receiving an answer when he pinned her with a level stare.

"I must plead guilty, sweet. There is a matter in which I've been less than candid with you."

Her lips compressed. She lifted her chin, hoping she appeared sufficiently annoyed by his evasiveness. "And yet you've assured me I can trust you."

"You needn't concern yourself on that score. I'd never harm you on purpose," he promised. "What I've been remiss in sharing concerns my place in society, not me as a man."

"That sounds ominous." She aimed for a light note that would encourage a quick account from him.

"Hardly." His long fingers scraped back the soft

black hair from his furrowed brow. "The long and short of it is that I possess a title, lands and the wealth bequeathed to such a heritage."

Though she'd anticipated his announcement, hearing the truth fall from his own lips sent a frisson of panic through her limbs. Somehow it hadn't seemed real that *her* Drake was a high and mighty lord of the British realm.

Quite suddenly he seemed like a mysterious stranger, foreign to everything she believed and held dear. With a delicate cough, she cleared her tight throat. "The soldier referred to you as 'Your Grace?'"

He tipped his noble head. "The fifth duke of Hawk Haven at your service, *Your* Grace."

She flinched as though he'd cast a slur upon her name. Light pierced the window lace, creating a silvery, speckled pattern that ebbed and flowed with the swaying coach. The curtain whipped in the breeze and she reached out to straighten it, grateful for something to fix upon besides his dark looks and her darker thoughts.

Elise knew she should exhibit some kind of emotion—joy, dismay, even anger for having such important information withheld from her—but at the moment her emotions were a torturous web of confusion.

The liberation she'd expected upon hearing his confession eluded her. A crushing weight settled on her shoulders and a perverse sense of guilt churned her stomach. How could she accept his confidences when she harbored so many secrets of her own?

"My situation is a trifle complicated," he continued. "I hoped you would view your new status in light of the honor it is. But, I dare say, you appear less than gratified."

"I'm sorry. I'm a touch overwhelmed." Reminding herself that he *would* see the gift of a title as an honor, she fiddled with the ivory lace that edged her light green sleeve. "When were you going to share this news with me? Surely, it would have been more fitting *before* we wed?"

His eyes shifted to the window. "It may have been more opportune, but I had my reasons for silence."

"I must confess, I'm faint with curiosity. Why would you wish to keep something so important from me?"

"I wanted to be assured you wed me for no other reason than you cared for me alone."

"I do care for you," she was quick to assure him. "But if you're a duke, how can you wed *me,* a simple colonial girl?"

His expression softened. "You're anything but simple, though I *have* wondered why you play the simpleton on occasion."

She shrugged. "Most men prefer a woman of little brains."

"I don't. I prefer you just as you are. Don't ever hide yourself from me, Elise."

She nodded even as guilt washed through her. She'd never felt more of a liar. How she wished she could tell him all her secrets, but her loved ones' safety hung in the balance.

As the coach rumbled through the streets, he sighed. "Where was I?"

"You were explaining why you didn't tell me you're a peer."

"Ah, yes. My first wife married me because the king desired an alliance between my family and hers. She was in love with someone else and resented me from the first day of our marriage. As you can probably guess, there was no warmth between us. After she died, I was hard-pressed to notice she was gone."

Elise sat forward and took hold of his hand. Drake was a proud man. She knew it cost him to admit what must seem like a monumental failure in his eyes. "She didn't deserve you."

His grim smile said otherwise. "I should have tried harder."

"It takes two to try," she whispered.

He nodded and released a wary sigh. "Last year, I acquired a fiancée."

She gasped. "What happened?"

"I found her with a lover. She had agreed to wed me at her family's insistence—for my fortune and title."

"You must have been devastated!"

He shook his head. "Not in the least. My pride was bruised and I was angry, but not hurt. I'd sought to wed her for my own less than heartfelt reasons, though I would have been faithful and trustworthy."

"The girl must be an imbecile." She snorted. "Both of them were. I don't see how any sane woman couldn't help but love you."

He smiled, his white teeth flashing in the coach's dim interior. "Are you sane, then?"

Her cheeks flushed. "I was until I met you. Now, I'm just crazy about you."

"And I adore you," he assured her with more honesty than she'd ever encountered. "For the first time in my life I've found love."

Her heart swelled with tenderness and her throat closed with emotion. "It's the same for me, too."

He bent his head to kiss her, but the coach began to slow and rolled to a stop. Drake flashed a wry grin.

"Barring the possibility of additional overzealous red-coats, I believe we've arrived at the house I arranged for our use. We'll be residing here until we make for England."

Elise peered out the window for a better view of the whitewashed brick three-story townhouse. Aged magnolia trees provided shade in the trimmed front yard, and potted white roses flanked either side of the gleaming red front door. "And how long might that be?"

"God willing, not much longer," he said. "I've been absent from Hawk Haven for half a year. My sister will be anxious to see me."

"Why must we remain in South Carolina at all?" She tried not to sound overeager, but she wouldn't feel completely safe until she and her family were far away from everyone who knew their secrets. "Why not sail for London as soon as possible?"

His sculpted face turned hard as flint. "Soon, sweet. I'm not quite finished with a few business matters here in Charles Towne."

The driver opened the coach door, eyes averted to the road. Drake jumped down first, then raised his arms to help Elise alight.

The moment Drake's hands encircled her waist, her nerves jangled in giddy alarm. Without pause, he swept her into his arms. The air whooshed from her lungs in a hearty, startled laugh as she looped her arms around the strong column of his neck.

His joy palpable, he raced up the brick walk to the front door. The door swung wide as though welcoming them of its own accord. The scents of roses, herbs and roasting beef greeted them. They were inside the wide entryway before Elise looked over Drake's shoulder to see who'd opened the door.

A stout woman of about three score or more thrust the door closed, casting the front hall into twilight. Her broad smile made her eyes mere slits above her weathered apple-red cheeks. Wiping her hands on her apron, she bobbed curtsy after curtsy while she spoke in brisk German.

"What did she say?" Elise whispered from her lofty height in Drake's arms. "I didn't understand."

Drake grinned down at her. "This is Frau Einholt, the housekeeper. She's welcoming us to our new home. She said there's a light repast ready for us to enjoy whenever we like, and the trunks you sent from Brixton Hall have been unpacked."

He paused, listening as the robust woman chirped with animated enthusiasm. "She's congratulating me on my fine choice of bride."

Elise smiled and thanked the housekeeper for the compliment. The beaming woman curtsied again, obviously understanding some English even if she didn't speak it.

When Drake answered in German, Elise waited for the translation, but none came. He'd started up the curved staircase before she asked, "What did you tell her just now? I know it was something improper. The two of you shared a most mischievous laugh."

They reached the second floor and he placed her on her feet. "She wished us good fortune, long life and a house full of sons. I thanked her, 'tis all."

Elise eyed him with playful suspicion. "There's something more. I'm sure of it. What else did you tell her?"

Drake chuckled. "It's ill indeed when a new wife distrusts her husband."

She tried to sound stern. "Tell me what else you said, Drake Amberly."

He didn't answer. Instead, he caught her to him, pressed open a door behind him, and pulled her into a large candlelit chamber. "I merely mentioned we plan to begin work on filling the house full of sons tonight."

Chapter Fifteen

The next morning Elise dressed and left the room to join Drake downstairs for breakfast. Her cheeks heated when she recalled Drake's tenderness as he'd made her his wife. She'd never felt more cherished. With a grateful heart she thanked the Lord for letting them find each other. It truly was a miracle when she considered their opposing circumstances.

Drake met her at the bottom of the stairs. The riding crop he held suggested he'd been to the stables. His billowy white shirt open at the neck revealed a hint of bronzed throat. His golden eyes searched her face with tender concern. "Hello, sweet. How do you fare this morn?"

"I'm most well," she said, a little breathless. "And you, my dearest husband?"

His smile warmed her heart. He took her hands in his and brushed his lips across her knuckles in a gentle kiss. "I've never been happier. I knew you were the woman for me that first day we sailed for Charles Towne."

"So soon?" she asked in surprise. "How did you know?"

He led her across the hall to the morning room and

seated her at a table laden with fresh bread, cheese and fruit. "When a man's been searching for his match as long as I have, he knows her the moment he spies her."

The word *spy* sent a shiver of fear down her spine. Some of her merriment dimmed. A pessimistic voice in her head reminded her that Drake loved Elise Cooper, the ward of a Tory plantation owner, not Elise Cooper, the patriot spy. What would he do if he ever discovered her past as the Fox? Would he understand and move on with their lives, or would he see her treason to the crown as an unforgivable betrayal and set her aside?

"Elise?" Drake knelt on one knee beside her chair. "Did I say something wrong?"

Her gaze slipped to his face and his concerned frown. Thick dark lashes fringed his questioning eyes. The thought of losing him formed a painful lump in her throat. She cupped his cheek with her palm, determined to cast off the haunting questions and do her best to make him happy.

"No, you've said everything just right."

He stood and pulled her to her feet. "Good, because I have one more gift for you before we eat."

"Another gift?" She ran her thumb over the back of the smooth wedding band he'd given her to mark their marriage. "But I don't have one for you."

He nuzzled her neck and nibbled her ear. "I want you, nothing else."

Her gaze softened as she traced the sculpted line of his lower lip. "You really are the most wonderful man I've ever known."

His eyes glowed with love. "Come, sweet, your gift is outside." He held out a hand to her and led her down the wide hall and past the sitting rooms. She might as well have been floating, she felt so light and happy. He held the back door open as she emerged into an open-air courtyard of curved brick walkways and a circular center garden. Fresh, fragrant herbs, including her favorite, rosemary, perfumed the warm summer morning.

A stable stood across the courtyard some distance away, and the faint whinny of horses drifted across the expanse toward them. Drake led her onward. The earthy smell of horses and hay grew stronger the closer they came. Once inside, Drake lit a lantern, illuminating the stable's spacious interior. Drake's shiny new coach sat to the left. Huge bales of hay stood stacked to the beamed ceiling, and various articles of horse tack hung along the walls.

Drake's pair of matched grays stood in individual stalls next to each other, but it was the bay gelding toward the back that brought tears of happiness to her eyes. "Freedom? You're giving me Freedom?"

He shrugged fluently. "I know you love him. Seemed a bit of lunacy to leave him behind."

Elise shrieked with joy and threw her arms around Drake's neck, squeezing him tight.

Freedom whinnied and kicked at the door of his stall. She crossed the sandy floor and reached out to stroke his forehead. The onslaught of happy tears tickled her nose. "Hello, my dear friend. I thought I'd lost you."

The horse nickered and pressed the side of his head into her palm.

Drake moved close behind her and settled his hands on her shoulders. "I believe he missed you, too."

Elise melted into Drake's embrace. "How did you convince Zechariah to sell him? When I tried to buy him, he wouldn't hear of it."

Drake kissed the top of her head, and stroked her hair. "You're not as persuasive as I am, apparently."

"Drake, how much—"

"Truth be told, Sayer seemed almost desperate to be rid of you. When I told him I refused to consider marriage without the horse included in the bargain, he seemed quite eager to part with the old boy."

She gave him a watery smile and sniffed. "I couldn't ask for a more perfect gift."

"Then why the tears?"

"I don't think I've ever been this happy. Thank you," she whispered, standing on tiptoes to give him a kiss. "Thank you with all my heart."

"Isn't Moira the most beautiful child you've ever seen?" Tabby chirped with maternal pride. "It's hard to believe she's seven weeks old."

"Indeed, it is," Elise said, cradling the Smiths' new arrival. "Such wide blue eyes and what perfect, cherubic cheeks. She's a darling. Don't you agree, Prin?"

Prin turned from the window of Tabby's parlor, where she'd been watching the quiet street. The blue-and-yellow striped curtains fluttered into place as she moved toward the unlit fireplace. "She's sweet as maple sugar, that one. You and Mister Josiah should be peacock proud."

"We are." Tabby beamed. She scooped the baby from Elise's arms and sat in a nearby rocking chair.

Elise leaned back on the settee and patted the seat next to her. "Come sit with me, Prin. There's plenty of room for us both."

When her sister joined her, Elise gently squeezed her hand in encouragement. She knew that along with feeling ill from her pregnancy, Prin longed for Kane. A cloud of melancholy followed her sister no matter how much she tried to be strong and act as if nothing were wrong.

"You know," Tabby said to Elise, "you've been married nearly two months. Folks will be expecting you to be with child before too long."

Elise's cup clattered as she returned it to the saucer. "It's too soon, surely."

Tabby and Prin shared a telling glance.

"After weeks of marriage with your dazzling husband," Tabby teased, "I can't believe you've not considered the possibility."

"I try not to think about it," Elise said, her unease with the topic difficult to conceal. "I may not have a choice, but until I know Prin and I are completely out of danger, I'd rather not have to consider a babe."

"That's wise," Tabby agreed as she ran a fingertip along her daughter's cheek. "I don't think there's anything I wouldn't do to keep this precious girl from harm. But as you say, you may not have a choice."

The discussion struck a chord of fear in Elise. If she became pregnant, Zechariah would have one more weapon in his arsenal against her. He'd used her love for Prin enough times in the past to convince her he wouldn't be above using her child. She could hear his threats in her mind. "Elise," he would say, "bring me this information or I may be forced to turn you over to the British. Think. What will your child do without his mother?"

"Elise?" Tabby intruded her troubling thoughts. "Is all well with you? Why, you look positively violent."

"Do I?" She pasted on a smile. "I'm fine, really. Just a little tired."

Her friend giggled. "Not been getting enough sleep, eh?"

Prin set her cup aside and studied Elise with concern. "Perhaps we should be headin' home?"

"Don't leave yet." Tabby stood and placed her sleeping daughter in a cradle dressed with frills and white lace. "Zechariah will be arriving soon. He wishes to speak with you."

Elise bit her lower lip. She'd been avoiding her spymaster and wished to continue in that vein. While at a dinner party a fortnight ago, she'd learned news that might be of interest to him, but her loyalty to Drake made her loath to share it. "Why didn't you tell me, Tabby?"

"He asked me not to." She tucked baby Moira in one of the blankets Elise had knitted for her. "I thought it strange, but then supposed there must be a reason."

A light knock sounded on the door and a servant stepped through once Tabby called him in.

"Ma'am, Mr. Sayer is here to see you."

"Thank you, Henry. Show him through."

A few moments later, Zechariah waddled in. After he performed a shallow bow, Tabby motioned him into a chair, which barely held his girth once he rolled into it.

"Prin," Tabby said. "Let's you and I take the baby and our tea tray to the garden. The oaks will give us plenty of shade to escape this dreadful heat."

Prin waited until Elise nodded her approval before picking up the tray and following Tabby into the hall. Henry followed and closed the door.

Zechariah studied Elise, his gaze as sharp as a well-honed dagger. He leaned forward and rested his hands on the ball of his walking stick. "You look fit enough, girl. Marriage seems to agree with you."

She folded her hands in her lap and held his gaze without flinching. "Yes, it does."

"That lad you married is treating you well, then?"

"Very well indeed."

There was a slight pause as Zechariah inspected his shoe's square, brass buckle. "You may not believe this, m'dear, but I've been most concerned about you."

Elise's brow rose in cynical inquiry.

"You may think I enjoy manipulating your life, but such is not the case. I—"

"Forgive me, Zechariah, but I've been the subject of your machinations more times than I can count. You've conspired against me so often I find it hard to believe you have a true care for my welfare."

"'Tis why I'm here, Elise. I have news you'll wish to hear." He tapped the tip of his walking stick against the floor, giving her time to snatch in several breaths. "Actually, I've come for two reasons today."

"I'm surprised you haven't come to call before now."

"I might have, but you've been avoiding me since you wed. Don't think I haven't noticed. It's a shame I had to trick Tabby into helping me or I doubt I'd be seeing you today."

Elise reddened, but didn't deny it.

Zechariah cleared his throat. "You've had ample time to retrieve information to aid the cause. I'm here to collect it."

Elise jumped to her feet, her bountiful green skirt swirling as she swung toward the open window. "I have little to tell you."

"Some is better than nil. Spit it out, and be quick about it. If you think to break our bargain I'll be forced—"

"To call in the British," she sneered with ferocious bite. She wondered if she'd ever be free of that particular threat. "I'll have you know I do have news I'm willing to impart. Not because of your threat, but because contrary to what you suppose, I love this land as much as you. From the beginning, I would have freely shared the knowledge I gleaned, but you chose to dangle Prin's freedom over my head and use threats to bend me to your will."

"By what other means could I be sure—"

"Be quiet," she snapped.

To her surprise, he fell back in his chair, sputtering and indignant, but eventually silent.

"Before I share what I've uncovered, I'm adding to our bargain." She straightened her spine and thrust back her shoulders in a silent dare for him to refuse her. "I wish to purchase Kane from you."

"Impossible." The old man shook his head, setting his jowls to flapping.

"'Tis a simple transaction, why is it impossible? I'm willing to pay you double his worth."

His gaze slunk to the floor. "I may have need of him yet."

Elise narrowed her eyes, savvy to his ways enough to suspect he'd planned something reprehensible.

"You think I don't know about him and Prin or the *illegal* marriage you arranged for them. But I assure you, girl, I know everything that happens on my plantation."

She threw up her hands. "I can't believe it! You intend to bargain with his freedom in order to bend me to your will at some future date?"

"I know you and your soft heart," he admitted. "If Prin longed for him enough, you'd do whatever was required to get him for her."

"You're despicable." Her upper lip curled in disgust. "Always playing with people's lives as if they're pieces in some game."

"On the contrary. I'm just determined," he said without remorse. "But that's neither here nor there. You've mentioned you have news. I believe the war situation is desperate enough for extreme measures. My contacts tell me Washington is stalemated with Clinton in New York and Cornwallis is like a plague of fire weaving his way through Virginia. Share your information and I'll have Kane, his freedom papers signed and sealed, sent to you this eve."

Hope sparked in her chest. She lifted her chin. "How can I be certain?"

"You wound me, child. You may not like my methods, but when have I ever lied to you?"

He hadn't that she knew of. "I have your word?"

"Aye." He held out his palm. "You have it. Your information in exchange for Kane's freedom."

Wary, she shook his hand. "At dinner a fortnight ago, I heard it mentioned that General Clinton has called Cornwallis to leave the southern colonies altogether and aid him in New York. It seems Clinton fears Patriot forces plan to attack before the onslaught of winter."

"It will take weeks for Cornwallis to march to New York."

She shook her head. "No, he and his army are to wait in Yorktown for the British fleet to transport them north."

Zechariah slapped his knee suddenly and hooted

with excitement. "Do you know what this means, my girl? Lafayette is camped in Virginia. If I can send word to him and his army there, he can notify Washington and Rochambeau's combined forces farther north. If the armies converge—"

"We might win a major battle this year."

"God willing, we might capture Cornwallis's whole army and win the war." His eyes began to twinkle with excitement. He levered himself to his feet and made his way for the door. "Good day to you, Your Grace." He grinned as he reached for the brass doorknob. "I knew wedding you off to Amberly would bring us a bout of luck."

"Wait. You said you had two items to discuss with me. So far, we've spoken of just one."

"Ah, yes, I forgot. The Fox is in trouble."

"The Fox is dead," she said adamantly. "He ceased to exist the day I married."

Zechariah clamped his hands behind his back and rocked on his heels. "That may be, but it seems he has a persistent admirer who refuses to let him rest in peace. Several months back I received reports that an individual was offering a reward for the Fox's capture. At the time, I thought nothing of it. After all, who among the British wouldn't like to see the Fox hang? But, a short time ago, just a few days before your marriage, in fact, it seems that original sum was tripled."

"Tripled?" she asked curiously. "What was the original amount?"

He paused. "Five hundred pounds."

"Five *hundred?* You must be jesting!"

"I wish I were, my dear, but there it is. Whoever is hunting you means serious business. Fifteen hundred pounds is enough to make any man consider.... Why, even I was tempted to turn you in for such a fortune."

Elise dropped into a nearby chair.

"Don't go all female on me, girl. You've lost every scrap of color. I'm not likely to do it, you know. At least, not without good reason."

Robin Goss shivered in the moldy dampness of his warehouse cell. Rats squeaked in the dark, and their scurrying feet scratched along the wood floor. He bellowed in frustration as he strained against the rope around his wrists, but the dank rag in his mouth muffled the feral sound.

He cursed the day he'd found the woman's traitorous letters in his carriage. His last remaining hope was that he would someday escape, hunt her down and make her pay.

A key rattled in the lock. Disgusted by the stab of excitement that lanced through him, he realized he'd been held in this pit long enough to appreciate the sight of any human face, even one of his hated captors.

The door swung wide. One of his kidnappers, the one he'd heard called "John," entered carrying a lantern and tray of steaming food. A homespun mask covered his face. Black gloves protected his ham-sized hands. The smell of mustard greens, bacon and cornbread briefly cloaked the smell of rotting fish, making his mouth water.

"How's our pris'ner, this fine night?" John snickered under his breath as he dropped the tray on the table. "I'm thinkin' you must be hungry considerin' I'm late this eventide."

Robin tried to swallow. He was starving. His eyes

followed the movement of the dishes as John laid them out on a rickety bench, the cell's only piece of furniture.

John crouched before him and removed the gag. Robin heaved in a lungful of salty air. "Can I eat?" The words burned over his parched throat.

"'Course, but there'll be no exercise tonight," John said, untying the ropes that bound Robin's wrists and ankles. "I'm wantin' a pint before I head home to the missus."

"Sorry to be such an inconvenience," Robin muttered. "Let me go and I won't bother you again."

John grunted with laughter. "Don't be daft." His huge hand jabbed toward the food. "Now, eat up a'fore you lose your chance."

Robin stood slowly, his leg muscles tight from sitting in one position on the hard floor all day. He eyed his captor, studying the big man, wondering, not for the first time, if he could take him in a fight.

"Don't even think it," John warned, patting the pistol that bulged in his pocket. "Matthew is waitin' just outside the door. He's armed heavier 'an me and hankerin' to shoot himself a traitorous spy."

"I'm not the traitor," Robin sneered. "These colonies belong to King George. I'm doing my part to see they stay that way."

John's nostrils flared with obvious fury. "Well then, it does my heart good to know you're tied up in here where you can't do more damage. Now, eat the food and shut your stupid mouth! I got no patience for your Tory prattle."

Robin shoveled the food with his fingers while he fumed. Each hearty mouthful fortified him a little more. He washed the meal down with the provided mug of ale.

"I need to relieve myself," he told John. John stretched and ambled toward the door. "I'll count to thirty. You'd best be high and dry by then."

Raising his hand in a mock salute, Robin waited for his captor to leave before he positioned himself by the door. Ole John had grown lax. He'd never left him untied and alone before. When his captor returned to bind him this time he was in for a nasty surprise. Once he escaped, Robin promised Captain Beaufort would get an earful.

"…twenty-eight, twenty-nine, thirty." John shouted as he burst through the door, his pistol at the ready.

Robin pounced from the corner. His arm wrapped around John's thick neck, snapping it so quickly the man didn't have a chance to cry out. John wilted to the floor, dragging Robin with him. The pistol bounced on the planks. Robin yanked his arm from around his captor's neck, grabbed the pistol, and rolled to his feet.

Matthew burst into the room, brandishing his own weapon. Robin fired. Matthew yelped. When the smoke cleared, Matthew was on his knees, gasping for breath, a look of stunned horror on his ashen face.

Robin spared a moment to watch Matthew's lifeblood drain from the hole in his chest. He couldn't help smiling. He was free again after months of rotting in this pit.

Matthew slumped face-first to the floor. Robin stepped over the dead man and raced out the door.

Chapter Sixteen

Robin Goss pushed his way through the jostling crowd of the smoke-filled Ax and Hammer tavern. The Scottish barkeep, Michael MacClean, set down the stein he was drying and eyed him with suspicion.

"Don't you recognize me, Mac? It's Robin," he yelled over the fiddle music and raucous conversation that threatened to dislodge the rafters.

"*Robin?* Robin Goss?" the barkeep hollered as though blinders had been ripped from his eyes. "I didna' recognize you with that bedraggled mane hidin' yer face. Where you been, laddie? It's months since I saw you last."

Robin's buckteeth bit into his lower lip. His fingers clenched the sticky counter. "Rebels nicked me off the street and stowed me in a warehouse not three blocks from here."

"Those filthy traitors!"

"Aye, they were, but they've seen the light," Robin said darkly. "What's the date, Mac?"

"The twenty-ninth of September." The Scot glanced at the mantel clock. "For another few hours anyway."

"Two stinkin' months." Robin wiped his bearded chin with the back of his filthy hand. His confinement had given him plenty of time to recall the day he'd been kidnapped, the traitorous female spy he'd uncovered, and her accomplices at The Rolling Tide, including its owner, Josiah Smith. He had no doubt that she and Smith were behind his imprisonment.

Killing John and Matthew had only whetted his appetite for vengeance. Hatred burned in his belly until the need to strangle the wench threatened to tear him in two. "They kept me locked in that rat hole over two rotten months!"

"I believe you." Mac stepped back, picked up a towel, and began to dry a stoneware plate. "Nothin' else would explain why you look so beastly and smell vile enough ta make yer mother cry."

Robin's lips compressed in vexation. "Keep your sweet talk to yourself and pour me a drink, old man. I'm so dry I've got sawdust clogging my veins."

Mac slid him a pint, sloshing foam over the mug's pewter rim.

Robin took a long swig of the bitter brew. He leaned back against the counter as he looked over the sea of English revelers. Sailors jigged to the Irish fiddles while a group of army officers gambled in the protective shadows of a corner table.

Robin cocked his head, studying each officer through the lantern light and smoky haze.

"Who you lookin' for?" Mac boomed over a bagpipe that wailed in competition with the fiddles.

"Captain Beaufort," Robin shouted. "I went to his office across the way, but he's quit for the night. I thought I might find him here."

Mac shook his head as he handed a barmaid a tray full of overflowing mugs. "I havna seen him in nigh a month."

Robin drained his tepid ale, but it did little to quench the rage in his belly. He slammed the empty mug onto the bar and turned to leave.

"Have a care, laddie," the Scotsman warned, staying Robin with a tight grip on his wrist. "That'll be two pence."

Shaking free of the barkeep's tight grip, Robin warned him off with a level stare and jammed his hand into his grimy pocket, remembering too late he was poor as dirt. "I'll have to owe you, Mac."

The barkeep's eyes narrowed with anger. "And will you be askin' yer pa for funds then?"

"No." Robin's voice landed with finality. His father had told him to put his education to use. He wasn't to return to Lowell Plantation until he'd made something respectable of himself. Becoming a Tory spy, disguised as a carriage driver, was a far cry from what his patriot father considered acceptable. "I'll get Beaufort to lend me a bag of coin."

Mac guffawed. "He won't be handin' out silver unless you become one of those Fox hunters of his. You've been away, so you may no' have heard—the ransom's tripled. Fifteen hundred pounds is enough to make the soberest of gents tipsy with the want of it."

"Fifteen hundred pounds!"

"Aye. You heard me right, laddie."

"And no one's found the scum yet?"

"No one." Mac picked up another mug to dry. "You'd think that amount o' money would spark some clever soul into finding the vermin, but from the whispers

I've heard, the leads have all dried up. Most think the Fox has left Charles Towne altogether. Perhaps gone to Williamsburg or the swamps to aid that other sly one, Francis Marion, and his militia of rebel slime."

Robin's imagination teemed with possibilities as he stroked his matted beard. Could the spies he'd uncovered at The Rolling Tide somehow lead him to the Fox? Could he watch Josiah Smith, wait him out until he learned enough of the tavern owner's secrets to force him to his will? For fifteen hundred pounds, it was worth a try.

A current of elation danced through Robin, bringing a sudden, hateful smile to his lips. The promise of combined retribution and revenge spurred him to the tavern's iron-hinged front door. Over his shoulder, he shouted, "I will repay you, Mac—with interest. I just need a little time."

Alone in the parlor, Elise attempted to read her well-worn Bible. The rays of the late afternoon sun flooded through the windows behind her, illuminating the yellowed pages, but her mind refused to concentrate and the words blurred together.

Dropping the book on her lap, she spread her hands over her flat stomach. Tabby's banter yesterday had made Elise admit the truth. She was with child. Last month she'd missed her monthly and now she was a week late again.

Joy flickered to life deep inside her. She was carrying Drake's child. A soft smile turned her lips as she imagined the tiny hands and feet knitting together within her womb. Even the threat Zechariah posed to her happiness couldn't snuff out the wonder lifting her spirits.

"Hello, sweet." Drake strode into the room as though her thoughts had called him home. His exuberant energy brought the large, airy parlor to life. Tall and strong, he lacked only an earring and cutlass to personify a pirate she'd once read about. Black breeches and leather riding boots molded the muscular length of his calves. The embroidered neckline of his stark white shirt highlighted the swarthiness of his skin and silky black hair. He was a dessert for the senses and he simply stole her breath away.

He deposited a leather satchel on the mahogany desk near the door and poured himself a drink. The smoldering look in his honeyed eyes told her how glad he was to see her.

"I must say, Your Grace, you look tempting enough to eat."

She rolled her eyes, but couldn't stop the smile that spread across her lips. Sliding the Bible onto the table beside her, she blushed under his affectionate perusal.

He tipped the glass in her direction. "What were you reading?"

"My Bible."

His brow furrowed in surprise. "What passage?"

"Romans eight. It's one of my favorites." Her hand caressed the worn leather Bible. "I find it's a true comfort in times of trouble to know no matter where I go or what I do, I can never be separated from Christ's love."

"Are you troubled, Elise?"

"Not when you're here," she said with a smile. "And what of you? Do you have a favorite passage?"

He turned thoughtful. "I supposed of late, it would

be the story of the prodigal son. When I was younger, I trusted in the Lord. After my sour marriage and the untimely deaths of my parents and older brother, I stopped believing in God's mercy. Then I met you, and I've had much cause to thank Him ever since."

The knowledge warmed her. "I'm glad I've had a part in bringing you back to your faith."

"You've brought about a good many things in my life."

Touched that he should think so, she blinked back sudden tears. "Just promise me you won't turn your back on God again if something should happen to me in the future."

His cheerfulness faded. "I refuse to think of my life without you."

"Please promise me," she insisted.

He nodded. "I promise."

"Thank you." She smiled brightly. "Now, tell me where you have been all day. You were sorely missed."

He leaned against the mahogany cabinet behind him and regarded her with a spark of mischief in his eyes. "'Tis good to hear. A man *should* be missed by his wife."

She plucked at the gold fringe of a pillow she held and watched him from under her lashes. "I didn't say *I* missed you."

His brow arched with mock severity. "How in the world did I acquire such a lippy duchess?"

"I don't know." She grinned. "Good fortune?"

His rich voice took on a husky timbre. "Indeed, the very best."

Sweet affection filled her senses. She'd been more than blessed to wed such an excellent man. The terror she'd had of marriage thanks to her mother's misfortune with Roger was well and truly gone, buried under the onslaught of Drake's constant love and attention.

She patted the seat beside her. He prowled toward her like a man intent on ravishment. Her heart hammered against her ribs in anticipation of his touch.

As he brushed aside the layers of her skirt and petticoats, he claimed his share of the plum-and-gold-striped settee. "To answer your question, I've spent an unfortunate day in Beaufort's witless company."

She wrinkled her nose in distaste. "You told me he's your cousin, but if he irritates you, why must you spend so much time with him?"

"Before we wed, I mentioned that I'm hunting for someone while I'm here in the Colonies. Beaufort is supposedly aiding me. The longer I'm here, I grow less and less certain."

"Ah." She laced her fingers with his and brushed her thumb across his knuckles. "Who is the unfortunate soul you're looking for?"

His expression turned dark, almost savage. "My brother's murderer."

She gasped. Sympathy welled up inside her. Through their talks she'd learned how much Drake loved his family, how protective he was and how serious he took his duty toward them. She twisted in her seat and cupped his cheek with her palm. "I'm so sorry. You told me you'd like to find the culprit, but didn't say you were looking for him here. Tell me more. Perhaps I can help in some way."

He stretched out his long legs and crossed them at the ankles. "There's nothing you can do, sweet, and frankly, I refuse to dwell on the miscreant any longer today. I have more enjoyable things in mind. Come here."

Eager to obey, she swayed into his arms. He smelled of warm spices and sunshine. Beneath her palm, his heart picked up speed. His arms banded about her, pulling her close as though he'd been waiting all day just to hold her.

A sharp rap on the door made Elise jump. Prin burst into the room.

"Lisie, I… I'm sorry." Her sister reversed course, yanking the door closed as she backed out in embarrassment.

"Prin, wait!" Elise struggled off Drake's lap.

Prin peered around the door, a look of apology in her huge brown eyes. She massacred a curtsy and bowed for good measure. "I'm sorry. I thought you were alone. I jus' wanted to let you know that me and Kane are headed to the market. It's late, but Frau Einholt says she's needin' some cornmeal if we can come by any. Did you want me to fetch anythin' special for you?"

"I need nothing at the moment." Elise looked to Drake, who studied Prin with narrowed eyes. "Do you, darling?"

Drake declined and Prin hurried to leave. When the door clicked shut, Drake called Elise back to her place on the settee beside him. Something in his manner was different. She couldn't put her finger on what, but she suspected it had to do with Prin.

His arm tightened around her shoulders and tucked her close to his side. "Something intrigues me, Elise. I hope you can help me puzzle it out."

The room's mellowed light made it difficult for her to see his expression. She drew a pillow back onto her lap and hugged it to her middle. "I'll always aid you whenever I can."

"It has to do with your maid."

"My maid?" she braced herself. "What would you like to know about her?"

Quite deviously, as if he thought she wouldn't notice, his fingers eased one of the pins from her hair and then another. "There. That's better."

He sounded so pleased with himself. She shook her head in amusement, causing the thick skeins to tumble around her shoulders. She'd grown used to his obsession with her hair. Since the first week of their marriage, she'd given up on having it arranged in a decent style if Drake was within arm's length.

"Now, about your maid," he continued. "I'd like you tell me the truth about her."

"The truth?"

"Yes, the truth." He stroked her hair. "Mind you, I haven't seen her often, as she seems to hide from me, but I have noticed a marked resemblance between the two of you, except for her darker skin and curly hair, of course. Is she somehow a relation? It strikes me that she's much too familiar with you and rarely behaves like a maid if she believes I'm absent. When she does stumble upon me, she regards me as if I'm his majesty's master of the whipping post come to whisk her away for a sound lashing."

Elise didn't know whether to laugh or cry, but the time had come to tell him the truth about Prin. "She's my half sister, and you might as well know, the giant trailing her about is her new husband. They were married in secret the week before you and I met. Zechariah allowed me to buy Kane yesterday. They're expecting a child this winter." The words flowed with more ease than she'd imagined, lifting the heavy weight of one of her secrets from her shoulders. "I apologize if Prin's made you uncomfortable. She doesn't know how to behave around you. She loves you for making me happy, but neither of us knew how you'd react to the truth. I've wanted to tell you a hundred times—"

"Then why didn't you?"

She searched his face, but could read nothing in the lean, hard lines of his expression. She grappled for the right words, tried to explain without making him angry. "Can't you guess? I've never known anyone to understand my feelings for Prin. Even Tabby was scandalized when I first told her. It's as though no one sees beyond the shade of her skin. She was a slave so I'm expected to ignore our sisterhood, forget she's the one person I've loved and depended on all my life.

"Our family's past is ugly," she continued. Embarrassed, but determined to admit the full truth, she left his side, afraid to see his reaction. "Prin's mother belonged to our father. She was his housekeeper and he forced her to be his mistress. Prin is four years older than I. When we were children she protected me from father's…unpleasantness."

His silence greeted her confession. She glanced up to find his reflection in the looking glass. Fury glittered in his gaze before he stood and turned his back on her. She clutched the pillow she'd brought with her from the settee like a shield; afraid she'd misjudged how he'd react.

She shouldn't feel betrayed, she reminded herself. She'd been the one to keep secrets. It wasn't acceptable to claim a slave as a relation. Why, when no one else had ever understood her loyalty and love for Prin, did she expect Drake to feel any different? Worse, he was a duke. His family tree stemmed back to Creation, mingled with royalty and most likely had nary a hint of scandal in its branches.

She turned and studied his back. Poker-straight, his legs braced and his hands locked behind him, he took a deep breath before he faced her. His ire emanated in waves. She cringed. All her past experiences with this kind of anger had resulted in a beating or a tongue-lashing. She set down the pillow and backed away, primed to escape.

Drake must have guessed her intention. "Where are you going?"

"I'm not blind to your fury, Drake. I won't stay here and allow you to unleash it on me."

He could not have looked more stunned if she'd punched him in the nose. "You must be joking. I would never raise my hand to you. I think, however, I've finally hit upon the truth as to why you didn't confide in me about your sister—you still don't trust me."

"Not true!" she protested. "I do, but—"

"Don't think I haven't noticed there's a part of yourself—a secret self—you keep hidden away from me." He dragged his fingers through his hair, his shoulders stiff with tension. "I am more than angry, I am furious, but not with you, you silly woman."

"Not with me?" Her throat convulsed over a jagged lump of shock. "Then who?"

He shook his head as though he couldn't believe he'd wed such a simpleton. "Your father, your neighbors, anyone who has ever caused you the slightest amount of pain." His fist slammed into his open palm. "I'd like to crush them all."

Disbelief held her in thrall. Never had anyone been outraged on her behalf. With the greatest care, he pulled her against him. His voice dipped low and brushed along her nerves, soothing her as though she were still the child who'd hid in fear from her father's drunken rages.

"Elise, there's nothing you needn't tell me. I want to know your every thought, your every dream. I would do battle for you, fight for you until my dying breath."

Snuggling against him, she basked in his embrace while her thoughts lined up like opposing armies within her head. He could make promises because he didn't know her darkest secrets. She trembled at the thought of him discovering her past and turned her back on the mental promptings that advised her to confide in him. Her love for Drake was too precious to risk losing with a confession that, she reminded herself once again, would soon be moot.

"I'm glad to hear it," she whispered, warmed by his declaration that he would fight for her. "Our child and I couldn't bear to live without you."

"You would never have to, I…" He stopped, blinking in stunned amazement. "What child?"

She looked up into his face to judge his reaction as she pressed his palm flat against her stomach. "This one," she said softly. "The one we're expecting in about seven months' time."

His delight was immediate. Joy reflected in his eyes, his smile, the gentle, almost reverent way he clasped her to him. "My life improves each day you're a part of it. Thank you, my love, for making me the happiest of men."

Elise sat at the opposite end of the dining-room table, too far away for Drake's liking. He wanted her within arm's length, close enough to touch her at all times.

He picked up his goblet, admiring how her green eyes were bright and lively, her soft cheeks rosy with happiness.

The knowledge that she carried his child filled Drake with enormous pride and a primitive need to protect her. Love, hot and fierce, rippled through him, growing with each beat of his heart. She was everything to him. A gift from God to heal his jaded soul and bring his heart to life again.

Wanting to please her, he'd shunned convention and insisted Prin and Kane join them for dinner that night. They'd just finished their coffee. Prin had begun to relax, another blessing from the Lord. Her fidgeting had resulted in only a few minor spills—nothing that soaking the starched white tablecloth in lye soap for a week wouldn't fix.

Drake turned to Kane. "So, my good man, now that you're free, how do you plan to earn your way and support my lovely sister-in-law here?"

Elise stilled. Prin went round-eyed with curiosity, whilst Kane's hand shook as he set down his sterling silver spoon, careful not to clang it against the delicate rim of his fruit bowl. Squaring his shoulders, the former slave spoke with quiet dignity that didn't quite conceal his worry on the matter. "I don't rightly know, suh. I been a slave all my life. I worked the Sayers' fields since I was a child and for the last five years, I managed 'em under the overseer's guidin' hand. Thanks to Miss Lisie and Prin, I knows how to read and write a little. I can do sums in my head and on paper, but—" he looked Drake straight in the eye "—I don't know a white man in the whole south who'd hire a black man when he could buy hisself one."

"You may be right," Drake leaned back in his chair. He stole a glance at his wife, amazed by her strength of character and generous nature. He suspected there were few who would bother teaching a slave how to read. "I suppose it's a good thing I'm English. I have a proposition for you."

Confusion marked Kane's weather-worn black face. "I'm sorry, suh, but I don't take your meanin'."

"I'd like to offer you employment. Not here in Charles Towne, you understand, but in England. My wife and I will be returning to my estate in Oxfordshire as soon as possible. I hope you and Prin will accompany us there. Once we arrive, I'd like you to train under my estate manager, Peebles. If you agree, you will assume his position when he retires in two years' time. The wages are excellent and a comfortable house is provided on the grounds of the estate."

A huge smile split Kane's plump lips and he was already nodding his head in eager acceptance, but Drake continued. "While we remain here, I'll expect you and your bride to honeymoon, of course. I sent my man this afternoon to inquire about renting one of the houses flanking this one. I know my wife won't be happy if her sister isn't close at hand. As a belated wedding gift, I'd like to pocket your expenses whilst we're all waiting to leave South Carolina. What say you? Is that acceptable?"

Kane's smooth head pivoted to find Prin, who had huge tears rolling down her cheeks.

"Yes, suh. Thank ya, suh. That's mighty generous of ya, suh." Gratitude radiated from Kane's stunned dark eyes. "Mighty, mighty kind."

"No need to thank me," Drake said. "We're family."

Kane's smile wavered. A proud man himself, Drake

understood. "Don't think of this as charity, for it isn't. The honeymoon is a belated wedding gift. The rest I wouldn't offer if I didn't believe you capable of making a success of the position. I've seen the Sayers' crop fields. They not only rival those of many English estates, they surpass some. I'd like to put your knowledge to use at Hawk Haven."

Kane gave a solemn nod. Drake knew he'd just earned the giant's undying loyalty, but it was the love reflected in Elise's delighted expression that pleased him most.

Frau Einholt entered the dining room. Atop the silver tray she carried lay a crisp white note sealed with a blob of red wax and the stamp of the letter *B*.

Drake took the missive, broke the seal and began to read:

Sir,
It is with a glad heart that I send you word. Our efforts to locate the Fox, though fallow until now, have begun to bear fruit. As of a few moments ago, one of my most trusted sources, the carriage driver you met in Charles Towne, has returned as though from the grave. He claims he has reliable information concerning the whereabouts of our mutual foe. My contact assures me the rebel spy will be ours within one week's time.
Your diligent servant and most faithful cousin,
Beaufort

"Drake?" said Elise. "Is everything well?"

He looked up, taking in her innocent face and the question puckering her soft brow. "Everything is superb, my dear." He placed the corner of Beaufort's missive in the candle flame nearest to him and watched it burn until the heat forced him to drop it in his bowl for the servant to remove. "The note is from Beaufort. He assures me the noose is tightening around the throat of my nemesis. Anthony's murderer should be bagged by week's end."

Chapter Seventeen

The hall clock chimed noon just as Elise made her way to the downstairs parlor. A messenger awaited her. Dressed in a white gown embroidered with lavender flowers, a lavender stomacher and yards of white petticoats, she hoped she looked cool and fresh—the exact opposite of how she felt.

In the week since she'd told Drake of her condition, she'd begun to suffer slight bouts of morning sickness. So far, though, today was the worst. Cold chills skimmed over her skin. Moisture broke out on her upper lip. She'd already retched twice, and a third trip to the chamber pot loomed large in the foreseeable future.

Plastering a smile on her lips, she entered the parlor. The messenger's sour stench turned her delicate stomach. She pressed a hand to her mouth and waited for the queasiness to pass. "I… I apologize for your wait, sir. I'm a bit under the weather this morn."

He raised his head. She fell back a step, caught off guard by the man's venomous, yellow eyes.

"No matter, ma'am. I'm only here to deliver this missive from your friend Mr. Smith."

She reached for the extended note, leery of touching the grimy fellow. "What's your name, sir?"

The messenger's mouth tightened ever so slightly. "Brody, ma'am."

His name didn't sound any warnings in her memory and she was certain she'd never seen his skeletal face before. She turned her attention to the message. Breaking the wax seal, she unfolded the stiff white stationery and scanned the tremulous script.

> *I have grave news which I must give to you and only you. You are my last hope. The Dragon and Wolf are not to be found. I beg you. Meet me at quarter to nine at our usual rendezvous. It is a matter of life and death.*
> *Yours,*
> *J*

Elise crumpled the starched paper in her bloodless fingers. Dread seeped into her heart as she quickly deciphered the message. Josiah needed her to meet him at The Rolling Tide later that evening concerning a matter of life and death. Zechariah and Christian weren't to be found. Something was terribly amiss. Josiah knew she'd ceased spying as the Fox. He wouldn't call on her without enormous cause. He'd put his life on the line too many times to protect her. She wouldn't ignore his cry for help.

She set aside her misgivings and focused on the eerie messenger. "Tell Mr. Smith I'll do as he bids."

In a fine mood, Drake rapped once on Beaufort's door and entered the Captain's dockside office. Bright midday sun glinted on the polished pine floors, momentarily blinding him. As his eyes adjusted to the light, the harsh smells of fish and salt from the nearby wharf assaulted his nostrils.

"Your Grace." Beaufort scrambled to his feet behind a corner desk piled high with stacks of crumpled papers and unopened envelopes.

Drake strode to the window and adjusted the shutters to block out the glare before commanding a seat on the ball-and-claw-footed sofa. "I've just returned from my ship, *The Queen Charlotte.* After receiving your assurance on the Fox's capture sometime this week, I'm having her readied to sail."

Beaufort collected a set of crystal goblets and a bottle of port from a nearby cabinet. He offered Drake a drink, but Drake declined. "So soon to quit America? How I envy you, sir. Is your wife reluctant to leave her homeland?"

Drake shrugged. "As a matter of fact, she seems more than eager to be on our way."

"Strange," commented Beaufort. "Christian Sayer gave me the impression she rather fancies Charles Towne."

The bottle clinked on the rim of a glass as the captain poured himself refreshment.

Drake leaned back in his seat. "I've grown to quite like the place myself. 'Tis lush country even if it is hot as blazes and everything is rather primitive compared to England. In truth, I find its relaxed attitudes a pleasant change from the formality of London and even Hawk Haven, for that matter. With fewer servants milling about, privacy abounds."

Beaufort returned to his chair and drank from his own glass. "As a newly wedded man, I'm positive the chance to be alone is much appreciated, eh, Your Grace?"

Drake was in too grand a mood to take offense at

his cousin's flat attempt at wit. "Indeed, Charles, I'm the happiest of men. My wife pleases me more every day. Have I told you I'm to be a father in the spring?"

"Brilliant news, Your Grace!" The captain raised his glass in congratulations. "Perhaps Anthony's death is a blessing after all."

Drake's good mood vanished along with Beaufort's mirth. He watched his cousin pale as Charles realized how tactless he'd been. Drake gritted his teeth. "Enlighten me to your meaning, Captain."

"I meant nothing disrespectful. Just that if Anthony had lived 'tis unlikely you would have met your lovely wife."

Muffled cries of the gulls outside filled the tense silence. "I prefer to think of it as God returning good for evil."

"I couldn't agree more, sir." Obvious in his attempt to return to Drake's favor, Beaufort picked up an open letter from his desk. "It seems there's even more good fortune in store. I received this letter minutes before you arrived. Robin Goss has done it. He says we must meet him at The Rolling Tide at nine this evening. The Fox will be ours tonight!"

When the clock chimed seven, Elise dressed with the rain and danger in mind as she prepared to leave for The Rolling Tide. Fortunately, her sickness had receded after lunch and no longer plagued her.

Word arrived from Drake earlier in the afternoon, explaining that business would keep him away until the next morning. As she tied the laces of a black wool dress over black petticoats, it struck her as coincidental, his being away the very night she would have had to make an excuse to leave, but she wasn't one to question good fortune in tight circumstances. Instead, she laced up a pair of sturdy boots, slipped a loaded pistol into her skirt pocket, and sat down at her writing desk.

When she finished a message to Zechariah she called for Prin. "Is my coach ready?"

"You asked for it, didn't you?"

Elise didn't acknowledge her sister's surly tone. Dear Prin was *not* happy. "I need Kane to carry this correspondence to Brixton Hall. He must wait until he can give it to either Zechariah or Christian, no other."

Arms crossed tight across her chest, Prin's face creased with unease. "I don't like this whole business, Lisie. I don't like it one bit. I want you to stay home and for once take care of yourself instead of everyone else."

Elise set aside her own reservations and patted her sister's hand in reassurance. Pressing the envelope into Prin's palm, she gave her a tight hug. "Don't be such a handwringer. Josiah's asked for my help and I'm not about to withhold it after all the times he helped me. Just do as I ask, please, and all will be fine."

"You know I will," Prin grumbled.

A short time later, Elise dodged the rain and stepped into the waiting coach. As it bounced into motion and gained speed, rain drummed on the roof and blew against the lead glass window.

Outside The Rolling Tide, the coach rocked to a halt. Elise opened the door herself and stepped down, splashing in a puddle on the street. Cold water soaked her boots and the hem of her skirt, making the layers of her clothes cumbersome and difficult to maneuver. She reached up, gave the dark shape of the driver a handful of coins and instructed him to wait for her around the corner.

For several long moments, she observed the tavern from a covered doorway across the street. Smoke poured from the chimney and mingled with the mist rolling in from the harbor. Josiah must have trimmed back the ivy. Light coursed through the front windows and illuminated the slick, wet street. Fiddle music spilled from the doorway as an occasional patron came or went, but she noted nothing out of the ordinary. Even the number of redcoats seemed less than usual.

Taking a deep breath, she waited for a carriage to pass before sprinting across the brick street and into the dark alley that led to the tavern's back door. Rain doused the front of her dress and poured from the wide brim of her hat. Skimming her fingers along the alley's rough brick wall to guide her, she saw nothing in the darkness, only heard the scurrying of rodents as they fled her swift steps.

When she reached The Tide's back door, she yanked it open and rushed inside the kitchen, savoring its instant warmth. The cockney barmaid, Louise, sliced a ham before the blazing fireplace.

"Louise," Elise said as she removed her hat and shook it under the eaves outside. "Where's Josiah? I'm to meet him in a few minutes' time."

The barmaid ceased her work and wiped her sweaty brow with the back of her hand. "'E's above stairs. Said to tell ye 'e's waitin' for ye in the last room to the right."

Elise thanked the blonde as she crossed the kitchen and darted up the tavern's back steps. She ignored the peculiar feeling that all was not well, but considered that she hadn't spied in months. Most likely she was out of practice and her nerves more jumpy than normal.

At the landing, she turned to the right. Simple pewter sconces lit her path down the empty hall, past the room where Hawk had died. The faded memory of that cursed night rushed to the forefront of her thoughts, dousing her with guilt.

Dear God, how she hated this place and its painful memories. After tonight, she would *never* return here. If Josiah needed her, he'd have to make arrangements to meet her somewhere else.

When she arrived at the designated door, she tapped out three soft knocks, the signal she and Josiah had agreed upon long ago.

"Come in," she heard him call through the door. Slowly, she lifted the latch and pressed open the portal. It was dark in the small room except for the slice of light cutting in from the hall behind her.

"Josiah?"

Her friend sat behind a small square table, his face in shadow. He seemed tense and rigid, when she knew him to be a relaxed sort. "Why are you in the dark? Shall I fetch some candles?"

He hesitated over the simple question. "No…there's no need. I have some here."

With the tips of her fingers, Elise shoved the door inward, broadening the scope of light. She winced when she saw her friend's battered countenance. Purple bruises and fresh cuts covered his face and throat. He looked as though he'd fought a berserk mule and lost. One eye swollen shut, tears sliced paths through the dried blood on his cheeks.

"What happened to you?" she gasped as her concern pulled her deeper into the small room.

A heavy hand grabbed hold of her, yanking her forward. The door slammed, trapping her as the room went black. Arms, thick and hard as mighty oaks, banded about her, crushing the breath from her lungs before she could scream. Panic paralyzed her for a timeless second. Josiah had betrayed her!

Disbelief and terror churned her stomach. What would they do to her? Fear for her unborn child chilled her heart. She tried to scream for help, but a second captor shoved a rag into her mouth and tied the ends behind her head.

A forceful slap burned across her cheek. A pair of fists pummeled her ribs, and knocked the wind out of her. As she gasped for breath, tears of pain pricked her eyes, but she shook her head and squeezed them tight to stem the flow. Whoever these monsters were, they wouldn't make her weep!

Forcing her brain to function, she kicked her legs in a ferocious attempt to break free. Her heels found her attacker's shins, his instep, his knees, but the brute might as well have been fashioned from steel.

In the dark, Josiah begged piteously for her forgiveness. "I had to do it, Elise! They threatened to murder Tabby and Moi—"

"Shut up, you mangy dog!" a hoarse voice commanded. A moment later the sound of something heavy met human flesh with a sickening thud. Josiah grunted and fell silent.

White-hot fear seized Elise. She was trapped by an unknown number of adversaries, bagged by enemies violent enough to threaten an innocent woman and child be slain for their purposes.

Her cheeks throbbed where she'd been hit. Her bruised ribs ached. Behind her someone struck flint. A spark of fire glowed to life.

Elise's gaze flew to the table, where she saw Josiah knocked cold, tied and leaning forward in his chair.

"Give me a lantern," one of her captors demanded. Glass pinged against metal. The light bloomed. Four simple-hewn chairs and the small table where Josiah slumped made up the furnishings in the otherwise stark room.

The hulk behind her slammed her into a seat. Another man tied her. She kicked at him with all her might. He grunted several times as her feet found their target, but he wouldn't be stopped until her hands were bound tight behind her back, and each of her legs was lashed to the chair.

Elise straightened her spine as much as the thick hemp rope allowed. She focused on the framed landscape hanging on the far wall, desperate to clear her thoughts, but fear clawed through her brain. What if these ruffians had somehow learned Drake's true identity and planned to use her as bait to snare him? Just as bad, what if he found her missing and searched for her only to end up hurt or killed? Her imagination tortured her.

Please, dear God, please, she prayed. *Whatever Your plans for me, please protect my husband!*

A man in a simple white shirt and rough tan breeches placed himself between her and the wall. "Look at me, Fox."

A river of relief flowed over her. These lunatics wanted her, not Drake. Perhaps he would stay safe.

"Fox? I don't know—"

The man laid a fisted blow to her jaw. Bright spots of light danced in her vision. He struck her again with the back of his hand. Warm blood trickled from the corner of her mouth.

"When I give you an order, you best do it quick," her captor growled. "Now, look at me, wench. Don't you recognize me?"

The man was deranged. Elise would give him no cause to strike her again. Quickly lifting her gaze, her eyes widened in horrified recognition.

"Robin Goss, at your service, ma'am. I'm happy to see you remember me. For certain, I could never forget *you,* Fox. I have yet to thank you and Mr. Smith properly for my stay at the wharf. Two months is a long time and requires that I show you a great deal of gratitude."

His fingers threaded painfully into her hair. With a violent yank, he jerked her head back and lowered his face to within an inch of hers. His rotten breath spread across her face and invaded her nose, making her gag in reflex. "If you promise not to scream, I'll remove the rag."

Eager to get the putrid cloth out of her mouth, she nodded.

"Once I'm done showing you my thanks," he said, untying the gag, "I plan to give you to your *worst* enemy."

With the rag gone, she dragged fresh air into her lungs. She ran her thickened tongue over her split bottom lip and tasted blood. Her words slurred. "My *worst...?*"

"Oh, yes. I suppose you can be forgiven in thinking I'm him, but there's one more. Someone willing to pay fifteen hundred pounds for your sorry hide."

Something in his words rang in her memory, but her limited powers of concentration gave her no chance to dwell. A pair of men moved from behind her. Brody's shifting image she recognized. He'd brought her Josiah's message earlier that day, but she'd never seen the human mountain next to him before.

"Meet my lads." Goss's fleshy lips parted in a smirk that revealed his rodent teeth. "But then you've met Brody, haven't you?" He waved his palm in the direction of the mountain. "This here's Clancy."

"For—forgive me when I say it's no pleasure to meet you."

Goss backhanded her across the face. "I expect better manners from a *lady,* even if you are nothing but a filthy, traitorous spy."

Head spinning, ears ringing, Elise could no longer concentrate. She knew his words should mean more to her, but consciousness seemed like a luxury she could barely hold on to. One of her eyes was swollen shut and her vision blurred in the other.

Pain became her one sensation as what seemed like fist after fist rained down in stunning blows. The dim light began to fade. Sound came to her as though from a distance. The netherworld beckoned.

They're going to kill me for certain.

Her mind fought against the agonized haze overtaking her and savored the vision of Drake for a moment of sweet solace. A sob caught in throat. She couldn't bear to leave him.

Using the last ounce of her energy, she squirmed in the chair, but escape was futile. Another slap across the face brought a wave of darkness. Believing she'd met her end, she prayed one last time for forgiveness. As she lost consciousness, her heart broke on the thought she would never again see her husband.

Chapter Eighteen

The swiftly moving coach wasn't traveling fast enough for Drake as it splashed through the dark, narrow streets. A keen sense of anticipation gripped him until he thought he might leap from his skin. He snapped open his filigreed pocket watch and held it up to the small interior lantern. A few minutes more and he'd have the Fox by the throat.

Thunder rumbled ominously. Cold air blew in through the partially raised window and whipped the curtains. Drake shut the window and pulled his cape closer around him. His gaze shifted to his cousin fidgeting in the opposite seat. "Pray, Charles, why so down in the mouth? Are you worried Goss has somehow led us false?"

Lantern light flickered over Beaufort's glum face. "Oh, no, Your Grace, I've a touch of indigestion, but it shall pass. My spy knows if he leads us astray, the reward is forfeit. It's not a risk he's willing to take, nor does he need to. He found the Fox's weakness, you see, a friend and frequent contact willing to turn Judas."

A bolt of lightning struck overhead, washing the coach's leather seats and tufted velvet walls with a moment of clear, white light. He thought of Elise and worried the storm might frighten her. He would be over-joyed when he could return home to keep her safe. "I'm eager to have this business over and done."

Beaufort nodded. "Unless the Fox manages to flee again, we'll have all we need to condemn him."

Drake's eyes narrowed. "Is his escape a concern, Charles?"

"I don't believe so, but the Fox is a wily creature. He escaped your brother once, and Robin Goss is not the clever chap Lord Anthony was." The captain swallowed nervously. "I have redcoats surrounding the tavern. They'll follow us once we go inside to give us aid if need be."

As the coach driver slowed their breakneck pace and reined the horses to a halt, Drake wiped the foggy window with the lace curtain and pressed the cloth out of the way behind a hook.

Beaufort leaned forward, scanning the front of The Rolling Tide. "Aha! There. You see it? They've just lit a light in the second-story window. That's our signal, sir."

"Then let us delay no longer." Drake's heart pounded with the thrill of the hunt. Finally, he would avenge Anthony's death. He bounded from the coach, ignoring the sting of cold rain on his face.

Inside the tavern, his quick pace led him through the maze of occupants, past carousing sailors and a drunken fiddle player who smelled as if he'd soaked himself in rum. Taking the stairs two at a time, he glanced over his shoulder to see Beaufort huffing his way up the steps several paces behind him. Four redcoats, one of whom Drake recognized as Lieutenant Kirby, followed farther behind the captain.

When Drake reached the landing, he didn't hesitate until he passed the room where Anthony died. Righteous fury fueled him onward. As he drew closer to the room that held his nemesis, the unmistakable thud of heavy blows meeting human flesh and the low, mewling cries of a trapped victim penetrated the red haze of his anger. A few steps from the door, he tasted victory.

"That's enough, Brody," a vaguely familiar voice said from inside the room. "We only get the full reward if the Fox is turned in alive."

"We got in three or four licks, is all. She could take another half dozen and live to tell the tale," a second voice argued.

Drake's hand froze on the doorknob. *She?* He hesitated, listening. The voices were muffled by the door. Perhaps he'd misheard?

"I said *enough,* Brody. Any more and you'll break her bones. Use Smith for punchin' practice. It won't matter if he gives up the ghost."

"While he takes Smith, how 'bout I have a little fun with the wench?" a third, deeper voice asked.

"Not enough time, Clancy," the first voice said. "That lummox Beaufort'll be here any minute."

"Lummox?" Charles hissed behind Drake. "Goss is nothing but a weas—"

"Quiet!" Drake insisted.

"He's bringing the soul who's offering the reward." Robin laughed. "Can't wait to see the surprise on his face when he finds out the Fox is a wom—"

Drake thrust open the door, cutting off Goss, who whirled sharply to see who entered.

"You!" Goss choked. Blood fled his face, leaving him as gray as a gravestone. "Anyone but you!"

Drake ignored Goss's horrified exclamation. His gaze flew about the room, looking for the woman Robin claimed to be the Fox. Surely Anthony hadn't been killed by a female? And even if such a circumstance were somehow possible, what kind of woman would perpetrate so vile a crime?

Two oil lanterns cast enough light for him to see the spare furniture and the battered hulk of a man slumped over the table. With the windows closed the smells of blood and sweat permeated the hot, stuffy room. From the corner of his eye, Drake saw Goss's henchmen close ranks in front of a second trussed individual hidden in the shadows.

"Get out of my way," Drake growled as he shoved a human mountain from his path.

"Wait!" Robin shouted. It was too late. Drake recognized Elise's luminous hair the moment he saw her bowed head. Stunned disbelief robbed his body of breath. What was she doing here? Numbed by the sight of his battered wife, all feeling drained from his limbs until overwhelming pain roared back with a vengeance.

She didn't move. Terror warned she might be dead. Begging the Almighty for mercy, Drake staggered forward and dropped to his knees in front of her chair. He laid a shaky hand on her chest and felt the rise and fall of her shallow breaths. Relieved beyond measure, his eyes closed on a prayer of thanks.

Behind him, an argument ensued between Goss and Beaufort. The captain ordered the spy and his henchmen to sit, then brought in the redcoats to enforce his command when the angered trio rebelled.

Drake ignored them all. A dozen questions buzzed in his head, but nothing mattered in that moment save

Elise. Not his pride, not his quest for vengeance. His whole being focused with frantic intensity on his wife as he gently tucked a bloodied strand of hair behind her ear.

With the greatest care, he tested her jaw and found, by some miracle, it wasn't broken. He lifted her chin, wincing when he saw the dark bruises forming on her precious face.

Frantic with worry, he ripped off his white linen cravat and dabbed at the blood streaking her cheeks and cut, swollen lips. He held her head to keep it from lolling while his other hand untied the ropes that bound her to the chair. Freed but unconscious, she sagged against him and would have slipped to the floor had he not held her tight against his chest.

As he gathered her into his arms and stood, a new kind of rage brewed within him to rival the intensifying storm outside. How dare these filthy animals abuse his duchess!

He turned toward the shouting behind him. Kirby and three other redcoats held Goss and his comrades at bay with weapons drawn, while Beaufort stood over them like an affronted rooster. "You've done it this time, Goss. I've heard enough—"

"But she *is* the Fox!" the spy shouted.

"Don't be a fool," Beaufort scoffed. "Her Grace is as much the Fox as I am."

Drake refused to consider the possibility of Robin Goss's accusation. The whole idea of Elise being the Fox struck him as absurd. There must be some other explanation.

"Cease your bickering!" With great care, Drake adjusted Elise in his arms. "Captain, I want these men arrested and taken far beyond my sight."

A chorus of alarmed protests rose from Goss and his duo of cutthroats. Robin leaped to his feet. "On what charge?"

One of the redcoats silenced him by slamming the butt of his musket into the spy's middle. Drake took perverse pleasure in watching Goss double over and drop to his knees, moaning in agony.

Beaufort quickly obeyed Drake. "Lieutenant Kirby, arrest these men on charges of kidnapping and attempted murder. I believe one of the prison barges will have plenty of space to host them."

The three men spewed obscenities and fought like fish trying to escape a net, but the redcoats made quick work of subduing them and prodded the prisoners out the door.

"What about Smith?" Beaufort asked.

In his concern for Elise, Drake had forgotten the tavern owner. He glanced down at his wife, who'd grown paler during the last few moments. There was no time to dwell on Smith. "Convey him to my home, but put a guard at his door. This man must have lied about my wife and betrayed Elise into Goss's clutches. I should like to know the reason."

Downstairs, Drake left the tavern by way of the back door. He hunched his shoulders against the cold driving rain and held Elise close to keep her as dry as possible. A stiff wind snatched at the edges of his cape as his expeditious steps took them around the brick building to his waiting coach.

Quick to help him, the driver opened the door. Drake

placed Elise on the velvet bench as if she were a piece of priceless crystal.

Climbing in, Drake shook off his wet cape before taking the opposite seat, then lifted her onto his lap. He held her tight with one arm while he covered her with his cape, hoping the warm lining would fight off the chill.

"Your Grace?" Beaufort popped his head inside, water dripping from the brim of his hat. "I've stowed Smith in a hired carriage. We'll follow you back to the townhouse."

"Fetch a physician on your way," Drake ordered. He cradled Elise close, her heated forehead pressed against his jaw. Already her skin grew hot with a rising fever. "Make haste, there's not a moment to lose."

"Stop your pacing, young man." Doctor Hardy glared over the rim of his spectacles. "You're becoming a distraction."

Drake raked his fingers through his hair as he swung on his heel. A sharp retort born of anxiety teetered on the tip of his tongue, but he bit it back. Elise's care was his main concern. If he was disrupting the doctor, he'd position himself in the corner and wait stock-still if need be.

Heavy of heart, Drake watched Elise where she lay with a deathly pallor in the four-poster bed. Prin had washed her battered face and applied an herbal salve to her chafed wrists, but there'd been no time to cleanse her hair and it was still caked with blood. After building a fire to keep her warm, he'd exchanged her black garb for a fresh dressing gown. There was little else he could do to fight his feeling of uselessness.

Sick with worry, he rasped, "Will she recover?"

Doctor Hardy, a severe fellow with a disapproving manner, looked up from checking her pulse. "It's too early to tell. I've examined her, and fortunately her bones are undisturbed. These cuts and bruises on her head and face will heal in a few weeks, but we'll have to wait and see if her brain has suffered any ill effects."

Drake swallowed the lump in his throat. "And the child?"

"I've no way of knowing if your wife is damaged internally. As of yet, there's no evidence she'll miscarry." The doctor replaced his instruments into a worn leather bag. "Perhaps the next time you lose your temper, you'll refrain from releasing it on your lady."

Incredulous, Drake found himself speechless for the first time in his life. "You don't think *I*—"

"The law may not frown on a man chastising his wife, and I have no wish to come between you, but when tempers rise, you must remember that self-control is the order of the day. Your lady is too delicate to take this kind of abuse."

The physician had his mind made up. Gritting his teeth, Drake called Prin to see the doctor out.

Drake crossed the room to the footboard and gripped the smooth mahogany rail. His gaze touched on Elise's beaten face and a sharp lump of emotion gathered in his throat. Where she wasn't bruised or cut, her pale skin blended with the white sheet and pillows behind her.

His chaotic thoughts were nearly unmanageable. The doctor was right. Drake may not have abused her, but he'd not been home protecting her as he should, either. Elise had wanted to leave for England weeks ago. With his obsession for revenge, he'd made her stay. Now he might lose her and their child.

Torment swirled around him. Grief and helpless frustration bit deep. He sank to the edge of the bed and took her hand in his. Ropes had made her wrists raw, and the glossy sheen of the foul-smelling salve Prin applied earlier glistened in the candlelight. Raising her slender fingers to his lips, he blinked excess moisture from his eyes. He hadn't wept since he was a boy, but his heart was shattering from the tightness of his chest.

A soft knock sounded on the door. He quickly wiped his cheeks. "Come in."

Prin entered carrying a cup of steaming coffee. The aroma churned his stomach. Cool air from the hall streamed through the open door, causing the fire to dance in the hearth.

"I thought you might need this."

Drake took the cup, but set it on the side table untested. "Do you think she'll be all right?"

"I'm believin' the Almighty will see her through. She's been treated worse and survived it." Prin's eyes shone with unshed tears. "She may look as fragile as a dove, but she's stubborn as a mule and tough as an ox."

"What do you mean, she's been treated worse? How? Who?"

Prin straightened the edge of the bed sheet. "I don't know what Lisie told you 'bout our pa, but he was a vile man with no good qualities I ever saw. He'd drink like a pack of sinners on Saturday night, then get mean. I did my best to protect her, but sometimes, he'd catch her and I couldn't do nothin' to stop him from hittin' on her."

Drake shook his head, wondering what kind of barbarian would beat an innocent little girl.

"Then there was that ruckus last winter, but it wasn't near as bad as this."

An alarm bell went off in Drake's head. "What happened?"

Prin's face turned anxious. Clearly she'd spoken out of turn and regretted it. She crossed to the pitcher on the writing desk. "I think we best keep water going down her if we can. I'll get a clean cloth. We can keep it moist and wet her lips if nothing else."

"What happened last winter?" he persisted. "Did one of the Sayers abuse her?"

"It's not my place to say."

He'd come to the end of his patience. "I'm making it your place. What happened?"

Prin shifted nervously. "She was in a tussle with a man who tried to kill her. She fought with all her might and he ended up dead."

Lightning flashed in the window. In an instant all the questions he'd sought to deny crystallized into one clear, horrifying picture.

"You're not lookin' so good, your Grace."

He ignored her. "Where did this happen—The Rolling Tide?"

"How did you know?" she asked in surprise. "Did Elise tell you 'bout it already?

He closed his eyes, absorbing the agony that sliced through him like a bayonet. "No, I'm afraid she never did."

"Then how did you know about her troubles at the Tide?"

"Captain Beaufort mentioned it some time ago." Drake allowed the silence to linger as he gathered his wits. His gaze slid toward the bed where Elise lay in frightening stillness.

Worry, shock and betrayal vied for precedence in his mind. The one woman he'd believed in most deserved his faith the least. His hands clenched into fists of indignation. How could he have been so gullible? He deserved a flogging for his blindness. "How long has Elise been the Fox?"

"I… I can't say." Prin backed toward the door. "You'll have to talk to her 'bout that when she wakes up."

Drake had suffered one too many blows in the last few hours to forego issuing threats if necessary. "Prin, answer me or you and Kane gather your belongings and go."

Prin froze. Surprise etched her mocha features. "Would you really cast us out?"

"If you force me to it." He crossed his arms over his chest. Tension vibrated under his skin. He leaned against the cool windowpane where rain beat against the glass.

She nodded, her face solemn as if she'd learned a valuable lesson concerning his character. "I was a fool. I never guessed you'd be so heartless."

His laugh was cold and grated with bitter irony. "I believe this business has duped us all in one way or another. I want the truth. *Now.*"

Chin quivering, his sister-in-law sat heavily in the wing chair before the fire. As she wrung her hands, she spoke to the mantel and avoided looking in his direction. "She's been a spy since the winter before last."

"To whom does she report her findings?"

"I don't know."

Embers crackled in the fireplace. Drake didn't believe her, but he let the lie pass. His suspicions pointed toward the Sayers, despite Beaufort's assurance they were loyal to the crown. No matter, he would find out eventually. "Why did she resort to espionage? Is she really such a traitor she would risk her life for so futile a cause?"

Prin buried her face in her hands as though she'd suddenly come to the end of her tether. Rocking back and forth in the chair, she fought back sobs until she broke down and wept. When she lifted her head, tears streamed from her pleading eyes. Drake refused to soften. "Answer me!"

She wiped her cheeks with her palms and sucked in several deep breaths. "She's a patriot who believes in liberty, but…but mostly she spied to save *me*."

Chapter Nineteen

"It's been two days, sir. I suggest you pray. She's in God's hands now."

Through the pain piercing her skull, Elise heard the cryptic announcement as though a thick portal stood between her and the speaker. Something smelled foul, like lard mixed with herbs. She remembered the beating. Her mind snatched at disjointed memories of Goss and his henchmen, but the images swirled together in a gruesome haze. Sharp blades of agony sliced her skull and limbs, preventing the slightest movement. Her tongue felt thick against the walls of her lacerated mouth, making it impossible for her to speak.

"There must be something else you can do. You're supposed to be the best surgeon in the city!"

Drake's voice penetrated the fog. She wanted to reach out, console his obvious distress, but her arms felt as though someone had bolted them to the bed.

"I can't lose her."

The despair in Drake's voice broke her heart. She tried to reassure him, but the darkness beckoned, and she was too weak to fight its call.

* * *

Drake prowled the solitary confines of the bedchamber, willing Elise back to consciousness. His concern for her outweighed his feelings of anger and betrayal. After three ghastly days to ponder Prin's disturbing revelations, he was ready to climb the walls. Exhausted by the vigil he'd kept at his wife's bedside, he stayed close nonetheless. Leaning over her supine form, he ascertained her breathing for the hundredth time. He reached for a cloth and dipped it in cool water to wet her lips.

In his heart, he ached for her, cursed the hardships she'd braved to create a better life for herself and Prin. He admired her loyalty, a quality he'd never known in any other woman, but her role in Anthony's death tormented him. He feared without the Lord's help his faith in her might never recover.

Elise fought to open her eyes, but her weighted lids declined to obey. As she came to wakefulness, she listened for some indication of where she might be. A window must be open. She could hear the faint chirping of birds. The lightest of breezes brushed her sensitive cheeks, chilling her heated skin.

A dull ache pulsed through her limbs, her jaw throbbed and her head pounded. She wiggled her toes. The fingers of her right hand moved, but those of her left felt crushed. She couldn't fathom how, but she thought it might be broken.

"Elise?"

Drake. Anxious to see him, she found the will to open her eyes. As she struggled to focus, his dear face swam into view. He looked haggard, unshaven. His brilliant golden eyes were dull. Had he lost weight? She tried to smile, but the muscles of her face were stiff and sore.

"Thank God you're awake!" He brought her left hand to his lips, and she realized he'd been holding it all along.

"Are you well?" she asked in a reedy whisper.

"I?" He swallowed thickly and raked his fingers through his hair. Strain pinched his mouth and lined his eyes. "You're the one who has given us all a fright."

She licked her scabbed lower lip. "Our child?"

With great care, he lifted her head and held a glass of water to her lips. "The child lives. Just as you will."

She heard his determination and clung to it. Using all her strength, she lifted her hand to clasp the back of his. "I… I love you." She wanted to say more, but her eyelids grew heavy and slid shut as weariness claimed her.

Drake dismissed the guards from Josiah Smith's door and strode into the guestroom. He found the rotund tavern owner in a clean white nightshirt, lurching about the comfortably appointed room in a state of palpable distress. The man's head was bandaged and his round face battered, but at least he was on his feet, Drake thought bitterly. More than he could say for Elise.

Smith's face lit with fear the moment he saw Drake. He slumped on the edge of the bed. "How is she?"

"Little you care, Smith. My wife fares far more ill than you, apparently."

Josiah's hands shook until he clutched the rumpled sheets on either side of him. "Will she be all right?"

Drake chose to ignore the man's concern. He nodded. "No thanks to you and your loose lips."

"I had no choice!"

He bit back an infuriated growl. "I'm waiting to be enlightened on that score. How much were you paid to betray the Fox?"

Josiah sighed in resignation. "You know the truth about her then?"

Drake inclined his head.

"I'd never betray Elise for coin. I had to protect my family. Robin Goss and one of his minions broke into our home. They threatened to murder my wife and child if I refused to lure Elise into their net."

"Where is your family now?"

Josiah hedged. "I've been told they're safe."

"Ah, I assume that means you've talked with Prin."

Smith's silence was an affirmative answer. He stumbled to his feet, his face crimped by the pain of his movements. "I need to see about their welfare myself."

"Beaufort's men are posted outside your door and yonder window. There's little you can do to escape."

"I can try. Wouldn't you do the same in my position?"

"I wouldn't be in your position, Smith. I know how to be loyal." Drake paused at the door. His fingers gripped the frame as he regarded Josiah with scorn. "Do you happen to remember a spy known as Hawk?"

"Aye, I remember the pompous scoundrel well. He was an arrogant fool with a hateful sense of humor. Elise was the only person with any patience for him. I believe she considered him a friend." Josiah's face contorted with disgust. "The greedy Judas sold her out for silver. His betrayal nearly broke her. She hasn't been the same since he died, but if you ask me, he deserved what he got."

Unable to tolerate another moment in the colonial's

company, Drake turned to leave. "I suggest you rest and rebuild your strength, sir. As weak as you are, you'll offer no sport when they hang you."

A fortnight later, Elise sipped her hot tea in contemplative silence. Prin had warned her that Drake knew about her previous life as the Fox. Though he hadn't mentioned it yet, she was convinced he despised her. Before he'd quit visiting her a week ago, the accusation in his eyes had been enough to make her tremble.

With a sigh, she ran her palm over the slight mound of her belly, thanking the Lord for His mercy toward her child. After the beating she'd endured, she knew how fortunate she was the baby lived.

Turning to face the window, she fortified herself with a breath of crisp autumn air. Since the night of her clash with Goss, she'd regained her strength bit by bit, but this morning was the first she'd felt recovered enough to confront her husband.

Her chamber door opened. Prin entered the room carrying a fresh set of candles to replace the spent ones beside the bed. She grinned. "Except for that sad frown, you're lookin' mighty fine this mornin', Lisie. Them yellow bruises are still faint round your eyes and along your jaw, but at least you don't look like a kicked raccoon anymore."

Elise cast off her doldrums and offered a smile for her sister's sake. "That's good to hear. I think I'll be healed before the week is out."

"I doubt it," Prin said matter-of-factly. "Sit forward and let me plump your pillows."

She did as Prin bid, grimacing when her movement shot a twinge of pain through her ribs. "Where is Drake?"

"Probably in that study of his downstairs. He don't come out much."

"What do you suppose he's doing in there?"

"Broodin', I expect." Prin shrugged. "He holed himself up the afternoon he talked to Josiah. Didn't come out for 'bout a week. Now, at least, he sometimes goes ridin' on one of them fine horses of his."

Tears misted her eyes at how much he must be hurting. *Please, Lord, don't let this mess cause him to turn his back on You again.*

"I wonder what he and Josiah discussed?" she said.

Prin shrugged. "I'm not sure. That same day I was told not to speak to Josiah anymore. I'm not even allowed to take him his food. Frau Einholt does that now. By the way, you best be careful what you say to that one. She acts like she don't understand much English, but more than once I caught her with her ear to a door."

Elise made a mental note to be careful around the housekeeper, then steered the conversation back to the Smiths. "Josiah must be distraught about Tabby and the baby." She bore her friend no ill will for his part in handing her over to Goss. With his wife and child's life at stake, Josiah had had little choice but to protect them. She was convinced no other inducement could have enticed him to betray her. "I know you said Kane found them and saw them to her parents' home, but Josiah must be anxious."

"I imagine so. He's got to be frettin' the British plan to hang him, too."

Elise raised her hand to her throat. "I must say I've been concerned about that same fate myself."

"Oh, bosh." Prin rubbed her lower back, her stomach protruding now that she was further along in her pregnancy. "That husband of yours might have a temper a bull would envy, but he isn't gonna let anything happen to you."

"I'm not so sure." Elise tipped her head against the pillows. She closed her eyes for a moment, her head throbbing with tension. "I'm a traitor in my husband's eyes. What if he decides he can't abide that fact?"

"He'll forgive you." Prin sat beside her on the bed and brushed the hair from Elise's brow. "I never saw a man care for his wife so much."

"You don't know him like I do. Both his first wife and former fiancée betrayed him, but he gifted *me* with his trust anyway." Tears sprang to her eyes. "Now that he knows the truth, I'm sure it's killed all his love for me."

Later that afternoon, Elise was supposed to be napping, but she couldn't sleep. Instead, she left her bed, pulled on a robe and went in search of Drake. Itching with nerves, but weak from weeks of little activity, she made slow progress down the stairs. She was gasping for breath against the smooth, wooden banister when the door of Drake's study swung open. He entered the central hall.

"Elise!" He ran to her. "What are you doing out of bed?"

"I need to speak with you." She clutched at the soft material of his shirt, basking in his strength. She'd missed him desperately. It felt so good to have him hold her.

"Why didn't you wait until I came to you?" He cradled her in his arms and started back up the stairs.

"Now that you know about my past as a spy, I thought you might never come again."

Hearing the hurt in her voice, Drake winced. He watched over her every night while she slept, but she had no way of knowing about his nocturnal visits. "I see Prin has told you of our conversation."

"Yes," she whispered. Her soft hair brushed his throat and her lavender scent tugged at his senses.

"Then perhaps you can understand why I have no wish to speak with you at present."

"I know you're angry," she said in a small voice. "You must feel betrayed. But have my worst fears come true? Have I lost your love forever?"

He said nothing as he stalked across the second-story landing and into the bedchamber. The tight grip he'd maintained on his temper began to unravel.

"What do you expect of me?" he demanded, placing her gently on the bed. "You played me for a fool." He turned his back on her. "You deceived me without conscience, but all of that fails to compare with—"

"What?" she cried. "Tell me, Drake. Tell me all the crimes you think I've committed. If you ever loved me, give me a chance to explain. Allow me to set right the wrongs between us."

If he'd ever loved her? Was she insane? Loving her was a malady, and he had no cure. He berated himself for his weakness. His need for her was part of the war raging within him. Anger twisted him in knots. He shouldn't love her, but he did with an intensity that bordered on madness.

He turned to find her sitting on the edge of the bed. Her lovely hair wreathed her face and fell in thick tendrils over her narrow shoulders and down her back. He should loathe the sight of her. His pride should prevent him from having the smallest thing to do with her. As it was, her beauty stung. Her faded bruises shone like badges of her deception. She was a traitor to England and all he held dear. But that wasn't the worst of her sins. "Do you remember the Hawk?"

She blinked in confusion, then paled. "Hawk? What do you know of him?"

"I know it all, Fox. Including something you do not. His real name was Lord Anthony Amberly. He was my brother."

"Your brother...?" The blood drained from her face by slow degrees. She shook her head in silent, shocked denial. Her hand slipped over her mouth as though she might be sick. Tears welled in her bright green eyes and spilled down her cheeks. "No. It can't be!"

Thinking she might faint and topple off the mattress, he lunged forward in an involuntary bid to catch her. She scrambled to her feet and dodged his reach. He saw her grimace and judged her injuries protested the speed of her escape.

Icy cold swept through him. His hands clenched into fists. "You're the killer I've been hunting these many months."

"I didn't kill him! I promise I didn't." Her face was wild, filled with the fear of a trapped animal. "You *must* believe me. He tried to hand me over to the enemy. I had no choice but to fight for my life. We struggled for his weapon. *He* fired the pistol, not I. It was an accident. I never meant for him to end up dead."

Her confession touched him at his core. He could see the truth reflected in her face, but his pride fought the yearning of his heart. "So you say. Next you'll try to convince me you had no knowledge of my station when we wed. Tell me the truth if you're able. Did you marry me to work your wiles and spy on me?"

"I did know you were a duke, but I married you because I love you."

He wanted to believe her, but he'd be a fool if he did. "And Prin's fate had nothing to do with it, I suppose?"

Trembling, she grasped the bedpost for support. "By marrying you, it's true, I assured her freedom sooner, but nothing could have forced me to pledge my life to you if not for love."

"Surely you don't expect me to believe—" Her pallor concerned him. "Sit down, Elise."

"No." She shook her head. Perspiration beaded her upper lip. "I want you to hear me out."

"I can listen while you're sitting down." He moved with such speed he had her cornered before she could flee. He pressed her onto the feather mattress and covered her with a quilt. "I admire your determination, but you've the babe to consider. He's the only good left in this charade of a marriage."

She flinched as if he'd smacked her. The saner part of him regretted the cut, but under the circumstances it would have rung hollow to apologize.

Elise squared her shoulders and schooled her delicate features. Her chin quivered. "If you truly believe our union is a sham, then all is lost. How can I make you see the truth when your mind is already set against me?"

What *could* she say to ease the battle that raged within him? He should set her aside, end their marriage in whatever way possible. To choose her would be an insult to his brother's memory, yet an unthinkable, unforgivable part of him burned toward Anthony for putting her in harm's way all those months ago. He cleared his tight throat. "Indeed, what is left to say? Perhaps farewell is our only option."

Shattered, Elise watched him storm from the chamber. Without considering the consequences, she ignored her protesting muscles and followed after him. He'd traversed most of the stairs by the time she crossed the landing and grasped the mahogany rail. "Drake, wait! You can't be serious. We have much to say, and none of it includes goodbye."

Spine rigid, he continued his exodus without a backward glance. Desperate, she ran down the steps, nearly tripping on the hem of her dressing gown. "Drake, please come back. I *love* you."

To her relief, he halted before entering his study. He faced her. In her eyes, he'd never looked more like a duke. Cold and intimidating, his frigid manner belied the heat burning in his eyes.

"Don't say those words to me again," he said through clenched teeth.

"Why? You say you want the truth." She refused to let him push her away. "Drake, please. Hear me out."

Remembering the guards at Josiah's door upstairs, she pursued Drake into his study, where the faint scent of leather provoked her already throbbing head. He slammed the door behind her. "You deceived me about Anthony."

"No! I had no knowledge of Hawk's relationship to you until you told me minutes ago. I didn't kill him," she repeated, eager to reach him now that he might listen. "Even so, I've agonized over his death."

"You expect me to believe you suffered over the death of an enemy?"

"We were friends of a sort," she hurried to explain. "He was a spy much longer than I, the first agent I was ever sent to meet. Everyone trusted him. Over time I felt I could trust him, too."

"Yet you never allowed him to view your face."

His sarcasm stung. "I needed to protect the fact that the Fox was a woman. I don't know why Hawk wore a mask, only that he did. Perhaps he meant to conceal his identity as a lord."

"Perhaps," Drake conceded coldly. "Espionage is a shameful business."

His steely condemnation hit her with dizzying force. Her fingers clenched the back of a green leather chair for support. She cleared her throat, frantic to cross the chasm widening between them. "I learned he had a lively, sometimes hateful sense of humor. More than once he played at turning me over to the redcoats. That night he threatened the same. At first, I thought he must be up to his usual tricks."

Drake looked away. "That sounds like Anthony. Always enjoying a prank only he would find amusing."

"I realized he meant serious business when he placed a pistol to my head."

"What? I don't believe you!" His gaze flashed to her face. "He put a pistol to your head? He could not have known you were a woman."

"He learned within minutes, but cared not a whit."

Drake clawed his fingers through his hair in a gesture that betrayed his anguish. She'd never imagined such a decisive man could look so torn.

Shaking with trepidation, she rounded the chair and took a hesitant step closer. "After I came to lov…after I agreed to wed you, I didn't know how to tell you of my previous life. Truthfully, I didn't want to. I convinced myself there was no need. Prin and Kane were free. I had you—everything I dreamed of. Even leaving America was not too high a price to pay for the life I longed to share with you. I reasoned the war would be over soon one way or the other, and none of what I'd done would matter in the end."

"You planned never to tell me." It wasn't a question. "What other secrets have you concealed?"

"None, I promise. I don't know how to convince you, but consider what you would have done if I *had* told you. I believe you would have sent me to the gallows. In fact, were I not carrying your child, I think you would see me there now."

He stepped closer. A muscle ticked in his jaw. Waves of tension emanated from him, encircling her. His eyes were hard as flint. "It's what you deserve. You've no remorse for your spying. My duty to my family and country require I turn you in."

She blanched, but held her ground. "And our child? What will you tell him? That you had his mother hanged moments after he was born?"

He swung away, but not before Elise saw a glimpse of his inner torment. His pain stretched between them and pierced her own heart.

Outside, shouting erupted, giving them both a start. Elise looked toward the open window. She saw nothing except magnolia trees swaying in the cool breeze. A door slammed at the back of the house, pounding footsteps echoed along the central hall.

Drake whipped open the study's door to find Kane sprinting up the stairs. "Miss Lisie! It's over," he shouted. "It's over."

"What's all the clamoring about, man? What's over?" Drake demanded.

Kane stumbled to a halt.

Elise looked past the foyer's chandelier to see one of Josiah's guards come into view on the upstairs landing. Kane spun on the step to face Drake. "The war, suh! Everyone's hollerin' it's all over. The Patriots has won."

"Blimey! You must be mad!" the soldier exclaimed.

Elise's heart stopped in an instant of joy. She schooled her features to belie her excitement and sent up a prayer of silent gratitude. "How do you know, Kane? Where did you hear the news?"

As Kane's dark gaze darted from Elise to each of the two Englishmen, and back to her again, his enthusiasm waned. "I jus' come from the wharf, ma'am. News arrived by ship this mornin'. The British done surrendered at Yorktown, up Virginia way. General Washin'ton got 'em all tied up by land and the French fleet cut 'em off by sea. They had no where else to go."

"When?" Drake asked in transparent disbelief.

"From what I heard, las' week, suh."

"The entire Southern army?"

Kane gave a quick nod. "That's what everybody's sayin'."

Drake groaned. Elise's gaze flew to the guard upstairs. He'd paled a shade lighter than his pristine white breeches.

"Lieutenant, I'm off to Captain Beaufort's. Reposition your men," Drake ordered. "If pandemonium breaks out in the city, I want my wife well-protected."

The young soldier jumped to do Drake's bidding. Kane had disappeared in the confusion. Elise guessed he'd gone to find Prin.

At the door, Drake gathered his tricorn and cape from the rack. He raised his eyes to meet Elise's in a moment of heartrending silence. What could she say to soothe him? He believed the worst about her. And if Kane's report were true, England, the greatest power in the world, had lost the jewel in its crown to a ragtag force of upstart colonials.

With no words to ease Drake's heart or his pride, she stayed rooted to the spot, pleading silently for him to come to her.

He turned away. With haste, he took his leave, shutting the door between them on a note of haunting finality.

Chapter Twenty

Elise awakened the moment a heavy hand covered her mouth. Her eyes flew wide and a jolt of panic raced up her spine. Eyes straining to see in the moonlit parlor, her startled cry died in a palm that stunk of sour ale. Fear crippled her as she imagined Goss or one of his henchmen had escaped the prison barge and come to finish her off.

Kicking furiously, she met empty air as she clawed at her captor. She rolled her head and gritted her teeth, but her shadowed assailant managed to gag her. He wrapped her in a quilt and stuffed her into a large box. Her mind raced. A trunk? A coffin? With her legs bent at the knee to fit her in the confining space, she couldn't even kick in protest. A scream borne of panic welled in her throat, but she choked it back, determined to keep her wits about her when she had her child to think about.

The strength of her fear crippled her. The quilt made it difficult for her to breathe. Anger and frustration began to override the terror. Muted male voices penetrated her shroud, alerting her to more than one captor. One of them took pity and uncovered her face. She could see nothing in the dark. Cool air bathed her skin, but the reprieve ended when the lid banged shut.

Agitated, Drake popped his head out of the coach window in an attempt to judge the traffic. The cloak of night made it difficult for him to determine accurately, but if the noise and number of coach lanterns were anything to go by, a week would pass before he traveled half a mile.

His meeting with Beaufort had concluded an hour ago, and he would have been home already if not for the congestion. As it was, he pondered his quandary with Elise. Truth to tell, he'd thought of little except her since he'd left the house that afternoon. The need to see her had grown to unmanageable proportions. What information his brain happened to filter from Beaufort's ramblings happened by chance. The captain had droned on, blubbering on more than one occasion as he confessed Britain's ghastly state of affairs in North America.

Mayhem outside drew Drake's attention to the window. Small bonfires blazed along the street, illuminating the hornet's nest of humanity to be found there. So far that evening, he'd seen as many revelers celebrating the British surrender as protesters. Drake hated to admit the unthinkable, but Cornwallis's surrender at Yorktown signaled England's certain withdrawal from the Colonies. The loss was no small thing. It was humiliating and vexed his pride, much like finding out his traitorous wife was entangled with his enemies.

In principle, he could make no excuse for Elise's actions. Had she been a man, he would have seen her hanged at the first opportunity. But she wasn't a man.

She was his wife, the other half of his soul, the mother of his unborn child.

He wouldn't give her up. He defied anyone to try to take her from him.

Old bitterness began to swell in his chest and he could feel himself slipping back into the darkness that had plagued him so long after the deaths of his family. Anger rose inside him like a fountain of acid. "I thought she was a gift from You, God. Now I see You only meant to torment me."

The box landed with a thud that rattled Elise's bones. The lid lifted and candlelight glowed above her like a celestial orb.

"Elise?" Christian said, incredulous. "Are you all right?"

She squinted as her eyes adjusted to the blinding glow. Seeing a friendly face, she sagged in relief. With her trepidation gone, her temper flared. Her entire body screamed with the agony of her cramped position. She struggled to sit up, but the quilt hobbled her.

"What have those idiots done to you?" He reached in and untied the gag.

"Help me up," she sputtered, gasping for a deep breath of air. "Why…why have you brought me here?"

He set the candelabra he held to a side table and helped her from the box. "I sent Adam and Hargus to rescue you and Josiah."

"How did you know we needed help?"

"Several days ago, Father received a letter from Tabby explaining the whole story of Goss's duplicity. She's been worried sick. She and the baby have joined her parents at their plantation up river."

"They're both safe then?

"Yes."

"Has Josiah been taken to join them?" she asked, unable to conceal her worry.

"No. The lads sent a missive with Captain Travis when he brought you upriver from Charles Towne. According to the letter, Josiah's being kept on the second floor of Amberly's house. They weren't able to reach him."

"Yes, he is upstairs. It's been impossible to speak with him. What's to be done? We can't abandoned him."

"We won't." Christian stooped to unwind the quilt from around her legs and helped her to the parlor's settee. "Tabby feared Amberly had learned of your past as a spy. Is it true? Does he know you're the Fox?"

She nodded, unable to say more as sensation clawed up her legs like a thousand stabbing needles. She held her breath to keep from crying out.

"Are you all right?" Christian asked worriedly.

Rubbing the cramps from her calves, she frowned.

He backed away. "I know that look."

"An eternity passed in that box. I thought I would suffocate."

"There were holes in the top," he said quickly. "You weren't in danger."

"Why didn't they tell me you'd sent them?"

"I don't know. Perhaps time didn't allow or they feared any noise might alert someone to their presence." His gaze settled on her rounded stomach. His jaw tightened. "But considering the similarities in your girth, I think we should be grateful the lads didn't confuse you with Josiah and send you to Tabby."

She sent a pillow flying straight for his head. "I'm

with child, you lummox. And I'm nowhere near the size of Josiah."

Christian ducked just before the pillow hit the wall behind him. Chuckling, he sauntered to the cabinet and poured them both a glass of water.

"Thank you," she said when he handed her one. "That gag made my mouth as dry as a bale of cotton."

She sipped the refreshment, revived by the cool liquid on her parched tongue. Once she'd had her fill, she asked, "How did they sneak me past the soldiers?"

"By getting rid of them first, of course."

"They didn't kill them, I hope."

"I didn't order them to finish anyone, but I won't know if it came to that until I've talked to Adam and Hargus. After putting you on the ferry they stayed in town in case they were followed."

A nippy breeze blew through the room, carrying with it a faint, familiar song from the direction of the slave cabins. Elise shivered in the chill and handed her glass back to Christian. "Where have you been? It's been weeks since I saw you last."

"I returned from Virginia this morning," he said, his face suddenly animated. "Thanks to the information you gave father, I made it to the Marquess de la Fayette in time for him to send word to Generals Washington and Rochambeau. Rochambeau notified the French fleet under Admiral de Grasse in the West Indies. de Grasse did not disappoint. He sailed up the Chesapeake, cutting off Cornwallis's escape by sea. I stayed throughout the siege, then took part in the battle."

"I'm glad you weren't hurt."

"As am I, though I had a close call. A redcoat tried

to skewer me with his bayonet, but my pistol took off his face before he succeeded."

She grimaced at the grisly picture he described, but he continued with verve, "As everyone's talking about it, I believe you know Cornwallis surrendered. It's too soon to be certain, mind you, but word is that England will petition for peace."

"'Tis excellent news," she said, remembering she'd given Zechariah the information concerning the British encampment as a means to secure Kane's freedom. She sighed. There was another reason for Drake to despise her.

Christian's brow furrowed. "I expected you to be pleased. The war will soon be done."

"I'm overjoyed, I promise you." She stood and moved to warm her hands at the fireplace. The scent of warm cloves rose from a bowl of pomanders on the mantel. "As a patriot, I'm overcome with pride. If I seem melancholy, it has nothing to do with the political situation."

"It's Amberly, isn't it? Kane mentioned—"

"Kane mentioned?" She faced her friend. "When did you see Kane?"

"A short time after I docked. He was at the wharf."

"Ah, yes, he told us he'd been there when he reported Cornwallis's surrender. I take it you were the one to apprise him of events?"

He nodded. "In return, he told me little is well under your roof. Faint though they are, I see the bruises on your face. If Amberly's abused you, I'll take pleasure in avenging your honor and beating him to a pulp."

As she watched Christian grind a fist into his open palm, she wondered why he seemed so eager for an excuse to throttle her husband. "He hasn't beaten me yet. However, he may before too much longer."

"That's a rather cryptic reply, dearest."

She picked up the pillow she'd thrown and ran her palm over the expensive blue silk. "Not only does he know I'm the Fox, but Hawk was his brother. Drake believes I killed him."

Silence reigned. For the first time since she'd known him, Christian grappled for words. "It's worse than I imagined. After I spoke with Kane, I sought out Beaufort. He told me one of his spies claimed you were the Fox, but that no one believed it. If Amberly knows the truth, why is Goss rotting on a prison barge instead of being hailed as a hero?"

She repeated the story as Prin had told her. "After Goss beat me senseless, Drake arrived to collect the Fox. When he found me, he believed in my innocence. I've yet to determine if Beaufort wished to curry favor with Drake or if he found it impossible to believe the Fox was a female. Whatever the case, he sent Goss to the barge for assaulting me. Drake saw me recovered, though Prin made the mistake of telling him I'm the Fox a few weeks ago. He confronted me this morning."

"And?" Christian jumped to his feet. "Tell me you did the intelligent thing and lied through your teeth."

She tossed the pillow to a nearby chair and rubbed her pounding temples. The headache from earlier in the day had grown worse. She'd spent the whole afternoon wishing Drake would return while deep down she feared he would never come back. "Of course not, you idiot. I told him the truth."

"Did he inform you of his plans? Has he deduced

the identity of your spymaster? What of Brixton Hall?" he said, displaying an anxious side she'd rarely seen.

Returning to the settee, she mulled over what Drake had said. "I believe he must have worked out Zechariah's role in my escapades because he's aware that I spied in part to win Prin. However, both your reputation as Tories and friendship with Beaufort speak well for you. He must not have solid proof of your activities or redcoats would be breaking down the door by now."

"God be praised." Christian picked up the poker and stoked the fire. "Where is the duke now?"

"When he left me, he said he intended to seek out Beaufort. Perhaps my abduction was a blessing. For all I know, they may have returned to the house with a noose to see me hanged."

"That bad, is it?" The taut line of his mouth softened with compassion. "He must have been angry enough to say the vilest things if you believe he would consider such treatment when you're expecting his child. Did you try to explain?"

"Of course." She swallowed hard and bit her lower lip to stop its quivering. "He refused to believe me. I don't blame him. I'm not certain I'd believe me either if our positions were reversed." She stood and began to pace the Oriental rug. "I've contemplated the situation from every possible angle, but I've come up with no acceptable solution. How can I convince Drake of my innocence when he believes I'm the worst sort of trickster? As quickly as he decided to marry me, it seems he's determined to leave."

Christian rammed the poker in the fire, causing the flames to flare and pop. "Then let the fool go and stay here with me. I'll care for you and the child as if he were my own."

She quit her pacing, not sure she'd heard him right. "But Christian, I'm a married woman. You and I are naught but friends. I couldn't ask you to—"

"Friends we may be, but I love you, too." His intense blue eyes lifted to hers. "I have for quite some time."

The fire crackled in the silence. She couldn't mistake his sincerity. Stricken with shock, she sank to the edge of the settee behind her. "Some spy I am. I never guessed."

"I'm as good at concealing information as you are at uncovering it," he reminded her. "I should have declared myself long ago, but you viewed me as you would a brother or...or some sort of harmless pet." Sitting beside her, he leaned his head against the back of the settee and closed his eyes. "I've been in agony watching you fall in love with that arrogant *Englishman*."

She'd been an insensitive clod. "Oh, Christian, I'm so sorry. You know I'd never purposely hurt you. Please forgive me."

He grasped her hand in his and gave it a light squeeze. "Don't fret, Elise. I know you wouldn't hurt a fly. I also know you want Amberly back. I can see it in your eyes. If you wish, I'll send word to him that you're here. Just know I'll protect you and your loved ones if his high and mighty is too stiff-necked to come to his senses."

She clutched his hand. "Thank you, my dear friend. Your kindness won't be forgotten."

Compelled by his craving to see Elise, Drake abandoned the stalled coach to the capable hands of his driver and walked the remaining miles home. Midnight had come and flown by the time he reached the front steps. Much to his surprise, no guard stood watch as he'd ordered. Candlelight poured from the front windows when he expected everyone to be abed. The stillness of the place warned of something dire.

Tearing up the front steps, he crossed the threshold, calling for Elise.

Prin appeared in the parlor door to his left, her face pinched and reproachful. "She's not here."

Momentary alarm stole his breath. "Where...?"

"I don't know. Last I checked on her, she'd finally fallen asleep after spendin' the whole day frettin' over you." Her voice sizzled with accusation. "Me and Kane went to enjoy the cool air in the courtyard. When I came back an hour later, I found Lisie gone."

Cold fingers of dread took hold of Drake. Goss's promise of revenge came to mind at speed. What if the ferret had somehow escaped the prison barge and sought out Elise to finish her? Thoughts racing, he refused to think on that possibility. He was determined to find Elise and bring her home, he would never forgive himself if she came to harm. Once he found her, he swore he would never let her out of his sight again.

Please, Lord. Protect her.

"What's been done to secure her return?"

"Very little, if you ask me."

Drake flinched under her condemning glare.

"Whoever was here trussed up the guard at the front door and the one outside under Josiah's window. Kane cut 'em loose. They run off as soon as he did. The kidnappers left the guard outside Josiah's door alone. He didn't hear nothin', and neither did we. We thought maybe the other two was goin' for help. When nobody came, Kane went lookin' for Lisie himself. He's been gone over an hour. If he don't find her soon, he'll probably aim for Brixton. The Sayers won't mind helpin' to find one of their own."

Drake felt off-kilter enough to disregard her accusatory tone. "You believe I wouldn't aid in the search?"

Her chin trembled. "Forgive me for speakin' my mind, but I do wonder. Lisie told me what happened between the two of you earlier. Don't seem like you cared enough to listen to her side of things. If you ask me, it don't seem like you love her very much at all."

Her censure hit a raw nerve. "Cease your prattle, madam, you go too far. My feelings for my wife are none of your concern. Regardless, I can't condone her treachery."

"What treachery?" she said, tears slipping down her dark cheeks. "All she did was for the love of her country and to save me from slavery. I told you that weeks ago, but you're holding it over her head like an ax about to fall. What would you have done in her place?"

Drake made for his study without answering. Undeterred, Prin followed him. "Maybe the treachery you can't forgive has to do with your brother? She said you think she killed him."

In the brightly lit study, Drake yanked open the top desk drawer and removed his leather pistol box. Opening the lid, he lifted one of the matched set from the case's blue velvet lining. He loaded the ornately carved weapon before shoving it into the depths of his coat pocket. If Goss had dared to take his wife, the rat-faced vermin was dead.

"Maybe you think she shouldn't have defended herself when your brother tried to kill her?" Prin said from behind him. "Would you be happier if she was the one to die?"

"No!" Drake growled. "How can you even suggest such a thing?" Racked with grief, he collapsed into the seat behind him. Rampant frustration and bitter regret rattled him to his core. His gaze flicked to Prin, where she stood crying beside the desk, her slender fingers clenching and unclenching with tension. "Get out of my sight," he ordered.

Flinching, Prin collected herself with dignity and wiped the tears from her face. "You're too proud, Your Grace. That pride's gonna cost you more than you're willin' to pay, if you're not careful."

"I said get *out*." Drake stared at the cold fireplace until he heard the soft click of the door closing. Images of Elise bombarded him. Her startling green eyes and luscious hair, her soft smile, the sound of her laughter, and the memory of her touch all conspired to torture him. He couldn't lose her. As he'd known months ago, to lose her would mean going back to the cold, joyless existence he'd known in England.

"Dear God, please help me!" he cried out from the depth of his soul. He remembered the promise he'd made to Elise not turn his back on the Lord again. Remembering how easily he'd allowed renewed bitterness to creep into his soul, he realized he'd broken his word like a spoiled child throwing a tantrum when he didn't get his way.

Another wave of anguish swelled over him. It had been Elise who'd reminded him of God's grace, that no matter what he did or where he went, nothing could separate him from Christ's love.

He bowed his head in his hands, desperate for the Lord's guidance. "Lord, *please* forgive me and my stiff-necked pride. Prin was right. My arrogance kept me from giving Elise a proper hearing when I should have remembered she is a blessing from You. *Please* help me find her, to listen to her, to understand Your will for us."

More at peace than he'd been since learning Elise was the Fox, he stood and crossed to the open window. The streets had calmed, though an occasional coach continued to rattle past. As he gazed at the starlit sky, he silently acknowledged he hadn't wanted to learn the truth about Anthony when he'd known it all along. Ever since Kirby arrived at Hawk Haven with the news of Anthony's death, Drake had sought to remember naught but the good in his brother. Elise's version of events challenged those memories and forced him to see Anthony for the man he really was: a man loyal to no one but himself, a spy willing to kill a woman for a reward and a fleeting taste of glory.

He fingered the scar along his jaw. On more than one occasion, he'd been the target of his brother's wrath. It wasn't difficult to imagine Anthony exploding into violence when Elise resisted capture. How could he blame her for fighting back when anyone would have done the same? In truth, he could only admire her courage.

He could no longer make excuses for his brother's unbridled behavior. He'd love him, but he wasn't to blame for Anthony's decisions. Since the death of his parents, Drake had done his best to protect his family. Elise was his family now, and she was out there somewhere, believing he despised her. He had to find her if only to tell her how much he cherished her.

He weighed the loaded pistol in his pocket once

more. Intent on finding Beaufort, he left the house and collected a horse from the stable. The captain would know if Goss had somehow escaped. With no other clues concerning his wife's disappearance, it was the only place to begin.

Drake returned from Beaufort's quarters just as the clock struck six. Exhausted but unwilling to relent in his search when Elise remained in peril, he'd returned to the house for a fresh horse and any available news.

Prin met him at the front door. By her haggard appearance, he could see she'd slept little, if at all. Lines of stress ringed her full mouth and her eyes were bloodshot. The aroma of breakfast sausage drifted through the house from the kitchen. His stomach growled, reminding him of his hunger.

"Did you find her?" Prin asked, her anxiety unconcealed.

He shook his head. "Has Kane returned?"

"Aye, he's sleepin'. I drilled him for you, but with all the goings-on last night, he had nothin' to follow 'cept a cold trail."

Drake ground his teeth in frustration. "What of the guards who deserted last night?"

Prin straightened her apron. "They came back 'bout an hour ago. Said they was gone so long 'cause of the ruckus in the streets."

"I can believe it."

"They wouldn't tell me nothin', but they might have some information they'll spill to you."

"Get them for me," he said as he sprinted up the stairs. "I'll see what they know, if anything."

Drake entered the bedroom he shared with Elise.

The emptiness of it tore at his heart. The scent of lavender she always wore teased his senses until he thought he might go mad. Regret twisted in his chest when he thought of how they'd parted.

Please Lord, please let me find her.

After changing his clothes, he went to his study, where the two soldiers awaited him. Both denied hearing an intruder, and neither could tell him anything to aid his hunt for Elise. Drake dismissed them to their duties, though he doubted their competence. Dashing off a note to his cousin, he requested fresh guards to replace them.

Prin delivered a plate of sausage and eggs. "You gotta eat somethin' or you'll be no good to anybody."

He accepted the plate and handed her the note with instructions for Kane to deliver it the moment he woke. Eating quickly, Drake made plans to go to Brixton Hall. The very idea of procuring help from rebel spies offended his sense of honor, but Elise's safety hung in the balance, and she was more important than his pride or his principals.

A rooster's crow awakened Elise. Red streaks of the rising sun painted the Eastern sky. The muted chatter of servants in the hall beyond her chamber door spurred her to dress with haste. A quick look at the clock told her the ferry was due. She needed to be on it when it returned to Charles Towne.

Locating one of her old dresses in the wardrobe, she changed from her nightgown and tied her hair in a ponytail. Downstairs, she traced Christian to his father's study, where she heard the two men arguing. With a loud rap on the partially opened door, she announced her arrival.

"Come in," Zechariah bellowed from where he stood by the window.

She took a seat in front of her spymaster's desk. "My goodness, the atmosphere is ripe this morn. May I inquire as to why?"

"We're deciding what to do with you," Christian said matter-of-factly. "Father says we should use you as a lure to capture Amber—"

"You wouldn't dare!" Elise hopped to her feet in protest.

"I assure you I would, girl." Zechariah sent her a sidelong glance. "Alone, Amberly is worth a fortune in ransom. Think of the sum I could command by holding both of you."

"Think of what you'd lose, you cold-hearted old goat. The war may be winding down, but the British still hold Charles Towne. My husband would have all the evidence he needs to see Brixton Hall seized and you dangling from the gallows."

"The voice of reason," Christian quipped beside her.

"I'm glad you agree with me," she said. "The idea is plain foolishness."

Christian leaned forward in his seat. "Exactly. A better plan is to exchange you for Josiah, *then* kidnap Amberly."

Elise's eyes nearly popped from their sockets. "You must be jesting. How dare you even suggest it?"

"We won't hurt him."

"No, you won't, Christian, because he won't be touched."

"You're being too hasty, dearest. The war is almost

over. By ransoming your duke, we'll gain additional funds to aid wounded Patriots and their families. Josiah will be freed, and you will be reunited with your Englishman. Everyone benefits."

Livid, Elise began to prowl the study, aware that Zechariah remained riveted by the view outside the window. "*I'll* see Josiah freed somehow, but you must leave my husband out of this nonsense."

He's been wounded enough already.

A low, sinister laugh emanated from Zechariah, sending a shiver down Elise's spine.

"What is it?" Christian stood and went to the window. He groaned. "It seems our discussion is at an end. His high and mighty has arrived."

"What?" Elise pushed her way through the two men blocking her view. When she located Drake striding up the path from the ferry landing, a shot of joy brought a smile to her lips, but it was quickly replaced by a deep concern for his safety. "When did you send him word of my arrival here?"

"I didn't," Christian grumbled.

"Then how?"

He shrugged. "You'll be able to ask him yourself in a moment."

Elise spun on her heel to leave, but Zechariah clamped a staying hand on her elbow. "Don't betray me, girl. Amberly is worth a fortune to me dead or alive. His family will ransom him either way. You can help deliver him to me and keep him alive or today you will see him dead. A British aristocrat in a cold grave will warm my heart. The choice belongs to you."

With a sidelong glance to Christian, Elise fled the study and arrived at the front door before the footman.

She opened it wide and crossed onto the portico just as Drake mounted the steps.

A burst of cool morning air surrounded her, tugging the tendrils of her hair and whipping it around her face. Brushing it back, she searched Drake's face. She held her breath, unsure of his reaction to finding her there. Blatant surprise scored his features and a relieved smile spread across his lips. For one sweet moment it was though no impediments stood between them.

Elise descended a step.

He climbed two, his golden gaze roaming over her in an anxious inspection that conveyed his deep concern for her.

Zechariah cleared his throat behind her, splintering the moment of ease between them. "Good day, Amberly. I see you received my message. So good of you to respond with such haste."

"I received no word from you, Sayer." Drake's deep voice blistered with skepticism. "When did you send it?"

"Why, as soon as Elise arrived yesterday, of course. If you ask me 'tis unseemly for a wife to abandon her husband."

Gasping at the lie, Elise pivoted on her heel to face the spymaster. His narrowed gaze warned her to hold her tongue. "Would you care to come in and discuss the matter?"

"We've decided to take a stroll," Elise interrupted.

"Then you'll need to fetch a shawl," Zechariah replied with the timing of a seasoned thespian. "'Tis a clear enough day, but we wouldn't want you to catch a chill in your condition."

Drake noticed the silencing glance Sayer cast toward

Elise. His anger burned toward the old man. According to Prin, Zechariah had bent Elise to his will for years by using her sister as a hostage. Drake was determined to see his wife freed from the old man's clutches once and for all.

Sprinting up the remaining steps, Drake reached into his coat pocket to feel for his pistol just in case he might need to make use of it. "My wife is right, Sayer. The morn is too fine to waste indoors. However, with all this wind it's perfect for a sail. I thank you for keeping her safe for me, but we'll be taking our leave on the ferry."

His right hand clutched the pistol in his pocket. He set his left arm around Elise's waist and started down the steps. The sharp click of a gun being cocked stopped them the moment they reached the gravel path. Zechariah waited for them to face him before he spoke. "I hate to disrupt your plans, Amberly, but we have much to discuss. Either return indoors with me now or die in the dust where you stand."

Elise knew Zechariah would carry out his threat. Without hesitation, she threw herself in front of Drake, determined to keep him safe.

Just as quickly, Drake thrust her behind him. "What are you doing, woman? Have you lost your mind?"

She grabbed hold of his shirt and refused to let go. "I won't see you hurt. Yesterday when you left me, I faced what life would be like without you. I'm not strong enough to do it again."

He twisted around to face her. Admiration glowed in his eyes as he tucked a wisp of hair behind her ear. "It breaks my heart to think of how we parted, my love. I can only pray you'll forgive me."

"But I'm the one who needs forgiveness," she said,

full of regret. "I didn't tell you of my past. What of Anthony?"

He placed a soft, lingering kiss on her brow. "Let's speak of it later. In the end, though, I suggest we forgive each other and start afresh."

"The two of you are about to give me a case of the vapors," Zechariah complained.

Unconcerned, Drake slid off his coat and draped it around Elise. As he faced Zechariah, he tucked the pistol he'd eased from his pocket into the back waistband of his breeches, careful to keep Zechariah ignorant of his actions. With a flight of stairs between them, he couldn't rely on his weapon's accuracy. He would have to move closer in order to insure a clean shot. He raised his hands in a show of surrender and sighed as though Sayer had him over a barrel. "You leave me no choice, old man, I'll come with you. However, I insist Elise be allowed to return to Charles Towne without further hesitation."

Elise clutched the back of his shirt. "No," she whispered fiercely. "I'll not leave without you."

Zechariah aimed his pistol at the center of Drake's chest. "I'm afraid you're not in a position to negotiate, Amberly. As I told Elise before you arrived, the two of you are more valuable as a pair."

"What is it you want to secure our freedom, Sayer?"

"I believe ten thousand pounds, the freedom of Josiah Smith and your silence concerning my and Christian's identities will do."

"You've thought of everything," Drake said, undaunted. "If I agree, Elise and I must be free to go at once. I'll have to arrange for the funds to be delivered to you. You'll have to accept my word your demands will be met."

The blustery morning rang with Zechariah's laughter. "I think not. You and Elise will wait in my study. I'll have you write and sign orders for Josiah's release. Once I'm assured of his freedom and the ten thousand pounds is delivered safely, I'll set you both free. Not a moment before."

Drake opened his mouth to reply, but the words died on his lips when Elise slid the pistol free of his waistband. She shoved the barrel into his back. The click as she cocked the hammer sent the hair rising at the back of his neck.

"I'm sorry, Drake, but I'm doing this for both our sakes," she said, her voice as hard as flint.

The old man guffawed with delight. "You thought to shoot me, eh, Amberly?" To Elise he said, "I knew you'd see reason, my girl. Bring him inside and let's have this business done."

Palms sweating, Elise prodded Drake with the weapon. He started a slow ascent of the steps. Without taking her eyes off Zechariah or the gun he directed at her husband, she waited until the precise moment, then, using surprise to her advantage, thrust Drake out of harm's way and pulled the trigger. The explosion echoed on the wind. A cloud of smoke enveloped her.

Through the acrid haze she watched Zechariah fumble his weapon and fall. He squealed in pain before clutching his hand. Christian burst from the house. Shouting for a servant, he bent down beside his father, aiding him as best he could.

Drake extracted the smoking pistol from Elise's

bloodless grasp, then pulled her into his embrace, where she trembled against him.

Christian helped his moaning father to his feet. Blood dripped from Zechariah's hand, but she saw he maintained all of his fingers.

"I'm sorry Zechariah, but you left me no choice," she said. "My loyalty is to my husband."

"Come, sweet, we're leaving," Drake said. "The ferry is prepared to sail."

"Elise, wait!" Christian called as they turned go. "Things were never intended to come to this. Remember Josiah. Most of all, never forget what I told you last night. It will always hold true."

Elise choked back the sob that swelled in her throat. Christian wouldn't keep them from leaving because of his feelings for her. Combined with the events of the morning, it was too much to say a final goodbye to one of the dearest friends she'd ever known.

Before she could respond, he turned his back on her and led Zechariah's groaning form inside the mansion.

Drake tugged on her hand. "Swiftly, love, it's time to go."

On board the ferry a few minutes later, Captain Travis inquired about the shot he'd heard. Elise assured him all was well, and asked after his mother to distract him.

Cap in his hands, Travis studied her with concern. "She's right as rain, Miss Elise, but I hope you don't mind me sayin', you don't look so good. Maybe you should sit a spell in my cabin."

"My thoughts precisely, Captain." Drake led her away. "Your kindness is appreciated."

The cabin was a dusty cell, but Elise welcomed the privacy it offered. Sitting on the narrow bed, she watched Drake close the door. White-lipped and face taut, he reminded her of a storm cloud. "Don't be angry with me, Drake."

"Angry?" He sank to his knees before her. "'Tis more like I'm in the throes of shock. Please don't ever endanger yourself like that again."

"I had no choice." She brushed her fingers through his silky hair and cupped his cheek, grateful they'd escaped unhurt. "I knew we had to move closer if I hoped to have a clear shot."

"You are the most brilliant, bravest woman—"

"No, but when he aimed at you, I wanted to kill him, Drake. God forgive me, I would have if he'd caused you harm."

His eyes caressed her face. "I'm the most fortunate of men to have a loyal wife such as you, my love. From the depths of my heart, I thank you for your care. It shames me to think of what I said to you yesterday."

"It broke my heart, but I understood." She ran a fingertip along his full bottom lip. "I want no distrust between us. Will you allow me to explain?"

"There's no need," he assured her. "I didn't want to face it, but I've known the truth since Prin set me to rights weeks ago."

She searched his face for the truth. "You believe me about Hawk?"

He nodded without hesitation. "I loved Anthony and I always will, but with the Lord's help, I was able to remember him as he really was, not the idealized version I'd clung to these many months. Once I realized what I'd done, I had no trouble believing your version of events, especially when you've proven by word and by deed what a woman of honor you are.

"As for your spying, I admit I wish it were otherwise. For your sake, I wish you'd been spared the painful choices that led you down that path. As it is, I can only thank the Lord for bringing us together and I stand amazed at your courage, for I've never met the like."

He stood and slowly, as if he feared she might reject him, drew her into his embrace. "I love you, Elise. I love our child. There's nothing I want more than to spend the rest of my life loving you."

With a prayer of thankfulness, she snuggled close, breathing in his comforting scent. Drake knew her secrets and loved her anyway. Love for him filled her heart to the brim and spilled over. At long last, she knew the meaning of peace.

Epilogue

Hawk Haven Manor, England
August 1782

Elise clipped her long hair at the nape of her neck and checked her appearance in the mirror one last time. Drake would be coming to find her soon. The thrill of anticipation seized her. She was looking forward to a lazy afternoon with him and the picnic the servants had set up near the estate's large fish pond.

God had been faithful, just as His word promised. The Lord truly had seen them through their darkest hours. Now their lives overflowed with goodness. In the eight months since she'd arrived at Hawk Haven, the sprawling estate had become the home of her heart. Though she occasionally missed the warmer climate of South Carolina, England possessed its own lush beauty. Prin, Kane and their new son, Robert, thrived in their own spacious cottage down the lane. Elise had made friends, including Drake's impish sister, Eva, whom she'd come to love as her own.

She smelled one of the vases of sweet red roses displayed in artful arrangements on the side tables and atop the mantel. When the clock struck noon, she grew impatient and went in search of her husband.

She found him in the nursery across the hall. Through the open window, light streamed into the luxurious space decorated in soft shades of yellow and cream. His black hair loose around his shoulders, Drake rocked their sleeping daughter in the crook of his arm, despite the capable nanny who read a book in the corner.

At three months old, Olivia was the darling of the household and the axis of her parents' world. A wave of tenderness engulfed Elise as Drake slipped his large fingertip into the baby's tiny grasp. She memorized the loving expression on his face and wished somehow she could capture the unguarded moment on canvas.

Not wanting to interrupt him, she turned to go, but the floor creaked, giving her away. He looked up and smiled with obvious pleasure. "At long last." He placed the sleeping baby in a crib frothed in cream lace and yellow silk before gently covering her with a soft blanket.

Meeting Elise in the doorway, he pulled her close and bent to nibble her ear. "Are you ready to leave? I'm starving."

"I've been waiting for *you*," she whispered with a smile, careful not to wake Olivia.

"You were reading a letter when I came to find you earlier."

"That was ages ago."

"How odd." He grinned. "I thought it less than half an hour. Who wrote to you?"

"Tabby," she said. He held her hand as they walked down the hall. "She says all is well in Charles Towne. Moira's nearly a year old and as fat as a sausage. Josiah is well. The Rolling Tide is flourishing. Zechariah has use of his hand again and Christian has left to come here for a visit."

Drake's brow arched. "Come again?"

Elise tried not to laugh at his aghast expression. "Drake, please don't make a fuss. Christian has been my friend for a long time."

His brow drew together. "I don't like it. I still say he's in love with you—"

"Don't you trust me?"

The scowl returned. "Don't be a simpleton. You know I trust you. I love you more than words can say."

"Then don't worry about Christian." They started down the grand, winding staircase lined with the portraits of Drake's noble ancestors. He seemed to relax and Elise continued her account of Tabby's letter. "Tabby asked me to thank you again for releasing Josiah last fall. She'll be your loyal friend forever."

"It made you happy. That's all that mattered to me."

Elise's merry laughter filled the foyer as he swept her off her feet and out the door the butler held open. Bright sunshine surrounded her the same as her love for Drake filled her heart. She flung her arms around his neck, savoring the knowledge that he was hers.

He glanced down at her, a smile warming his face. "Love me, sweet?"

Her arms tightened. "You know I do, my darling. Today and every day for the rest of my life."

* * * * *

Florida author **Louise M. Gouge** writes historical fiction for Harlequin's Love Inspired Historical line. She received the prestigious Inspirational Readers' Choice Award in 2005 and placed in 2011 and 2015; she also placed in the Laurel Wreath contest in 2012. When she isn't writing, she and her husband, David, enjoy visiting historical sites and museums. Please visit her website at louisemgougeauthor.Blogspot.com.

Books by Louise M. Gouge

Love Inspired Historical

Four Stones Ranch

Cowboy to the Rescue

Cowboy Seeks a Bride

Cowgirl for Keeps

Cowgirl Under the Mistletoe

Cowboy Homecoming

Cowboy Lawman's Christmas Reunion

Lone Star Cowboy League: The Founding Years

A Family for the Rancher

Ladies in Waiting

A Proper Companion

A Suitable Wife

A Lady of Quality

Visit the Author Profile page
at Harlequin.com for more titles.

THE CAPTAIN'S LADY

Louise M. Gouge

I am my beloved's, and my beloved is mine.
—*Song of Solomon* 6:3

To my beloved husband, David, who encouraged me to keep writing these books even as he was enduring radiation and chemotherapy treatments. May our God grant us another forty-five years together.

And to my insightful editor Melissa Endlich...thanks!

Chapter One

March 1776
London, England

Lady Marianne peered down through the peephole into the drawing room while her heart raced. Against her back, the heavy woolen tapestry extolling one of her ancestors' mighty deeds pushed her into the wall of her father's bedchamber, nearly choking her with its ancient dust. Yet she would endure anything to observe the entrance of Papa's guest.

Often in her childhood she and her closest brother had evaded the notice of Greyson, Papa's valet, and crept in here to spy on their parents' guests, even catching a glimpse of the prime minister once when he called upon Papa, his trusted friend, the earl of Bennington. But no exalted politician captured Marianne's interest this day.

Her breath caught. Captain James Templeton—*Jamie*—entered the room with Papa, and warmth filled her heart and flushed her cheeks.

The two men spoke with the enthusiasm of friends

reunited after many months of separation and eager to share their news. Unable to hear their words, Marianne forced herself to breathe. Jamie, the Loyalist American captain of a merchant ship. How handsome he was, taller than Papa by several inches. His bronzed complexion and light brown hair—now sun-kissed with golden streaks and pulled back in a queue—gave evidence of long exposure to the sun on his voyages across the Atlantic Ocean. In contrast to Papa's blue silk jacket and white satin breeches, Jamie wore a plain brown jacket and black breeches. Yet to Marianne, he appeared as elegant and noble as Papa.

Hidden high above the drawing room, she could not clearly see the blue eyes whose intense gaze had pierced her soul and claimed her heart less than a year ago. Jamie, always honest, always forthright. No wonder Papa took an interest in him, even to the extent of calling him his protégé, despite his utter lack of social position *and* being an American.

Marianne suspected part of Papa's interest stemmed from wanting to secure the captain's loyalty now that thirteen of England's American colonies had rebelled against the Crown. But last year she had seen that the old dear truly liked Jamie, perhaps even more than his own four sons, a fact that stung both her and Mama's hearts. Yet, despite that affection, the earl's patronage might not extend to accepting a merchant for a son-in-law.

How she and Jamie would overcome this prejudice, Marianne did not know. At this moment, all she knew was that her own affection for him was unchanged. Last summer, against the better judgment of both of them, their friendship had intensified through shared interests, from reading Shakespeare and Aristotle to spending hours sailing on the Thames. On a short excursion with Papa aboard Jamie's large sloop, the *Fair Winds,* Marianne and Jamie had whispered their confessions of undying love. Then he had placed the sweetest, purest kiss on her lips, sealing her heart to his forever. Now her pulse pounded at the sight of him, and her heart felt a settled assurance that no other man could ever win her love.

Wriggling out of her hiding place between tapestry and wall, Marianne brushed dust from her pink day dress and hastened to the door. She escaped the bedchamber undetected and hurried down the hallway to her own quarters.

"Lady Marianne." Emma emerged from her closet, her hands clasped at her waist. "Why, my lady, your dress." She took hold of Marianne's skirt and shook dust from it, then glanced up. "Oh, my, your hair." Her youthful, cherubic face creased with concern.

"Yes, Emma, I am a fright." With a giddy laugh, Marianne brushed past her lady's maid to sit at her dressing table. "Make haste and mend the damage. Oh, dear, look at this." She removed a silvery cobweb from her hair, pulling several long black strands from the upswept coiffure Emma had created earlier. "Please redo this. And I shall need another of my pink gowns." More than one dandy had told her pink brought a pretty blush to her cheeks, so she wore the color often.

Her appearance repaired and Emma's approving smile received, Marianne clutched her prayer book and hurried from her room. With a deep breath to compose herself, she held her head high and glided down the steps to the front entry hall. A quick glance revealed

Jamie and Papa seated before the blazing hearth, deep in genial conversation.

Marianne opened the book and mouthed the words of the morning prayer as she entered the room, not looking their way. Last year, Jamie's parting words had encouraged her to greater faith, and she must let him know she had followed his advice.

The rustle of movement caught her attention. She cast a sidelong glance toward the men, who now stood to greet her.

"Why, Papa, I didn't realize—" She stopped before completing the lie, while heat rushed to her cheeks. "Forgive me. I see you have a guest. Will you excuse me?" She could not look at Jamie for fear that her face would reveal her heart.

"Come, daughter, permit me to present my guest." Papa beckoned her with a gentle wave of his bony, wrinkled hand. "You may recall him from last summer. Lady Marianne, Captain James Templeton of the East Florida Colony." His presentation was accompanied by a shallow cough, and he held a lacy linen handkerchief to his lips.

Gripping her emotions, Marianne permitted herself to look at Jamie. His furrowed brow and the firm clenching of his square jaw sent a pang of worry through her. Was he not pleased to see her? Worse still, his gaze did not meet hers. Rather, he seemed to stare just over her head. Surely this was a ploy to divert any suspicion from the mutual affection they had spoken of only in whispers during his last visit.

"Good morning, Lady Marianne." His rigid bow bespoke his lower status, but his rich, deep voice sent a pleasant shiver down her spine. "I hope you are well."

Offering no smile, Marianne lifted her chin. "Quite well, thank you." She closed her book and turned to Papa, her face a mask. "Will you be busy all day, sir?"

The fond gaze he returned brought forth a wave of guilt. "I fear that I must go to Whitehall for most of the afternoon. Is there something you require, my dear? You have but to ask." His blue eyes, though pale from age, twinkled with his usual eagerness to please her.

Marianne's feigned hauteur melted into warm affection. Truly, Papa did spoil her. Yet she lived in dread that he would never give her the one thing she desired above all else: the tall *should*-be knight who stood beside him. "No, dear. I am content." She sent a quick look toward Jamie, who continued to stare beyond her. "I will leave you to your business affairs."

Before she could turn, Papa coughed again, and she stepped closer, frowning with concern. He waved her off. "Never mind. I am well. But I have need of your assistance." He clapped a pale hand on Jamie's shoulder. "Captain Templeton has just arrived, and I have offered him lodging. Your mother is occupied with one of her charities, and your worthless brother has not put in an appearance for several days. Would you be so kind as to make certain the good captain is taken care of?"

A laugh of delight almost escaped Marianne, but she managed to release a sigh intended to convey boredom. "Very well, Papa. I shall see that he has accommodations." She graced Jamie with a glance. "Do you have a manservant, or shall we procure one for you?"

A hint of a smile softened his expression. "My man awaits out front in our hired carriage, Lady Marianne."

"Very well, then. I shall instruct our butler, Blevins, to receive him." She reached up to kiss Papa's wrinkled cheek, breathing in the pleasant citrus fragrance of his shaving balm. "Do not let His Majesty weary you, darling."

"Humph." Papa straightened his shoulders and pushed out his chest. "I am not yet in my dotage, despite what you and your mother think." Another cough accompanied his chuckle. "You have to watch these women, Templeton. They like to coddle a man."

"Yes, sir." Jamie's tone held no emotion.

Marianne resisted the urge to offer a playful argument back to Papa. The sooner he left, the sooner she would have Jamie to herself. Yet how could she accomplish that and maintain propriety? She lifted the silver bell from the nearby table and rang it. A footman stepped into the room. "Tell Blevins we have need of him."

"Yes, Lady Marianne." The footman bowed and left the room.

"Blevins will attend you, Captain Templeton." Marianne kissed Papa's cheek again. "Enjoy your afternoon, Papa." She shot a meaningful look at Jamie. "I am going to the garden to read."

Gliding from the room with a well-practiced grace, she met Blevins in the entry hall and gave him instructions regarding Captain Templeton. "I believe the bedchamber at the end of the third floor is best. Do you agree?" With the room's clear view of the garden, Jamie would have no trouble knowing when she was there.

"Yes, Lady Marianne. I shall see to it." Blevins, of medium height but seeming taller due to his exceptionally straight posture, marched on sticklike legs toward the drawing room, his gait metered like a black-clad soldier who heard an invisible drummer.

Seated on the marble bench beneath one of the barren chestnut trees, Marianne drew her woolen shawl about her shoulders and tried to concentrate on the words in her prayer book. But at the end of each Scripture verse, she found herself beseeching the Lord to send Jamie to her. As a guest in their home, he could visit her here in the garden without impropriety. Anyone looking out any of the town house's back windows could see their actions were blameless.

After a half hour passed, Marianne shivered in the early spring breeze, closed her book and stared up at Jamie's window, willing him to look out so that she might beckon him down. Perhaps he did not know they could meet here without censure. Yet had Papa not requested her assistance in making him feel welcomed? Tapping her foot on the flagstone paving in front of the bench, she huffed out an impatient sigh. She had told him she would be in the garden. Why did he not come?

A rear door opened, and Marianne's heart leaped. But it was John, one of the family's red-and-gold-liveried footmen, who emerged and approached her with a silver tray bearing a tea service and biscuits. "Begging your pardon, Lady Marianne, but Blevins thought you might like some refreshment." John set the tray on the marble table beside her. "May I serve you, Lady Marianne?"

"Thank you, John. I can pour." Perfect. An answer to prayer. "I should like for you to inform my father's guest that he has missed his appointment with me. Please send Captain Templeton down straightaway."

"Yes, Lady Marianne." The ideal footman, John bowed away, his face revealing no emotion.

In a short time, Jamie emerged from the house. But

instead of striding toward her with all eagerness, he walked as if facing the gallows, looking beyond her toward the stables, the hothouse, the treetops, anywhere but at her. By the time he came near, Marianne had almost succumbed to tears. Instead, she stood and reached out both hands to greet him.

"Jamie." His name rushed out on a breath squeezed by joy and misery.

"You summoned me, Lady Marianne?" He stopped far beyond her reach and bowed. "I am at your service."

She clasped her hands at her waist and laughed softly, but without mirth. "Such a cold tone to match a cold day. Where is the warmth that once graced your every word to me?"

For several moments, he stared at the ground, his lips set in a grim line and his jaw working. He seemed to compose himself, for at last he lifted his gaze to meet hers.

"My lady, I beg your forgiveness for my inappropriate conversations with you last summer."

"But—"

"Please." He raised his hand in a silencing gesture. "I will not betray the trust of Lord Bennington by arrogantly presuming an equality that would permit us… permit me…to pursue a lady so far above me." For an instant, a sweet vulnerability crossed his eyes, but then all light disappeared from his face, replaced by the same blank expression John or any of the household servants might employ, a facade that bespoke their understanding of status and position. "You must not ask me to do that which would dishonor you, your family and my faith." He gave her a stiff bow. "Now, if you will excuse me, my lady." Jamie spun around and strode back toward the house with what seemed like eagerness, something clearly lacking when he had come to meet her.

Chapter Two

The last time Jamie had felt such grief was beside his mother's grave in Nantucket some sixteen years ago, when he was a lad of nine, struggling then not to cry. Now his jaw ached from clenching, and his chest throbbed as it had when a young whale had slammed him with its tail, trying to escape his harpoon. No, this was unlike any pain he had ever endured aboard his uncle's whaling ship. He could not seem to pull in enough breath, could barely manage to climb the wide front staircase without clutching the oak railing.

In the third floor hallway, a footman cast a glance at him, and one eyebrow rose. Jamie stiffened. He was no faint-hearted maiden who swooned over life's injuries. He'd seen the harm he'd just inflicted upon Marianne... *Lady* Marianne. Yet despite the pain pinching her fair face, she had not swooned. Or had she? Perhaps after he tore himself from her presence, she'd succumbed to her distress.

With some effort, Jamie drew air into his lungs and strode down the hallway, bursting into the elegant bed-chamber assigned to him. He ignored his friend Aaron's shocked expression and dashed to the window to peer down into the garden where he'd left her. There she sat beneath the leafless tree, staring straight ahead, her shawl carelessly draped over the stone bench.

Pain swept through him again, but this time for her. How brave she was. No tears. Even at this distance he could see her composure. Was this not one of the reasons he loved her? As he had prayed, her unfailing good sense prevailed. She knew their romance was hopeless, and would not protest his declaration that it must end. *See how she clutches her prayer book. Perhaps even now she is seeking God's consolation.* His parting admonition last year had influenced her as he hoped. Surely now she would cling to the Lord, as he did, to ease the agony they both must endure. No doubt she would manage better than he.

She lifted her gaze toward his window, and he jumped back, chiding himself for lingering there. She would survive the dissolution of their love, but only if he stayed true to his course. If she sensed he might waver, she might pursue him, which would lead to their undoing. No, far more than their undoing. Nothing less than the failure of his mission for the American Revolution.

"You'd best sit down, Jamie." Aaron tilted his head toward an arrangement of green brocade chairs near the roaring fireplace. "You're looking a mite pale." Worry clouded his expression.

"Aye, I'll sit." He staggered to a chair and fell into it, clutching his aching head in both hands as warmth from the crackling logs reached him. The itchy collar of his brown woolen jacket pressed against his neck and generated sweat clear up to his forehead, while a cold, contradictory shudder coursed down his back.

Aaron sat in an adjacent chair and clasped Jamie's shoulder. "You've got it bad, lad, no mistake. But you'd best gird up your mind straightaway, or General Washington will have to send someone else to spy on Lord Bennington and his East Florida interests. And by then it'll be too late for any useful information to reach home." His bushy brown eyebrows met in a frown. "I thought you'd worked this all out before we sailed."

Jamie swiped his linen handkerchief across his forehead. "Aye. I thought it, too. Then I saw her."

"Well, you'd best deal with it." Aaron sat back and crossed his arms. "I didn't sail over here to get hanged. My younger brothers aren't yet old enough to manage my lands, you know."

His words sank deep into Jamie's mind, and the unsaid words sank deeper. In truth, now that he'd broken with her, a certain peace began to fill his chest. He lifted a silent prayer of thanks for God's mercy. Determined to shake off personal concerns, he gave Aaron a sidelong glance and snorted. "If you aren't keen on hanging, then you'd best quit pestering me and start playing your own part." He punched his friend's arm. "Up with you, man. When does a valet sit beside his master? And no more 'Jamie.' It's Captain Templeton to you, and don't you forget it."

"That's the way, Cap'n." Aaron jumped to his feet. "And I'm Quince to ye, sir. So watch what ye say, too." He spoke with the affected accent that augmented his guise as Jamie's valet.

The good humor lighting Aaron's face improved Jamie's spirits. Together they could complete their mission and be gone in just over a fortnight. Surely he could evade Lady Marianne for that short time.

* * *

Shivering in the brisk breeze, Marianne clutched her prayer book to her chest and stared unseeing toward the back entrance of the house. Over and over, Jamie's words repeated in her mind: *You must not ask me to do that which would dishonor you, your family and my faith.*

Dishonor? Did he truly believe loving her would cause such dishonor? Had all his ardent declarations of last summer meant nothing to him? Where was his honor if he broke his promise to love her forever? She could not think. Could not feel. His words hammered against her heart, numbing her to all, even tears, even to the biting March wind.

The memory of his cold facade burned into her like a fire, reigniting her senses. She tightened her grip on the prayer book. How could he cause her such pain? In answer, his face appeared in her mind's eye. For the briefest moment, she had seen misery there. What his lips would deny, his eyes revealed. He did love her. Of that she was certain. Serenity filled her heart, and she dared to cast a gaze upward toward his window. She gasped. There he stood, looking directly at her. Then he was gone.

Marianne's heart soared like the song of a nightingale, and warmth swept over her despite the wind. Oh, yes, indeed. Jamie Templeton loved her. And if he thought she would let him slip away because of some misplaced sense of honor, then the good captain had an important lesson to learn. She would begin teaching him this very evening.

Marianne's father always insisted on supper in the formal dining room with all his family and followers gathered around the table. No one could escape. Even her brother Robert usually managed to appear and stay sober for the meal, after which he would go off with his friends for a night of activities about which Marianne tried not to think…or worry.

That evening as usual, Papa sat at one end of the long oak table, and Mama at the other. In her seat at Papa's right hand, Marianne was delighted to see he had placed Jamie on his left, a singular honor that she prayed would not grate on her brother, who really should sit beside Papa. While it would be unacceptable for her to speak across the table and address Jamie, perhaps she might comment on his conversation with Papa.

According to his custom, Robert arrived several minutes late, but no hostility clouded his dark, handsome features. Instead, seated beside Jamie, he greeted him as a long-lost friend and insisted nothing would do but that Jamie must accompany him on his nightly exploits.

At Robert's outlandish proposal, Marianne almost spewed her soup across the table, but managed to swallow and force her gaze down toward her plate. *Please do not permit Jamie to go.* Her silent prayer was directed to both her earthly and heavenly fathers. Before she could fully compose herself and observe Papa's reaction to Robert's plan, the gentleman seated to her right cleared his throat.

"Lady Marianne," Tobias Pincer said, "how exquisite you look this evening." As he leaned closer to her, his oily smile and the odors of camphor and wig powder nearly sent Marianne reeling off the other side of her chair. "Do tell me you plan to attend the rout this evening. I shall be nothing short of devastated if you do not."

With the tightest smile she could muster, she muttered her appreciation of his nightly compliments. "You must forgive me, Mr. Pincer, but my mother and I have prior plans." Did this man actually think she would consort with his crowd, even if Robert was a part of it?

"Of course." His smile turned to a simper, but before he could say more, Grace Kendall claimed his attention from the other side.

"Why, Mr. Pincer, you are neglecting this delicious soup." Her pleasant alto tones dropped to a murmur as she shared a bit of harmless gossip. Mr. Pincer bowed to propriety and turned his full attention to her.

Marianne wanted to hug Grace. For the past three years, Mama's companion had frequently sacrificed herself to deflect unwanted attention Marianne received from suitors. Although more than pretty herself, Grace had no fortune and no prospects. At six and twenty, she would likely remain an old maid, but her selfless companionship always proved a blessing to both Mama and Marianne.

Freed from polite necessity, Marianne looked back across the table just in time to see Papa's approving nod in Jamie's direction.

"We shall see to it tomorrow," Papa said.

What had she missed? Would Jamie go out with Robert this evening? From the defeated look on her brother's face, she guessed he would not. Even as her heart ached over the way Papa often crushed Robert's spirits, she could not help but rejoice that Jamie would not be dragged into the gutters of London.

"Papa," she ventured in a playful tone, "what plans are you making? Have you and His Majesty already subdued those dreadful rebels in America?" She saw Jamie's eyebrows arch, and she puckered away a laugh.

Papa chuckled in his deep, throaty way. "You see, Templeton, these women have no sense about such things." He leaned toward her. "Would that it could be done so easily, my dear. No, I have another project in mind, one in which Captain Templeton has agreed to participate. Our good Reverend Bentley—" he nodded toward the curate, who sat at Mama's right hand "— has agreed to school the captain in some of our more tedious social graces."

Marianne turned her gasp into a hum of interest. "Indeed?"

The color in Jamie's tanned cheeks deepened, and charming bewilderment rolled across his face.

"Yes, indeed." Papa straightened and puffed out his chest. "If this partnership goes as planned, I shall be introducing Captain Templeton to other peers and gentlemen. Through our mutual business efforts, we will make East Florida the standard of how to prevent a rebellion, shall we not, Templeton?"

"That is my hope, sir." Jamie's attention remained on Papa.

"Furthermore, daughter," Papa said, "I am enlisting your assistance, as well. Your mother can spare you for a while. I want you to take the captain to see the sights about the city." He glanced down the table. "I suppose Robert should go along for propriety's sake."

She could hardly believe her ears and could not call forth any words to respond. Jamie blinked and avoided her gaze, perhaps as stunned as she was.

Robert stopped balancing his spoon on the edge of his soup plate and stared at Papa, his mouth agape. He shook his head slightly, as if to clear his vision, and a silly grin lifted one corner of his lips. Marianne would have laughed if her brother's reaction did not seem almost pathetic. Papa never entrusted him with anything.

"Humph." Now a wily look crossed Robert's face, and he studied Jamie up and down, then sniffed. "Well, for gracious sakes, Father, before I am seen in public with this fellow, do let me see about his clothes. Look at him. Not a length of ribbon nor an inch of lace. And this awful black. And not even a brass buckle to catch anyone's attention. Gracious, Templeton, are you a Quaker? Who makes your clothes? No, never mind. I shall see that you meet my tailor."

Jamie's narrowed eyes and set lips, if visible only for an instant, steadied Marianne's rioting emotions. How she would love to thump her dear brother right on the nose for his rude words, spoken so shortly after his own invitation to take Jamie out for the evening. But Marianne could see the resolution in Jamie's face. Her beloved could take care of himself. And although he was at least five years Robert's junior, she had no doubt Jamie would have the greater and better influence on her brother. She would make that a matter of most earnest prayer.

"I thank you, Mr. Moberly," Jamie said to Robert with all good humor. "I shall look forward to any improvements you might suggest."

What graciousness he exhibited. Was that not the epitome of good breeding and good manners? Marianne blushed for the rudeness of her father and brother for suggesting that he needed anything more.

As for the favor Father was heaping on Jamie, she felt her heart swell with joy. If he considered Jamie a partner and an ally in saving the colonies for the Crown, this could be regarded as nothing less than complete approval of the man, perhaps even to the point of accepting him into the family, despite his being a merchant. Her parents had never insisted she marry. Was that not very much like permission to marry whomever she might choose? Hadn't they themselves married for love, despite Mama's lower status as a baron's daughter and no title other than Miss Winston? But in the event she was mistaken, Marianne must take great care to hide her love for Jamie, at least for now.

Chapter Three

For the first time since he had set out on this mission, Jamie began to wonder if General Washington had chosen the wrong man. As a whaler and merchant captain, Jamie had learned how to employ patience and strategy to accomplish whatever goal was at hand. But the gale brewing around him in Lord Bennington's grand London home just might sink him.

He had no difficulty maintaining his composure when the earl offered to introduce him to some important people. After all, that was why Jamie had come. But this scheme for improving his manners almost set him back in his chair, especially when the earl instructed Lady Marianne to help. Now he would be forced into her company and that of her foppish brother, a dark-haired fellow not exactly corpulent, but on his way to it. Jamie had only just met the curate, a slender, compliant fellow, but he preferred the clergyman as a tutor, for every minute in Lady Marianne's company would be torture.

Bent over his roast beef, he wondered if he was doing anything amiss. Not that he cared whether someone pointed out a blunder, for he would welcome a chance to learn better manners for future use in such company as this. But he also would like for Lady Marianne to think well of him. *Belay that, man.* He must not think that way. Yet, without meaning to, he lifted his gaze to see how she wielded her cutlery. Her lovely blue eyes, bright as the southern sky, were focused on him, and he could not look away.

She glanced at the earl. "Papa, have you asked Captain Templeton about Frederick?"

Lord Bennington cast a look down the table at his wife. "Later, my dear. Your mother will want to hear the news of your brother, too."

"Oh, yes, of course." Lady Marianne resumed eating, stopping from time to time to speak with the man beside her. From the prim set of her lips and the way she seemed unconsciously to lean away from the fellow, Jamie could see her distaste, especially when the man tilted toward her. If some dolt behaved thus toward a lady aboard Jamie's ship, he would make quick work of the knave, dispatching him to eat with the deckhands. But civility had its place, and this was it. Jamie watched Lady Marianne's delicate hands move with the grace of a swan, and he tried to copy the way she cut her roast beef and ate in small bites. When he swallowed, however, the meat seemed to stick in his throat, and he was forced to wash it down with water in a loud gulp. Anyone who may have noticed was polite enough not to look his way.

Beside him, Moberly chose a chaser of wine, several glasses of it. As the meal progressed, his demeanor mellowed. "I say, Templeton, do you ride?"

Moberly's tone was genial, not at all like his insulting reference to Jamie's clothes, a matter of some injury. Jamie's beloved cousin Rachel had spent many hours sewing his travel wardrobe, and her expertise could not be matched.

"I have never truly mastered the skill, sir."

Moberly snorted. "Ah, of course not." A wily grin not lacking in friendliness creased his face. "Then you must permit me to teach you. 'Tis a skill every gentleman must have."

If Jamie could have groaned in a well-mannered tone, he would have. Having grown up at sea, he could ride a whale with ease, but not a horse—something Moberly clearly did not believe. *Lord, what other trials will You put before me? Will this truly serve the Glorious Cause in some way?* He lifted one shoulder in a slight shrug and cocked his head to accept the challenge. "Then if I am to be a gentleman, by all means, let us ride." The more time he spent with Moberly, the less he would be in Lady Marianne's alluring company. The less he would be tempted to break his vow not to use her to gain information from her father.

Jamie managed the rest of the meal without difficulty and afterward joined the family in Lord Bennington's study, where the earl held court from behind his ornately carved white desk. Lady Marianne's brother and his slimy friend had excused themselves, no doubt for a night of carousing, for both Lady Marianne and Lady Bennington seemed disappointed as they watched Moberly leave.

"Now," the earl said, "we shall see how my youngest son excuses his mismanagement of my money in East Florida." He opened the satchel Jamie had brought and pulled out several sealed documents.

Jamie flinched inwardly. His good friend Frederick Moberly had made a great success of Bennington Plantation, as proved by the large shipment of indigo, rice, oranges and cotton Jamie had just delivered to Bennington's warehouses. Not only that, but Frederick served well as the popular magistrate of the growing settlement of St. Johns Towne. Jamie had already apprised Lord Bennington of both of these matters in no uncertain words. Yet the earl referred to all of his sons in singularly unflattering ways. Had Jamie been brought up thus, he doubted he could have made anything of himself. As he had many times before, he thanked the Lord for the firm but loving hand of his uncle, who had guided him to adulthood, first in Nantucket and then on his whaling ship.

Jamie's widowed mother had died when he was nine and his sister, Dinah, three. Uncle Lamech, his mother's brother, had secured a home for Dinah with kindhearted friends, then took Jamie along as his cabin boy on his next whaling voyage. Uncle taught him how to work hard, with courage, perseverance, and faith in God, all the while demonstrating confidence that Jamie would succeed at whatever he put his hand to. Would that the four Moberly sons could have received such assurance from their father.

The earl broke open the seal of the letter addressed to him, and once again Jamie cringed. In his spoken report to Lord Bennington, he had omitted one very important fact about the earl's youngest son.

"Married!"

Marianne and Mama jumped to their feet as one and hurried to Papa's side, as if each must see the words for herself. Mama practically snatched the letter from

Papa, who stood at his desk trembling, his face a study in rage. Eyes wide and staring at the offending missive, cheeks red and pinched, mouth working as if no words were sufficient to express his outrage.

Mama did not mirror his anger, but her sweet face clouded as it did when she was disappointed. "Oh, my. And to think I have found no less than six eligible young ladies of consequence who would gladly receive Frederick now that he has done so well for himself."

"Papa, do sit down." Marianne took his arm and tried gently to push him back into his chair. He stood stubbornly rigid and waved her away.

Reading the letter, Mama gasped, and her puckered brow arched and her lips curved upward in a glorious smile. "Why, they are expecting..." She blinked and glanced toward Jamie. "I shall be a grandmamma by July," she whispered to Marianne and Papa. "How exquisitely delightful." Her merry laughter brought a frown of confusion to Papa's face.

"Do not tell me that you approve of this match." Papa's cheeks faded to pink, but his trembling continued.

"But, my darling, approve or not, the deed is done." Mama touched his arm and gave him a winsome smile. "Do be reconciled to it. A sensitive young man can endure rejection from the ladies of his own class for only so long. His every word indicates that this Rachel is above average in wit and temper. Did he mention her family?" She lifted the letter to read more. "Ah, yes. 'Her father owns...'" Her eyes widened. "Oh, my. He owns a mercantile. Tsk. Not even a landowner."

"What?" Papa's voice reverberated throughout the room.

Marianne jumped once more.

Mama scowled. "Now, Bennington, please do not shout."

Marianne noticed that Jamie had moved across the room and was staring at a painting. Once again, his flawless manners manifested themselves through this tactful removal from the unfolding drama.

"I will shout in my own home." Papa's trembling increased, and he raised one hand, a finger pointed toward the ceiling. "I will shout in the streets. From the halls of Parliament I will proclaim it. For all the world can clearly see that I have spawned nothing but fools for sons." He slammed his fist on the desk. Documents bounced. A bisque figurine of an elegant lady fell to the floor and shattered. "The daughter of a merchant. Not even an Englishman. An American. The next thing he will be telling me is that he approves of that infernal colonial rebellion."

Mama quickly perused the letter. "No, dear. He speaks only of his little wife—"

Papa snatched the letter from her. "I was not in earnest. Should that day come, I would sail to East Florida and execute him myself."

"Oh, look, Mama." Marianne's voice came out in a much higher pitch than she intended. "Frederick wrote to you and me, too." She picked up the letter bearing her name. "You do not mind, do you, Papa? I shall tell you if he has written anything you must hear."

Papa's shoulders slumped, and his reddened eyes focused on her. "You see, Maria," he said to Mama. "The Almighty saved the best for last." He set a quivering hand on Marianne's shoulder and bent to kiss her forehead. "Our wise, beautiful daughter gives us only joy." He pulled her closer in a gentle embrace. "Would that I could leave all to you, Marianne, for never once in your life have you grieved me."

Marianne's eyes stung mightily. At that moment, she was very near to vowing to God that she would surrender Jamie forever, that she would never hurt her parents as Frederick and Robert and Thomas and William had done. But she gulped back the promise. To vow and to break it would be a sin. To vow and to keep it would mean a lifetime of bitter loneliness.

She stared across the room toward the man she loved, willing him to turn her way, to give her some direction, some wisdom to bear this situation.

But when he did turn, Jamie's wounded frown seemed to shout across the distance that separated them. *You see? I was right. We have no future together.*

Jamie struggled to secure his turbulent emotions to their proper moorings. As captain of his ship, he often managed numerous life-threatening situations concurrently and with haste and acuity. But never had his heart and wits been so at odds in the midst of a tempest. Never had so many threats loomed over all he held dear.

Lord Bennington's rage over Frederick's marriage might extend to Jamie, especially when he discovered the bride was Jamie's beloved cousin, Rachel. Even if the earl did not cast blame on him, Jamie still felt a bitter ache at not being able to comfort Lady Marianne in her distress. Or to declare his love for her. Or to seize her hand and dash from the room, the house, the country, and to make a future with her in the far reaches of America.

Parallel to these agonizing thoughts streamed the keen awareness that this very room might hold documents outlining Lord Bennington's involvement in British defenses of East Florida. Yet this little meeting could scuttle the mission for which Jamie had been sent to England.

He inhaled a calming breath, relaxed his stance and unclenched his hands. Then, just as Lord Bennington looked his way, he directed a sympathetic frown across the room to the earl. If the man had caught him staring at Lady Marianne—

"Templeton, I will see you in private." The glower Lord Bennington directed toward Jamie softened as he gave his countess a slight bow. "My dear, you will excuse us." He turned to Lady Marianne with the same gentleness. "And you, my child."

"But, Papa—"

"Come along, Merry." Lady Bennington used the fond address Jamie had heard Lady Marianne's parents and brother using. Indeed, her sky-blue eyes and merry disposition—subdued now in her unhappiness—warranted such a nickname. Jamie dismissed a fleeting wish that he had the right to address her with such affection. That right would never be his.

As mother and daughter walked toward the door, Lady Marianne cast a quick glance at him. He forced all emotion from his face and gave them a formal bow, then turned to the earl as if the two ladies had never been there.

"What do you know of this?" Lord Bennington lifted Frederick's letter from the desk.

This was trouble Jamie could manage. Man to man. The earl had commended him for his forthrightness, and now he would receive a goodly portion of it. Jamie crossed the room and held the man's gaze.

"They make a handsome couple, milord. Mrs. Moberly is a lady of spotless reputation, pleasant disposition and considerable courage."

Lord Bennington inhaled as if to speak, so Jamie hastened to continue. "You may have heard the account of how she rescued Lady Brigham from being dragged from a flatboat by an alligator."

The earl's wiry white eyebrows arched. "Indeed?" Puzzlement rolled across his face. "When Lady Brigham speaks of her near demise in the jaws of a dragon, she says her husband saved her. She makes no mention of another woman being involved." He studied the letter as if it would set the story straight.

"An oversight, I'm sure, milord. Frederick recounted the incident to me himself." Jamie pushed on with the more important issue. "Mrs. Moberly is the perfect wife for a man who is carving a settlement out of the East Florida wilderness." His own words struck him. Would Lady Marianne be able to survive in that same wilderness after her life of ease? Not likely. Breaking with her was best for her, if not for him, for far too many reasons to count.

"You seem to have some affection for this young woman." Suspicion emanated from the earl's narrowed eyes.

Jamie gave him a measured grin. "I have great affection for her." The earl's eyes widened with shock, so Jamie kept talking. "She is my cousin, reared with me like a sister."

Lord Bennington's face reddened. He placed his fists on the desk and leaned across it toward Jamie. "Are you responsible for this ill-advised union?"

Jamie still stared into his eyes. "No, milord. I was here in England when they formed their attachment.

However, I will confess that when Frederick asked for my help, I complied. They were married aboard my ship by an English clergyman."

Lord Bennington straightened, but his eyes remained narrowed. "You could have omitted that information, and I never would have known it."

"That is true. But our shared business interests will prosper only if we are honest with one another, do you not think?" Honor and duty clashed in a heated battle within Jamie's chest, as they always did when he considered his plans to spy on this man. He quickly doused the conflict. "As I told you earlier, your youngest son is performing his duties admirably as magistrate in St. Johns Towne. Bennington Plantation is prospering prodigiously, as you can see from the oranges we were served at supper tonight. Your warehouse is bursting with the indigo, cotton and rice harvests from East Florida, all grown under Frederick's oversight." Jamie paused to let his words reach the earl's business sense.

Lord Bennington's brow furrowed and his jaw clenched. Again he stared at Frederick's letter, but said nothing.

Jamie decided to press on. "Milord, he has found in Rachel the perfect helpmate for who he is and what he is doing for you." Again, Jamie permitted a cautious grin to grace his lips. "Their mutual devotion proves the truth of the proverb, 'Whoso findeth a wife findeth a good *thing,* and obtained favor of the Lord.'" He wondered if it would be going too far to mention the similar devotion he had noticed between the earl and his countess. But Lord Bennington stiffened, and his white eyebrows bent into an accusing frown.

"And you, Templeton, where will you find *your* wife?"

"Ha!" Surprise and shock forced a too-loud laugh to burst forth, and heat rushed to Jamie's face. He grasped his wayward emotions once again. "I am a seaman, milord. 'Twould be cruel to marry, only to leave my wife alone during my voyages. And of course the sea is no place for a woman." Speaking that truth solidified his decision. He would pry from his heart every fond feeling for Lady Marianne, and marry Lady Liberty and her Glorious Cause.

Lord Bennington studied him with a hardened stare. But gradually, the old man seemed to wilt before Jamie's eyes, and soon he slumped down into his chair as if defeated. "I'll not doubt you again, my boy. Your honesty has proved your worthiness." He waved his hand in a dismissive gesture. "You may go. And if you decide to accompany my reprobate son on his nightly jaunts, do remember that Robert is not Frederick."

Several responses formed in Jamie's mind, not the least of which was that the earl's comment seemed to imply a measure of approval of Frederick and perhaps even Rachel. But the man appeared spent from his emotional evening, so Jamie withheld his remarks. "Very good, milord. Good evening."

As he climbed the stairs to his third-floor suite, a grim sense of satisfaction filled him. He had gained Lord Bennington's trust and could begin his search for information regarding Britain's planned defenses of East Florida. And memories of his tender but short romance with Lady Marianne had been safely tucked away in a remote corner of his mind, to be fondly recalled when he was an old man.

Yet a dull ache thumped against his heart with each ascending step.

Chapter Four

"Your hair is so easy to work with, Lady Marianne." Emma's sweet, round face beamed as she set the silver-handled comb on the dressing table.

"My, Emma." Marianne drew over her shoulder the long braid her maid had just plaited. As always, the work was flawless. "What makes you so happy this evening? Could it be Captain Templeton's handsome young valet, whom I saw you talking with earlier?"

Even in the candlelight, she could see Emma's cheeks turning pink. "Why, no, my lady. I mean—" Her smile vanished, and she chewed her lip. "We spoke for only a few moments. No more than a half hour."

Marianne gave her a reassuring smile. "Do not fear. Mr. Quince seems a pleasant fellow. And being in the good captain's employ, he is no doubt a man of character." A tendril of inspiration grew in her thoughts. "You have my permission to chat with Quince as long as you both have your work completed *and* you meet only in the appropriate common areas of the house where anyone passing can see you. I will tell Mama you have my permission."

Happiness once again glowed on Emma's face. "Oh, thank you, my lady." She curtsied and then hastened to turn down the covers on Marianne's four-poster bed and move the coal-filled bed warmer back and forth between the sheets. Once finished, she returned the brass implement to the hearthside. "Your bed is ready, my lady. Will that be all?" She started to douse the candles beside Marianne's reading chair.

"Leave them." Marianne retrieved her brother's letter from her desk drawer. "I wish to sit and read awhile."

Emma seemed to blink away disappointment. "Shall I wait, my lady?"

"No. You may go." Marianne pulled her woolen dressing gown around her, shivering a little against the cold night air. "I can warm the bed again if I need to. Thank you, Emma."

Her little maid fairly danced from the room with a happiness Marianne envied. How wonderful to find a suitable man to love, one of equal rank, whom Papa and Mama would approve of without reservation. But the heart was an unruly, untamable thing, as evidenced by Frederick's marriage and her own love for Jamie Templeton.

After she and Mama left Papa and Jamie, it had been all she could do to keep from pleading for her mother's support for that love, especially since Mama seemed reconciled to Frederick's marriage. But Mama had excused herself to attend to household matters, leaving Marianne to languish outside Papa's study in hopes of seeing Jamie again. That is, until her brother's missive began to burn in her hand. Here was her ally in the family. Frederick would support her love for Jamie, of that she was certain.

Seated now in her bedchamber in her favorite place to read, Marianne broke the seal on Frederick's letter and unfolded the vellum page. A small, folded piece fell out, so she quickly perused the first one, which repeated the information he'd written to Papa. The details about his dear wife assured Marianne that she would love Rachel and call her "sister" the moment they met.

Wishing that meeting might happen soon, she opened the smaller page—and gasped at the first words. "You must not think to do as I have done, dear sister. For reasons I cannot now explain, other than to say it is for your own happiness and written because I am devoted to you, you must release our mutual friend from the premature vows you traded with him on his last visit to London. To continue this ill-advised alliance will bring only heartache to you both. While he is a man of blameless character, he will not make a suitable husband for the daughter of a peer of the realm. I cannot say more except that you must, you *must* heed my advice, my beloved sister."

Scalding tears raced down Marianne's cheeks. Never had she expected such a betrayal from Frederick. Had they not been the closest of friends all their lives? Had she not frequently stood beside him against their three older brothers, the sons of Papa's first wife, when they sought to bully him? Why did he not wish for her the same happiness he had claimed for himself?

Trembling with anger and disappointment, she resisted the urge to crumple the entire letter. Frederick had signed the first page as if it were the only one, no doubt knowing she would share its contents with Mama. But she reread the second one just to be certain she had not mistaken his cruel intentions. No, she had not. So

Marianne ripped the page to shreds and fed the pieces to the hearth flames, then watched as the fire's ravenous tongues eagerly devoured them.

Childhood memories of Frederick's devotion sprang to mind. His comfort when she fell and scraped her chin. Their forays into Papa's chambers to spy on guests. His gentle teasing, edged with pride, when she emerged from the schoolroom and entered society. Why would he abandon her now? She knelt beside her cold bed and offered up a tearful prayer that she might understand why God would let her fall in love with Jamie and then deny them their happiness.

The response came as surely as if the Lord had spoken to her aloud. *Be at peace. This is the man you will marry.*

"Lord, if this is Your voice, then guide my every step."

Joy flooded her heart—and kept her awake into the early morning hours, planning how she would bring God's will to pass.

Following an afternoon visit to an elderly pensioner who had served the Moberly family for many years, Marianne sat at supper wondering at the different opinions people held about Papa. The old servant had extolled Papa's generosity and kindness, calling him a saint. Yet across the table from Marianne, Robert practically reclined in his chair, his usual protest against Papa's nightly berating. Beside him sat Jamie, in the place where the ranking son should sit, his admiration of Papa obvious in his genial nods and agreeable words to everything Papa said. Doubtless Jamie had no idea that Robert should be sitting to Papa's left. Of course Mama, as always, gazed down the length of the table at Papa with the purest devotion, a sentiment Marianne felt as deeply as a daughter could while still seeing his flaws.

Tonight the topic was the Americans and their foolish rebellion against His Majesty. Some anonymous colonist had written a pamphlet entitled "Common Sense," which was causing considerable stir in London, and Papa seemed unable to contain his outrage.

"Common *non*sense," he huffed as he stabbed a forkful of fish and devoured it. "What do these colonists understand about the responsibilities of government?"

While he fussed between bites about His Majesty's God-given duties to rule, and the Americans as recalcitrant children, Marianne glanced directly across the table at Jamie, whose thoughtful frown conveyed his sympathies for Papa's remarks. Eager to turn the conversation to more pleasant topics, Marianne patted her father's arm.

"But, dearest, if these colonies are so much trouble, why does His Majesty not simply break with them?"

From the corner of her eye, Marianne could see Jamie's own eyes widen for an instant, but she turned her full attention to Papa. He returned a touch to her arm, along with a paternal smile.

"Ah, my dear, such innocence. You had best leave governing to the Crown and Parliament."

Any other time, this response might have soothed Marianne. But for some odd reason, irritation scratched at her mind. She was not a child who should have no opinions, nor should she fail to seek information to enlighten her judgments. She knew of some ladies who expressed their political opinions without censure, including Mama's acquaintance, the duchess of Devonshire.

"I agree with Marianne." Robert's voice lacked its

usual indolence, a sign that he had not yet succumbed to his wine. "Let the colonies fend for themselves for a while without the Crown's protection. Then when they're attacked and plundered by every greedy country on the Continent, they'll come crawling back under His Majesty's rule."

Marianne sensed the bitterness in his wily wording. His break with Papa had lasted less than three weeks before he came "crawling back."

Papa regarded Robert for an instant, then dismissed his words with a snort and a wave of his hand. "Templeton, what do you think of this rebellion?"

While her heart ached for her brother, Marianne could now study Jamie's well-formed face without fear of who might notice her staring at him. A sun-kissed curl had escaped from his queue and draped near his high, well-tanned left cheekbone. His straight nose bore a pale, jagged scar down one side that added character rather than disfigurement. She wondered what adventure had marked him thus, and would ask him at the first opportunity.

"I find it a great annoyance, milord." Jamie's brown eyes burned with indignation. "East Florida is prospering and should soon prove to be the most profitable of England's American colonies. But shipping goods back and forth from London has become difficult since King George declared the wayward thirteen colonies to be in open rebellion. I cannot sail five hundred leagues without one of His Majesty's men-of-war stopping me to be sure I have no contraband."

"Hmm." Papa leaned back in his chair and rubbed his chin. "Have my flag and my letter of passage been helpful?"

"Yes, sir. They have saved me more times than I can count. But every time I am forced to heave to—no less than four times on this last voyage—especially when I'm ordered to change my course for whatever reason the captain might have, it delays shipments. This isn't a problem when I carry nonperishable goods. But our orange and lemon cargos can spoil if not delivered in a timely fashion." Jamie bent his head toward the fragrant bowl of fruit gracing the table. "We barely managed to reach London with these still edible."

As he spoke, Papa's smile broadened. "That's what I like about you, Templeton. No interest in politics. Just business. If those thirteen guilty colonies were of the same mind, there would be no rebellion."

Marianne enjoyed the modest smile Jamie returned to Papa, but Jamie did not look at her. While the two men continued to talk, she cast about for some way to gain his attention. When the perfect scheme came to mind, she knew the Lord was continuing to lead her.

"Papa, may we discuss something other than business and the war?"

His wiry white eyebrows arched in surprise. "Forgive me, my dear. I believe your mother is of the same mind." He bowed his head toward Mama, who had sent more than one disapproving frown his way during the meal. "What would you like to discuss?"

"Why, I wonder if you recall that Mama and I plan to visit St. Ann's Orphan Asylum for Girls tomorrow." She could not keep her gaze from straying to Jamie, who seemed to be particularly interested in the aromatic roast beef the footman had just set before him. "Would you like to make a small contribution to our efforts?"

"Of course, my dear. I shall see to it before I leave

for Parliament tomorrow." He cut into the meat before him, but paused with a bite halfway to his lips. "Why do you not take Templeton with you? I'm certain he would enjoy seeing more of London, and I would feel more at ease if you had the protection of his presence."

Jamie coughed and grabbed his water goblet, swallowing with a gulp. Marianne did not know whether to laugh or offer sympathy. But as long as her plan worked…

"I say, Merry." Robert sat up and leaned across his plate, his cravat nearly touching the sauce on his meat, "My tailor is coming tomorrow to fit Templeton's new wardrobe. You know how petulant these Dutch tailors can be if one misses an appointment, which, I might add, I had a deuce of a time arranging so quickly. Can you not take Blevins or a footman or someone else on your little excursion?"

"It is not an excursion, brother dear. It is ministry." Marianne knew she must continue talking before Papa began to berate Robert, for she could hear Papa's warning growl that always preceded such scolding. "In fact, I do believe you would enjoy it, too. Why not join us? I am certain Mama will not mind waiting until Captain Templeton has been measured. All of us could go." For the life of her—and even to save Robert's dignity—she could not think of another thing to say.

"Just the thing, Moberly." Jamie appeared to be taking up the cause, and Marianne's heart lilted over his kindness. "Let's accompany the ladies. I still don't have my land legs, so the walking'll do me good."

Robert's eyes shifted in confusion, and he blinked several times before his gaze steadied. "*Rather,* my good man. A splendid plan." His grin convinced Marianne he knew they had saved him. But now mischief played across his face in a lopsided smirk. "Shall we not ride, then? You did agree to riding, you know."

Marianne saw the dread in Jamie's faint grimace. One day she herself would see to his riding lessons, for her brother would be merciless in the task. "But, Robert," she said, "you know Mama and I must take our carriage, for we have many items to carry."

"No doubt too many items to leave room for Templeton and me." Robert nudged Jamie. "Do you not agree?"

Jamie's jaw clenched briefly. "I thank you, Lady Marianne, but tomorrow is none too soon to begin my acquaintance with a saddle."

She could not stop a soft gasp. Would he deliberately avoid her? Somehow she managed a careless smile. "Of course, Captain Templeton. Whatever you prefer."

The footman behind her removed her half-eaten meat course and replaced it with a bowl of fruit. Marianne glanced at Papa, who was absorbed in his own bowl. Once again she had deflected his anger and thus defended one of her brothers.

But who would work in her defense? Who would see that her dreams were accomplished? Despite the verse in her morning reading, "Be still and know that I am God," her heart and her faith dipped low with disappointment.

Jamie had thought his heart was settled in the matter of Lady Marianne, especially after his first session with Reverend Bentley, who'd expounded on the nature of British social structures and everyone's place in it. As he'd left the good curate, Jamie had felt certain he'd conquered his emotions. But this supper turned everything upside down. The impossible choice set before him demanded an instant decision, and he could see how his words had wounded her. Ah, to be able to comfort her. Yet there could be no compromise, even though by choosing Moberly's invitation, he was now forced to risk his neck to keep his distance from her. Jamie could not bear the closeness that a carriage would afford, even with her mother present.

He'd never had cause to trust or not trust Moberly. But youthful experiences had taught him that privileged gentlemen found great amusement in putting other men through the worst possible trials to test their mettle. In truth, he'd suffered the same treatment as a cabin boy, and inflicted the same on youths under his command. How else did one become a man?

But did his latest trial have to be on horseback?

Chapter Five

Jamie had always dressed himself, and Quince employed his own manservant, who had remained on his farm in Massachusetts. So it was a challenge for both men to go through the motions of acting as master and valet. But they each put on their best performance for Jamie's fitting with Moberly's tailor.

Soon, however, the tall, finicky man irritated Jamie to the extreme as he roughly measured him, tossed about colorful fabrics and barked orders at his harassed assistant, a dark-skinned boy of no more than thirteen. Other than his helper, the man spoke only to Moberly and only in his native tongue—French—clearly regarding Jamie as less than worthy of being addressed. Just as clearly, the tailor had no idea Jamie was fluent in his language and was having difficulty not responding to his insults.

When he turned at the wrong moment, the slender thread of a man lifted his hand as if to cuff him, but Jamie warned him off with a dark scowl.

"I thought you said he's Dutch," he said to Moberly through clenched teeth.

Sprawled out on the chaise longue in Jamie's suite, Moberly gave the remark a dismissive wave. "If Bennington knew I used a French tailor, the old boy would have apoplexy. All that unpleasantness with the Frogs, you know."

At his words, Jamie's crossness softened. Moberly had a deep need in his life, yet how could Jamie speak to him of God's grace while spying on his father? He lifted a silent prayer that somehow Lady Marianne might deliver the message of God's love her brother needed to hear.

Jamie ducked to avoid the long pin the tailor wielded like a rapier to emphasize his ranting. Used to home-spun woolen and linen, Jamie chafed at the idea of wearing silk, satin and lace, but he'd decided to tolerate Moberly's choice of fabrics and styles. That is, until the tailor unrolled some oddly colored satin and draped it across Jamie's shoulder. What a ghastly green, like the color of the sea before a lightning storm. He would not wear it, no matter what anyone said.

As if reading his mind, Moberly rested a finger along his jawline in a thoughtful pose. "No, no, not that, François. It reminds me of a dead toad. Use the periwinkle. It will drive the ladies mad."

"*Mais non,* Monsieur Moberly." François sniffed. "That glorious *couleur* I save for you, not this…this *rustique.*" He snapped his fingers to punctuate the insult.

"That's it." Jamie snatched off the fabric and flung it away, ignoring the derisive snort from Quince, who observed the whole thing from across the room. "My own clothes will do."

Moberly exhaled a long sigh. "Now, François, look what you've done. I shall have to find another tailor."

The middle-aged tailor gasped. "But, Monsieur—"

"No, no." Moberly stood and walked toward the door. "I shall not have you insult Lord Bennington's business partner and my good friend."

The man paled. "Lord Bennington's business partner?" Now his face flushed with color. "But, Monsieur Moberly, why did you not say so?" He turned to Jamie, his eyes ablaze with an odd fervor. "Ah, Monsieur, eh, Capitaine Templeton, for such a well-favored gentleman, *oui,* we must have the periwinkle." He snapped his fingers at his assistant. *"L'apportes à moi, tout de suite."*

The boy brought forth the muted blue fabric, a dandy's color if ever Jamie saw one. When François draped it over his shoulder, Quince moved up beside Jamie and stared into the long mirror with him.

"Aye, sir, that'll grab the ladies' attention, no mistake." The smirk on his face almost earned him Jamie's fist.

"Bad news about your ship, Templeton." Moberly's comment surprised Jamie. "What's all this about repairs?" Perhaps he'd noticed Jamie's difficulty in restraining himself throughout this ordeal. Indeed, Jamie knew the report about the *Fair Winds* had set him back, for it meant he and Quince would be in London for an unknown length of time instead of just a month.

"The hull requires scraping and recaulking." Jamie stuck out his arm so François could fit a sleeve pattern. "And the storm damage to the mast was worse than I thought. 'Twill take some time to fix it all."

"Ah, well." Moberly's grin held a bit of mischief. "Once we finish the charity bits with Marianne and Lady Bennington, we'll find ways to fill your time."

In the mirror, Jamie traded a look with Quince. When

his first mate, Saunders, arrived early that morning with disappointing news about the sloop, Quince reminded him of their prayers for this mission. God wasn't hiding when the *Fair Winds* received storm damage, and He'd brought them safely to port. The Almighty still had this venture safely in His hands. All the more time to secure important information, Jamie and Quince agreed, but too much time for Jamie to be in Lady Marianne's beguiling presence.

Once the torturous fitting session ended, the now-fawning tailor withdrew, and Jamie gripped his emotions for the coming events. After their midday repast, he and Moberly joined Lady Bennington and Lady Marianne for their visit to the orphan asylum. Yet, other than the brief quickening of his pulse at seeing Lady Marianne—dressed modestly in brown, as was her mother—he had only to deal with riding.

To his surprise, Moberly chose for him a large but gentle mare that followed Lady Bennington's landau like an obedient pup. Jamie began to feel comfortable in the saddle. Moberly also furnished him with a pistol and sword to keep at hand lest unsavory elements be roaming the streets.

The trip across town, however, passed with unexpected ease and some pleasant sightseeing under a bright spring sky. Although the cool March breeze carried the rancid odors of the city waste and horseflesh, making Jamie long for a fresh ocean wind, he did notice some of London's finer points. Upon catching a glimpse of the dome of St. Paul's Cathedral, he decided he must visit its fabled interior. Then some shops along the way caught his eye as possible sources of gifts for loved ones back home or, at the least, ideas for items to export to East Florida.

The carriage and riders entered the wide front courtyard of the asylum as though passing through a palace's gates…or a prison's. The wrought-iron fence's seven-foot pickets were set no more than four inches apart, giving the three-story gray brick building a foreboding appearance, a sad place for children to grow up, in Jamie's way of thinking. Not a scrap of trash littered the grassy yard, which still wore its winter brown, and not a single pebble lay on the paved front walkway. No doubt the denizens of St. Ann's had swept the path with care for the expected visitors. Dismounting with only a little trouble, he saw with gratitude a stone mounting block near the building's entrance. He would have no trouble remounting. Perhaps this horse riding would not be so bad, after all.

Robert assisted his stepmother's descent from the carriage and looped his arm in hers. Jamie had no choice but to offer the same assistance to Lady Marianne. Taking his arm, she gave him a warm smile that tightened when her mother glanced over her shoulder. But the lady's attention was on John the footman, who balanced several large boxes in his arms as he followed them. She gave the man a nod and turned back toward the door. Lady Marianne squeezed Jamie's arm, and a pleasant shiver shot up to his neck. He tried to shake it off, to no avail. Wafting up from her hair came the faint scent of roses, compounding his battle to distance his feelings from her.

"Mama takes such delight in these visits," Lady Marianne whispered as she leaned against his arm. "She loves the children dearly."

He permitted himself to gaze at her for an instant, and his heart paid for it with a painful tug. "It seems you do, too, my lady." Indeed, her eyes shone with an affection far different from the loving glances she'd sent his way. How he longed to learn of all her charitable interests. But that could not be.

"Oh, yes." Her strong tone affirmed her conviction. "They do such fine work here, rearing these girls and teaching them useful skills. My own Emma came from this school."

"Ah, I see." Jamie was glad they reached the massive double front doors before he was required to comment further. He had yet to discover just how deeply Quince cared for Lady Marianne's little maid, but he knew his friend would not play her false. Still, both men would likely end up sailing home with broken hearts.

As the group moved through the doors and into the large entrance hall, which smelled freshly scrubbed with lye soap, the soft thunder of running feet met them. Some hundred and fifty girls of all sizes hastened to assemble into lines, the taller ones in the back ranks, with descending heights down to the twenty or so tiny moppets in front. Each girl wore a gray serge uniform and a plain white pinafore bearing a number.

Jamie swallowed away a wave of sentiment. An orphan himself, he, too, might have been a nameless child raised with a number on his chest, had his uncle not taken him in.

A middle-aged matron in a matching uniform inspected the lines, her plain thin face betraying no emotion as she turned and offered a deep curtsy to their guests. As one, the girls followed suit.

"Welcome, Lady Bennington, Lady Marianne." Another matron, gray-haired and in a black dress, stepped forward. Authority emanated from her such as Jamie had witnessed in the sternest of sea captains, but he also noted a hint of warmth as she addressed the countess.

"Mrs. Martin." Lady Bennington's countenance glowed as she grasped the woman's hands. "How good to see you." Her gaze swept over the assembly. "Good afternoon, my dear, dear girls."

Mrs. Martin lifted one hand to direct the children in a chorus of "Good afternoon, Lady Bennington, Lady Marianne." One and all, their faces beamed with affection for their patronesses.

While the countess made some remarks, Jamie noticed Lady Marianne leaning toward the little ones as if she wished to go to them. The countess then gestured to John the footman, who brought forth one of the boxes. Jamie followed Moberly's lead and moved back against the wall while the two ladies disbursed knitted mittens, scarves and caps they and their friends had made. The children's joy and gratitude punctured Jamie's self-containment, and he tried to grip his emotions. Still, breathing became more difficult as the scene progressed.

When Lady Marianne knelt on the well-scrubbed wooden floor among the smallest orphans, gathering in her arms a wee brown-haired tot to show her how to don her mittens, Jamie's last defenses fell away, and a shattering ache filled his chest.

Lord, forgive me. I love this good lady beyond all sense, beyond all wisdom. Only through Your guidance can I walk away from her. Yet if, in Your great goodness, You could grant us happiness—

Jamie could not permit himself to complete the prayer. He would neither request nor expect the only answer that would give him personal joy. Not when there was a revolution to be fought and a fourteenth colony to draw into the mighty fray. If he must lose at love, so be it.

But he must not lose at war, for in that there was so much more at stake—nothing less than the destiny of a newborn nation.

Chapter Six

"Captain Templeton looks quite presentable in his new riding clothes, do you not think, Grace?" Marianne sat in the open carriage beside Mama's companion, whom she had borrowed for today's outing to Hyde Park. "Robert approves, or he would not have agreed to bring the American with us." She herself had been stunned when Jamie walked into the drawing room just an hour ago, for the cut of his brown wool coat over his broad shoulders and the close lines of his tan breeches over his strong legs emphasized his superior masculine form. Why, if not for his colonial speech, he could pass for a peer of the realm.

Grace looked toward the two men, who rode their horses slightly ahead of the open black landau. "Yes, my lady. The captain has the appearance of a true gentleman." She pursed her lips, and her eyes took on a merry glint. "And I do believe with a little practice, his horsemanship will improve."

Marianne responded with a knowing smile as she searched Grace's face. But the lady's countenance bore no hint of feeling for Jamie other than her usual kindheartedness. A modicum of shame warmed Marianne's cheeks, despite the brisk March breeze that fanned over them. She need never be jealous of dear Grace.

"I agree. But I am not altogether certain my brother can be trusted to see to Captain Templeton's riding lessons."

A shadow flitted over Grace's face. "Surely you do not think Mr. Moberly would permit the American to be harmed." She gazed at Robert, her eyes glowing with a softness that Marianne had never before noticed.

Withholding a gasp of realization, she forced her own gaze to settle on Robert. This morning she had observed the usual shadows beneath his eyes and his languid posture, which bespoke his many nights of intemperance and little sleep. Could pious Grace care for such a reprobate? Marianne hated to think of her brother in terms their father would use, but Robert truly met that description.

Before she could respond to Grace's concern, Robert hailed another open carriage passing from the other direction. "Ho there, Highbury. Do stop for a chat." He waved to Wiggins to stop Marianne's conveyance.

The young man called to his driver, who reined his horses to a stop. Beside Mr. Highbury sat his sister, Lady Eugenia, and Marianne felt a rush of pleasure at seeing these friends. Due to Lord Highbury's Whig politics, Papa no longer associated with him, and out of loyalty, both families deferred to their patriarchs.

Robert presented Jamie to the Highburys, and pleasantries flew about the little group.

"I see you and Lady Marianne have taken advantage of this rare sunny day, too, Mr. Moberly." Lady Eugenia gave Robert a warm smile, and her eyelashes fluttered.

Marianne heard Grace's soft sigh beside her. It was clear Eugenia was flirting with Robert. But Lord Highbury would never permit her to marry a second son.

Robert, all charm and energy now, bowed in his saddle. "My lady, it must be Fate that brought us together."

"I absolutely concur." Mr. Highbury's gaze settled on Grace, and he nodded to her. "Even the ground is dry. We simply *must* take a turn around the park."

With all in agreement, the ladies were assisted from their carriages. While Eugenia maneuvered her way toward Robert, Marianne managed to edge close to Jamie. Mr. Highbury seemed more than agreeable to pairing with Grace, bowing and offering his arm to her.

"Your riding has improved, Captain Templeton." Marianne gave his arm an expectant look.

"Thank you, my lady." He offered it without meeting her gaze. "I would not call myself a horseman, but at least I've remained astride."

A light laugh escaped her, as light as her heart felt over walking beside him on this fine day. "Your modesty is as refreshing as today's weather." Indeed, the invigorating air in Hyde Park carried no hint of the unpleasant city odors.

"It is a good day." He lengthened his stride, as if eager to catch the other two couples walking several yards ahead of them on the brown grass.

After several seconds of trying to keep up with him, Marianne tugged at his arm. "Perhaps when your ship is repaired, we can enjoy a short voyage on the Thames, as we did last year."

Jamie stopped, but his gaze remained on the others as the distance between them widened. "I am sure Lord Bennington will be too busy for such an excursion."

Again, Marianne laughed, a strained sound she hoped Jamie would not notice. "Of course Papa will be too busy. But Robert—"

"Ah, yes. Robert." Jamie looked at her, and his eyes filled with concern. "My lady, I would not wish to presume…anything. However, Moberly seems to regard me as a friend. It may be that I can have some good influence on his, um, habits." He glanced away. "Please continue to walk with me."

"Yes, of course." Her heart dipped in disappointment.

They resumed their stroll across the almost empty park. She did not wish to discuss Robert, but he was very dear to her. Jamie's Christian charity toward her brother moved her.

"I have often spoken to my brother about his lack of spiritual interest. Our brother Frederick is also concerned about him. But Robert assures us he will take care of that matter when he grows older."

"An error too many people make, if I may be so bold, my lady."

A hint of dread touched Marianne's heart. "I hope you will be bold enough to speak to him of Christ's redemption."

Jamie's expression grew thoughtful, but he did not seem inclined to say more. Her heart heavy for more than one reason, Marianne gazed around the landscape, where trees had begun to bud and tiny shoots of green appeared in the brown grass.

"Moberly would benefit from our prayers." Jamie's deep, rich voice resounded with concern. "In truth, though I would not judge the man, I fear that his immortal soul is in danger."

Gratitude for his observation filled Marianne. "I have the same fear. Oh, Jamie—"

Wincing, he stopped again, but avoided her gaze. "Please, my lady."

The pain and censure in his voice cut into her. "I—I mean, Captain Templeton." She resumed her stroll, and he followed suit. "What can we do for him?"

"I would not wish for Lady Bennington to think ill of me, since I am a guest in her house, but I have considered going to one of these routs with Moberly. They're all he speaks of, and seem to consume his life." Jamie paused. "What does a rout involve?"

The tightness of his tone almost made Marianne laugh. "Why, a rout is just a gathering at someone's home. The hostess invites a huge number of people who want to be seen and to see others." She sobered. "But Robert only says he's going to a rout to avoid stating his true plans. Oh, he may indeed attend one, but he then goes gambling and—"

"You need not continue, my lady." Jamie cast a quick glance her way and patted her hand, sending a pleasant shiver up her arm. "I understand your meaning." He studied the ground before them. "Nevertheless, I feel compelled to go with him."

They walked in silence for a few moments. Jamie's large form blocked much of the breeze that fluttered the edges of her cape and carried the scent of his woody shaving balm in her direction. She could not resist the temptation to lean against his arm, as if she could absorb some of his strength. But he seemed to sway away from her to a degree so small she might have been mistaken.

"You would put yourself in temptation's way...for

Robert?" Marianne felt tears forming. Jamie's godly goodness and selflessness were just two of the reasons she loved him.

"By God's grace, I have so far resisted such temptations. The Book of Proverbs fully addresses the subject, and it is my guide."

"But there are other dangers." Marianne shuddered to think of the vicious packs of wellborn miscreants who wandered the night streets of London filled with evil intentions. Thievery, beatings, even murder were their games, and if they chose their victims carefully, they never had to pay.

Jamie nodded. "I'm sure there are. But our Lord dined with the worst of sinners that He might demonstrate God's love to them."

"Oh, Jamie… Captain…" She again tugged him to a stop. "Our Lord knew when and how He would die. He was in full control of everything. You are not. Why would you risk your life this way?" She argued against her own heart, for she did love Robert and longed for his salvation.

Jamie drew himself up to his full height, yet his gaze into her eyes was gentle and full of conviction. "Lady Marianne, there are causes worth giving one's life for. Christ died to free us from sin and give us eternal life. Should I not willingly give *my* life for another man… and for freedom?" He clamped his lips closed and shook his head. "We should join the others."

Confusion filled her. Jamie seemed to think he had spoken amiss, yet she found no fault in his words. "I am deeply grateful for your willingness to befriend Robert. I will pray God will bless your efforts." *And that He will protect you both, my love.*

* * *

Jamie was surprised so little time had passed during his torturous walk at Lady Marianne's side. A few more minutes alone with her would be his undoing. He could see she understood his concern for Moberly and that she truly loved her brother. This, along with her earnest words of faith—and the heady scent of her rose perfume—created in him a powerful yearning to confess his love that he was scarce able to deny. His weak, silent prayer for strength brought no relief, and the journey across the park left his emotions ravaged by the time they reached the others.

Not one of the four seemed to have missed Lady Marianne, and certainly not him. With great effort, he forced his mind to address this fortuitous meeting with young Highbury, a lad of perhaps twenty-one. Jamie had learned Lord Highbury was a prominent Whig who, with others of his party, opposed King George's vile treatment of the colonists. In fact, their opposition extended to refusing to take their seats in the current session of Parliament. Jamie's orders from General Washington included uncovering any allies among the Whigs who might help the Revolution, but Bennington's social circle excluded those very men.

"Captain Templeton." Lady Eugenia gazed at him, her eyelashes fluttering. "You must tell us all about the conflict in the colonies."

A pretty girl somewhat younger than her brother, she had a merry disposition, and her flirting was harmless. Yet Jamie would remember his station, at least the way these aristocrats might view it, and be pleasantly formal. He had long ago rejected any plans to deflect Lady Marianne's affections by showing interest in someone else. If he must break her heart and his own, it would not be through deceit.

"You must forgive me, Lady Eugenia." He bowed to her. "My travels at present do not take me to the troubled areas."

"But, my good man," Mr. Highbury said, "surely you hear news of the war…or at least rumors." An intense look flickered in his eyes, and he leaned toward him.

Jamie smiled and lifted one shoulder in a light shrug. "Sir, the North American continent is vast. An entire war can be fought at one end without a ripple reaching the other." He observed the disappointment in Highbury's expression, but could say nothing more. The lad might indeed be sympathetic to the Cause, but his emotions were too much in evidence to invite Jamie's trust.

"Oh, bother." Moberly emitted a long sigh. "Must we talk of politics? It is beyond enough that our fathers engage in their tedious debates over such things."

"I agree, dear brother." Marianne put one arm around Lady Eugenia's waist. "For my own part, I have missed dear Genie very much these past months. We simply must have more time together. I think Mama should give a ball. Everyone has been in London since October, and here it is March. Yet she has not done her share of entertaining."

"Oh, a ball at Bennington House." Lady Eugenia's voice trilled with excitement. "Indeed, that would be lovely."

"*Rather,*" Mr. Highbury said with a chuckle. "That is, if you don't think Lord Bennington will cast us out for disloyalty." He sent Jamie a meaningful look.

Jamie returned a placid smile and looked to Moberly

to respond for them. But inwardly, he groaned. In his search for allies, the last thing he needed was a foolish young pup who might ruin everything.

Chapter Seven

"Lord, I trust You to bring them safely home." Bundled in her warmest woolen dressing gown, Marianne sat by the window of her bedchamber and watched the darkened street two stories below. Her prayer, which she had repeated countless times over the past several hours, soothed her emotions each time anxious thoughts beset her. Why this night was somehow different, she could not guess, but it seemed something sinister hung in the air.

After supper, Jamie had accompanied Robert and his friend Tobias Pincer on their nightly wanderings. Marianne had been hard put not to ask their destination, but such a question would have been beyond propriety. Perhaps they had indeed gone to a rout. In her first season, she had attended one and found it a crushing bore. But other than an occasional supper at the home of some friend, Papa preferred for Mama and her to stay home in the evenings, saying the night was for the devil and his dark deeds. Never mind that much of London's social life occurred after sunset or that many political compromises were made over a fine supper.

This very evening, from Billings House across Grosvenor Square, soft sounds of party merriment reached through Marianne's slightly open window.

She yawned and snuggled into her wrap to ward off the night chill. Perhaps she was being foolish. But after going to bed she had lain awake for well over an hour, at last rising to light a candle and find comfort in the Scriptures. Her eyes fell on Psalm 27:1. "The Lord is my light and my salvation; whom shall I fear? The Lord is the strength of my life; of whom shall I be afraid?" Whether or not Robert sought God's protection, Jamie would, and in the coal-black streets of London, the Lord would be his light.

Her eyelids grew heavy, and she rested her head against a pillow on the windowsill. A cold breeze sent images of ships floating through her mind, and she dreamed of standing beside Jamie aboard his *Fair Winds* while the sails filled with wind and carried them to faraway shores.

Sitting up with a jolt, she realized that noise no longer came from the party across the Square, and silence ruled the night. But, no, distant sounds drew nearer. The muted thuds of a horse's hooves on the dirt street, the rattle of carriage wheels. Hurried whispers. Jamie's deep voice. And John the footman, who had kept vigil at the front door at Marianne's request. She shoved the window farther open and leaned out to see a hired hackney driving away and forms disappearing through the front door beneath her.

She dashed from her room and downstairs to meet them in the front entry.

"Milady, 'tis Mr. Moberly." John's bushy eyebrows met in a frown as he and Jamie struggled to half carry, half drag Robert into the light of a single candle illuminating the hall.

"Go back to bed, Marianne." Jamie jerked his head toward the stairway as he knelt and let Robert slump against his chest. "We can manage."

Jamie's breath came in deep gasps. Robert lay silent.

"Let me help." Marianne knelt in front of her brother, whose forehead bore a bloody lump. "What happened?" Did Jamie realize he had not used her title?

"Go upstairs." Jamie used a stern tone, one that must cause his sailors to quake, but only made her cross.

"I will not. John, take Mr. Moberly into Papa's library. We can tend him there." She could see the footman's hesitation. "Do as I say."

"Yes, milady." John sent Jamie an apologetic look.

Still working to catch his breath, Jamie shook his head. "To his bedchamber."

"No," Marianne said. "We would have to pass Papa's door, and he might hear us."

Now Jamie leaned toward her, and she could see the raw emotion in his eyes. "Madam, it may turn out that Lord Bennington would actually want to have some final words with his son."

Marianne drew in a sharp breath. She stared down the length of Robert's drooping form and saw a scarlet stain oozing through a slash on the left side of his yellow waistcoat. "Oh, Robert—" She clamped down on her emotions. Tears would not help him.

Jamie glanced up the wide front staircase and released a weary sigh. "You're right. To the library, John."

While Marianne took charge of the candle, the men carried Robert down the dark hallway beside the staircase to Papa's library. Inside, she pointed. "On the settee."

"Milady, the blood," John said.

"Never mind. Mama is planning to redo this room." Perhaps not soon, but she did redecorate often.

With Robert on the long settee, Jamie fell to his knees beside him, still breathing heavily.

"John, fetch clean rags and water." Marianne hurried to the hearth for more light, bringing back a candlestick with three candles. She placed it on a table in front of the settee. Robert smelled of sweat and brandy…and blood. "What happened?" She unbuttoned his waist-coat and shirt to reveal a one-inch red gash on the left side of his pale, doughy chest. Although it still oozed blood, the color was crimson, not dark as from a deeper wound. Refusing to succumb to the horror of it, she rolled his linen shirttail and pressed it against the cut.

Jamie leaned against the settee arm. "Thank You, Lord. It's not as deep as I feared." He shook his head as if to clear it, and studied Robert's forehead. "This is why he's unconscious. I feared the stab wound was—"

"Yes. No doubt the blade was aimed at his heart." Relief soothed Marianne's ravaged emotions, and she released a few tears. "What happened?" she asked again.

Jamie blinked, as if struggling to focus his eyes. "It is sufficient to say that Moberly's gambling luck did not follow him into the streets."

"Footpads?" She could not think anyone would attempt to murder the son of an earl. It must have been true criminals, not bored aristocrats up to no good.

"Aye. And a scurvier bunch I've never seen." He grimaced. "Forgive me."

She laughed softly. "I am not so fragile that I cannot bear such words. My brothers—"

"Lady Marianne." Blevins marched into the library

wearing his usual black livery, but his sleeping cap instead of his periwig. Behind him, John carried the requested items and more. "Please permit me to attend Mr. Moberly."

"Yes. Thank you." Marianne stood and moved back.

Jamie struggled into a nearby chair, grasping his left forearm with his right hand. His blue wool coat was torn in several places and lightly splattered with bloodstains.

"Jamie!" She reached toward his arm, but he pulled it away. "You must let me look at your injury."

"Just a scratch or two." His eyes still did not focus. "I'm not injured." Belying his words, he touched the back of his head and winced. "Not badly, anyway." He glanced at Blevins and John, who were huddled over Robert, and sent her a warning frown. "Please, my lady, go to bed."

She settled into a chair next to him. "When I am assured of Robert's—and *your*—health, I shall retire. Until then, you will have to endure my company." She would have given him a mischievous smirk had not Robert been lying there having his side sewn together by the incomparable Blevins.

Jamie watched the butler's doctoring methods with interest and growing respect. He himself had stitched up numerous wounds during his whaling days. But he was in no condition to do this job. He'd certainly not expected to see such violence on the streets of London, especially against the son of an earl. Jamie couldn't be altogether certain Tobias Pincer had not orchestrated the attack. At the very least, the man proved to be a worthless coward. If Moberly recovered, as it now seemed he would, Jamie would give a full accounting of his gaming companion.

After they had eaten supper at Lady Bennington's table, the three of them had attended a strange gathering at a large private home, one of those routs, during which a throng of people milled about with no apparent purpose. Jamie met several people but was never presented to a host. Afterward, Moberly and Pincer insisted their next stop must be a gambling establishment. While Jamie stood near a window in the dim and smoky room, the two sat at cards downing drink after drink. Or perhaps Pincer didn't drink all that much.

With minimal knowledge of the game, Jamie still could sense that Pincer was helping Moberly to win. When they decided at last to leave, Moberly's pockets bulged with notes and gold coins. And it was he whom the footpads attacked. If Jamie hadn't been last out the door, he might have suffered the same fate. As it was, he'd been able to drive away the scoundrels with a few blows of the ebony cane Moberly had loaned him for the evening. As many attackers as there were, perhaps three or four, Jamie thought he and Moberly had come out of it fairly well, especially since Pincer disappeared the moment they exited the gaming hall. But then, footpads generally proved to be cowards if their victims fought back.

Sitting in Lord Bennington's library generated an instinct in one part of Jamie's mind. He should be trying to locate a chest or hidden compartment where maps or plans or royal communications might be kept. But another part of him could think only of Moberly and his near encounter with death.

Jamie's dizziness began to clear, but the injury on

the back of his head still pounded deep into his skull. He touched it, drawing Lady Marianne's anxious gaze. Dropping his hand to the chair arm, he decided he'd have to ignore the sticky lump until he could get to his quarters and have Quince check the damage.

Still, a surge of pride rolled through him. He'd never imagined Lady Marianne would be awake, much less that she would view her brother's injuries without swooning. His lady had courage and pluck.

His lady? Try though he might, he couldn't dislodge the pleasant notion nor stop the accompanying warmth spreading through his chest. If not for the blood on his hand, he might have reached out to grasp hers. Thank the Lord for the blood.

Before a new day dawned, he must speak to Moberly about his eternal soul, which so far the Almighty had mercifully spared.

Marianne insisted upon overseeing Robert's transfer to his bedchamber, and informed Blevins that she would sit with her brother until morning. "You and John must retire for the night so you both can see to your duties tomorrow."

In the dimly lit room, she noticed just a tiny flicker in the butler's eyes, perhaps wounded pride, for he never failed in any of his duties no matter how late he had labored the night before. But he gave her a perfect servant's bow. "Of course, Lady Marianne. Shall I summon Miss Kendall to accompany you?"

Marianne glanced toward the small side chamber where John had gone to wake Ian, Robert's young valet. If she, Jamie and Ian were to keep watch over her brother, propriety demanded the presence of another lady in the room.

"Yes, please."

Ian soon emerged fully dressed and began to assess the situation. Like Blevins and John, he demonstrated no emotion, but Marianne could see concern in his eyes as he arranged Robert's dressing gown, pillows and covers.

Jamie excused himself to wash up, and Marianne settled into a chair beside Robert's bed just as Grace joined her for the vigil. Within a half hour, Jamie returned, but gently refused Marianne's request to check the lump on his head.

"Quince cleaned it and says it's nothing, my lady." Jamie settled into a chair across the room. When he fell asleep, with his long legs extended out in front of him and his head resting back on a pillow, Marianne spent half her time watching him and half watching Robert.

In the early morning hours, her brother became delirious, thrashing and mumbling nonsensically. Jamie awakened, and he and Ian held Robert fast so the stitches would not tear. Soon he quieted. Marianne wiped his face and freshened the cool, damp cloth on his forehead. The crisis passed, but she could not be certain another would not strike. All the while, she was aware of Grace's soft prayers…and her tears. Assured of her brother's progress, Marianne moved to the small settee where Grace sat.

A slim horizontal thread of gray appeared on the floor beneath the window, announcing dawn's arrival. Marianne looked over to see Jamie stir awake, then walk to the bedside just as Robert opened his eyes.

Relief swept through her, and she clasped hands with Grace.

"Well, old man," Jamie said. "I believe you got the worst of it."

Robert coughed out a weak laugh, then grimaced and grabbed at his wound. "Ahh. Hurts. Never thought—"

"Shh." Marianne rushed to him. "Rest easy, Robert dear." She dampened another fresh cloth for his forehead. "You're safe at home."

He turned his bloodshot eyes toward her. "Merry." Then beyond her. "Miss Kendall. Ian." A wry smile lifted one corner of his lips. "I say, have you all kept vigil? Am I going to die?" A sardonic tone accompanied his gaze around the room. "What, Father did not come to bid me farewell?"

"No, Robert." Her heart aching for him, Marianne applied the compress. "We did not wake him."

"No, of course not." Robert grunted. "By all means, do not disturb the patriarch." His bitter tone cut into her. "Fine Christian father that he is." He closed his eyes and leaned into the cold cloth as she pressed it against his temple.

She swallowed an urge to reprimand him. "Shh. You must rest."

"Hmm." He rolled his head toward Jamie. "I say, Templeton, how did you enjoy your first night out in London?" He chuckled, then coughed and again clutched at his injury.

Standing on the opposite side of the bed, Jamie glanced at Marianne and then frowned down at Robert. "Can't say I'd like to repeat it." Again he looked at her, this time with a question in his eyes.

Without a word spoken, she understood him and quietly resumed her place beside Grace. Surely after this night, Jamie would see how well they worked together. How they could communicate without speaking. How their very souls were knit together in purpose.

A sense of urgency pulsed through Jamie. Many times he'd seen a wounded man become receptive toward God's call at the height of his pain, only to recover and forget his mortality. Jamie had not a single doubt that the Lord had permitted this attack to capture Moberly's attention. But where to begin? Jamie already had learned much from Reverend Bentley's tutoring, especially that these aristocrats could take offense if wrongly addressed. But he must not lose this opportunity. *Wisdom, please, Lord.*

"You must forgive us for not waking Lord Bennington. Our main concern was tending your wounds and seeing you rested."

Moberly shrugged against his pillow. "I doubt he would have been concerned." The pain ripping across his face appeared more like damaged emotions than an injured body.

Jamie sat on the edge of the bed, hoping to set a mood of familiarity. Hoping Moberly would not be offended. "My friend, even the tenderest of earthly fathers can disappoint us."

Moberly snorted, then cried out and grabbed his chest. "What is this? What happened to me?" Teeth gritted, he shoved away the goose down cover and clawed at his nightshirt.

Jamie grasped his hands. "I recommend you leave it alone, sir. You received a nasty knife wound, but

Blevins stitched it together very nicely. Let's don't break it open."

Moberly's eyes widened. He touched the area with his fingertips. "Right over my heart. I might've died." He slumped back and looked vacantly toward the bed's canopy. "I might have died."

"God's mercy was on you," Jamie said. "No mistaking that."

"Yes," Moberly whispered. His gaze returned to Jamie. "Yes." A stronger tone. "Thank God. And you." His eyes grew red and moist. "You saved my life."

Jamie leaned a bit closer. "Perhaps. But I was merely God's instrument. You're right to thank Him."

Moberly gave out a mirthless laugh. "But why would He bother when my own father regards me as a parasite and cares not whether I live or die?"

His words slammed into Jamie's heart. How could anyone understand why Lord Bennington treated his sons so callously? "My friend, God desires to be a father to you. He longs to save your eternal soul. This is why you didn't die in the street last night."

Moberly appeared to consider the idea, and fear filled his face. "No. I have waited too long, done too much—"

"No." Jamie gripped his arm as he would a drowning man's. Moberly's words indicated he comprehended his own sinfulness. Surely that meant it wasn't too late for him. "Don't believe that lie. The blood Jesus Christ shed on the cross covers every sin. God's grace is offered as a free gift to you right now. All you need to do is accept it."

Moberly seemed to fold into himself. "No. It cannot be that simple." His gaze hardened. "There are rules and rituals and *righteousness.*" His lips curled. "All the things I despise about religion and—"

"No!" Jamie prayed Robert wouldn't take his stern tone as an affront. "Christ's death and resurrection are sufficient to save the worst sinner. If we were required to do even one small thing other than accept His grace, none of us could be saved. Did He not say to the thief who was crucified beside him 'Today thou shalt be with me in Paradise'?"

Moberly's dark eyebrows met in a frown, and his left eye twitched. "I thought perhaps the man received a special dispensation."

Jamie shook his head. "I believe, in fact I am more than certain, that thief was meant for an example to us. As he was saved, so we can be saved." He leaned close again. "Believe in the Lord Jesus Christ, Moberly, and you *will* be saved."

A long, narrow swath of light shone from beneath the drapes onto the Wilton carpet at the center of the room. The smell of sweat vied with the scents of soap and lavender for preeminence. Moments passed without a sound in the room, not even a rustle. Some hours ago, a maid had started a fire in the hearth, and Ian kept it burning. A barely audible sigh came from across the room, and Jamie guessed both ladies were praying. He wondered how much longer he could sit up without rest.

"I will try," Moberly whispered.

Jamie's energies vanished, and his posture drooped. This was useless. The man did not grasp God's truth at all. Jamie's head pounded, and he ached to go to his own chambers, his own bed. He glanced at Lady Marianne. Her eyes reflected the same weariness he felt. But Miss Kendall, who always carried herself with reserve, now sat at the edge of her seat and stared toward Moberly with her jaw set firmly and fire in her eyes. Jamie shook off his lethargy, which he realized was nothing less than the work of eternal darkness. He would, he *must,* continue his struggle for Moberly's soul.

"Faith is not something you can try, Moberly. Accept God's gift of eternal life, or reject it. There is no middle ground."

Moberly blinked. He opened his mouth...and closed it. Another moment passed. "I see. Yes, I think you are right about that."

"Well, then?"

He chuckled, but winced as if the effort pained him. "A bit pushy, aren't we?" Another chuckle, then he sobered as a tranquil expression smoothed the premature lines around his eyes. "I feel...there is...*peace*... here." He touched his chest and spoke in a hushed voice. "Peace such as I have never felt in my life. It floods me, floods my very soul." His eyes glistened with hope. "I have always known about God. I have seen His goodness in my stepmother and my sister. But now I *believe.* I accept Him. Why, Templeton, I think if I were to die at this moment, God Himself would take me up in His arms."

Jamie experienced his own flood of emotions—joy, gratitude, tranquility—and he cleared his throat. Before he could offer an affirmation to his new brother in Christ, Lady Marianne appeared at the bedside and kissed Moberly, pressing her cheek against his and blending her sweet tears with her brother's. Beyond her, Miss Kendall stood with lifted chin, her tear-filled eyes ablaze with victory. Jamie gave her a nod. When his energies had failed, her prayers had infused him with strength enough to complete his mission.

A sharp thump on the bedchamber door caused them all to jump. Before anyone could respond, Lord Bennington threw open the door and strode into the room, staring about at the occupants. Rage rode on his wrinkled brow, and his lips curled in a snarl.

"*What* is going on in here?"

Chapter Eight

Marianne stood like a shield in front of Robert's bed. Behind her, she heard his quiet groan, the sound of a man wounded deep within his heart. She had no doubt that if Papa had entered the room one minute sooner, her brother's immortal soul would still be in danger, perhaps lost forever.

"Robert was stabbed and robbed by footpads last night." She grabbed a quick, quiet breath that she might appear calm. "If not for Captain Templeton, he would have died."

Papa stared at her as if she were crazy. "Footpads, you say? Common street ruffians dared to assault a son of mine?" He strode toward the bed. "Move aside, daughter." His eyes blazed as he inspected Robert from head to toe as he would a piece of furniture. "Well, boy, are you going to live?"

Marianne saw a flash of anger on Jamie's face—fiery eyes and lips clamped shut. But she moved close to Papa and slipped her hand in his, hoping her presence might soften him. Robert's eyelids drooped with feigned laziness, and his lips formed a smirk, the bored expression he wore when Papa was present.

"I suppose I must live," her brother muttered. "If only to show my gratitude to Templeton here. 'Twould be deuced bad-mannered of me to pop off after all his trouble."

Papa looked across the bed at Jamie. "Are you injured?" His eyes blazed.

Jamie shrugged and returned a crooked grin that caused Marianne's heart to skip. "I believe we did more damage than we received, my lord."

"Ha!" Papa fisted his free hand and pummeled the air. "That's the spirit." He looked at Robert again. "Do plan to survive as best you can. With these despicable wars going on, I do not have time for a funeral."

Marianne thought she detected a tiny crack in Papa's voice, but perhaps it was wishful thinking.

"Marianne." He patted her hand. "You and Miss Kendall are dismissed. I commend your interest in your brother's welfare, but in the future, leave such ministrations to the servants."

She bit her bottom lip to keep from responding with anger. This was the closest to scolding her Papa ever came, but it was inconsequential in light of Robert's tragedy.

"Yes, Papa." She nudged past him and bent to kiss her brother's cheek. "I love you, dear one. Please rest until you are healed." The responding tear in the corner of his eye nearly undid her, and she hurried from the room to hide her own tears.

If Jamie had held the slightest scruple against spying on Lord Bennington, it just vanished. No decent man should treat a son so callously, no matter how that son behaved. But, like their king, these English aristocrats seemed to think their ranks and titles granted them the right to use all other beings in any manner they chose. From everything Jamie had seen, he could only conclude that, instead of seeing Moberly as a son to nurture and guide, Bennington had let him grow up like a weed and then despised him for it.

"Captain Templeton." His tone sounding almost jovial, the earl spoke across the bed as if Moberly were not there. "Lady Bennington has asked my permission to give a ball in your honor. She says your dancing master has given his approval for you to participate in some of the less complex dances. What do you say?"

Remember why you are here. Swallowing his bitterness on behalf of Moberly, Jamie forced a smile and a bow. "I would be honored, my lord."

"Very good. Now, I am off to Whitehall." The earl looked at Moberly with a bland expression. "See if you can keep my son from doing further damage to himself."

"Yes…my lord."

Bennington clearly did not notice Jamie's clenched teeth, for he strode from the room with his head held high, wearing his importance like a crown.

Moberly chuckled softly. "Let it go, Templeton. That's what I have to do. The old man is…what he is."

Jamie regarded his friend. Weariness once again deepened the premature lines on his face, and his pale, blotchy skin gave evidence of many late nights and much drinking. But a soft new light shone in Moberly's eyes, encouraging Jamie. He felt a pressing need to examine its cause.

"Before Lord Bennington came in, we were having a discussion—"

"Ah, yes." Moberly breathed out a lengthy sigh and tugged his covers up to his chin. "About my *new* Father..." He yawned, then winced, perhaps in pain. "We must talk about that soon...." His voice faded, and his eyelids drooped.

The young valet hovered near, so Jamie walked to the door. "I'll leave him in your good care."

More than exhausted, he trudged up the staircase to his own chamber, where in spite of his best efforts to keep quiet, he woke Quince.

"Did you learn anything?" Quince jumped up from the trundle bed and inspected Jamie's head wound, tsking his concern.

"No." Jamie waved him off and walked to the window to close the heavy velvet drapes. "The Lord seems to have altered my mission for the time being." He watched his friend, whose clownish smile hinted at some secret. "All right, then, out with it."

Quince cleared his throat, obviously pleased with himself. "If you want to learn what's going on with the aristocracy, it pays to fraternize with their servants."

Jamie threw himself on the four-poster bed, neglecting even to remove his shoes. "Brilliant. Absolutely brilliant." He rolled over and burrowed beneath the counterpane. "That's why you took leave of your considerable properties in Massachusetts and are acting as my valet." Sleep beckoned, but he could feel Quince tugging off the heavy footwear. This business of having a body servant had its advantages.

"Ah," Quince said, "but when one discovers where

the master keeps his important papers…and the best time to access them—"

Jamie bolted up in the bed, fully awake and fully aware of the lump on the back of his head. He grunted, but shook off the pain and punched Quince's arm. "Good work, man. Tell me everything. How do we get to them?"

Chapter Nine

"Do listen to me, Robert." Marianne mustered the crossest look she could manage while feeling so happy. "It is far too soon for you to be riding again." Seated at the smaller of two oak tables in the sunny breakfast room, she turned to Jamie, who stood serving himself at the buffet. His dashing appearance in his newest gray riding clothes pleased her very much. "Captain Templeton, you must speak reason into my brother's barely healed head."

"Nonsense." Across the table from her, Robert waved his hand in a dismissive gesture. "I have lain about for nearly two weeks while the weather gets warmer, the grass becomes greener and everyone who's anyone is out and about." He popped a bite of toast and jam into his mouth.

The twinkle in her brother's eyes heartened Marianne. He truly did seem to have recovered, as evidenced by his voracious appetite. He would soon regain those few pounds lost during his convalescence.

"Then at least ride in the carriage with Miss Kendall

and me." Marianne tilted her head toward Grace, taking in the scent of her lavender perfume.

"Lady Marianne," Jamie said, "the surgeon has given Mr. Moberly permission to resume his activities as he wishes. Doubtless he'll be happy to be out in the fresh air."

As he took his place beside her, amusement lifted one corner of his lips, and again Marianne was encouraged. And even more in love with him than before. Since Robert's injury, Jamie had spent hours with her brother every day, discussing Scriptures and other pleasant topics. The result was that, in these recent days, Robert had made every effort to be at the supper table on time, had borne up under Papa's comments well and had completely stopped drinking spirits—all due to Jamie's influence. If the good captain thought to dissuade her from her affections for him, he was certainly going about it in the wrong way.

"Very well, then." She sniffed, still pretending to be cross. "Just remember that I have advised a better course."

But she felt anything but cross. Today's early morning sunshine promised a grand April day at Richmond Park, where the four of them would meet with friends and enjoy a picnic. A longing struck her to make the most of the day, for she did not know when Jamie would be returning to East Florida. Although she could never wish him ill, she could not help but be happy that his ship required serious repairs before sailing back across the vast Atlantic. And fortunately, Papa seemed content to continue hosting him here in London.

"But since you insist upon riding," she said, "I shall ride, too."

Eyebrows shot upward, and if she was not mistaken, Grace's soft gasp held a modicum of delight. Marianne guessed she had not ridden in some time, for Mama no longer rode.

"Splendid," Robert said. "I'll warrant Templeton here hasn't ridden since our last foray to the park."

Jamie's smile flattened, and Marianne hoped she had not put him in an awkward situation.

"Of course you understand, Templeton," Robert said with a smirk, "that Miss Kendall will have Bess. We shall have to find another horse for you."

True alarm filled Marianne. Why had she failed to think this through? Bess was their gentlest horse. In fact, the only one they could depend upon always to be gentle. She noticed Jamie was concentrating on his plate and chewing his boiled eggs with fierce determination.

Without lifting his head, he shot a look of irritation her way. "I shall endeavor not to embarrass you, my lady."

Heat rushed to her face. These men would ever strive to prove themselves to one another, no matter what the cost.

She glanced across the table at Robert. He looked at Jamie, then back at her, and his eyes widened. One eyebrow lifted with an unspoken question. She could not stop her continuing blush, nor think of a single thing to say or do to divert the all-too-correct deduction written across his face. What would he do with the information? Would he protect her interests, as she had always tried to protect his? Or would he rush to Mama, or even Papa, and betray her, possibly causing Jamie to be banished from the house and Papa's good graces? Glaring at her brother across the table with her chin lifted and lips a determined line, she dared him to do his worst.

He grinned broadly and shook his head, and the tender look in his eyes washed away all her fears. But if Robert, with all his self-centeredness, could see that she and Jamie loved each other, surely others in the household could, too.

Jamie gripped the prancing gelding with his knees and secured his black riding boots into the stirrups. If he thought of the horse as a ship on an undulating sea, perhaps it would become easier to stay in the saddle. A lifetime of keeping his balance on rolling vessels had strengthened his leg muscles, a fact that now aided him as he sat on this chestnut horse aptly named Puck. The rascal was as full of mischief as Shakespeare's impish elf, not unlike Moberly.

Jamie could not fault the man for this choice of horses, for Bennington's town stable housed only so many mounts. But he felt certain Moberly chose this particular one to test Jamie's mettle. If that night outside the gaming hall wasn't sufficient, Jamie would show this coxcomb what he was made of…and enjoy every minute of it as he did. The lump he'd received at the hands of the footpads still ached from time to time, but his thick hair hid it from view. Moberly was thriving under all the attention his injuries attracted, and Jamie wouldn't diminish that by calling attention to himself.

Leading the group, Moberly rode his bay stallion next to Miss Kendall on Bess. Jamie followed beside Lady Marianne, forcing his attention away from her to the houses and businesses they passed. He'd learned that this part of London had burned to the ground over a hundred years ago, but the past century had erased all signs of the fire. The twoand three-story wooden or stone buildings were packed close together. In the streets, vendors hawked their wares, and dusty little shops hummed with customers. The smells of fish and bread, horses and garbage assaulted the senses.

"Captain Templeton." Lady Marianne nudged her spirited mare close to him. "Robert said we'll take a ride through Hyde Park before we go to Richmond Park, where the servants await with our picnic." Her wine-red woolen riding dress brought a rosy color to her smooth cheeks, and the fresh breeze carried her jasmine perfume his way. "Hyde Park has riding paths, and at this early hour, there will be no crush of riders."

"Very good, my lady." He risked a second glance in her direction, and a familiar pang struck inside his chest. His service to the Revolution notwithstanding, he was enjoying this prolonged stay in London because of the beautiful lady beside him. Perhaps it was not too wrong to permit himself the luxury of relaxing a bit in her presence.

They'd fallen into a pleasant companionship, at least when Moberly or Miss Kendall or one of Jamie's tutors was present. Under Mr. Pellam's supervision, he'd even managed to practice his dancing with her as his partner without succumbing to an excess of feeling. Of course, at that moment, his attention had been focused on his own two feet. At this moment, however, with the warmth of the April sun shining on their little group, all things seemed possible. And he confessed to himself that he loved her.

"Captain," Lady Marianne said, "may I speak to you about a matter of some delicacy?"

Had she read his heart? *Lord, please don't let her speak of it.* Jamie forced a bland expression to his face. "My lady?"

Her eyes sparkled with...playfulness? "Have you noticed that my brother and Miss Kendall seem quite compatible?"

Relief swept through him, and he shrugged. "I try not to concern myself with matters of the heart." Wrong thing to say. "Of other people's hearts. I mean—" He clamped his mouth shut, and heat shot up his neck. He rarely suffered a loss for words, except with this lady.

Her delightful laughter seemed to echo around him. "But can you say you have no concerns about your Quince and my Emma?"

He cleared his throat. "It is my understanding Miss Emma has your permission to...*speak* with Quince." How odd, the way these aristocrats ruled their servants' every move. Even if Quince were truly Jamie's servant, he could love whom he pleased. Nor would Jamie ever concern himself with his crew members' affections.

"Indeed she does." She exhaled a long sigh. "They, of all of us, have the least possibility of their hearts being broken."

"I don't understand. Why should Moberly and Miss Kendall not form an attachment?"

Marianne glanced sideways at him. "Why, now that you mention it, I cannot think even Papa would mind. But one never knows with him, and without his permission..." Her gaiety vanished into a frown. "I envy their freedom to love whom they will. Emma and Quince, I mean."

"My lady, please." Jamie envied that freedom, too, but it would be unwise to confess it to her.

"I would become a lady's maid if it meant I could marry as I wished." Her voice took on an edge, maybe even tears.

"Lady Marianne." He doubted he could withstand her crying. "You don't know what you're saying." A quick look about the street revealed that none of the inhabitants were close enough to hear them. On the other hand, some scruffy fellows stared at Lady Marianne as they rode by, and Jamie's riding crop burned in his hand at their boldness. If they dared to come near her—

"Here we are," Moberly called over his shoulder.

At last. Drawing in a deep breath as the party emerged from the crowded street into the fresh air, Jamie gazed around the park's wide green expanse edged with blooming trees and blossoming bushes.

With a wave of his riding crop, Moberly directed them to circle their horses. "Shall we walk a bit and smell the flowers?" The fond look he cast at Miss Kendall showed his preference for that activity.

"Hi ho, Moberly." Young Highbury galloped up on a fine looking brown gelding. "Imagine meeting up with you here. Lady Marianne. Miss Kendall." He bowed to each in turn. "Hi ho, Templeton. How's our favorite American today? You look right well astride old Puck. What do you think of the news of our General Gage being driven out of Boston by your General Washington? I hear Washington generously permitted our troops safe passage to sail to Nova Scotia."

Jamie's belly clenched. If Bennington had not spilled this news the night before, Jamie might have given himself away just now with a great huzzah. "Such are the fortunes of war, I suppose. No doubt Gage will not sit idly in Canada for long."

Highbury laughed in his high-pitched way. "My father says the colonials will send all of our troops packing. What do you think?"

"I say, Highbury." Moberly reined his horse between Jamie and the pesky youth. "I care nothing for the troubles in America, but do have some respect for His Majesty's position. At least in front of the ladies."

"Very well." Highbury laughed again. "Tell you what. You and Templeton join me in a race around the park. These horses have not had a good run all winter, and my Socrates is eager to show what he's made of."

"A grand idea." Moberly's face brightened. "A race is precisely what I need."

"Most certainly not." Lady Marianne moved her horse beside Jamie. "I will not permit it."

Jamie ground his teeth. "If you please, my lady, I believe a race is exactly the thing."

Despite her continued protests, Moberly and Highbury marked out a course by pointing their riding crops.

Jamie's mouth felt as dry as last year's dead leaves littering the ground, but he forced down a swallow, forced down his fear. A familiar excitement and sense of competition began to fill him, and he set his feet more firmly in the stirrups. Puck nibbled grass, oblivious to what would soon be expected of him.

"Now," Moberly said, "since my beloved sister protests, I shall leave it to Miss Kendall to drop the handkerchief." He drew a silk one from his pocket and handed it to the lady. "When it hits the ground, we're off."

Miss Kendall's face was a mirror of Lady Marianne's, and both wore their fear like a mourning veil. The few denizens of the sparsely populated park somehow got wind of the event and gathered beside the pathways.

Her hand raised, Miss Kendall cast an apologetic glance toward Lady Marianne and dropped the handkerchief.

With merry cries, Moberly and Highbury dug in their heels, and their horses sprang away. Jamie swatted Puck's flank, but the gelding merely danced around in a circle. Lady Marianne reined back her own horse, which seemed eager to join the party. She eyed Jamie and shrugged, then swatted Puck across the flank with a cry of "Off you go, you silly nag."

Puck lurched into a run, knocking Jamie off center. He felt his upper body careening toward the ground, but tightened the grip of his knees and grabbed the opposite edge of the saddle to right himself. Again in the saddle, he crouched low on Puck's neck. The pain rattling his lower back soon numbed, and he gasped for breath, pulling in the odors of horseflesh with an occasional whiff of the nearby flowers.

Puck now seemed to realize what it was all about, so Jamie trusted the race to him as he would trust his ship to a seasoned helmsman. They galloped after the other two horses and soon gained on them. Cries and cheers met Jamie's ears as he thundered past a blur of people.

After what felt like an endless chase around the park, Jamie saw Lady Marianne ahead. Throwing up a prayer that Puck would know when to stop, Jamie felt a mad desire to win. He slapped the crop against Puck…to no avail. Highbury's horse pulled away and soon crossed the line scratched across the dry pathway by some enthusiastic bystanders.

Jamie tugged on the reins and brought Puck to a stop

some twenty yards beyond the finish. Energy pulsed through him, almost lifting him from the saddle with the same elation, the same sense of victory he'd felt after a successful whale hunt. He'd done it. He'd conquered his fear and run the entire course. If he'd known riding a horse could be so invigorating, he would have taken up the practice long ago. Excitement, a sense of personal accomplishment and pure joy crowded his mind and heart as Puck trotted back to their waiting group.

Once there, he slid his feet halfway out of the stirrups and began his dismount. On the way down, he discovered his left boot would not come free. Puck shifted his massive weight, and Jamie felt a jolt of panic as he rolled toward the ground. The back of his head hit the hard-packed dirt in the exact spot where he'd been struck by the footpads, and pinpoints of light stabbed his eyes. The last thing he heard was Marianne's voice.

"Jamie!"

Chapter Ten

"So there Templeton lay, dazed as a duck, with my sister and Miss Kendall nearly undone thinking we'd murdered Father's protégé."

Even Marianne found herself joining the laughter as Robert regaled their friends at Mama's ball. For Jamie had recovered and was none the worse for his accident, as evidenced by his flawless dancing in the first two sets.

"Permit me to say—" Jamie lifted his hands to quiet them "—landing on one's back in the ocean, even surrounded by thrashing whales, is much less dangerous than landing on hard English soil."

Laughter erupted again, and Marianne felt a measure of pride in how well he blended into this exalted company. Wearing his new periwinkle silk coat and white satin breeches, and his long blond hair held back in a queue with a black satin ribbon, he looked every bit as noble as any titled man in attendance. Perhaps even more so, for his sun-browned skin bore a healthy glow and set him apart from the powdered, foppish men around him. His dark brown eyes gleamed as he spoke, his American accent was giving way to English pronunciations, and his every gesture was filled with grace. Papa had outdone himself with Jamie Templeton. He had made him into a true gentleman and proudly introduced him to several exalted politicians and lords this very evening, each of whom had commended his loyalty to the Crown.

"Do tell us more about whaling, Captain Templeton." Miss Martin, the pretty daughter of a baron, who would one day inherit her own fortune, stood near Jamie sipping ratafia. Her green-eyed gaze never left his face, even when Robert was speaking. Marianne felt a twinge of annoyance. Last season Miss Martin had played with Robert's affections, then cut him. Everyone knew she was looking for a titled husband, but she would ever torment those whom she considered unsuitable. The game was played by several of the young ladies in this crowd. Jamie's good looks and graceful dancing brought them buzzing around him like bees, but not one would think twice about stinging him merely for her own amusement.

Jamie appeared to consider Miss Martin's question about whaling, but before he could answer, Mr. Highbury wedged himself into the group.

"I say, Templeton, I'm all keen on the happenings in America. Have you heard anything new?"

Several ladies tittered. Several gentlemen groaned. Marianne gave Jamie a sympathetic smile, for he blinked at Mr. Highbury as if he were some odd creature.

"Mr. Highbury," she said, "do you have any idea how difficult it was for me to secure an invitation for you and Eugenia? If my father hears you spouting your Whig opinions, he will be most displeased."

Robert nudged him with his elbow. "Indeed, perhaps you should stay out of Bennington's vision altogether." He tilted his head toward Papa, who stood across the room talking with Lord Purton.

As the musicians began another tune, Mr. Highbury winked at Jamie and ducked away. A surge of anger swept through Marianne. Mr. Highbury was more than a little obnoxious, and his casting aspersions on Jamie's character was simply too much. He would not even have been invited if not for his sister Eugenia, whom Robert now approached to claim a dance. The very idea. Thinking Jamie was disloyal to the Crown simply because he was an American.

The others dispersed, most taking their places on the dance floor. Marianne had declined an invitation so she could remain beside Jamie. She sipped her lemonade and moved closer to him, almost brushing his sleeve with hers as they watched the dancers.

"A very fine ball, Lady Marianne." He smiled down at her, but his eyes held caution. "Lady Bennington seems to be having a grand time."

Marianne saw Mama, with Grace Kendall beside her, chatting away in the midst of the older women seated in the far corner of the ballroom. "Yes, she does. And so does Papa." She noticed Papa chatting with his friends and laughing heartily, a good sign. "But I have not stayed with you to speak of them."

His smile dimmed. "Indeed? Then how may I be of service, madam?"

His formal tone, as devoid of emotion as John the footman's, stung her. "I require nothing. But I should like to warn you that Miss Martin and her friends may decide to make sport of you. Please guard your...your heart."

"Guard my—" Jamie gazed at her, and his formal facade melted into tenderness. "My lady, thank you for your concern. And please be assured that my heart is... well-guarded." A light sparked in his eyes, then vanished as he turned away and cleared his throat.

If she had even the slightest doubt about his love, it now disappeared. But even more, she stood in awe of his confidence and poise, surely the results of his being a self-made man. In this society, where birth and rank meant everything, her wellborn friends might scoff at such a notion. But she saw within Jamie something they would never possess. Now more than ever she knew she would give up everything for him. Could he not do the same for her? Could he not cease this foolishness and confess his love?

Jamie wondered how long he could stand beside Marianne—*Lady* Marianne—without surrendering to the constrained emotions swelling within his chest. Her curly black hair framed her porcelain cheeks, and her modest pink gown outshone the garish, wide-skirted fashions of many other ladies in the room. She wore jasmine perfume tonight. He liked the jasmine better than the rose, but the rose also—

Think of something else, man. Of the *Fair Winds* now being serviced across the Thames in the Southwark shipyard, under the watchful eye of his worthy first mate, Saunders. Of his crew, who had sworn themselves to good behavior as they awaited their return to East Florida. Of the cargo he would deliver there— fabrics, leather goods, perfumes, plows and harnesses, dishes…and several dozen crates of muskets from Spain that Lord Bennington knew nothing about.

"Have I commended you on your dancing, Captain Templeton?" Lady Marianne interrupted his thoughts with more than words. Her sweet smile contrasted with the tears at the corners of her eyes.

He looked away. "You have, my lady. Thank you. And you may thank Mister Pellam for his fine skills in teaching me."

"Yes, I shall do that." She lifted the delicate lace fan hanging on her wrist and began to wave it slowly.

The ladies of East Florida would appreciate fans. Fans, parasols, bonnets in the latest fashion—

"Have you recovered from your fall?" Her voice took on a higher, softer pitch.

"Yes. Very well, thank you." *No.* Sometimes his head pounded like Puck's hooves on the dry ground, especially at the end of the day. Especially when he was in her presence. Perhaps he'd suffered a concussion. He'd seen a man succumb to such repeated injuries—

"You cannot imagine how frightened I was when you fell off of Puck."

Yes, I can. You've shown me nothing but kindness and goodness. Your concern is everywhere in evidence, even to the protection of my heart against your friends. He forced a chuckle. "I was a bit alarmed myself."

Her responding laugh was more like a squeak. His resolve almost shattered.

"Would you excuse me, my lady." His own voice sounded thin. He knew it was bad form to leave her alone. But as he bowed to her, he looked into those blue, brimming eyes and knew he could not stay in her presence.

"Yes. Of course." She returned a curtsy. "Lord Good-wyn will soon claim his dance."

Unreasoning jealousy joined the warring emotions within Jamie's heart. "Ah, yes. The thin fellow." *Whom I could break like a stick.*

She smothered her laugh with her fan. "Shh. Here he comes."

The young viscount, dressed in green and blue, strutted toward them like a peacock about to spread its tail. He greeted Jamie, then offered his hand to Marianne, and off they walked to the dance floor. While her expression was pleasant enough, Jamie could see her sway away from Goodwyn when the man leaned near to speak to her. *Lord, forgive my unreasoning jealousy.*

With a mixture of relief and a sense of loss, Jamie forced his attention away from her to concentrate on the large ballroom's decor. The polished wooden floor gleamed in the light of hundreds of candles whose flames were magnified by exquisite girandoles, ornate candlesticks hung before tall mirrors to intensify the light. The tall windows had been opened wide, and red-and-gold-liveried servants waved large feathered fans to keep the crisp night air moving. The room was awash with the scents of countless perfumes. A table laden with punch, cakes and various liqueurs offered refreshment to the guests between dances. And among the powdered wigs and ceruse-covered faces were some people who had eschewed those hideous, impractical fashions. But with or without their masks, he could not discern the political leanings of any of them. Except for Highbury, who was becoming a serious nuisance. Fortunately, he was busy with the newly begun country dance in partnership with some young lady Jamie hadn't met.

The ballroom itself had seemed much larger during Jamie's dance lessons, but now, despite the brightness, the walls seemed to close in around him. In the midst of this mass of people, he longed for the open sea, where he could breathe again.

Across the room, Lord Bennington had lost his pleasant demeanor and waved his hands about, as he did when expounding on the Revolution. Even if that was not his topic, his familiar gestures brought to Jamie's mind his purpose for being here. This would be the perfect time to slip away and locate the secret desk drawer Quince told him about. Earlier, Jamie saw Lord Shriveham hand a document to Bennington, who treated it like a treasure and briefly retreated to his study.

No one seemed to notice Jamie move toward the large double doors and into the hallway, where another crush of people milled about or stood talking in groups. He slipped through, not looking directly at anyone, but focusing beyond and smiling as if his destination was a particular acquaintance. With only two friendly greetings from those he passed, he managed to make it down the wide staircase to the brightly lit first floor.

He kept a casual pace, stopping to admire a painting hanging in the hallway leading behind the stairs, stopping to adjust his silk cravat in a mirror a few feet away. He had his hand on the study door when he felt a sharp tap on his shoulder.

Stifling his alarm, Jamie feigned calm as he turned around.

"Hi ho, Templeton." Hugh Highbury stood there with a wide grin. "I'm so glad to have found you alone. We simply must talk about the war in the colonies."

A mix of relief and irritation swept through Jamie.

He knew he should pretend to be insulted. But something in the younger man's eyes stopped him. He rested one shoulder against the study door, praying he would be able to find the right words. After all, this man and his father supported the Revolution in open defiance against their king and powerful men in Parliament, and he might know something of value. Jamie would be foolish to make him an enemy.

"Highbury, I came down here for a short rest." He touched the back of his head. "That blow when I fell off the horse still has me a bit off balance."

"I'm terribly sorry, my good fellow." Highbury reached up to pat Jamie's shoulder. "Had I known you did not ride..." He smirked. "I no doubt would have challenged you, anyway."

Jamie winced and offered a weak chuckle designed to confirm his need for rest.

Highbury glanced around the candlelit hallway and up the stairs, then sniffed the air and cupped a hand behind his ear. "Can't see anyone. Can't smell anyone. Can't hear anyone. We're in the clear. Why don't we step into the privacy of Bennington's library, and you can tell me what old Washington and his friends are up to. Is it true this entire rebellion began in a Boston tavern?"

Jamie swallowed a groan. Those words revealed far more than Highbury could possibly realize. If he knew anything of value about the Revolution, he never would have asked such a foolish question. Nor would he be so flippant about it.

"Listen, Highbury." Jamie stood to his full height, head and shoulders above the other man, and leaned toward him like the sea captain he was. The shorter man blinked and his jaw went slack, just the effect Jamie had hoped for. "For you this is a game. But I could be accused of treason merely for meeting privately with a Whig. Surely you realize, as Lord Bennington's guest, I will defer to him in all things. Now, I don't have anything against you, lad, but if you have any decency, leave me alone so I can rest." For further effect, he once again put his hand on the back of his head.

"I—I say, Templeton, easy on." Highbury's shoulders slumped. "I'm merely looking for diversion." He waved in a dismissive gesture. "You cannot imagine how boring life can be when one is on the outs with the cream of society."

Comprehension swept through Jamie. He'd almost trusted this man. This silly, pampered pup. He clamped one hand on Highbury's shoulder harder than he needed to, and was rewarded when panic swept over the man's youthful face. "But look around, lad. You are right here among that cream of society tonight. Why are you wasting time with me when fifty eligible young ladies are no doubt awaiting your attention upstairs?"

Highbury shrugged. "I suppose." He brightened. "Yes, that's just the thing. I believe the minuet is up next, and I would loathe to miss it. You see, Miss Martin actually promised to dance with me, and she would never speak to me again if I stood her up."

Jamie gave his shoulder a hearty shove. "By all means, go. You must not keep Miss Martin waiting."

Grinning broadly, Highbury dashed toward the stairs and ran up them two at a time. Jamie waited until certain the young pup was gone for good, then ducked into the library, praying no one else would accost him.

The dark, quiet room was cool, with just a hint of Bennington's favorite tobacco in the air. Outside the velvet-draped windows, torches lit the street so guests could make their way to the door. Jamie could see drivers tending their carriages and footmen standing by to assist latecomers. At any time, one of them might peer in the window. In the torchlight, Jamie saw his own shadow flicker on one wall, but when he moved to Bennington's desk, darkness covered him. He sat on the tapestry seat of the ornately carved white chair and felt around the edges of the drawer. Quince said it was well known among the staff that this desk had a secret compartment where the earl stowed his latest missives from the king. In fact, Jamie had seen such a hiding place in the desk of Bennington's youngest son in East Florida.

Underneath the drawer, toward the back of the desk, he felt a latch and tried to open it. *Locked.* But a small bit of paper stuck out through the tiny slit between the compartment and the drawer. Jamie eased the sheet through, careful not to tear it, and slipped it under his waistcoat. He felt again to see if he could unlock the latch. A click echoed throughout the room, but instead of coming from the desk, it sounded from across the library. The wide door opened slowly, and a dark form entered, eerily lit from behind by the hallway candles.

Chapter Eleven

Jamie eased down in the chair, rested his head against the carved back and stretched out his legs. Surely no one would believe he'd chosen this place to sleep, but he had no other option but to pose that way.

As if in a familiar place, the person moved to the center of the room without bumping into any furniture.

"Jamie?"

He bolted to his feet. "Lady Marianne?"

She hurried to the desk and found a candle to light. "Mr. Highbury said you were ill." The flame revealed her lovely face pinched with worry. The scent of flint blended with her jasmine perfume.

He ached to comfort her, to reassure her, but shoved away that impulse. "And so he sent you instead of your father or brother or a servant?" Jamie thought he might strangle Highbury.

Lady Marianne laughed softly, but a little catch in her voice cut it short. "No. I asked him if he had seen you, and he told me you came in here to rest." She lifted the candle high. "Do not be alarmed. No one knows we are alone."

His heart pounded as if it would leap from his chest. If they were discovered, all would be lost, especially if the paper in his waistcoat was found. "And we shouldn't be alone, so I'll just say good-night, my lady." He strode toward the door.

"Jamie."

He stopped, all senses heightened by his near discovery. But he would not turn back to face her. "My lady?"

"How long must we pretend?" Her voice thick with tears. "My love for you did not diminish in your absence. It has grown stronger with you here." The sound of her soft footsteps on the Wilton carpet drew nearer. "And I believe you love me still."

Her tears had ceased. Jamie wished that gave him more relief than it did. But her words shattered the last of his reserve. "Yes, I do love you still." He still would not look at her, though at this moment he could cast his entire future to the wind just to proclaim that love to the world. *No.* One of them must be strong.

She touched his arm, and he covered her hand with his—an instinctive gesture he could not undo.

"Jamie." Her voice caressed his name.

He turned and pulled her into his arms, resting his chin on her head. Ah, the comfort of her responding embrace swept through his entire being, even as his heart ached for their impossible situation, even as he feared she might notice the crinkle of the stolen letter.

A soft, shaky laugh escaped her. "Will you kiss me?"

Shoving away every thought of intrigue, he pressed his lips against her smooth white forehead. "My beloved."

"But I meant—"

He cut her short, bending to kiss her lips gently, then firmly. "Will that do?"

Another shaky laugh. "Yes. It tells me what I wished to know." She moved out of his embrace and took his hand, leading him to the settee in front of Bennington's desk.

And now he sat there holding her white-gloved hands and thanking the good Lord they both had a strong measure of self-control. But it was those very hands that made marriage impossible for them. If he took her back to East Florida, no matter how his business prospered, she would have work to do, as did every person in that wilderness, whether wealthy or poor, master, mistress or servant. She would not be able to wear gloves for her work, and soon her hands would become callused like everyone else's. He could not do that to her.

"What are we to do, Jamie?" The innocence and trust in her voice stabbed into his heart.

He reached out to caress her smooth cheek. "Beloved, you realize there is nothing we *can* do, don't you? We are not well suited. Therefore, we must pray for strength to follow the paths God has chosen for us. For as surely as we sit here, He has ordained separate paths for us."

"No." She gulped back a sob, and he could see she was trying not to cry. It was no use. A flood of tears poured down her cheeks, and she grasped his hand tighter. He bent close and touched his forehead to hers. *This too shall pass,* he told himself. *One day this pain will subside.* But he'd never been successful at lying to himself.

Marianne could not stop her tears, but with deep breaths, she managed not to sob. She would save that for later in her bedchamber. Despite her denial, she knew

Jamie spoke the truth, although it stirred a bitter rebellion within her. There simply must be a way for them to share a future together.

"I do wish to follow God's path." She reached for the handkerchief in her sleeve and dabbed her cheeks. "But I am not convinced His will is to separate us."

Jamie took the handkerchief and finished the job of patting away her tears, a tender gesture that calmed her. "He's already separated us through our births, and the work He's given each of us will take us to different places." Sorrow creased his broad forehead.

"Yes, you have important work to do. But what work has God given me? I am pampered by my parents and society, and I know full well my uselessness on this earth."

"How can you say that?" He reached out as if to touch her cheek again, but then withdrew his hand. "Your charitable work among London's orphans is an example to that same society, and I know it comes out of a true Christian heart."

"But are there not poor people everywhere? I can minister to the needy wherever the Lord sends *you*."

"Not at sea. Not to my crew." His words were a whisper, yet she flinched at this truth.

"But will you always sail your own ship? As you prosper, will you not hire others to import your wares so you can settle in comfort either here or in East Florida?"

He started to speak, but she touched a finger to his lips. "Would we not have a lovely life there? You and I, Frederick and Rachel. Oh, Jamie, I so dearly long to know my brother's wife, my own dear sister. Will you not take me there to meet her?"

Jamie moved back, staring beyond her as if contemplating her words. But then he shook his head. "Lord Bennington will never approve our marriage."

"Perhaps we should give him a chance to approve or disapprove. He surely thinks well enough of you. He has made you like a son, even favored you over his own." She felt like a traitor to Robert for saying it. William, Thomas and Frederick had all found their places in life, but dear Robert was still far from it, even with his recent improvements. "We have not been fair to him. We must give him a chance to say yes or no."

"But what if it's no, as it likely will be?"

"I cannot think he would deny me my happiness when he himself has been so happy in marriage with Mama."

A loud sneeze came from the room's other settee, which faced the hearth. Marianne jumped, and Jamie drew in a soft breath. The man chuckled as he peered over the settee back. His face was shadowed, but the well-formed shape of his head was unmistakable.

"Well, isn't this a pretty pickle?"

"Robert!" Marianne thought she might faint. "What are you doing here?"

Robert sat up and scratched his jaw. "I came to escape the ball."

"But you were having such a grand time." Marianne feared some lady had wounded him.

"Perhaps I should say I came to escape trouble." He rose and crossed the room. "The brandy looked all too inviting, and Tobias Pincer was there waving a glass under my nose." He gave Jamie a weak smile. "I turned him down, but somehow I do not feel as if I entirely won that battle."

"Pincer." Jamie's voice resounded with disdain. "I thought you got rid of him."

"I did, but his father has some influence with Bennington, so I certainly could not avoid him." Wearing a teasing grin, Robert sat on the chair next to the settee and looked back and forth from Jamie to Marianne. "So my suspicions are correct. What are we going to do about this fine mess?"

Jamie cringed. Things were getting far too complicated. He'd nearly lost his life—twice. His love for Marianne had no future, he felt the burn of an important document against his chest, and now Moberly was putting himself in the mix. Had he heard Jamie examining the desk? What a fool he'd been for not searching the dark corners of the room first. Moberly hadn't made a sound, nor had the scent of his bergamot cologne carried across the room.

Jamie must turn this conversation away from delicate matters of the heart. "Why don't you feel as if you won the battle against the brandy?"

Moberly slumped in his chair. "Strange, is it not? I turned away from it, but I wanted it very badly. I went away feeling deprived and cross that other men can drink and I cannot. Once I begin, I cannot stop." He rested his elbow on the chair arm and propped his chin on his hand. "Even now, my mouth waters at the thought of brandy."

"Oh, Robert." Marianne reached out to squeeze her brother's arm. "I am very proud of you. I had the lemonade. It is quite tasty and has a splash of strawberries. Will you not have some of that?"

He gave her a paternal smile. "Yes, I should do that.

Next time I will." He straightened and patted her hand. "But for now, here we are, and you two still have not answered my question."

Jamie permitted himself to feel a bit relieved. Moberly didn't seem in any way suspicious of him. The best way to handle the other situation was straight on. "If you heard our conversation, my friend, you know of our feelings for each other. But you also know the impossibility of our being any more than friends. Please help me convince your sister of this painful truth." How he regretted his confession of love to her. He should have walked right out of the room.

"Well…" Moberly drawled the word. "You could elope. There would be a bit of a scandal, but then, society needs one of those from time to time. Eventually it would die down, and you could live on in bliss, oblivious to it."

Jamie stiffened. "Lord Bennington has done nothing but good for me. I would never do that to him." Except for advising the king to send thousands of soldiers to quash the Revolution.

Moberly's laugh was sardonic. "Ah, my good man, I would do *that* to Bennington. But then he would disown me completely, and my ladylove would suffer for it."

"Speaking of your ladylove." Jamie grasped this diversion. "You and Miss Kendall enjoy each other's company." He glanced at Marianne for her confirmation.

She nodded and gave Moberly a mischievous smile. "You do indeed."

Moberly snorted. "And how will penniless I provide for penniless her?" A pained, wistful look overtook his shadowed countenance. "Indeed, how?" Again he snorted. "I should have gone into the church. Father could have found me a living among his friends. But alas, I came to faith far too late."

"Why too late?" The idea pulsed through Jamie. "You have your Oxford education. You know your Scriptures. With the proper mentor from among the clergy, you could become a very fine minister."

Moberly's frown lessened. "I was joking, but—"

"But why not?" Marianne's face glowed with love for her brother. "Do you have any idea how long Grace has prayed for you?" She bit her lip. "Oh, do not tell her I told you. She would be mortified. But if anyone would suit for a minister's wife, it is she."

A smile broke over Moberly's entire face. "I will... it seems strange for me to say this...*pray* about this matter. Yes, I will pray, first, that the Lord will show His will regarding my future. And second, that He will make Miss Kendall a part of that future."

"Well reasoned," Jamie said. "I'll pray likewise for you."

"And I, too." Marianne stood. "Now, we must return to the ball. Mama will be disappointed to find us shirking our hosting duties."

Jamie and Moberly rose, each offering her an arm. With a laugh, she took both of them, and the three proceeded to the door. "We look like a trio of conspirators, do we not?"

Her words sent a chill down Jamie's spine.

Marianne lay abed that night thinking of all that had transpired. Although Jamie had confessed his love, they had not settled anything. But if he thought she would give up on their future, he was quite mistaken. Robert's suggestion about elopement had long ago occurred to her, but that would ruin Jamie's partnership with Papa. Somehow she must find a way either to break his resolve against asking Papa for her hand, or throw all to the wind and follow him back to East Florida, which would protect Jamie and put all the blame on her shoulders.

How could it be accomplished? Her brother Thomas was an officer in His Majesty's navy. Perhaps he could see to her passage. No, Thomas was all rules and order. He would never help her against their father.

She stared through the darkness toward the little chamber where Emma slept. When Marianne came upstairs after the last guest left the ball, her servant seemed particularly happy. Upon examination, she'd confessed to a pleasant visit with Aaron Quince under the watchful eye of Mrs. Bennett, the housekeeper. As surely as Marianne trusted Jamie's integrity, she trusted his Quince not to play with Emma's heart. She fully understood that if they married, Emma would return to East Florida with him. While Papa might be mildly displeased to have a servant desert his household, he would not go against Mama, who had brought the orphaned Emma into their home.

Feeling far from sleep and more than a little envious, Marianne let her imagination wander. She could see herself bundled up in a plain brown cloak, boarding the *Fair Winds* as Emma's lady's maid. No one would know the difference, even Jamie, until they were far out to sea. She laughed into the darkness at the silly idea. Then sat straight up in her bed.

Perhaps the idea was not so silly, after all.

Chapter Twelve

The message, informally scrawled on foolscap, held helpful information, some of which General Washington might already know. The King's 60th Regiment of Foot, which the general might well have fought alongside during the French and Indian War, had been serving in the West Indies in the ensuing years. Now they would be removed to East Florida and serve under Colonel Thomas Browne, a colonial from Georgia who'd suffered at the hands of Patriots for his loyalty to the king.

Jamie chafed at not being able to get this vital information to Washington as soon as possible. But until his ship was seaworthy, he must remain in England. He and Quince often reminded each other that they were doing what they'd been sent to do, and must trust God to open opportunities where He willed. After copying the missive in the early morning hours, Jamie left it to Quince to slip back to the library with the stealth of his Shawnee grandfather and replace it in the desk. Now that they knew where information was to be had, they would check often. In the meantime, boredom often set in for both men.

Although Quince had worked his own farm in Massachusetts, with leisure times only in the dead of winter, Jamie was more used to long stretches of inactivity while his ship sailed from port to port. After crew drills and other exercises, he filled his time by reading the Scriptures or lighter fare, and keeping busy about the vessel. But most of these aristocrats seemed to have honed their skills at indolence. While they found contentment in sleeping half the day, visiting and gossiping with one another, and attending parties and balls, Jamie's hands ached to work. He feared that by the time the *Fair Winds'* hull and mast were repaired, his hard-earned calluses would be worn away.

He managed to spend some of his time traveling to various suppliers and arranging the goods he would take back to East Florida. In addition to household goods and luxuries for the wealthy, the plantation owners needed metalworks to build their own foundries now that they could not do business with the northern colonies. Jamie could supply some of their needs, such as the Swedish bar iron on order from Birmingham. The *Fair Winds* was being reinforced even now to carry the heavier cargo. But it would take many more ships and many more trips between the continents to import everything the burgeoning colony required to be self-sufficient.

Sometimes his divided interests wore him down, especially since he seemed not to be able to get back into Bennington's library alone. The earl had invited him to read any of the countless leather-bound books that lined two walls floor to ceiling. But when Jamie did so, Moberly or Miss Kendall or Marianne or the ever-present Reverend Bentley would also be reading there. Many evenings during supper Bennington would mention progress in the war against the colonists. But Jamie could not detect anything further regarding the Crown's plans for defending East Florida, or any helpful information about troop action in the northern colonies.

At least Marianne seemed to have reconciled herself to the impossibility of their going beyond friendship, for she no longer cast wistful glances in his direction, glances that cut into his soul and distracted him. In fact, her cheerful disposition had brightened the entire household these past weeks. For his own part, after those brief sweet kisses the night of the ball, he felt something settle in his own heart. To know such pure and tender love, though denied its fulfillment, was still a gift from the Lord. Jamie would treasure the remaining time with Marianne and thank God for every moment they spent together, however formally they must conduct themselves.

"How do you stand for it, my friend?" Quince folded Jamie's new gray jacket and placed it in a trunk. "If anybody told me Emma and I couldn't marry, we'd elope in the middle of the night."

"That's exactly what I'd expect of you, and I'd not fault you for it." Jamie stared out the window into the bright May sunshine. "But can't you hear me telling Bennington 'by the by, old man, in addition to my using our partnership to spy on you, I'm also stealing your daughter'?" He looked down on two servants sweeping the back terrace, and envied their industriousness… and the simplicity of their lives. "If spying on the man strains my sense of honor, elopement would destroy it altogether."

Quince grimaced. "Under the circumstances, it would be reprehensible, wouldn't it?" He brought another jacket from the wardrobe. "Are you going to help me with this?"

"You're the valet, not I." Jamie crossed his arms and leaned against the wall. "I think you've found your calling, my friend."

Quince glared at him, but there was mischief in his grin. "Shall I dump it all on the floor and let you pack for yourself?"

"Now, now. Let's not take offense." Jamie crossed the room and began to carry items from the wardrobe to the trunk. "I must say, I never expected to own so many clothes, nor such fine ones. Have Ian or Greyson told you what I'll need for country living?" Jamie laughed at his own words. "Lord, what've You brought me to? An orphaned boy and lowly whaler playing with the aristocracy."

Quince clapped him on the shoulder. "And you play the part well, Cap'n Jamie." He surveyed the growing stash of clothes. "Yes, we should take all of it. Ian says the family's months at the country manor are filled with even more activities than their season in the city."

"I suppose it depends on what you consider 'activities.' Other than their frivolous nonsense, they don't seem too full of activity," Jamie said. "I'll arrange with Moberly to have horses available for us to return to the city and see to the *Fair Winds*. When I was at Southwark yesterday, she looked well on her way to being mended. They can step up the mast in another month and start the rigging. What's our old friend François said about the arrival of the muskets?"

Quince snorted. "Who could have guessed that arrogant fellow hates the English so much? When he brought the gray jacket yesterday, he told me his sources require anonymity. But he also said his latest news from France indicates some important people are backing our Revolution. Of course, young Louis will want us to succeed if only to needle the English…and repel their interests on the Continent."

"That kind of help will be a blessing indeed. But what about the weapons?"

"We'll have the details of where to get them by the time the ship's ready to sail."

Jamie felt a sense of reprieve. Once he had the Spanish muskets, he might not be able to return to Lord Dennington's hospitality. And he was not yet ready to say goodbye to Marianne.

Seated in the family carriage with Mama and Grace, Marianne watched the passing scenery of the Surrey countryside with a mix of joy and sorrow. She longed to return to Hampshire and Bennington Park, for she preferred the country over the city. But she had no doubt this would be the last time she ever visited her childhood home. With this in mind, she treasured each sight, each fragrance, each moment with Mama and Robert.

With Robert especially. Her dear brother seemed a different man since Jamie had convinced him to trust in God's mercy. He confided his lack of confidence in approaching Papa regarding service in the church, but he did spend many hours with Grace. Marianne could see them growing closer, could see Robert growing in his faith. And while he said nothing more about her relationship with Jamie, he did his best to arrange times when the four of them could be together. Perhaps Mama sensed a romance for Robert, too, for she granted Grace an unusual amount of freedom.

On May Day, they had at last enjoyed their picnic at Richmond Park. What a lark it had been to spread out linen tablecloths on the green grass and enjoy cold chicken, salad, hothouse strawberries, and cakes, and to greet their many friends. With the social season soon to end, everyone seemed eager to gather as often as possible, and the next two weeks had seen a flurry of parties and balls, few of which members of Bennington's household attended. Marianne found she did not miss the events in the slightest.

Now, as the end of May neared, the closed carriage wended its way home through the pine forests that shrouded the Portsmouth Road, while Robert and Jamie rode alongside, their guns and swords at the ready in case highwaymen dared to attack. Papa would join the family as soon as Parliament adjourned.

Marianne experienced several moments of guilt over being glad for her father's absence from the family circle. Without pressing duties to king and country, he often bore down a bit harder on his family and might notice how often she and Jamie were together. She must find ways to avoid his scrutiny. Glancing out of the window, she watched Jamie riding beside Robert. Pride filled her over how well he had learned to manage Puck, and even seemed to have formed a friendship with the frisky horse.

As she watched, Robert reined his Gallant near Jamie. "Can I interest you in a race to Portsdown Hill?" He pointed with his riding crop. Marianne could hear her brother's teasing tone.

"Oh, Robert, do not—" She started to put her head out through the open window.

"Now, now, my dear." Mama touched her arm. "Do

let the men have their fun. Moberly is the picture of health these days, and I'll warrant Captain Templeton has learned to stay astride by now."

As the thunder of racing hooves met her ears, Marianne's heart dipped to her stomach. She glanced between Mama and Grace, and her face grew hot. Mama's mild expression revealed no deeper meaning beyond what her words conveyed. But Mama could surprise a person, and Marianne knew better than to assume anything. If she were twelve years old again, she would confess everything and cast herself upon Mama's mercy. But to do so would destroy everything. No, if Marianne planned to follow Jamie to East Florida, it must be without Mama's knowledge, for she would never approve of such a scheme. She had been heartbroken when Papa sent Frederick to the colony, and she would be devastated when Marianne left.

With a soft laugh that she feared sounded more giddy than casual, Marianne conceded Mama's assertion. "Yes, Robert has never been healthier…or happier." From the corner of her eye, she could see Grace's pink cheeks. "And I suppose the captain's riding has improved. But tell me, Mama, what plans have you made for our entertainment these next months?"

Mama's eyes lit up. "The viscount has accepted our invitation to summer at the Park. He and Lady Mary are bringing the children, so we may expect some lively games every day."

"How grand. I shall be delighted to see my nephew and nieces." Marianne's oldest brother, William, and his viscountess, Mary, were a bit stuffy, but their children made up for it with merry antics that amused the entire household.

"And you, my darling." Mama's eyebrows rose. "What are your plans?"

Marianne started. "My plans? What do you mean?"

Mama blinked. "Why, do you plan to have your usual parties for the village children? The sweetmeats for them after church each Sunday?" Again, her expression betrayed nothing.

And again, Marianne's laugh sounded a bit giddy in her own ears. "Oh, yes, of course. I would not wish to disappoint the children." *This will be the last summer I see them.* The thought made her heart ache. "And I'm looking forward to our traditional garden party in June."

"Ah, yes. The highlight of our summer."

The carriage emerged from the forest and slowed, soon to be surrounded by a flock of fluffy, bleating sheep.

Marianne waved her fan. "Ah, yes, the distinctive sounds and smells of Surrey."

Mama smiled but also tilted her head in a chiding fashion, for she felt that ladies should never complain. "But can you not also smell the rich fragrance of the earth? See how green the grass and trees are." She waved a gloved hand toward the window, which framed a view of Surrey's verdant hills. "Ah, how I look forward to working with my roses once again. And once Bennington comes home, summer will truly begin for me." Her eyes shone with anticipation. Mama always presented a picture of grace, but summers in the country brought out her very best.

Marianne forced a responding smile, but felt it waver, so she stared out of the window at the landscape. No doubt Jamie and Robert had completed their race and awaited the ladies at the top of Portsdown Hill, where they would disembark from the carriage to take in the view before making their descent. Crossing from Surrey into Hampshire was Marianne's favorite part of the ten-hour trip from London each spring. After months away from Bennington Park, she never failed to be awestruck over the beauty of God's creation visible in the vast panorama laid out before her. But this year, she felt only heartache. How could she leave it all behind?

Chapter Thirteen

If the invigorating race up Portsdown Hill wasn't enough to make Jamie breathless, once he and Puck reached the crest at Devil's Cleft, the spectacular scenery of the green, rolling hills of Hampshire viewed from this nearly five-hundred-foot elevation caused him to inhale in wonder. Then, with the intake of air, the familiar scent of the ocean met him, causing a painful ache in his chest. To his left lay Portsmouth, where the Royal Navy's vast fleet lay anchored. The sight was so impressive he could not help but question how the colonies' few ships would have any success against them.

A few miles beyond lay Southampton, where merchant vessels docked. The sight of countless vessels in both ports made him long for the *Fair Winds,* made him long to sail across the wide Atlantic toward home, where he could take a more active part in the Revolution. Perhaps he would offer to have his sloop more heavily armed for use in the war, for with his present defenses the smallest British man-of-war could sink him. But those thoughts were for another time. Right now, the splendor of the setting before him served as a reminder of all the beauties in England claiming a large portion of his affection.

"I say, old man." Moberly, equally breathless, reached the summit and reined his Gallant beside Jamie's Puck. "'Tis not wise to run a horse up such a hill."

Jumping down from his heaving, sweating mount, Jamie cringed. "Bad form on my part. I should have realized…" As captain of his own ship, he knew when to ease up on his crew. How foolish not to grasp the needs of this magnificent animal.

Moberly dismounted and came to check Puck's eyes and legs. "There, boy, you're all right. Never mind, Templeton. No harm done. I'm the one at fault. Should have warned you. Old Puck likes to run full out, but he's not always smart about hills and such. Do not give it another thought." He nodded toward their right. "Bennington Park, over there."

Only a little relieved by his words, Jamie followed Moberly's gaze toward a vast manor house in the distance, set on a lesser hill but nonetheless imposing. Once again, wonder stole his breath. So this was where Marianne grew up, where she became the genuine soul he loved so dearly. Even London's snobbish, irreverent society could not damage the purity of her character. In this place, Jamie would be hard put not to abandon all his resolve to maintain his emotional distance from her. But of course he must.

Rolling, grass-covered hills stretched before them to the north and east, with occasional rock and chalk outbreaks jutting to the surface. In the distance, countless sheep appeared as white dots on a carpet of green. At the sight of it all, peace swept through Jamie, and an assurance that all would be well.

The black-red-and-gold Bennington coach lumbered up beside them and stopped, its four horses echoing Puck's labored breathing. Wiggins, the driver, set the brake, and three footmen descended from the top.

"Lady Bennington." John the footman approached the coach door. "Will you walk down the hill today?"

The lady appeared in the window. "Yes, John. Thank you."

The footmen assisted the ladies from the conveyance, and Jamie and Moberly joined them. His senses already heightened by the race and spectacular view, Jamie felt a mad impulse to claim the right to escort Marianne down the steep incline ahead of them. Before he could put the plan into effect, Lady Bennington smiled up at him from beneath her broad-brimmed hat.

"Captain Templeton, may I take your arm?"

"It will be my honor, my lady." Indeed, it would. And he felt more relief than disappointment over not accompanying Marianne. Surely the Lord had intervened to keep him from a situation in which he might be tempted to say too much. Furthermore, in his two months as a guest in Lady Bennington's home, he had yet to have a private conversation with this kind, elegant woman.

Taking particular care to guide the lady to the smoothest parts of the rutted road angling down the hill, Jamie permitted himself to relax. He felt certain that manners dictated he should wait for her to address him, but words of praise for the landscape before them burned inside him.

"What a lovely day for travel." Lady Bennington spoke his very thoughts. "Tell me, Captain, what do you think of our Hampshire countryside?" Only a hint of pride edged her tone, and her face beamed. Without doubt, Marianne's gentle nature and flawless grace came from her mother, as did her beauty.

"Very fine country, indeed, madam."

She glanced up at him with eyes as blue as Marianne's. "Tell me about your home. Nantucket, I mean."

Jamie drew her off the road while the coach rumbled past. Two of the footmen walked beside the lead horses and held their harnesses, while Wiggins kept a hand on the brake. Dust flurried about them, and Lady Bennington brought up her fan to wave it away. Once the coach had passed them, they resumed their walk.

"Nantucket is a fine piece of land. Though it is more sand than grass, it still provides sufficient pasture for our sheep." He nodded toward the grazing flocks in the distance, and an unexpected thread of homesickness wove through his heart. His beloved sister still resided on the island of their birth. Now that the British navy had impressed most of the Nantucket whalers into English service, Jamie feared Dinah and his childhood friends would suffer terribly despite their neutrality toward the war. But he would not mention such unpleasantness to Lady Bennington. "The Quakers who settled the island in the last century have bequeathed it a legacy of faith."

"Ah, yes. The Quakers." Lady Bennington continued to wave her fan. "I have known several fine Christians who are Friends." She glanced at his brown riding clothes, complete with brass buckles and buttons. "May I assume you are not of that persuasion?"

"No, ma'am." Jamie's heart warmed. If the discussion was to be about his faith, he would gladly tell her everything. "While I respect their interest in seeking an inner light for spiritual guidance, I endeavor to de-

pend upon Scripture to guide me, lest my heart mislead
me." His own words reminded him that only in Scripture would he find strength for the days ahead.

"Ah, very good." Her smile was placid. "I noticed
your enjoyment of the services at St. Paul's. I hope you
will equally enjoy Reverend Bentley's sermons at Bennington Park."

Jamie stepped over a slight dip in the road. "The good
reverend has been most helpful in guiding me through
the complexities of the social graces." He wanted to
laugh, thinking of how his crew would mock his fancy
new manners on their return voyage. "I'm certain he
will prove equally proficient in his pastoral duties."

"You will not be disappointed." Lady Bennington
peered over her shoulder, and he followed her gaze. Several yards back, Robert escorted the other ladies, while
John the footman walked at the rear, leading Gallant
and Puck. John's diligent perusal of the surrounding
landscape was no doubt meant to check for any highwaymen who might be lurking nearby.

"And now you must tell me about East Florida." Lady
Bennington's eyebrows lifted, as though her words held
more than a surface meaning.

"'Tis quite a wilderness, madam, though not totally
uninhabitable." Jamie turned away with a grimace.
These were not soothing words for her. "But you may
be very proud of your son, for he is proving to be an
excellent force for good in St. Johns Towne."

"Indeed?" A tiny catch marred her melodious voice.

Her maternal tenderness brought a twinge to his
chest, and he wondered how it would have been to
grow up under his own dear mother's care. "Indeed,
my lady. Under Frederick Moberly's watch, civiliza-

tion spreads deep into the land. His father's plantation prospers under his management, and all of the people along the St. Johns River, whether plantation owner, merchant, slave or indentured servant, find him the most just of magistrates."

Moisture rimmed her eyes even as she smiled. "Yes, Frederick has always been diligent in his duties and fair to those under his care."

Ahead, at the bottom of the hill, the coach awaited them, but Jamie felt a strong impulse to tell her more. "My lady, please permit me a kinsman's pride over the good woman your son has married."

She gasped softly. "Why, yes, Bennington told me she is your cousin." Her smile grew radiant, and her face a lovely older version of Marianne's. "That makes us related by marriage. Dear Captain Templeton." She gave his arm a gentle squeeze. "If your cousin Rachel is anything like you—"

"My lady," Wiggins called from atop the coach. "Will you ride now?"

Jamie assisted Lady Bennington back into the coach, and the rest of the party all clambered back to their earlier places to resume the journey to Bennington Park. But as Jamie remounted Puck and urged him to follow the others, he felt an odd confusion stirring within him. Was it merely wishful thinking, or had Lady Bennington been interrupted just as she was about to bestow her approval upon him?

As they continued toward Bennington Park, Marianne could barely keep from squirming on the coach's red velvet seat like an ill-mannered schoolgirl. Questions and speculations scurried through her mind as she wondered what Mama had said to Jamie. Of course, Marianne could never ask Mama, but their little visit must have been pleasant, for when Jamie assisted Mama into the coach, they exchanged earnest pleasantries emphasized by sincere smiles. At the first opportunity, she must try to ferret out the information from Jamie.

Calming herself so as not to draw Mama's scrutiny, Marianne turned her thoughts toward Bennington Park. Unlike some of her friends, she found life to be much more engaging and enjoyable in the country than in the city. In anticipation of a last summer of gaiety, she longed to stick her head out and see the manor house as they approached it. The most she could do was lean close to the window as the coach hastened along the winding, tree-lined lane as if the horses and driver were as eager as she to be home again. Familiar woodlands, gently sloping downs, the private lake, and the village beyond the manor house all beckoned to her.

At last the coach broke from the last stand of trees and the gray stone mansion appeared in all its beauty. Marianne's heart jolted as never before. Home, if only for a few more months. And she had much to see, much to cherish before she said goodbye to it all forever.

Chapter Fourteen

"Bertha." Marianne hurried into the musty-smelling attic room of the manor house. "We are home for the summer." As she knelt by the heavy upholstered chair where her old nurse sat, her voluminous skirts puffed with air and then settled about her. There, light beams from the single window shone on airborne dust particles, sending them into a swirling tempest.

"Lady Marianne." The nearsighted woman dropped her knitting to her lap and reached out to take Marianne's face in her soft, wrinkled hands. "Oh, my child, how I have missed you." Tears slid down her lined cheeks, but her smile was radiant.

"And I have missed you, my darling." Marianne's heart ached at the thought of the sorrow Bertha soon would feel. Once Marianne left England, it was doubtful they would ever see each other again this side of heaven.

"Now, you must tell me all about your season." Bertha picked up the woolen scarf she had been knitting and resumed her work. "Did you meet any fine young gentleman worthy of my little girl?"

Marianne laughed. "No, dear, I did not meet anyone new." Her nurse had asked the same question for the past four years upon the family's return from London. But despite her gift of discernment, she had failed last year to realize Marianne's heart had been claimed.

"Ah, no one *new*." Bertha's eyebrows rose in thick gray arches. "But there is something you are not telling me."

Marianne seldom did well at keeping secrets from Bertha, who was more like a grandmother than a servant to her. But this time she must hold her own counsel.

"What I will tell you is that the orphans at St. Ann's were delighted with the wonderful mittens and scarves and hats you knitted for them. Many a child keeps warm because of these hands." She reached out to envelop and still the busy fingers that had cared for her since birth.

A glow softened the wrinkles on the old woman's face. "God is more than generous to permit me to perform this service in my last years. One longs to be ever useful, you know." Her gaze, while a bit unfocused, settled on Marianne's eyes. "You have not diverted me, my little lady. But I am so pleased to see you that I shall not press you." She reclaimed her hands and set to knitting again. "When you are ready, I will be grateful to hear it all."

Marianne leaned close and nudged aside the woolen scarf, laying her head on Bertha's lap and closing her eyes. How good it would be to have a confidante in her plans. But Bertha's loyalty extended beyond Marianne to Mama and ultimately to Papa, whose generosity provided her a home for as long as she lived. She would be bound by honor to report such a scheme as an elopement. Well, not exactly an elopement. A runaway? Marianne's insides quivered at the thought of what she was planning.

"Shh, my dear one." Bertha must have set aside her knitting, for she placed both hands on Marianne's head as she always had when praying for her. "Seek God's wisdom, and let Him guide your path," she whispered.

Even through her thick coiffure, Marianne felt the tender touch of those guiding hands. Warmth spread through her like the blessing of a biblical patriarch, sweeping aside her embattled emotions and replacing them with peace.

This is the man you will marry. Thus had her prayer been answered two long months ago, and thus she continued to believe. She had searched the Scriptures for some example of what to do, but none was to be found there. With no other recourse but to stow away aboard Jamie's ship so that honor would require him to marry her. How else could God's will be accomplished?

She permitted herself a few tears, enough to dampen Bertha's gray muslin skirt. But she would not burden the woman with her secrets. Lifting her head and brushing away the moisture from her cheeks, she patted Bertha's hands.

"Take up your knitting, for I have many stories to tell you." Marianne rose and fetched a straight-backed chair to sit beside her nurse. "Now, do not be alarmed, but Robert had quite an adventure. In the company of Papa's guest, a Captain Templeton from America…"

For the next half hour, Marianne recounted to Bertha the long winter's many happenings. She took care not to mention Jamie's name too often, but when she did, she noticed Bertha's eyebrows wiggling. Could the old dear discern her feelings for him? If so, Marianne feared that her heart might give away her plans.

"A common sea captain."

A woman's harsh voice brought Jamie to a halt outside the open door of the manor house's drawing room.

"And not even in His Majesty's navy." The voice continued within the chamber. "A merchant and an *American*. Really, Bampton, could your father not choose someone of rank, or at least an Englishman for his current pet?"

As quietly as he could, Jamie inhaled a deep, calming breath. So far Lord Bennington's friends had viewed him as just that, a powerful aristocrat's "pet," whose acceptance in their society was due to his sponsor's influence. He had an uncomfortable feeling he would not find that same acceptance from the earl's oldest son and heir.

"Now, now, my dear," a languid male voice responded. "We must let the old boy have his fun. And after all, the man did save Robbie's life."

"Humph." The woman sniffed. "Whatever else should a servant do? 'Twas his duty."

"He could have run." Moberly's voice. "As your good friend Mr. Pincer did."

Jamie ground his teeth. He'd been summoned to the drawing room to meet the viscount and his wife, but he would have difficulty managing his temper if they treated him with the contempt he now heard in their voices.

"Jamie?" Marianne appeared beside him and touched his arm. "We should go in."

He recoiled, moving several feet away from her, then

regretted it when dismay covered her lovely face. "For-give me, my lady," he whispered, "but we cannot enter together."

She winced but nodded. "Of course not." She moved past him and walked into the room. "William. Lady Bampton. How wonderful to see you."

A painful ache tore through him. He couldn't bear to hurt her, yet couldn't avoid it. Nor could he fail to notice the differences in her address to her oldest brother and to his wife. In her life of so-called privilege, Jamie's ladylove was forced to play many games.

He leaned against the wall and gazed around the vast entry hall. As grand as the Grosvenor Square town house was, this vast hundred-year-old mansion outshone it by far. Daylight streamed in through tall, narrow win-dows onto pale green wallpaper framed by dark oak woodwork. The requisite life-size ancestral portraits lined the wide, elegant front staircase, and brass can-dlesticks and delicate figurines sat on every table. The air smelled of roses, fresh from Lady Bennington's gar-dens. Jamie looked forward to touring the grounds, for Moberly had hinted at the many interesting sights and activities the Park afforded.

A footman walked past carrying a tray of refresh-ments, and cast a curious look in his direction. Jamie shrugged and rolled his eyes, playing on the camarade-rie he'd established with that particular rank of servant. The man puckered away a smile. Waiting a few seconds, Jamie followed him into the drawing room. Or, rather, he followed the aroma of coffee wafting from the ca-rafe on the tray. Although he rarely chose that drink, a good jolt of the dark brew should fortify him against the coming interview.

"Ah, here he is." Moberly rose from a brocade chair and strode to greet Jamie, shaking his hand as if it had been a week since they'd seen each other instead of merely since breakfast not an hour before. "Come, my friend, I want to present you to my elder brother and his wife."

Moberly's voice held a hint of strain along with its jollity. Could it be he feared his older brother because one day William would hold the title *and* the power? Jamie pasted on a smile, but not a wide one. He must perform a delicate balancing act in this company.

"Lord and Lady Bampton." Moberly guided Jamie to where the others sat in a grouping of furniture in front of a great stone hearth. "May I present Papa's…and *my* particular friend, Captain James Templeton."

"I am honored, Lord Bampton, Lady Bampton." Jamie bowed to each to the same degree he would to Lady Bennington, and cast a quick glance at the viscountess's hand to see if she would lift it to be kissed. She did not. Jamie tried to recall Reverend Bentley's instructions about such things, but nothing came to mind to indicate an error on his part. So he bowed to Marianne, who was seated in a nearby chair. "My lady." He then moved to stand by the hearth until invited to sit, though he guessed such an invitation would not come. He didn't want to sit, anyway, but rather to walk out into the fresh air and be away from all this stuffiness.

"Well, I must say…" Lord Bampton stared at Jamie up and down through a quizzing glass. "These Americans do grow tall." Though seated, the viscount appeared not to have inherited his father's height nor his slender frame. Like Moberly before his stabbing, he owned a well-rounded form and a pasty complexion.

"La, such height seems unnatural to me." The viscountess was her husband's mirror image in feminine form, although her round, smooth face did hint at the beauty she must have been in her younger days.

"Why, Lady Bampton, whatever do you mean?" Marianne held out a cup of coffee to her sister-in-law. Again, her use of the woman's title told Jamie much about their relationship. No wonder she wanted to go to East Florida and meet Rachel, who would be a dear sister to her. If only he could grant her desire.

"Why, nothing, Lady Marianne." Her voice edged with disdain, the viscountess used *her* quizzing glass to study Marianne before accepting the coffee. "What a question."

This couple was quite a pair. Jamie could only guess what tortures they put the earl's younger offspring through. He could not keep his gaze from straying to Marianne to see if the other woman's tone had hurt her feelings. Marianne wrinkled her nose so quickly Jamie thought he might be mistaken. He had difficulty not laughing. His sweet lady would take nothing from this pompous woman. All the more reason to love her.

"Well, then." Moberly moved closer to Jamie rather than sit back down, but he addressed his brother. "What shall we do today?"

"Oh, la," the viscountess said. Jamie wondered if that was her favorite word. "I must rest from the journey. Swindon is entirely too far from Hampshire. I shall be glad when we take up permanent residence here."

Marianne's jaw dropped, and Robert choked on his coffee. Yet the woman seemed not to realize what she'd said. Nor did her husband, if his approving nod indicated his attitude. Even Jamie comprehended that they would not inherit Bennington Park until Lord Bennington died. Yet how could they act as if the patriarch's death counted for nothing?

Jamie bowed his head as guilt crowded judgment from his chest. Was betrayal a lesser sin than wishing someone dead?

Chapter Fifteen

"Georgie." Marianne waved to the children on the far side of the duck pond, where her nephew and nieces frolicked on the lawn under the watchful eyes of their nurse, a maid and two footmen. "Katherine. Elizabeth."

"Aunt Moberly! Uncle Robbie." Eight-year-old Georgie ran around the pond. Behind him six-year-old Elizabeth raced to catch up, while twelve-year-old Katherine kept a more sedate pace.

Georgie slammed into Robert, nearly knocking him over, and Elizabeth leaped into Marianne's outstretched arms. Amid much laughter, the children traded targets and lavished kisses on the two. Even Katherine let down a bit of her reserve to embrace them with open joy. Then she glanced beyond Marianne and stood up straight, a perfect lady.

"Good afternoon, Miss Kendall." Katherine's sweet, inclusive manners sent a surge of pride through Marianne. Most people, and certainly Lady Bampton, utterly ignored Grace because of her status as a mere companion to Mama.

"Good afternoon, Miss Moberly, Miss Elizabeth." Grace curtsied to the girls and Georgie. "Mr. Moberly."

"I say, Aunt Moberly." Georgie smiled up at Jamie. "Who is this tall chap?"

"This, Georgie, is your grandfather's good friend Captain James Templeton. He is an American sea captain."

"I say, a sea captain. How dashing." He stuck out his hand. "Pleased to meet you, Templeton."

"My honor, Mr. Moberly." Jamie's bemused expression as he shook Georgie's hand made Marianne want to laugh. She had never asked him if he spent much time around children. And no doubt he wondered how many more Mr. Moberlys he would be meeting.

After all the proper introductions were made, Marianne beckoned to the children. "We were about to go visit the Roman ruins and—"

"Oh, do let us go."

"Please take us with you."

"What fun!"

The children jumped up and down and clapped their hands.

"Not this time," Robert said. "We will plan a picnic for you there soon."

Their whines and fussing ceased at his stern frown. Marianne wondered how long they would show such respect to this uncle when their parents treated Robert so shabbily. She wanted to give an extra kiss to each of them for their courtesy to Jamie. In fact, Katherine's gaze had not left Jamie's face. This pretty niece would soon become a young lady and already showed an interest in her future social life.

"Now run back to your play, my darlings." Marianne

gave little Elizabeth another hug. "You will see us often enough this summer."

The four adults walked toward the downs on the northwest end of the Park. Jamie and Robert had brought walking sticks, and each offered an arm to assist his lady with the ups and downs of the inclines. Once past the thatch-roofed outbuildings beyond the manor house, over a rise and around a stand of trees, they paired comfortably without a word or look, as if all were in mutual agreement.

Indeed, Marianne guessed that another silent concurrence had been reached, for she felt certain Grace was aware of her love for Jamie. Yet as much as Marianne longed to ask for Grace's prayers regarding her plans to follow Jamie, she dared not. A deeply spiritual woman, Mama's companion would surrender her claim on Robert before doing anything so drastic to marry him. If Marianne confided in her, Grace, like Bertha, might feel bound to speak to Mama or at the least urge Marianne to abandon her scheme. If they did not speak of the matter, Grace could honestly say Marianne had told her nothing. Thus, Marianne must be content with these stolen moments and find solace in her own prayers.

Enjoying the fresh spring breeze that carried the fragrance of honeysuckle and new-mown hay, the group ambled over the grass-covered chalk downs to a small cluster of trees a half mile from the manor house, wherein lay a clearing of hard-packed clay.

"Right there." Robert pointed to the familiar enclosure rising some eighteen inches from the earth. "This is the site of a Roman settlement of some sort."

"At least we think it is Roman." Marianne felt a rush of childhood memories. She and Frederick had discovered the outline of the stone structure during a family picnic. Their three older brothers proclaimed it a Roman ruin, and they all dug furiously to reveal how deep it went into the earth. Later, servants exposed the entire eight-by-eight-foot square with an opening on one side and even evidence of ancient fires that had burned within it. "Father said it might have been a forge built by earlier settlers whom the Romans conquered."

When Marianne and her brothers played here under the watchful care of servants, they'd dug around, trying to find other ancient structures. Those times of exploration had been happier days for the family, and Marianne could never discover what had changed…or when.

"Interesting." Jamie bent down to touch the rough surface of the wall. "What stories must dwell in these stones. Yet the people who built this structure are lost to history."

"How like the verses in Psalm 103," Robert said. "They speak of a man's days being as the grass of the field, flourishing one day until the wind passes over it, and it is gone. I think one of the loneliest sentences in all of Scripture is 'and the place thereof shall know it no more.'" His face grew sober.

Marianne felt so pleased with his new interest in the Holy Bible, and her heart warmed to think of this new spiritual depth, even though the passage seemed to depress him.

"But the verse continues with a hopeful promise." Grace hooked her arm around his and gave him a sweet smile. "'The mercy of the Lord is from everlasting to everlasting upon them that fear Him, and His righteousness unto children's children.'"

"Well quoted," Jamie said. "I'm sure you both recall

that the promise is to those who keep His covenant and do His commandments." He stood and stared beyond the ruins in the direction of Portsmouth and the sea beyond, as if deep in thought. "It seems we have all been moved by those Scriptures to realize how transitory our lives are and how important it is to obey His laws."

Laws such as honor thy father and thy mother. Conviction bore down upon Marianne, but she stiffened her back. Or perhaps it was not conviction at all, but guilt, when she had nothing at all to feel guilty about. Did not the Lord create marriage? Did not her father and mother have a rich and happy marriage to a person chosen of their own free will? Should she not have the same privilege?

"Are you all right, Marianne?" Robert's gentle questioning interrupted her inner turmoil.

Jamie and Grace turned her way, and tears scalded her eyes at their concern. She raised her parasol as a shield against their concern. "We should not stay out in the sun much longer."

"No, we should not." Grace's voice lost its cheerfulness. "And perhaps I should return to the house to see if Lady Bennington requires anything from me."

"My dear stepmother will not mind if we stay away a bit longer." Robert drew his linen handkerchief from his pocket and dusted portions of the wall. Jamie followed suit, and soon all were seated, Grace and Robert close together on one wall and Marianne and Jamie across from them—a full two feet apart.

The ever-present breeze rustled Marianne's muslin gown and blew black strands of hair from her already loose coiffure. She glanced at Grace, who was, as always, a picture of modesty and control, with her muslin skirt smoothed beneath her and her dark brown hair tucked perfectly under her white cap. Only a frown marred her lovely appearance.

At this rare mood, Marianne cast off her own concerns. "Grace, you must tell us why you have grown melancholy. Is something amiss?"

Grace shook her head, but tears formed as she looked at Robert.

"What is it?" Marianne studied her brother's face.

He shrugged. "She is put out with me because I did not speak to Father about a living before we left London."

"I am not put out, Mr. Moberly." Even Grace's protest was gently spoken. "Merely sad. You are a new man in Christ and, as such, you must not let fear keep you from doing God's will."

Marianne withheld a laugh at this new assertiveness, but Robert grimaced.

"Let me see if I understand." Jamie's eyes lit with playfulness. "You expect to have the boldness to preach the gospel to sinners, yet you can't gather enough courage to ask for your own father's sponsorship for your studies?"

"You know Bennington." Robert's wry expression matched his tone. "Why would he give me an egg when he can give me a scorpion?"

"Mr. Moberly." Grace shook her head.

"Robert!" Marianne would have smacked his arm if he had been closer.

"Now, now, ladies." Robert's light laugh held no mirth. "You well know Bennington showers you two— and Lady Bennington, of course—with nothing but kindness. But not one of his four sons will ever live up to his high standards, nor will we even comprehend what those standards might be."

"Nevertheless, Moberly," Jamie said, "you *must* ask him to sponsor your bid for a church post. Just ask yourself whether, at the end of your life, you'd rather have pleased your earthly father or your heavenly Father."

"Well put, Captain Templeton." Grace clapped her hands, another unusual display of emotion that surprised Marianne. "You see, Mr. Moberly, we are all with you in this. That is—" Her face grew pink. "I have said too much."

"Nonsense, my dear." Robert grasped her gloved hand and kissed it. "Very well, then, since I can count on all your prayers, I shall speak to Father as soon as he arrives from London."

"Perhaps the morning after, brother." Even Marianne had received a sharp retort when approaching Papa too soon after his arrival from a long journey.

The others laughed, and in the corner of her eye, she noticed Jamie looking at her. With all his talk of courage, she longed to ask why he could not exert the same daring and speak to Papa for her hand. "Now we truly must go home." She stood, and the others joined her.

As they left through the small opening in the stone enclosure, Robert chuckled. "I have been meaning to tell you all a very fine joke, but thought it best not to speak it within the hearing of others." His laughter grew. "Ah, if only those who think they are wise had any comprehension, they would discover us all too soon."

Marianne eyed him with curiosity. "Whatever are you talking about?"

"Why, do you not know, sister?" Robert clapped

Jamie on the shoulder and reached out to pat Marianne's cheek. "Your lovely mother and our exalted father think Miss Kendall and Templeton here have formed an attachment." More laughter, real and deep from his belly. "Isn't that rich?"

Marianne stared first at Robert, then Grace, her gaze landing at last on Jamie. "So that is why they permit, even encourage, the four of us to spend time together. Why, they expect Robert and me to be your chaperones."

Grace's smile held a great deal less amusement and a great deal more worry as she looked around their circle. "Oh, dear. Now what shall we do?"

Robert moved closer to her and captured her arm. "We shall enjoy our little secret, Miss Kendall. That is what we shall do."

So Jamie needed only to focus his attention on Miss Kendall when others were around, and no one would discern the true object of his love. The idea tantalized him. To think he could set aside his guilty feelings over the hours spent in this merry little group. He could feel free to enjoy Marianne's company as long as they were all together. After all, until Lord Bennington returned to his country home, bringing the latest news about the Crown's plans for defending East Florida, Jamie had nothing to do but wait for word that the *Fair Winds* was ready to set sail.

Halfway back to the manor house, the couples changed partners, and Jamie offered his arm to the compliant Miss Kendall. He gave her a teasing wink to lighten her mood. But the scarlet blush on her fair cheeks sent a dagger of conviction into his heart. Clearly their scheme did not please this Christian lady. And Jamie felt the same old guilt gnawing at his soul.

In the days following their excursion to the ruins, Jamie permitted himself to appreciate country living. Each morning he rode around the shire with Moberly and his brother, finding Bampton much more pleasant when not in the company of his snobbish wife. As weather permitted, afternoon walks afforded much-needed exercise. And each evening the adults gathered in the drawing room after supper to play whist or to read poetry.

The night before Bennington was to return home, Marianne brought out a leather-bound volume. "The sonnets of Sir Philip Sidney rival those of Shakespeare." She opened the book. "I have a favorite, and should I ever find a man worthy of my affections, I shall embroider it on a sampler for his wedding gift."

"Do read it, my dear." Lady Bennington's eyes lit with interest. "And do not despair over love, for the man of God's choosing will come into your life one day."

Jamie swallowed hard and turned to study a figurine on the table beside him, praying Marianne's audacity would not cause them both further heartache.

She settled in a chair and glanced around at her audience, pausing briefly to give Jamie a smile that sent his ravaged emotions tumbling. "'My true-love hath my heart, and I have his, By just exchange one for the other given.'" Her voice wavered, and she cleared her throat. "'I hold his dear, and mine he cannot miss. There never was a bargain better driven.'"

The tender words spun through Jamie's mind and reached his soul, pulling the breath from his lungs until he thought he might have to leave the room—an unfor-givable affront.

She continued. "'My heart was wounded with his wounded heart; For as from me on him his hurt did light, So still, methought, in me his hurt did smart. Both equal hurt, in this change sought our bliss, My true-love hath my heart and I have his.'"

Marianne closed the book, and her eyes glistened. Sweet, brave girl, she didn't look at Jamie. Yet for one mad moment, he longed to shout "amen." For she truly had his heart...and would have it forever, no matter how much it hurt.

Chapter Sixteen

Marianne ached for the pain in Jamie's eyes. Perhaps she should not have read the sonnet. But this was the closest she could ever come to announcing her love for him to her family. After everyone retired for the night, she lay abed as usual, reexamining all her plans. Tomorrow she would begin that sampler. And perhaps one day soon, everyone would know that Lady Marianne Moberly loved the American sea merchant, Captain Jamie Templeton, for he had her heart, and she had his.

Upon waking the next morning, she learned from Emma that Papa had arrived late the night before and retired to his apartment. As she expected, the morning atmosphere in the manor house became formal, almost somber. The housemaids hastened to clean common areas, then scurried out of sight, no doubt to avoid encounters with their early-rising employer. Footmen wore blank expressions rather than pleasant ones. The children stayed out of sight with their nurse until such time as their grandfather should summon them, an annual family ritual everyone dreaded. Marianne hoped this year their good behavior would win Papa's approval, but they often misbehaved in front of their parents. But her greatest concern was that Papa would somehow notice the unplanned, affectionate gazes she sometimes traded with Jamie. Of all the denizens of Bennington Park, it seemed only Mama was happy to have Papa home.

Jamie, Robert and William went out riding, a custom they had acquired of late and one which generally pleased Marianne. She hoped her eldest brother's better nature might show itself when he was away from Lady Bampton. But today she would find Jamie's company reassuring, and missed him terribly. As it was, Mama and Lady Bampton slept late, and even Papa did not come downstairs as early as usual. So Marianne and Grace ate a quiet repast in the breakfast room before taking up their needlework in the bright light of the south parlor.

"Bother." Marianne searched her sewing basket. "I have used all of my blue."

"Hmm." Grace held out a small ball of thread. "Will this do?"

"Thank you." Marianne laid the twine next to the indigo stitches on her sampler. "'Tis a bit too light, do you not think?"

"Indeed, yes." Grace could always be counted on to agree.

Marianne studied her new project, but last night's inspiration eluded her. In truth, she did not want to sew, and longed to be out riding with the men. Or out anywhere. "Nothing will suit but to take the carriage down to Portsmouth and shop."

"Or we could go to the village, which will not take as long." Grace's eyes twinkled. "We want to be back to welcome Lord Bennington."

"I suppose so." She truly loved Papa and always tried to please him. Never before had she feared or avoided him. But now she began to understand some of her brothers' foolish behavior in their vain attempts to satisfy their patriarch.

She looked at Grace, seated in the adjacent chair wearing a peaceful smile as she concentrated on her sewing—the very picture of serenity, much like Mama. She would be content with whatever God chose for her, even if it meant giving up Robert and breaking her heart. Yet, just as Marianne knew God had spoken to her about marrying Jamie, she believed Grace and Robert should be married. But how could either couple be wed when Papa stood before them all like the angel with the flaming sword who had kept Adam and Eve from reentering the Garden of Eden? In her own case, if she could not persuade Emma to help her board Jamie's ship, what other recourse did she have? Dress as a sailor? Hide in a barrel?

"Ridiculous." What a mad course her thoughts had taken.

"What is ridiculous?" Grace's fair face creased with concern. "Are you unwell?"

"I am well, thank you." Marianne released a long sigh. "But I shall be much better after we take our walk to the village." She set aside her sewing, grasped Grace's hand and stood. "Why waste a lovely day by staying indoors?"

Returning to her chamber, she summoned Emma to bring her walking shoes and shawl in case the day grew overcast and cool. As her maid helped her tug on the heavy leather shoes, a thought occurred to Marianne. At sea, this lace shawl would not keep her warm. She must have a new hooded cloak, heavily lined and black. A nervous thrill swept up from her heart to her throat at the idea of doing something tangible for her "flight."

Outside, the sun shone brightly, and a fresh breeze carried the fragrance of roses from Mama's garden to the narrow village road. Soon the musty smell of sheep became the stronger scent, and Marianne and Grace covered their noses with linen handkerchiefs. John the footman followed behind in case last year's gypsy band had again set up camp in the woodlands.

The small settlement of thatch-roofed cottages and businesses had been tidied up, probably in anticipation of Papa's arrival. Shop signs had been repaired and painted, and the single, rutted lane through the center of the village had been raked clean of debris and evidence of animals. Although Papa seldom went there, the citizens always took pride in being prepared in case their landlord varied his routine. Like a feudal thane, Papa served the king while his own tenants worked his land. Marianne had never considered such a thing before, but in truth they all were descendants of that time long ago when a serf could never leave the land of his birth, and daughters of the wellborn grew up to become bargaining tools in the world of politics. While these villagers were still dependent upon Papa's goodwill, at least he had never tried to force her into an unwanted marriage.

As though wafted on the wind, news of Marianne's approach must have carried from one building to the next, for in each doorway men bowed and women curtsied, all smiling their greetings. She waved and called each by name, stopping to inquire about a newborn infant or a child's progress in reading or the health of an aged parent. Each tenant seemed as pleased by her interest as if Father Christmas had paid a summer visit.

In the tiny mercantile shop, which sold a surprising array of fabrics, buttons, stays and needles, Marianne found her indigo thread, and Grace a card of buttons. Marianne also found a set of shiny brass shoe buckles engraved with three-masted ships, but resisted the temptation to buy them for Jamie. Then, while Grace chatted with the shop owner, Marianne gave whispered orders to his wife for a hooded black cloak made of wool from Papa's large flock of sheep. The woman, comprehending Marianne's need for secrecy, discreetly wrote down the order, her eyes twinkling. "A gift for yer mum's birthday, eh, milady?" she said. "Never you mind. We'll make it up good and proper and deliver it on the sly."

Marianne smiled and tilted her head in a noncommittal gesture, but felt as if she had just told a lie. Swallowing back her guilt, she thanked the woman. "Shall we go, Miss Kendall?"

As she and Grace walked back toward home, several children skipped along beside them. Marianne promised sweetmeats after Sunday services for any who could recite their catechism, and a party for them all one day soon. She thought one or two of them might have followed all the way to the manor house if their parents had not called them back.

"What an invigorating walk." Marianne inhaled the fresh spring air. "We must bring Mama next time."

"And perhaps Lady Bampton."

Marianne cast a glance at Grace, then a quick look over her shoulder. John the footman followed at a discreet distance, so she could be free in her conversation. "I doubt my sister-in-law would care to walk so far." She did not intend to be unkind, but the viscountess could make life insufferable, especially for Grace, whom she treated as a servant instead of Mama's poor but wellborn companion. Grace's inclusiveness of the woman revealed her sweet spirit.

Yet while Marianne admired Grace's Christian character, she could not help but think there were times when a person, even a woman, did not have to accept so submissively the pains and disappointments life meted out to her. Grace might find such thinking a sin, but Marianne was not so certain. Having ordered the cloak, she felt more than ever that her plan was right.

"How's this?" Jamie stood tying his cravat before the long mirror in his bedchamber, a larger, sunnier room than the one he'd inhabited in London.

Quince lounged in a brown leather chair. "You're getting better. Make it look good, because my reputation as a valet is at stake." He yawned and rolled his head and shoulders, as if waking from a long sleep.

"Get up, Aaron." Jamie took his gray jacket from the bed and shrugged it on. "You know how these servants come in to tend their duties with barely a scratch on the door. If one of them caught you sitting down while I'm dressing myself, it'd be all over the house in five minutes."

Quince groaned. "How much longer do we have to play this game? I'm ready to marry my Emma and take her home." He stood and stretched, then found a clothes brush and began to whisk nonexistent lint from Jamie's jacket and breeches.

A familiar ache throbbed in Jamie's chest. He longed to wed, too, and take Marianne back to East Florida, but that could never be. "Saunders'll send word when the *Fair Winds* is ready to sail. I've been thinking. Instead of our returning to London, I'll tell him to gather the crew and sail over to Southampton."

"Sounds pretty risky, if you ask me. After François delivers the muskets, do you really think Saunders should sail past Portsmouth and the Royal Navy docks?"

"Under the Union Jack and Bennington's flag, we shouldn't have a problem." Jamie pointed to his shiny black shoes with their large brass buckles. "Don't forget the footwear." He smirked at his friend.

Quince rolled his eyes but bent to brush the shoes. "I must confess I'm tied in knots now that the earl has shown up. Lady Bennington told Emma she would speak to the old man about our getting married. Of course, we'll get married with or without his consent. But if he gives permission, it might mean he'll give Emma a wedding gift." Aaron finished his job and rested an elbow against the mantel. "Of course, I don't need the money, but she doesn't know that, and it'll give her a measure of pride to bring something to our marriage."

"That's decent of you, my friend." Jamie punched his shoulder, then took a final glance at himself in the mirror. "How do I look?"

"Ready for an audience with the king, milord." Quince grinned.

Jamie chuckled. "From what Moberly and the viscount have said, it's very much like a king holding court when Bennington gathers his family here at the Park. Apparently the old man sits in his high-back chair as if it's a throne, and makes personal comments to each of his offspring. Bampton likened it to a whaler in the

midst of a pod of whales. Harpooning, he called it."
Jamie shook his head. "And not one of his sons es-
capes the lance."

A scratch on the door brought their conversation to
an end. John the footman entered. "Captain Templeton, sir, the earl has summoned the family and requests
your presence."

Jamie almost sent a knowing look to Aaron, but
stopped himself in time. Gentlemen, Reverend Bentley had taught him, did not engage in such camarade-
rie with their servants. Instead, he nodded to John and
strode from the room as if summoned before a king.

As with his bedchamber, the drawing room on the
first floor was larger than the one in town. Jamie had
enjoyed the evenings he'd spent there with Marianne
and her family for these past few days as they waited for
the earl's return. Her reading of Sir Philip Sidney's sonnets would always be a fond memory, and Jamie thought
he might have liked that noble Elizabethan courtier.
Lady Bampton cooled their laughter somewhat, but all
in all, it had been a pleasant start to the summer.

What was he thinking? He'd become entirely too
relaxed while he lived with this ruling class. He had a
duty to perform, and the success of the Revolution, or
at least his small part in it, depended upon his completing that duty. And yet the niggling sadness over his approaching separation from Marianne would not cease.

The afternoon sun beamed through the tall west windows and heated the drawing room, which would doubtless intensify the misery of the coming assembly. Only
the fragrance of the long-stemmed red roses in six or
seven vases around the chamber mitigated the close-

ness of the air. Jamie could only conclude that the earl liked to see his children sweat.

"Ah, Templeton, there you are." Moberly entered and strode to Jamie, his hand outstretched. "Well, here we go. The dreaded annual judgment day."

Jamie pumped his moist hand, an unmistakable sign that Moberly was already nervous. "Surely it can't be that bad." He clasped his friend's shoulder. "Buck up. You know what you have to do."

"Yes. My father's agreed to speak privately with me after he's finished with the family." Moberly's eyes gleamed a bit too brightly. "You cannot know what your support means."

"Three others are praying for you, friend." Jamie moved to the hearth, his usual perch. "And don't forget God Himself cares deeply about this. It is He whom you desire to serve."

Moberly's expression softened. "I have felt your prayers *and* the Lord's touch." He tapped his chest. "I must admit that feels far better than the 'touches' of brandy I've depended upon these many years."

Footsteps sounded outside the door. The younger members of the family entered in a group, all wearing solemn faces. Marianne sent Jamie a sweet smile, causing a swirl of emotions to churn through his chest. He put on a sober expression and gave her a formal nod, stopping himself in midwink. He really must drop that habit, at least in this company.

Everyone took their places, each seeming to know where they were expected to sit. Lord and Lady Bampton were more subdued than Jamie had ever seen them, and he was surprised to see the usually active children sitting primly on a settee, their hands folded in their laps. Even he felt his chest tighten in expectation, and for the first time in weeks, he worried that Bennington might have found him out. To ease such groundless speculation, he struck a careless pose, resting a foot on the pedestal of a five-foot statue of Zeus standing sentinel beside the hearth, and his elbow on the Greek god's shoulder.

Some minutes passed without a word among them, until at last the earl entered, a scowl on his noble visage, while the countess followed close behind, dispensing a beneficent smile to each person in the room. Facing the rest of the furniture, the earl's ornate wooden chair had a red leather cushion and a high back with a wild boar carved in the center, presumably to force its occupant to sit absolutely erect. Jamie wondered why a person would choose such a seat when he could have any of the comfortable chairs in the room. But the ways of these English nobles never ceased to perplex him. Did the man prefer to be as uncomfortable as he made his children?

Only seconds after Bennington settled in, and before he could begin his comments, little Georgie started to grasp Elizabeth's hair. As he pulled, Jamie coughed and let his foot slip from the pedestal so that his hard leather heel thumped loudly on the hearth's stone floor. All attention swung to him, with several gasps coming from the ladies. But Jamie kept his focus on Georgie, narrowing his eyes for the briefest instant. The boy snatched back his hand, sucked in his lower lip and stared down.

"Your pardon, my lord." Jamie gave the earl his best boyish grin. "Clumsy me."

The earl's eyebrows shot upward. "Do not give it a thought, my boy." As if the sun had emerged from behind a cloud, the man's expression brightened, and he gazed around the room. "Ah, 'tis good to be home with all of you."

"Welcome home, sir," Bampton said on the wind of a long-held breath.

"Father, dear." Marianne hurried over to kiss his forehead, and the children clambered after her before their parents could stop them.

The earl lifted Elizabeth up on his lap, tousled Georgie's hair and pulled Miss Moberly into a one-armed embrace. "And what mischief have you three been up to?"

The children spoke all at once, regaling their grandfather with their stories while the adults looked on. Bampton sent Jamie a grateful nod. Lady Bampton stared at him up and down through her quizzing glass, her expression unreadable.

"All right, now, let us see how tall you are." Bennington put Elizabeth off of his lap and stood, then measured the two younger ones against his waistcoat buttons. When it came to Miss Moberly, he shook his head. "Whom have we here? Where has my little Katherine gone? Who is this elegant young lady?" She giggled, still a child.

More clamoring ensued, with the earl laughing out loud more than once. Everyone in the room appeared surprised, relieved, even relaxed. Jamie noticed Moberly's hopeful expression, and Miss Kendall's serene smile. Marianne sent Jamie a wistful look, stirring his emotions again. Were they all thinking the same as he? In this pleasant, generous mood, perhaps the earl would grant each and every one of them their hearts' desires, if they would but ask him.

Jamie reined in his thoughts and turned from Marianne's sweet gaze to stare up at the painting above the hearth. While he could not ask for his own wish to be granted, he could pray that Robert Moberly would have the courage to ask for his.

Chapter Seventeen

Marianne gazed across the room at Jamie, her heart overflowing with love. This dear man had brought nothing but good to her family, and she longed to tell Papa how much she loved her American sea captain. How marvelous that a simple pretense for awkwardness could alter the entire atmosphere and everyone's frame of mind. Neither she nor her brothers would ever have tried such a trick to change the mood of the room, or to rescue their nephew from scolding and disfavor. Perhaps that was their trouble. They feared Papa needlessly.

She put herself in Papa's place, coming home to a family that seemed to dread his company, just like some of his opponents in Parliament. With all of them cowering before him, no wonder he had always been critical of his sons. Of course, she and Mama never had anything to fear, but they both always sympathized with the misery of their loved ones.

Now, in this moment of family amiability, she could envision herself asking Papa's favor for Jamie to court her. She looked again at her beloved and saw the longing in his eyes, which he quickly shielded from her by staring up at the painting over the mantelpiece. Tears scalded away her confidence, and prudence gripped her once more. And yet perhaps, just perhaps, if Robert's interview with Papa turned out well, she might dare to ask for her own heart's longing.

"There now." The earl slumped back in his chair and swiftly bucked away from that silly wild boar designed to force good posture. She winced for him, but his stoic facade gave no hint of pain. "You have wearied this old man." He patted Georgie's head and gave the girls another hug. "Run along now. Find your nurse. The adults must have some peace and quiet once in a while." His jolly tone belied his words.

The nurse must have been hovering outside the door, for she hurried into the drawing room and whisked the children away.

Immediately, Marianne sensed caution falling over the room like a curtain. But Papa merely asked after everyone's health, going from one to the next around the circle. He expressed regret over missing William and Lady Bampton in London during most of the season, but recalled their pleasant time at Christmas last. He brought news of Jamie's ship, which had been careened, scraped and recaulked, and would soon sport a new mast of sturdy live oak, a fact that startled Marianne, for it meant her beloved must soon sail away. Jamie thanked Papa, but she thought she detected a hint of hesitation in his eyes. Was he thinking her thoughts? Once his ship was loaded with the gathered cargo from the warehouses, nothing remained to keep him here.

Papa told Marianne that Tobias Pincer missed seeing her in town. She thanked Papa, but wanted to gag at the thought of Robert's former friend and all of his treachery.

Next, with the gentleness of a loving parent, Papa promised to enlist Grace's commentary on Reverend Bentley's upcoming sermons, for the minister would henceforth have the living at Bennington Park now that the old vicar had retired, something they had all expected and approved of. At last, he stood and kissed Mama's hand.

"And the happiest news, my dear, is that my son Thomas will soon arrive in Portsmouth, perhaps even in time for your summer garden party."

"Oh, Bennington, how delightful." Mama reached up to kiss his cheek. "Do you suppose he has been promoted?"

Father's countenance clouded. "I shall be greatly displeased if he has not been. With all our trouble with France and that nonsense going on in the American colonies, His Majesty's navy will need good commanders. Of all my sons, only Thomas possesses the courage of a military man." He pointed at the painting above the mantel, one Marianne had always loved, which showed Papa mounted on horseback in battle beside the late King George II. "When I served with His Majesty at Dettingen back in '43, we knew what a man was. We knew how to fight." He beat the air with his fist. "Yes, Thomas has what it takes to show those brigands who their master is."

Marianne could see William and Robert wilt, and she sent up a heartfelt prayer that Robert would not let these comments defeat him.

"Well, now," Papa said, "you are all dismissed except Robert." He strode over to Jamie and shook his

hand. "Good to have you here, lad. Have my sons kept
you entertained?"

A soft gasp escaped Lady Bampton, and Marianne
puckered away a smile. Her sister-in-law had never
spoken a civil word to Jamie, yet he saved Georgie—
and all of them—from Papa's sour mood. No doubt the
viscountess felt some degree of indignation over Papa's favor toward Jamie. Well, the disagreeable woman
would simply have to endure it.

Yet another thought struck Marianne. One day William would ascend to the title and Lady Bampton would
become Lady Bennington. How would she treat Mama,
who would become the dowager countess? Marianne
reminded herself that it would not do to make her an
enemy. But if Marianne followed Jamie to East Florida, she would have no say in how anyone treated her
mother back home in England.

As the company disbursed, Jamie escorted Miss
Kendall from the drawing room, and they joined Marianne beside the wide staircase in the entry hall. Miss
Kendall bowed her head, and Marianne chewed her
thumbnail, a habit she had taken up of late. Jamie longed
to grasp her hands to reassure her, but his own feelings
were loose from their moorings.

He'd had good friends all his life, but his friendship with Robert Moberly had been perhaps the most
rewarding, a fact for which he could take little credit.
God truly had touched Moberly, changing him from a
drunken prodigal to a man who desired to serve Him.
Jamie had no doubt that with further studies and Reverend Bentley's mentoring, he would make an excellent minister of the Gospel. But everything hinged on

Bennington's approval, and Jamie's nerves skittered about his stomach in anticipation of the outcome of this interview.

The earl's deep, hearty laughter rang from behind the drawing room's closed door. A good sign? Jamie and the ladies traded looks, mirroring each other with eyebrows raised in expectation. The drawing room was silent for several moments. Now the door opened and slammed against the entry wall. Moberly stalked out, his eyes wide and wild, and swiped the back of his hand across his lips, a gesture Jamie had not seen since the man quit drinking.

He stopped to stare at them briefly, yet no recognition lit his eyes. Then he strode down the hallway, cutting through the house toward the back. Marianne huffed out a cross breath, while Miss Kendall's sigh held a note of heartbreak. Anger roared up inside of Jamie, and he turned toward the drawing room, his jaw and fists clenched. He would tell that fool of a father what a mistake he'd just made.

"Jamie."

"Captain Templeton."

Marianne and Miss Kendall grasped his arms.

"You must not." Marianne's eyes swam with tears. "I will speak to Papa."

Jamie chewed his lip. "You're right. I'd only make matters worse."

At the slam of a door, Miss Kendall's gaze turned in the direction Moberly had taken. She turned to Jamie. "Please, will you…?" Her voice sounding clogged with emotion, but the plea in her eyes was clear.

He squeezed her forearm. "I'll look after him." With a nod to Marianne, he hurried down the hallway. He'd managed to figure out the maze of halls, rooms and staircases comprising the manor house. Guessing that Moberly had headed for the stable, he descended a small flight of stairs and exited through a back door. Across the wide backyard, where geese and chickens pecked the ground for bugs and a servant sat at a grinding wheel sharpening knives, Moberly entered the low-roofed stable. Jamie quickly closed the distance between them, entering the darkened building just as his friend slung a saddle onto Gallant's back.

"Mr. Moberly, sir." A slender, mop-haired young groom reached out to help him. "I'd be honored to saddle 'im for you."

"I can do it myself." Robert's bitter tone cut the air, and he waved the boy off with a sharp gesture that did not make contact, but nevertheless sent him reeling backward. "I *am* capable of a few things."

"Very well, sir." The groom watched with widened eyes.

Jamie clapped the boy on the shoulder. "Would you saddle Puck for me, lad?"

The groom gave him a quivering smile. "Aye, sir, be glad to."

"I do not require a nursemaid, Templeton." Moberly jerked the girth around Gallant's belly, and the massive horse snorted and danced on his heavy back hooves. "Hold still." His words came out through gritted teeth, but at least he'd not cursed, as had been his former habit.

"Of course you don't." Jamie stepped forward and rubbed Gallant's forehead, something Moberly had taught him to settle a horse down. "But I, too, would like an outing this fine afternoon." In truth, sullen gray clouds had begun to roll over the sky as if following the sun as it wended its way westward—a promise of rain if Jamie had ever seen one. His new jacket and shoes, neither made for rain or riding, might be ruined. But it was a small price to pay for his friend's well-being.

Moberly finished with the saddle. "You will not want to go where I'm going." Again he brushed the back of his hand across his lips. Jamie had seen many a drunkard do the same thing in his desperation for a drink.

He followed as Moberly led Gallant out of the stable, then watched him leap into the saddle, dig in his heels and gallop away. The groom seemed to take a long time to bring Puck, and Jamie paced about the yard, his nerves tightening as the minutes passed. The boy still looked stricken as he handed over the reins. "Here you go, sir."

"Thank you, my lad." Jamie lifted his foot to place it in the left stirrup, but Puck pranced around in a circle. He had the urge to swat the mischievous animal's flanks, but realized that would only make matters worse.

"Here, sir. Let me 'elp." The groom grabbed the bridle and secured it to a post, then gave Jamie a leg up into the saddle.

"Thank you, lad." His pride was a bit bruised by his needing help to mount this rascal. But pride was unimportant now, for Jamie had a far more important concern. He dug his heels into Puck's flanks and reined him toward the road to Portsmouth, where the dust from Gallant's hooves still stirred in the air.

"We must not stay here." Marianne could hear the sound of Papa's footsteps crossing the drawing room floor. She grasped Grace's hand, and the two of them scurried up the wide front staircase like frightened mice. Once they reached Marianne's bedchamber, they fell into each other's arms and wept. Marianne had never seen Grace so discomposed, but her own anguish was so severe she had no words to comfort her friend.

"My lady." Emma appeared from her little room wringing her hands. "Whatever is the matter? How can I help you?" She brought forth two fresh linen handkerchiefs and fetched glasses of water from the crystal pitcher on a side table.

"Thank…you… Em…ma." Struggling for control, Marianne sniffed and dabbed at her tears. In love herself, surely Emma had long ago noticed the other romances blooming in the shadows of the household. While Marianne had not yet confided her plans to her little lady's maid, she had not denied the girl's veiled remarks regarding her affections for a certain American nor her open remarks about Grace and Robert.

Grace breathed out a long shuddering sigh. "Forgive me," she whispered.

Marianne started to say there was nothing to forgive, but realized her friend was praying. Still, she could not think God would mind these heartfelt tears on Robert's behalf. Infused with a sudden fervor, she grasped Grace's and Emma's hands and led them to the chairs in front of her hearth. "We will pray together. Has the Lord not said that wherever two or three are gathered in His name, He will be with us?"

Grace gave her a trembling smile, and Emma's eyes grew round, as if she was startled by this unsettling elevation from lady's maid to lady's confidante.

"It is all right," Marianne said. "We are all equal before our Heavenly Father."

"Yes, my lady." Emma's eyes sparkled, and her smile held a bit of mischief. Marianne could not guess why.

With her head bowed, Marianne prayed first for Robert's and Jamie's safety, then for Papa to have a change of heart regarding Robert's future. The others lifted the same petitions in their own words. Emma added her request that, while the Lord was in the business of speaking to Lord Bennington regarding matters of the heart, He might also grant Aaron Quince favor in the earl's eyes. Then she gasped. Marianne and Grace raised their heads to look at her.

"I did not mean to be impertinent, my lady." Emma's round cheeks were pinched with worry.

Marianne shook her head. "Be at ease, Emma. I did not think you were at all impertinent."

However, the answering gleam in her maid's eyes threw up a caution in Marianne's mind. Mama had always taught her that God loved every person the same, whether rich or poor, mistress or servant, but each had her place in His plan. Servants who were granted too much liberty might one day misuse it, even a grateful orphan like Emma. Marianne must walk a delicate path while keeping Emma in her proper place, for one day soon her own happiness, her own future, would depend on Emma's good feelings for her.

Chapter Eighteen

Jamie bent low on Puck's back and urged him to a full gallop, taking care not to plow into people walking or driving carts on their way home from a long summer day's work. At least he did not have to stop to ask directions. In his early morning rides with Moberly and Bampton, he had seen Portsmouth in the distance, some five or six miles over numerous hills from Bennington Park. Late at night, from his bedchamber window, he could see the flickering lights of the growing naval town and Southampton to the west, where he must make arrangements at one of the public wharves for the *Fair Winds* to dock. Now that Bennington had informed him the ship was ready to sail, he would have to follow through on those plans, and the sooner, the better. Yet this evening, God had clearly shown him his work in England had not yet been completed.

Mindful of the danger he'd put Puck in a few weeks earlier, Jamie slowed the horse when the road rose over the hills, then gave him his head when they descended. As always, Puck seemed to enjoy their outing. Jamie wished he could say the same for himself this time.

Portsmouth had all the clutter of a town growing so fast it kept popping its seams. Some semblance of planning appeared in the residential area Jamie passed through. Fine brick homes and straight, tree-lined streets graced these outer edges. But that quickly gave way the closer Jamie got to the narrow, winding streets along the waterfront, where he hoped to find Robert.

Jamie prayed good sense would prevail, yet he had a foreboding that he'd find his friend already "three sheets in the wind," as they said in Nantucket, especially since Jamie had no idea where to find him, giving Moberly more time to drink to excess.

A typical navy town, Portsmouth boasted in what should be its shame—countless taverns large and small, and countless immodestly dressed women calling to sailors or any passing man in decent clothing to come into their lairs. Again, Jamie had cause to pray, for Robert had confessed an occasional visit to such places before he'd placed his trust in Christ. If Jamie found him returning to his old haunts, he'd beg Moberly on Miss Kendall's behalf not to return to such a vile custom.

In his many years among seafaring men, whether whaler, sailor or merchant, Jamie had learned that self-righteous preaching never accomplished anything. In the first few taverns he visited, he ordered a drink, then asked the serving wench about Moberly. Everyone in Portsmouth knew Bennington's second son, but he'd not been that way. Jamie paid his coin and left the rum on a table. In each place, he noticed how quickly someone grabbed his abandoned tankard. Finally, a clear-eyed wench who seemed entirely too young for her occupation said Moberly had been there, but had moved on to the Stowaway, unless he'd changed his mind.

Jamie hooked a finger under the girl's chin and stared into her pale blue eyes. "God loves you, child. I will pray He will show you a more worthy profession." He pressed a silver coin into her hand and enjoyed the shock and, perhaps, conviction covering her sweet face.

Outside, he took Puck's reins from the boy he'd engaged to tend him, paid the lad a coin, and continued down the street. This evening was becoming very expensive for a sober man who generally held on to his money. How much might it cost a drunkard whose pockets were filled with his father's guineas?

The Stowaway stood two blocks in the distance. As Jamie jostled his way through the masses, he saw a young man struggling to free himself from several sailors with clubs. *Press gang.* Jamie's heart hitched thinking of the terror he'd felt as a lad when the warning came that the British navy had sent out ruffians to gather crew members for their ships. Torn away from friends and family without warning, given no chance to say their goodbyes, the hapless victims seemingly disappeared, some never to return. Jamie looked closely to see if the young man was from Bennington's village. If so, he would intervene, warning the sailors of the earl's displeasure and reprisal. But the lad was not familiar, and although Jamie pitied him, he felt the Lord's prompting to continue on his mission.

Rain began to splatter the dust at his feet. The shoes would be ruined, all right. He'd never be able to talk Quince into cleaning them up, and it would be dangerous to ask the earl's valet how to do it. Greyson already eyed Quince as if he were an inferior servant. No need to give him reason to learn Quince employed servants of his own back home.

Ducking into the tavern just as the heavens opened in a deluge, Jamie saw Moberly seated in a corner, his back to the wall. He looked up and met Jamie's stare. But instead of a sullen or angry greeting, he gave a lazy smile and beckoned to him. Apparently, the drink had already done its job. As evidenced by the expression on his face, Moberly was feeling nothing but mindless bliss, from which he would come crashing down in the morning.

Ignoring the smells of sweat, rum and cooking cabbage, Jamie wended his way through the roomful of drinking men, and sat adjacent to Moberly. "You're a hard man to keep up with."

"Ha." Robert tossed down the last drops in his tankard, then lifted it toward a wench serving the next table. "When you can, Betty."

"Right away, milord." The plump woman left the other men, common sailors who apparently knew who Moberly was, for they made no complaint. Well past her prime, she gave Jamie a sliding look up and down and puckered her lips suggestively. "My, aren't you a pretty one. What can I do for you, milord?"

"I have all I need, thank you." He gave her a little smile, remembering Christ's kindness to women like this one, even as revulsion churned within him.

After she left the table, Jamie studied his friend, who closed his eyes and rested his head against the wall. "Miss Kendall sends her best wishes."

Moberly glared in his direction with unfocused eyes. "How dare you mention her name in a place like this?" His words were slurred, but his anger came through.

"How dare you come to a place like this when you have the love of such a good woman?" Jamie had never

truly crossed his friend, and questioned just how far he
should go. If he'd learned nothing else in the country,
he'd learned not to speak rudely to the aristocracy. Yet
these were the words God had given him, and he would
not back down.

Rage reddened and creased Moberly's cheeks, and
narrowed his eyes. "He laughed at me." He pounded the
table, splashing rum from the fresh tankard the wench
had brought. "All I have done, working like a fiend to
prove myself to that old goat, and he *laughs* at me. Said
I am not fit to be a minister."

Jamie prayed his next words were from the Lord.
"And so you promptly go out and prove him right.
You're *not* fit to be a minister."

Thunder crashed overhead and a bolt of lightning lit
the street, turning the raindrops into a million fireflies.
Jamie would haul this sorry sinner out into the deluge if
not for the lightning. As it was, he hoped the lad caring
for horses here had taken Puck to the tavern's stable.
What had Moberly done with Gallant? Jamie had more
than one creature to care for this evening.

"Grace…" Moberly stared vacantly across the room.

"Now who's saying her name unsuitably?" Jamie's
temper was rising, and he longed to pummel this man
who seemed all too willing to abandon his faith.

"No, I do not speak of Miss Kendall." Moberly's
voice sounded weary. He ran his finger around the rim
of the tankard, but did not drink. "Grace from God. The
prodigal son and all that. But when *I* returned home, my
father never noticed." He slumped on the table, prop-
ping his head on one hand. "I've always wondered why
the older brother became so angry. Did not everything
belong to him? All the younger son wanted was his

father's approval. Yet, in our family, 'tis the third son who's all the rage now because, like our august father, he fights for king and country."

Jamie could not quite follow Moberly's musings, but conviction for his own self-righteousness cut into him. He'd been willing to dispense grace to the young wench at the other tavern, but not to his fallen friend. *Give me words, Lord.* "Our fathers are human, even one as exalted as yours."

Robert's stare bored into him. "Did your father treat you like worthless baggage?"

Jamie shrugged but held his gaze. "No. My father died when I was six."

Moberly snorted. "Fortunate you." He put his head in both hands. "No, I do not mean that. Forgive me."

The rain abated somewhat, and Jamie decided they'd leave when it slowed a bit more.

"You're right, Templeton." Moberly gave him a crooked grin. "I am not fit to be a minister. But, as you have said, we've all sinned and come short of the glory of God. And—" he held up his index finger to stress his point "—as you also said, God will be a father to me. I will never, as long as I live, *ever* expect anything else from Bennington." He shoved the tankard away, put his hands to his temples and blew out a long breath that nearly knocked Jamie over for its smell of second-hand rum. "Lord, forgive me. Why did I drink all of that? And so quickly. And without anything to eat." He belched and placed a hand over his mouth.

In the dim daylight of the tavern, Jamie could see Moberly's face grow pale. "Come. I'll take you home." He gripped his friend's arm to pull him to his feet.

"Oh, no." He shrugged away. "Cannot go home

drunk." He leaned away and deposited the contents of his stomach into a cuspidor beside the table.

Jamie wiped Moberly's face with a handkerchief and grasped him again. "Come on, then, we'll get you sober." He began to move the two of them toward the door.

Moberly's lucidity seemed to have passed. "Shall we sing a song? How 'bout 'Rule, Britannia' or 'God save the king'?" He staggered along beside Jamie and would have fallen without support. "Rule, Britannia—" For a drunk, his baritone was not bad.

The sailors in the room lifted their tankards high and joined his song.

Jamie swallowed a retort. He and nearly every other American had suffered far too much of Britannia's rule. "I heard a new song. 'Amazing Grace.' Do you know it?" They reached the door none too soon for him with all that riotous singing behind them.

Moberly stopped and shook his head, as if trying to clear it. "No, but it sounds like an excellent song. Will you teach it to me? Perhaps Marianne can play it on the pianoforte. She is very good at playing, you know."

Jamie chuckled. No, he hadn't known that. He would have to ask her about it once this debacle was over. So many things he did not know about her, and so little time to learn it.

Outside, the rain slowed to a drizzle. The stable boy informed them that their horses were safely sheltered behind the tavern. Paying out yet another coin, Jamie started in that direction. On the way, he noticed a watering trough newly filled with rainwater. "Come along, my friend." He tugged Moberly toward it.

Robert must have guessed his plan, for he dug his feet into the mud. "Oh, no, you don't."

"Oh, yes, I do." Jamie gripped him around the waist and forced him forward, plunging his head into the cold trough and holding him there for a few seconds before releasing him.

Moberly came up gasping. And laughing. He tried to force Jamie into the trough, but slipped in the ankle-deep mud, grabbing Jamie's arm and pulling him down, too.

The two of them sat there in the mud for a few moments, then both burst out laughing. Jamie's new gray jacket and breeches were stained with splotches of brown and black dirt, and the buckles on his new shoes might never regain their shine. Indeed, neither the clothes nor the shoes would ever be fit for fine company again. But somehow, that no longer mattered to him.

What did matter was getting Moberly home and tucked into bed without the earl seeing him in this condition.

Chapter Nineteen

Marianne's stomach felt tied in knots. Papa expected the family to join him promptly at nine o'clock for his first supper at home. Like the drawing room gathering each year, he demanded strict adherence to these rituals. She cast about in her mind, trying to think of how to appease his anger when Robert and Jamie did not appear. It was bad enough for her brother to bring trouble on himself, but she was quite put out with him for Jamie's sake. Did he not realize Jamie was again risking his standing with Papa in order to rescue him from his mischief?

As the supper hour drew near, Marianne and Grace changed their gowns for the occasion, then watched together from the second-story parlor window for signs of the two men. On these long summer days, daylight lasted until late in the evening. While the afternoon storm had darkened the landscape, once the rain stopped, the sun burst through the clouds to cast its golden rays upon the green hills.

"The roads appear dreadfully muddy," Grace said.

"Even if Captain Templeton found Mr. Moberly, they will never make it home in time to freshen up."

Marianne nodded as she searched for riders on the lane. More than once a distant horse lifted her hopes, only to pass by the Park entrance.

"There." Grace pointed. "Two riders. I think…yes, they are coming." She clasped her hands to her chest, as if struggling to contain her joy.

Although they were far down the lane, their identities were unmistakable. "Oh, thank You, Lord." Marianne embraced Grace. "But undoubtedly they are covered in mud."

"Whatever shall we do?"

Marianne chewed her thumbnail for a moment. "Go to Robert's room and fetch Ian. Tell him to bring fresh clothes. We have just forty-five minutes to save my brother."

Grace released a giddy laugh. "Oh, my. Do you truly think we can accomplish this?"

Marianne tried to contain her rioting emotions, but a laugh escaped her nonetheless. "Yes, yes. But hurry. I shall fetch Quince for Jamie. Um, for Captain Templeton."

Grace gave her a knowing smile. "Yes. Captain Templeton." She hurried from the parlor with Marianne close on her heels.

Marianne raced up the stairs to the third floor and down the hallway toward Jamie's room. There outside his door stood Quince and Emma in a chaste embrace. At her hurried approach they broke apart. Quince looked oddly defiant. Or perhaps annoyed. Emma blushed scarlet. Marianne did not have time for this.

"Quince, you must come immediately and bring Captain Templeton a change of clothes. He will need everything." Marianne stopped to catch her breath. "He must be presentable and in the dining room by nine o'clock sharp. Is that clear?"

The man blinked, but did not move.

"Really, Mr. Quince, I cannot think why Captain Templeton retains you." Marianne's temper flared as it had not in many a year. "Do see to your duty and rescue your master, or I shall find someone who can." Only briefly did she think of how much her own future depended on the good opinion of these two people. For now, Jamie must be saved. "Will you come?"

"Aye, milady." Quince grinned, then tugged at a lock of his hair, a customary respectful gesture from an underling to a superior that somehow seemed impertinent coming from him. She would deal with that later.

"Very well. Hurry. Meet us at the back entrance nearest the stable." She rushed back down the stairs, her heart racing faster than her feet. "Please, Lord, help us to accomplish the impossible."

Jamie enjoyed the leisurely ride through the rain-washed countryside. The fragrance of wildflowers filled the air, and nuthatches sang their loud, simple songs, no doubt pleased to have survived the storm. Even the mud clinging to Jamie's hair and plastering his shirt to his body didn't spoil his appreciation for the glorious sunset over the distant hills. He noticed the cool breeze, which cut through his clothes and sent chills up his spine, seemed to have cleared Moberly's head. That and maybe his dunking in the water trough. What a lark that had been. Jamie enjoyed the friendly rowdiness. And now a good night's rest should cure the last of his friend's drunkenness. He felt certain Moberly would think seriously before drinking spirits again.

As the tall, gray stone manor house came into view, lit by a brilliant sunset of orange, purple and red, Jamie's chest filled with an unexpected and bittersweet pang. In the midst of all this beauty and in the aftermath of an event that might change the course of Moberly's life for the better, he knew nothing in this place held any future for him. With the *Fair Winds* repaired and seaworthy, he must send word to Saunders to load the ship with the goods from the earl's warehouse. His capable first mate would also complete the unwritten order to meet their Spanish allies and store the muskets and ammunition in the lower deck's secret hold. All of that and a short voyage from Southwark to Southampton would take perhaps a fortnight, perhaps a bit more. Then, after a short side trip to Boston to deliver his report about the troop movements, he would sail to East Florida, conveying a shipload of goods but an empty heart.

"I say, what is that?" Squinting, Moberly pointed his riding crop toward the east side of the manor house, where three people stood in the shadows, waving vigorously at them. "I pray nothing is wrong, but they seem a bit overwrought, do you not think?"

Without waiting for an answer, he urged his mount to a gallop, and Jamie followed suit. The horses' hooves flung up mud from the wet road, with Jamie being the recipient of Gallant's generous offerings. He'd not thought he could be any dirtier, but sure enough, now he was. He laughed into the wind. As long as he was here, he would toss away his gloom and enjoy himself.

Marianne permitted herself only a moment of horror as Jamie and Robert drew nearer. As they rode up the lane, she saw their clothing was caked and splattered and their hair grimy. But she had no time for emotions, only action. Nor had the men any time for baths, only cold buckets of water showered over them before they entered the house.

The instant they dismounted, she pointed them to the two footmen waiting beside her. "They will wash you by the back door. Your valets have your clothing ready in a room just inside, to save your going all the way upstairs. Make haste. You have a mere twenty minutes before Papa will expect you in the dining room."

"What—" Jamie stared at her in confusion.

"Oh, bother," Robert said. "Sorry, Templeton. The old man demands a strict routine here in the country. Family custom and all that. I quit paying attention years ago, but if I am to improve my lot, I'd best make an appearance on time."

Jamie grimaced. "You go ahead." He dismounted and handed Puck's reins to a waiting groom. "I'll take a light repast in my room."

"No, no," Marianne said. "He will expect you, as well. You saw today how Papa holds court. He will expect us all at the table at the chime of nine o'clock." Her pulse raced with anxiety. Jamie simply did not comprehend.

He had the audacity to laugh. "But shouldn't country living be a bit more relaxed?"

Marianne lifted her skirts and marched across the damp grass, glad that she had put on her leather walking shoes before coming outside. "Captain Templeton, you must defer to my father in this if you expect the rest of the summer to hold any relaxation for any of us."

"Indeed." He stiffened slightly and raised his eyebrows.

She had never spoken sharply to him, and she regretted it. It was she who was at fault for not informing him about the family tradition. "Please."

A glint of comprehension crossed his eyes. "Very well." He followed Robert around the side of the house, with Marianne not far behind.

The footmen had already begun to strip off Robert's jacket and shirt and loosen his muddy hair from its queue. Marianne hurried past them through the back door, praying the task would be completed in time.

Wafting up from the kitchen belowstairs came the aroma of roasted lamb and apple pie. She could picture the cook adorning the platter with sprigs of mint leaves, and the liveried footmen donning their white gloves in preparation for serving the sumptuous dinner. This was Papa's formal welcome-home celebration, a custom passed down in the Bennington household since feudal times, and she prayed Robert had not ruined the whole thing for all of them.

She found Grace in the upper parlor and reported the homecoming. "The footmen are doing all they can to help. Do I look all right?"

Grace studied her up and down, reaching out to tuck a stray curl into Marianne's coiffure. "Except for your shoes."

"Oh, dear." Looking down, Marianne felt a merry tickle inside and could not resist a laugh. "I have tracked mud all the way in here and shall have to apologize to the upstairs maid."

The mantel clock read ten minutes before nine, so the two ladies descended to the drawing room, where the rest of the family had gathered, except for the children, and Robert and Jamie. Surprised at her own thoughts,

Marianne tried to remember when she had begun to think of Jamie as part of the family. Would that Papa could regard him in the same light.

At the chime of nine o'clock, Blevins appeared in the drawing room doorway. "Lord Bennington, Lady Bennington, dinner is served."

Marianne and Grace shared a regretful look as they followed Papa and Mama, William and his lady from the room. But as the procession crossed the wide entrance hall, Robert and Jamie slipped around the staircase and, forefingers to lips to forestall any reaction, offered arms to her and to Grace, each choosing his friend's lady to escort. Although damp around the edges, with their shiny hair pulled back in wet queues, both men looked every bit the gentlemen they were. She did notice that Robert's eyes seemed somewhat blurry, but at least he could walk straight. Well, he did wobble a bit on her arm, but she managed to hold him up.

Papa seated Mama and then started toward his end of the table. At the sight of the two latecomers, Mama smiled serenely, William snorted out a laugh and Lady Bampton harrumphed. But all attention turned toward Papa. His eyebrows wiggled slightly, as they did when he was surprised. Then a slow smile crept across his lips, and a glint filled his eyes—a gleam that appeared only when he planned to skewer one of his sons with cutting remarks. Marianne knew that Grace was praying as hard as she that Papa would not be too cruel to Robert. For indeed, how much crueler could he be than to laugh at his son's desire to serve God?

Chapter Twenty

"East Florida is a fine place for a new beginning."
Jamie walked beside Moberly around Bennington
Pond, a long, narrow lake edged with cattails, ferns
and weeping willows, and inhabited by swans and
ducks watching over their hatchlings. In the distance,
a man from the village sat in a rowboat and fished the
black depths. "Marry Miss Kendall and come with me.
Your brother Frederick would be pleased to see you,
and there's no end of possibilities for new businesses."
Even as he spoke, he questioned the wisdom of his invitation. Moberly never expressed any serious views on
the Revolution other than to say it would be interesting
to see how it all turned out. Yet Jamie felt God's urging
to encourage him.

"You are a true friend, Templeton." Moberly found a
rock and flung it sideways into the lake. It skipped several times across the water, scattering a group of ducks,
who quacked in protest. "But Miss Kendall and I have
decided the Lord would have us stay here. These past
days, through her insights, I've come to realize my desire to go into the church was the misplaced zeal of a

newly converted man. Thus, I shall have to find a way to support us before we can marry." He exhaled a long sigh. "Of course, it will require another lengthy period of good behavior on my part so my next endeavor will meet with my father's approval. In the meantime, I shall plumb the depths of my interests and talents to see if anything pops to the surface."

"I understand." Jamie nodded. "You know we'll sail in just over a week. If you change your mind, I'll give you a berth aboard the *Fair Winds*." He found a smooth, flat stone, but once he threw it, it sank beneath the surface, much like his heart each time he thought about leaving Marianne. Up to now, his determination had held strong. Now that resolve wavered like the oak leaves fluttering in the wind on a branch above him. Somehow he must distract himself. "Tell me more about this garden party. Who's coming? What do you do?" Since Bennington had come home, the evenings in the drawing room had become more than boring. He hoped the upcoming event would be a good diversion.

"You may have noticed Lady Bennington loves to throw a party." Moberly chuckled, and his eyes lit with fondness. "This one began as a replacement for the annual Midsummer Eve festival, which of course is pagan in origin. Neither my stepmother nor Father could countenance such celebrations, yet they desired some sort of summer entertainment. They hit upon the idea of a garden party the week after Summer Solstice, so as to make a distinction. Theirs was to be decidedly more sedate—bowling, billiards, riding, grouse hunting, that sort of thing—an enjoyable way to gather like-minded friends for a week or so. They've hosted this event these past three and twenty years."

"Ah, what a fine idea." Jamie again considered the earl's contradictory ways—faithful in his religion, generous to his friends and to charity, but cruel to his sons. "Christians can always find ways to enjoy themselves without participating in godless merrymaking."

Moberly laughed ruefully. "I'm beginning to truly understand that…thanks to you."

Jamie shrugged. "More thanks to the Lord, I'd say." He looked across the lake toward the fisherman. "Any good fish out there?"

Moberly followed his gaze. "Sometimes. Want to give it a try?"

"I would. I haven't been on water since March, a sorry thing for a sailor to admit."

They found a rowboat and fishing equipment in the gray stone boathouse and rowed out to a likely spot. In the lazy quiet of the afternoon, both dozed beneath their wide-brimmed cocked hats, not minding in the least that no fish tugged on their lines to disturb their sleep.

Marianne threw herself into helping with the preparations for the garden party, as did everyone in the household. Mama spent a great deal of time with Cook planning a week's worth of menus to serve the expected thirty-seven guests. The men practiced their marksmanship in anticipation of the grouse hunting. Servants scoured the house until not a spot of dust could be found, nor a scuff mark on the floors, nor a frayed edge on chairs or drapes. The guest wing was opened, furniture uncovered and linens aired. Mama assigned Marianne the duty of planning for the evening entertainment of the younger set.

Papa did not permit the hanging of bunting or evergreen bows, but he approved of flowers, as many as could be gathered to decorate the house. Marianne and Grace enlisted Jamie's and Robert's help and secured the use of a dogcart to bring wildflowers from the woodlands and fields, and blooms from Mama's garden. The servants filled vases and scattered them around the manor, filling every room with delightful and varied fragrances. As much as Marianne loved Mama's roses and carnations, her favorite flower was the sweet pea, imported from her maternal grandparents' villa in Tuscany.

For all their enjoyment of Bennington House in London, it was Bennington Park the family claimed as home. And when Marianne considered all she was sacrificing for love, and how few days remained before she left, never to return, she found herself grieving the loss. But she had many more moments of giddy happiness—mixed with terror—over her own audacity. The ups and downs of her emotions left her exhausted at the end of each day.

In the evenings, she stared out of her bedchamber window, her gaze caressing the beloved countryside. She imagined her coming voyage and prayed she would not succumb to seasickness. She must secure some powdered ginger root from the kitchen. And, with a single small bag for all her possessions, she must decide what to take and what to leave. Some items she'd once considered treasures now proved to be foolish luxuries. She decided to take only two plain dresses. Would that she could ask Jamie which ones he preferred to see her wear.

But first she must get past the garden party. She drew out her volume of Shakespeare to design word games. In a moment of mad defiance, she considered presenting the elopement scene in *A Midsummer Night's Dream* to tease Jamie or to give a hint to her parents of her plans. Papa could play his counterpart, the heartless Egeus, while she and Jamie were well suited to portray the fleeing lovers, Hermia and Lysander. She could hear Jamie repeating Lysander's line, "'The course of true love never did run smooth.'" But such foolishness would ruin her flight. In any event, Papa did not care for that particular play because of its pagan setting. Instead, he preferred the Bard's histories, especially *Henry V,* which he likened to George II's courageous leadership in fighting for England and making the throne secure for the House of Hanover.

As her musing continued, a startling thought occurred to her. Jamie had never asked her to marry him. Did he love her as Lysander loved Hermia—enough to risk his entire future for her? What if, when they were far out to sea and he found her aboard his ship, he brought her back home in disgrace? Papa might be hurt by her desertion, but he would be destroyed to see his only daughter behaving like certain infamous society women whose affairs he had widely condemned. Before Marianne ran away to sea like a boy longing to be a sailor, she must force from Jamie the truth about the depth of his feelings for her, even as she gave no hint that she planned to sneak aboard his ship.

Chapter Twenty-One

As the carriages began to roll up the lane in a procession, Jamie grew morose. He'd become tired of these aristocrats with all of their frivolities. Yet he knew his irritation came more from a mixture of heartache over leaving Marianne and the limited information he'd gathered for General Washington. The best he could do for the next four days was watch the unfolding spectacle and try to enjoy himself in this hodgepodge of people.

Servants rushed around taking care of the incoming guests and their baggage. The aroma of cakes and meats wafted up from the kitchen, making Jamie's mouth water. Bennington's mastiffs—spoiled beasts—barked incessantly, while the children got loose from their nursemaid and ran about causing mischief. Through little Georgie's efforts, more than one vase of flowers crashed to the floor, causing extra work for the harried servants. But Lady Bennington insisted the children must not be punished, for everyone felt the excitement of the day.

In the midst of it all, Thomas Moberly came home to announce he had indeed been promoted and given command of a forty-four gun frigate christened HMS *Dauntless*. Jamie had hoped *this* Captain Moberly would be delayed until his own departure. But as numerous guests gathered in the drawing room, and Robert drew Jamie into the family circle, he was presented to a man who one day might very well try to blast his own ship out of the water.

"Another one of Father's pets, eh?" Captain Moberly, in an indigo uniform replete with brass buttons and gold braid, stood as tall and slender as his father, with broad shoulders, straight posture and a lift to his chin that suggested the man was full of himself—a younger version of the earl by some forty years. Like Marianne and Robert, he had thick black hair and sky-blue eyes. But whereas Marianne's eyes exuded gentleness, and Robert's earnestness, Thomas's icy stare bored into a man like a cold steel blade. Jamie could not fault him too much. He'd used the same stare himself on insubordinate sailors.

"Your father is a generous man." Effecting a humble bow, Jamie glanced beyond Captain Moberly and noted Marianne's dismay. The dear girl loved all of her brothers.

"Indeed." Captain Moberly turned away to speak to another guest. Several unattached ladies hovered nearby, but his stiff demeanor seemed to indicate he didn't welcome their attentions.

Marianne sent a quivering smile Jamie's way, and he returned a wink. If anyone but Robert or Miss Kendall noticed, he no doubt would have been sent on his way forthwith.

In the afternoon, the younger set moved outside to bowl on the leveled lawn. Jamie had bowled in Nantucket and Boston, and if invited to join the aristocrats, he would not embarrass himself. For the first hour or so, he had to be content to watch, until Marianne dragged him in to replace a wearied young lady.

"'Tis quite easy, Captain Templeton." Marianne placed the black wooden ball in his hands. "You only have to roll this ball across the lawn and try to knock down as many of the ninepins as you can." Her tutorial tone and the twinkle in her eyes sparked high spirits in him.

"Like this, my lady?" He held the ball in both hands over one shoulder, as if he would lob it through the air like a cannonball.

"No, no. Just one hand." She reached for the ball. "Let me show you."

He lifted it higher. "Ah-ah. 'Tis my turn, is it not?"

Murmurs erupted around them, intermingled with a few titters from the ladies. Had he gone too far to tease a lady of her station in front of them?

Marianne moved back and crossed her arms. "Very well. You have seen us play. Do it right." Her lips puckered, as if she was containing a laugh.

He longed to wink at her again, to secretly convey his love to her while everyone looked on. But he dared not risk such an affront, as they all would see it. Instead, he bowed. "I shall do my best not to embarrass you, my lady."

Gripping the ball in both hands, he held it up and eyed the pins some twenty-five feet away. He moved the ball to his right hand, swung it back and whipped it across the closs-cropped grass, knocking down all nine pins.

"Well done, captain." Marianne applauded, as did

several others. "You have played before. Tell me, what other hidden accomplishments do you have?"

Some in their audience again murmured their disapproval, but Jamie threw caution to the winds. "My lady, I have ridden the back of a whale in the South Atlantic and shot a bear in the wilderness of East Florida." He put a finger on his jaw in a thoughtful pose. "I have climbed a tree and rescued a kitten for your niece, Miss Elizabeth." His audience now began to chuckle. "But my most difficult accomplishment has been to dance the minuet without tripping over my own large feet and falling flat on my face."

The laughter grew, and the bowling continued, with others taking the center of attention. Marianne pulled up the fan on her wrist and waved it lazily. "After all of those amazing deeds," she said softly, her eyes sending a silent plea, "do you suppose you could brave the dangers of escorting me to the refreshment table?"

Not twenty feet away and near the house, servants had set up a long, linen-draped table and filled it with beverages, cakes and sweetmeats. The temptation to speak to her alone was too great. Perhaps this would be the last time they could talk privately before he left. Jamie bent low in a formal bow. "My lady, it will be my pleasure."

He offered his arm, and she set her dainty gloved hand on it. He couldn't resist the urge to cover it with his own. If anyone found this closeness inappropriate, he would declare himself a boor, and she would be blameless. He longed for the courage—or stupidity—to put an arm around her waist and draw her close to his side, where he wished to keep her forever. The ache he always felt at the edges of his chest now moved to the center, cutting deep into his heart.

At the table, they each took a crystal cup brimming with lemonade, then, as if they'd planned it, turned and walked the pathway down the hill toward the lake. One of the rowboats lay available for use at the water's edge. Nearby, in the care of nursemaids and footmen, Georgie and his sisters played with the dozen or so other little lords and ladies, offspring of the various adults who amused themselves around the vast estate.

The weather had bestowed its approval on Lady Bennington's garden party. Warm enough for outdoor activities, cool enough not to overheat the guests. Sunny enough to provide a profusion of light softened by a few puffy white clouds. The gardens bloomed in abundance, filling the air with varied pleasant scents and showing no evidence that many flowers had been plucked from them to grace the house.

If Jamie were a poet, he would pen the sentiments of his heart. At most, he could only think of Shakespeare's sonnet, "Shall I compare thee to a summer's day? Thou art more lovely and more temperate—" He could not remember the rest, and felt the fool for it. Perhaps he would memorize the Sidney love sonnet Marianne had read.

Now was the time. Now he must tell her how deeply he loved her, how leaving would be the hardest thing he'd ever done. Did she long to hear those words as much as he longed to say them? Or had their love been a mere pastime to her, the game of a bored, wellborn lady? Yes, she'd proclaimed her love and shown all the courtesies and generosities of such a sentiment. But had that merely been an amusement, safe for a young lady of her station to engage in because he would leave one day?

They came to a weeping willow and found refuge beneath its abundant tresses, a bower wherein he might speak the overflowing emotions of his heart. He turned to her and drew in a quick breath. Her eyes seemed like sparkling sapphires in her porcelain face, and tiny teardrops clung to her long black lashes. A rush of protectiveness overwhelmed him. He set both of their cups on the ground and pulled her into his arms.

"Marianne." He sighed.

"Oh, Jamie." Trembling, she laid her head against his chest and encircled his waist with her arms.

He held her for some time. When she tilted her head back and gazed up at him, he kissed her. The sweet softness of her lips, the innocent trust in her eyes, made him realize all the more that he *must* protect her from every danger, including himself. "If someone should see us—" He tried to move back.

She clung to him. "I do not care."

He brushed his hand across her cheek and kissed her again, breathing in her sweet jasmine perfume. *Lord, help us. How easy it would be to fall into the world's ways. But I will not corrupt her or myself, as difficult as it may be to resist the temptations of the flesh.* He lifted his head. "We must not do this, my lady."

Marianne gave him a playful smirk. "Yet you do not push me away."

"No, my lady, I would never do that."

"Enough of 'my lady'." She tapped his lips with one finger. "Have I not told you? I am your Marianne, and you are my Jamie. 'My true-love hath my heart, and I have his.'"

He shoved away his fond remembrances of Sidney's poem. "That was long ago in a dream world. Now we must live in reality."

Her broken sigh cut into him. "Would you marry me if you could?" In her eyes, he read the same despair his own heart held. Somehow, for both of them, he must lighten this mood.

"Yes, my darling daughter of a lord. If I were the eldest son of a prince or duke or whatever you English consider worthy, I would marry you." He gently removed her arms from around him and gripped both of her hands. "But I am not. I am a simple merchant sea captain, your father's business partner, a working man." He pulled off one of his gloves. "Do you see these calluses? I've worked hard all my life, and I'm proud of them." She reached out to touch his hand, but he pulled back and put the glove back on. "Please don't think me vulgar for it, but that is the essence of who I am. And I will never be what your family and your station require."

She stepped back and crossed her arms. "Lady Weston married her footman."

"Lady Weston was a widow whose reputation set no example for a Christian girl."

Marianne stared at the ground for a moment, then lifted her gaze to meet his. "But you do love me, and you would marry me if Papa gave his permission?" A strange gleam flitted across her eyes.

Jamie blinked. "Yes, of course. I've already said that."

She seemed to suppress a smile and instead released another long sigh. "Very well. I am content with that knowledge."

"Good." Yet he didn't feel very good. The conversation had shifted without warning, and he had the strange feeling she was neglecting to tell him something important. But he dared not ask what it was. Perhaps reality had settled in her heart at last, as it had in his, and she'd decided to make the best of it. But if she went to her father and declared their love, he'd simply have to beg the earl's forgiveness. "May I escort you back to the others?" He offered his arm.

As they walked beside the lake, her mischievous smile further unnerved him, making him reconsider his conclusions.

Suddenly she peered around him toward the water and gasped. "Georgie!"

Jamie followed her gaze.

There in the middle of the bottomless lake, the rowboat was foundering, and the earl's grandson flailed and splashed his arms.

"Help me!" The boy's gurgling wail sounded across the water.

Chapter Twenty-Two

"Georgie!" Marianne cried out and started toward the water, but realized she had no power to save her nephew. The horror of the drama before her swept away all thoughts of her own happiness. "Lord, save him."

Beside her, Jamie was already stripping off his gloves, shoes and jacket. He splashed into the lake where, several yards out, he dived in and swam with powerful strokes toward Georgie. Jamie would save the boy. She knew it as certainly as she knew he loved her.

She looked along the shore, where the family and guests had become a wailing throng. Nursemaids and footmen paced the edge, and John the footman stood knee-deep in the lake. Marianne ran to them. Tears ran down Lady Bampton's cheeks, and she wrung her hands. Marianne pulled her into her arms. Oddly, the woman held fast to her. Papa stood at the water's edge, his hand pressed against his chest and his legs drenched. Like the footman, he appeared to have stepped into the water, but must have drawn back when Jamie plunged in. She heard prayers around her and joined in with all her heart.

Near the water, Georgie's sisters held on to each other, and both were crying. "You see, Betts," Katherine said, "if you had gone with Georgie, you would be drowning, too." Elizabeth wailed all the louder.

Thomas came running from the house, with William close behind. Marianne had not seen her plump oldest brother run since they were children. While he took his wife into his arms, Thomas kept going, splashing into the lake several yards before he stopped, apparently realizing, like Papa, that Jamie was capable of the rescue. He turned to the earl. "We just heard what happened." He waved impatiently toward the footmen. "Can't any of those blokes swim?"

Papa's shoulders slumped, and he looked his age. "I have no idea. 'Twas never required of them...until now."

Jamie swam toward shore using one arm, while holding Georgie's head out of the water with the other. He stopped and gained footing fifteen yards out, then lifted the unconscious child and brought him to land. Breathing hard, he fell to his knees, gently laid the boy on his side and pressed a fist against his stomach.

The throng clustered close until Robert shoved in front of them. "Get back. Give him room to breathe."

The footmen seemed to remember their calling and herded the guests away, while the family knelt around Georgie. Lady Bampton—Mary—prayed. William prayed. Robert prayed. Even proud Papa pleaded with his Maker for his heir. Mama appeared and knelt beside Papa, and he accepted her comforting embrace. Thomas leaned over Jamie's shoulder, yet did not interfere with his ministrations.

Georgie's pale face frightened Marianne. In truth, he looked dead. Yet Jamie calmly rolled him on his back and breathed several long breaths directly into his mouth. A spasm shook Georgie, and he coughed out a stream of water, coughed some more, then started to cry. "Annie," he called in a choking voice to his nurse.

Mary scooped her son into her arms. "No, my darling boy, not Annie, but your dearest mummy, who loves you so very much."

Georgie rewarded the effort by coughing more water onto his mother, and then clinging to her. Mary did not appear to notice her ruined gown, another uncharacteristic behavior.

Great sighs of relief filled the air, along with giddy laughter, as the family rose to their feet, each member reaching out to touch the boy's back, or embracing someone else.

Assured of her nephew's recovery, Marianne went to Jamie, who was still on his knees, inhaling deep breaths after all his exertion. "You saved him." She knelt and kissed his cheek.

As if her touch burned him, Jamie jerked away and jumped to his feet, then helped her up. "By God's grace, my lady." He warned her with a stern look, but she returned a warm smile. Surely his courage in saving Papa's only grandson would change everything.

"Ask what you will, Templeton, and it is yours." Lord Bennington sat in his kingly chair in the drawing room, surrounded by family and guests, and chuckled a bit uncomfortably. "As the rulers in the Scriptures used to say, 'Up to the half of my kingdom.'" The lines on the old man's face had deepened since the afternoon's near tragedy, even after Captain Moberly sent to Portsmouth for his ship's physician, who declared the boy recovered from his ordeal. Jamie had not disputed the physician's word, but he had seen drowning victims seem to recover, only to die later of a brain fever. He prayed that would not happen to Georgie.

Jamie noticed the crowd leaning forward for his answer, and he surmised he truly was expected to ask for something. A flippant laugh rose from his belly and tried to escape, but he swallowed it. What would this august group do if he asked Dennington for his only daughter's hand? What would the earl do? Jamie tried not to look at Marianne. But she stood just behind her father's chair, and her widened eyes and hopeful smile made clear her hope. She knew how to manage her father, but on this one matter, Jamie did not trust her judgment. Like David in the Bible, he dared not ask the "king" for his daughter.

"My lord, if you would keep that fine gelding, Puck, in your stable for me, I shall enjoy riding him upon my return."

The crowd applauded and breathed out their approval, but Marianne's jaw dropped and the fine arches of her eyebrows bent into a frown. Jamie shrugged ever so slightly. Even the earl seemed a bit disappointed, if his "harrumph" was any indication.

"I see you are a diplomat, my boy." He leaned one elbow on the chair arm and rested his chin on his fist. "Well, it will not suit. What do you want? Money? Land? That's it." He snapped his fingers. "I shall arrange with His Majesty to grant you some land near St. Johns Towne, a plantation near my own. You are a friend of my son Frederick—"

"A friend of all your sons, Father," Thomas Moberly

said, a sentiment echoed enthusiastically by the viscount and Robert Moberly.

Jamie had no desire for a plantation, for he would never own a slave. Nor did he wish to settle anyplace until he'd succeeded in bringing East Florida into the Revolution, and all of the colonies were free from English rule. But he felt particular discomfort at the naval captain's praise. How could he call this man an enemy now?

"Yes, a friend of all my sons." The earl stood and clapped him on the shoulder. "And if a plantation does not suit you, we shall find something that will." He glanced around the room. "Well, now, everyone, go about your games." He waved one hand in a dismissive gesture. As the wellborn crowd disbursed, he stared into Jamie's eyes and squeezed his shoulder. "My boy, we must get you a wife." His pale blue eyes twinkled. "May I recommend Miss Kendall, whose company you seem to enjoy so much? While she is above you in rank, her lack of fortune precludes a more advantageous match. No doubt, the dear, compliant girl could be convinced that life in East Florida would suit her very well, for she has no other prospects."

Jamie opened his mouth to speak, but no words would come out. Bennington clearly thought he'd given Jamie a compliment by offering his wife's companion, and indeed the sweet lady would make the man of her choosing an excellent wife. But the earl had said far more than he realized. Did the man not comprehend how he had insulted both Jamie and Miss Kendall? Yet such was the attitude of these English lords and their king. Jamie thanked the Lord he'd not spoken for Marianne's hand.

After an awkward moment, he managed to find his voice. "Thank you, sir. I am deeply honored. But while Miss Kendall is a fine Christian lady, I would not burden her with the life of a sea captain's wife." He wished he could add that the earl would find a willing husband for the charming Miss Kendall among his own sons. "Nor would I settle such a gently reared lady in the wilderness of Florida." He glanced at Marianne, praying she comprehended the declaration was meant for her. Instead, she lifted her chin and wrinkled her nose in that quick little gesture he found so charming, despite its rebellious nature.

Lord Bennington chuckled. "You know your own mind, do you not, Templeton?" He wagged a finger at Jamie. "I shall continue to search for an appropriate reward for you. I am proud of my pedigree and my progeny. But a man my age with four sons should have a dozen grandsons by now. Thomas's young wife died with her child, and who would have Robert?" He coughed out a snort of disgust. "Of course, Frederick has received everything I'll ever give him, and his offspring will have nothing from me. But these others have not done their jobs in continuing my legacy. Even William should have more sons. So you can see why all my hopes for the family heritage lie in little George."

"Yes, my lord." Jamie's stomach turned at the earl's arrogant speech. This interview had done much to help him cut the cords of friendship binding him to this old man.

General Washington had insisted that Jamie maintain all his ties in England, which might mean he would have to return here to spy. But he would pray without ceasing that he might serve the Revolution in some other way.

Chapter Twenty-Three

"It would *seem* dreadfully scandalous," Miss Porter said. "But in truth, it would be completely innocent." The young heiress, Marianne's friend, sat primly in her chair, but her eyes were filled with mischief.

"Oh, dear." Marianne pretended shock. "My papa will be livid. The whole purpose of having Mama's garden party the week *after* Midsummer Eve is to avoid any association with pagan revelries, most of which take place in the middle of the night." Seated in the upstairs parlor with the younger, unmarried guests, she hoped no one would discover this entire game was her idea and Miss Porter her unwitting partner.

"Pagan revelries, ha," said Mr. Smythe, who everyone knew aspired to win Miss Porter's hand. "My father will think nothing of it. He has told me about some of his own youthful pranks, and this will be nothing compared to them. I rather think the old boy wants me to do something delightfully silly so he can brag about it to his friends."

"But is it fair to spoil the villagers' festivities?" Marianne looked at Robert, hoping he would contradict her.

"Their summer fair takes place this Wednesday, and their feast is in the evening."

"I do not see that it would spoil anything at all," her brother said. "'Tis a grand idea, a treasure hunt in the forest between here and the village. We will not disturb their merrymaking." He frowned and puckered his lips thoughtfully. "However, to maintain propriety, the ladies must go in twos or threes, with at least one gentleman as an escort."

Marianne's heart sank. If she was required to have a partner and an escort, how could she make her escape?

"I say, what a good idea." Mr. Smythe nodded with enthusiasm. "We can have teams."

Others chimed in with suggestions that came near to ruining Marianne's plan, and she scrambled to think how to amend it. "Very well. Since my brother gives his approval, I, too, shall play. But should we not wear masks?" She eyed Miss Porter's blue gown. Perhaps her friend would trade clothes with her. "Part of the fun can be not knowing who our fellow players are."

Everyone shouted agreement, and someone found pen, ink and vellum and began a list of the rules. With great care, Marianne added a few more ideas, all the while plotting her very different course. The treasure would be divided in many parts, and every item must be found before the hunt was declared over. Surely that would last until dawn. Some time before midnight, dressed as Miss Porter, she would whisper to someone that she had grown tired and would return to her room. After a night of games, none of the younger set would be expected to rise until afternoon. With Jamie sailing just after sunrise, no one would miss her until too late.

Excitement filled her chest and made her breathless.

Now she had only to enlist Emma's help, and her plan would succeed.

"I say, Moberly," Mr. Smythe said to Robert, "too bad your brother and Captain Templeton will be gone by then. They seem the sort of chaps who would enjoy such a romp."

Marianne smothered a gasp. She had not heard that Thomas would sail so soon, but this was all the better. Now, if Papa suspected her of going off with Jamie, Thomas could not pursue them. On the other hand, how else could she disappear other than to go with Jamie? Only one idea came to mind.

"Yes, it would be good to have extra men, for one never knows when the gypsies will return to the forest." She put on a worried frown. "Do be on the lookout, all of you."

Had she thought of every detail? Would something else come up to prevent her flight? Frequent twinges of guilt had struck her in the past few days, as if she had devised something evil, so Marianne had left off praying about her plan. Yet she could not help but think that God was directing her every step of the way.

"Flying Bennington's flag should keep you from unpleasant encounters with His Majesty's ships." Thomas Moberly, dressed in the full regalia of a British naval captain, stood with Jamie while the rest of the family began to gather in the entrance hallway. "If some officious fellow accosts you, you must use my father's name and mine and the letters we provided. But if you follow the heading I charted for you, you should reach East Florida without difficulty."

"Thank you, sir." Jamie forced a calm smile. If this

man knew of the hundreds of muskets and the ammunition hidden in the *Fair Winds'* secret hold, or if he knew Jamie would sail to Boston to deliver them before returning to East Florida, he would sink the ship before she reached the open seas.

"How many guns do you have?" Captain Moberly's dark eyebrows bent into a frown.

Jamie coughed to cover his shock. "Guns?" Had this man read his mind?

Captain Moberly snickered and chided him with a friendly shake of his head. "Cannons, man." He clapped Jamie on the shoulder. "Surely you do not sail unarmed when the seas are filled with pirates and privateers who are eager to seize your cargo."

Jamie shrugged and huffed out a sigh, trying to hide his relief by sounding annoyed. "Ah, yes, the bane of every merchant captain. I have ten six-pounders—five port, five starboard—a twelve-pounder at the bow, and a crew that knows how to use them, sir."

"Hmm. I suppose that will have to do. 'Tis better than none at all." Thomas leaned closer. "You will be pleased to know that Governor Tonyn has been granted an admiralty commission and is issuing letters of marque to a dozen or more Loyalist sloops to protect the St. Johns River and the inland passage from Georgia." A measure of controlled anticipation filled his eyes. "A former Royal Navy officer, Captain Mowbray, has been contracted to lead the waterborne defense. This will deter the rebels from invading East Florida. In fact, on your next voyage, no doubt Tonyn will commission you to carry naval stores to the area. What do you think of that?" Patriotic pride shone from the captain's eyes. "We'll rout those scoundrels soon enough and put an end to this rebel nonsense."

"Very good, sir." During Captain Moberly's little speech, Jamie somehow managed to maintain his calm. This was the very information he needed to complete his mission. Now the Patriots would know what they were up against—that Tonyn had the orders, power and means to fully prosecute the war in East Florida—and could plan their assault accordingly. "And I'll deliver these letters to Governor Tonyn and tell your brother Frederick all you've said." Jamie sent up a prayer of thanks and contrition. He should have known the Lord would supply everything he needed to complete his mission for General Washington. Once again he knew without doubt God was on the Patriots' side.

While Marianne and the others clustered around Captain Moberly, Jamie played the part of a servant, bowing away to leave the family to their private adieus. Strange how he had grown used to effecting such poses, except when he and Marianne, Robert and Miss Kendall, had gone beyond sight of the manor house. But soon he could fully straighten his shoulders and once again be the captain of his own ship, an American Patriot answering only to God, conscience and the Continental Congress, with fealty not to a feudal-like lord but to a new nation of free men.

That afternoon, Jamie, Marianne, Robert Moberly and several household servants accompanied Quince and Emma to the church at the edge of the village, where Reverend Bentley led them in their marriage vows. Jamie stood beside his friend while Marianne stood beside her maid. More than once he gazed at the woman he could never have, to see tears glistening in her lovely blue eyes. Even though he rejoiced at seeing his friend happy, his own heart felt like a cannonball in his chest.

Afterward, they walked back toward the manor house, where a small wedding celebration was to take place in the kitchen among the household staff. Then Jamie would gather his belongings and travel to South-ampton. Quince and Emma would follow later in the evening, after Emma had seen to the last of her duties as Marianne's lady's maid.

Chafing at the misery soon to visit Marianne and him, Jamie offered his arm to her and fell back behind the others. His heart overflowed with love, as it had a few days before beneath the willow trees. Who knew the wedding of a friend could move a man so deeply?

"What a lovely bride Emma makes." Marianne's own loveliness was enhanced by her affection for her servant.

"Yes, and I've never seen Aaron… Quince grin so broadly." His emotions rioted within him. Grief must not cause him to slip from his role as Quince's master. "My lady…"

"Yes, my Jamie." She looked up and gave him a smile that was strangely serene.

"Tsk. Be careful." He winked at her, not feeling the slightest bit playful. "I won't have another private moment with you, but if you will permit, I'd like to tell you something."

"Of course." Her perfect eyebrows arched with expectation.

He cleared his throat, fearing he was treading on dangerous ground, fearing his words might inspire her to some foolish action. Yet he could not restrain himself.

"If the course of history should ever level the ground beneath us to permit an equality made clear in Scripture, then perhaps by God's grace we can somehow be united." He prayed she would not notice the rebellion implicit in this declaration.

She stared at the ground before them as if hiding her widening smile. "What will it take to level the ground? Will you perform some gallant deed for His Majesty and be made a knight?"

"You know that's not possible." Why had he said anything? "I merely meant…it is my way of saying… I shall never love another."

She tugged him to a stop and faced him, no longer smiling or teasing, but staring up at him with misery in her eyes. "Nor shall I. And you must know this—if I cannot marry *you,* I shall not marry at all." Her lovely, full lips formed a pout of determination.

He stared down at her for only an instant before pulling her into his arms and kissing her with all the fervor burning in his heart. Right here on the village road. Right here where they could be seen, should someone look out of a manor house window. This moment of bliss could not be wrong, at least not before God, not when they had just pledged eternal love to each other.

A harsh whistle met Jamie's ears, snapping him out of his euphoria. He and Marianne looked up the road. While Moberly stared at them with fists at his waist, the others continued their walk toward the house. Now he beckoned sharply, his every move a warning. So this was it. Jamie might never see his love again. But he would carry her in his heart forever. *My true-love hath my heart, and I have hers.*

Chapter Twenty-Four

"Mr. Saunders, you have done your duty admirably." Jamie's heart swelled with pride as he gazed at the *Fair Winds*. The ship had arrived in port the day before, but events at the manor had kept him from coming to Southampton any sooner to greet his crew. "She looks trim and fit, more than ready to take us home tomorrow at sunrise." In addition to recaulking and scraping and sporting a new mast, the ship wore fresh coats of paint inside and out. Her sails had been mended or replaced, and sheets and halyards restored good as new. "You've done a fine job all around." He eyed Saunders, his sea-weathered first mate, whose response to this praise seemed strangely subdued. "Is there something you're not telling me?"

"Well, sir…" Saunders scratched his brown-and-gray-bearded chin and stared up at the new mainmast, then over toward another merchant ship, then toward the town, his eyes seeming not to focus on any of them. "Ye see, sir, uh, well, sir, I—I've taken me a wife. Sir."

"A *wife*." Jamie thought the top of his head might explode. "What do you mean you, you've taken a wife?"

Saunders's pained grimace and cowering posture, so uncharacteristic of him, sent a wave of nausea through Jamie. He'd always prided himself on having a good relationship with his crew, especially someone as responsible as his first mate, who could very well captain his own vessel. "Does that mean you plan to stay here in England?" This man's patriot fervor had always been unmatched. Had some clever wench turned his mind from the Revolution?

"Well, sir, that all depends on you, sir." Saunders rolled his hat in his hands.

"On me?" Jamie could not think of losing this valuable sailor. "What—?"

"Well, ye see, sir, I want to bring me wife along." He moved closer to Jamie in a confiding pose. "Ye see, sir, Molly wants to go to America. She's willin' to throw her lot in with us, if you know what I mean, sir." He tapped the side of his nose to indicate he could say no more.

Jamie huffed out a cross breath. First Aaron and now Saunders. His friends could marry their ladyloves, but he could not. "What does the rest of the crew think of taking a woman aboard?" He looked around to see several other men standing close. They tried to look busy, but bent near, as if all too interested in this conversation between their captain and his first mate. A thread of worry wove into Jamie's chest.

"Well, sir, it seems there was several ladies of the same mind as my Molly." Saunders shrugged, and twisted his pie-shaped cap so hard it resembled a sausage.

"Several?" Now true horror swept through Jamie, that and a large measure of anger. "Do you mean to tell me that all this time you and the men have been *court-*

ing?" Could it get any worse? He shook his head and exhaled a hot breath.

"Well, sir—"

"Saunders, if you say 'well, sir' one more time—" Jamie fisted his hands at his waist "—I'll not be responsible for my actions." Indeed, he felt like pummeling someone or something.

"Sorry, sir. But ye have to know a healthy man can't be expected to lie low in a town such as London and not seek out the comforts of a lady's presence." Saunders gave Jamie a gap-toothed smile.

"Just exactly how many 'ladies' are we picking up in London?" More nausea gurgled in Jamie's belly. Had his entire crew been bamboozled by tavern wenches? They should get out on the open sea right away, not sail back to London.

"Well, sir—" Saunders clapped a hand to his mouth, a gesture Jamie had never before seen him employ. "I mean, well, we don't need to pick up our wives in London. They're already aboard. All four of 'em."

"Four!" Rage filled Jamie, and he thought he might breathe out fire. Swinging away from Saunders, he strode to the gunwale and gripped it with both hands. Beyond Southampton lay Portsmouth and the vast British navy, countless sloops, frigates, ships of the line and men-of-war, vessels that could sink the *Fair Winds* if any hint of its true cargo and mission should be discovered. And, as if bringing Aaron's Emma weren't enough, adding four more souls, *female* souls, to this voyage made Jamie even more responsible to his Maker for their care. He took off his round-brimmed hat and brushed a hand over his hair down to his queue.

"Captain Templeton." Saunders came alongside him.

"Jamie." He set a hand on Jamie's shoulder. "I can't say I'm sorry, sir. We're honest men, and our wives are the decent sort. Christian ladies, every one of 'em."

Jamie gave him a sidelong glance, this plain, muscular, bowlegged fellow who'd weathered the change from whaler to sailor to patriot without so much as asking for a single boon, except that he might remain in Jamie's crew. Seeing his friend's crooked grin, Jamie thought he might like his Molly for loving this homely but stouthearted man. Yet he could not stop the grief that gripped his own chest so hard he almost couldn't breathe. Why, if he must love a lady, did she have to be someone so utterly unattainable?

"Very well, Saunders." A dull ache of resignation rolled through Jamie's chest as he turned to complete his survey of the ship. "Just keep the women below and out of the way until we set sail." A true gentleman would call them forth to be introduced, but Jamie wasn't feeling much like a gentleman right now.

"Aye, sir." Saunders strode toward the crew, all of whom were grinning like fools. "Avast, me rowdies. Let's get this ship ready to sail at sunrise."

At their cheer, Jamie swallowed hard, as if this action could dislodge the cannonball in his throat.

"Emma, do you have room in your trunk for some of my things?" Marianne had pared her belongings down to the essentials, but they still made a bundle too heavy for her to carry.

"No." Quince answered for his bride, and without so much as a "my lady" to soften his curt tone.

Marianne stared across her bedchamber at the couple. If she ordered Emma to obey her, they doubtless would leave her behind.

"No, of course not." Tugging her new black cloak about her, she gave them a trembling smile. "Forgive me."

Quince came closer, and in the shadowed room, his dark visage appeared ominous. "If not for my good friend's happiness, we would not risk taking you. If you cause even the slightest trouble, we'll say you forced us to take you with us."

"Your friend?" Marianne recalled some of this man's actions, hardly those of a well-trained valet. Yet Jamie defended him. Perhaps this was an American custom, to treat one's servants as friends. "Yes, of course. And do not be concerned, Mr. Quince, I shall follow our plan—"

A knock sounded on the door, and she gasped. Before anyone could move, Mama opened it and entered. "Emma, I brought you a little gift… Marianne!" She looked from her daughter to Emma to Quince. "What's this?" Even in the shadows, Marianne could see comprehension come over her mother's face.

"Oh, my lady," Emma trilled, "Lady Marianne is so kind to interrupt her games to see me off."

"Ah, I see." Mama looked down at Marianne's bundle, then stared at her, tears filling her eyes. "Well, then…" She closed the door behind her, swallowed hard and crossed the room to take her in her arms. "My darling girl." Her voice was thick. "I have known… I could see. I understand." She held Marianne in a death grip. "I was prepared to console you after his leave-taking, but you seemed so strong. I did not think you would… Why did you not tell me?"

Marianne sobbed against her mother's shoulder. "You know why."

Mama nodded. "Yes, I am grieved to say I do." She moved back and touched Marianne's cheek. "Now I understand why you embraced your father and me so fervently this evening." She laughed softly. "We thought it was gratitude for letting you and your friends have your treasure hunt." Another laugh, a sad one. "But you go to seek another treasure."

"Yes." Marianne felt a rush of anxiety and tried to pull away. "We must go, Mama. I love you…and Papa."

Mama held her fast. "Tomorrow I shall divert him as best I can. I will not tell him anything until absolutely necessary."

"You would face his wrath?"

Mama nodded again. "If I must. But I will also remind him that many frowned on our marriage because of my lower birth." She drew back, her eyes wide. "He will marry you, will he not?"

"Jamie Templeton is a man of honor." Quince stepped closer. "He'll do what's right. Now, my lady—" his every word conveyed anxiety "—we must go."

Mama gripped Marianne quickly, then released her and stared down at her bundle. "Oh, mercy, is that all you are taking?"

She shrugged, refusing to look at Emma or Quince.

"Gracious, child, take a valise or even a small trunk."

"There's no time, Mama." Marianne felt her knees quiver. For all the emotional benefits of Mama discovering her plan, would she now ruin the whole escape?

Emma hurried to the small chamber where she had slept for seven summers, and brought out a satchel. "Here, my lady." She quickly stuffed Marianne's extra belongings in it, in spite of Quince's fearful glances toward the door.

"Mr. Quince," Mama said. "I came to bring this one last gift to Emma." She retrieved a small leather bag from her pocket. As she handed it to him, the coins within it clinked, and his eyes rounded. "From Lord Bennington and me."

"Oh, thank you, my lady." Emma curtsied.

Quince blustered briefly. "Thank you, my lady." This time, his tone held true respect.

Mama kissed Emma's cheek. "Despite Lord Bennington's crossness at losing such a fine servant from his household staff, he sends his blessing on your union." She eyed Marianne wistfully. "I wonder if we'd had more courage, he might not have come around for another marriage. Oh, dear." Her eyes widened. "Do you have money?"

"Yes. I have been saving my pin money for some time." Marianne flung herself into her mother's arms. "I shall miss you, my dear one."

"I shall miss you, my darling girl." Mama sniffed back tears. "But I knew one day I would have to surrender you to some good man." She brushed a hand over Marianne's cheek. "How good to know that the man you chose is also the man who saved your father's grandson." She gave her an unladylike wink. "I shall remind him of that as often as I dare."

Chapter Twenty-Five

A week out of Southampton, the *Fair Winds* sailed into a storm that buffeted the ship for three days and nights. Once it abated, the vessel caught a rare northeasterly wind that swept it toward America at a good speed, as if the Almighty Himself hastened their journey. The gale had been appropriate weather for Jamie's unending tempest of emotions and a good immersion back into the sailing life. He'd expected his feelings to soften once he stood at the helm and felt the sun and wind on his face. But each time he thought the pain was all behind him, one or more of the brides ventured forth from below deck to catch some fresh air, and Jamie's anguish began all over again.

The only consolation he could claim was the information Thomas Moberly had bestowed on him, confident it would be safe with him. Yet even that was painful when Jamie contemplated his betrayal of people who had trusted him. He'd lived in the bosom of Bennington's family, given every benefit but adoption. And, of course, Marianne's hand. Still, his heart twisted within him. How could a man of honor be a spy? He prayed General Washington would find another use for him in the Revolution. Even turning the *Fair Winds* into a warship to meet the enemy face-to-face would be more honest than making friends only to betray them.

Becoming a battle-ready ship would not be the first change for this fine old vessel. For fifteen years she'd admirably performed her original purpose—whale ship. Then Captain Folger had refitted her as a merchant vessel, turning her over to Jamie as they made plans for serving the Revolution in East Florida. With her newly reinforced decks, she could carry more guns and many more sailors to fight for the Cause. The sloop even had three private cabins in addition to his captain's quarters to accommodate the officers a warship would require.

At the thought of the cabins, Jamie grunted. Quince, who wasn't a crew member, had paid for his cabin as a contribution to the Revolution. He and his Emma resided there. Naturally, first mate Saunders deserved one, and there he and his Molly slept. The other three wives were crowded into the third to protect their feminine privacy. They and their husbands would have to wait until they reached land to enjoy all the felicities of marriage.

Ten days out, Jamie sat in his cabin writing in his logbook. Other than the storm, the voyage had been uneventful. The previous day, a British man-of-war had sailed past, some two hundred yards off to starboard, but she'd merely saluted and gone on her way. No doubt her captain regarded the Union Jack flying on the *Fair Winds*' mainmast, and Bennington's banner beneath it, as sufficient to dispel any need for searching a merchant ship. Jamie duly noted the non-incident in his log.

A rap sounded on the cabin's door just as Jamie closed the book. "Come."

The door opened, and Demetrius, the ship's Greek cook, peered around it. "'Morning, Cap'n Jamie. Sorry to disturb you, sir."

Jamie beckoned to him. "Not at all. Come sit down." He put the logbook on its shelf.

Demetrius shuffled into the cabin and placed his bulging form into a chair in front of Jamie's desk.

"Did you learn any new dishes in London?" Jamie asked.

"Naw, Cap'n, nothin' new. Them English just cook roast beef." Demetrius smirked. "It's a shame what they do with a good piece of lamb."

Jamie joined his laughter, but he could think of more than a few fine dishes he'd eaten at Bennington's table, including an excellent leg of lamb. "What can I do for you?" He noticed the concern in the middle-aged man's eyes. "Did you forget to pack enough flour or sugar? Are we out of fresh vegetables already?"

Demetrius's shrug was more like a wince. "Not yet, sir, though we're goin' through 'em faster than I thought we would." He clicked his tongue and gave his head a shake. "Thought I'd brought aboard plenty of stores. Even counted the wives as I planned, knowing you wouldn't have the heart to put 'em off the ship when you saw how happy the lads were. But with six ladies, two of 'em needing to eat for two, if you get my meaning, we'll be eating a bit slimmer 'till we reach Boston." He eyed Jamie. "Just thought I should let you know so you won't think I'm trying to starve anyone."

"Thanks." Jamie pulled a book from his shelf, planning to read for the rest of the afternoon. Then he started. "Wait. Did you say *six* ladies? You mean there's a wife I haven't met?" Whoever this female was, she'd better be a wife, or Jamie would thrash the man who'd brought her aboard. He'd never countenanced wenching among his men, and certainly not aboard his vessel.

Demetrius's eyes grew round. "Not that I know of, sir. I just know I been deliverin' breakfast and supper to four grateful ladies in their cabin."

"Thank you, Demetrius." Jamie gritted his teeth. "Was there anything else?"

The cook stood. "No, sir. Just wanted to warn you about the stores."

"Very well. Don't say anything to anyone about our talk." The charge wasn't necessary. Jamie's cook did not engage in gossip.

After Demetrius left the cabin, Jamie shelved his reading and considered the situation. This crew was comprised of good men, every one. They knew his rules and abided by them.

But who was this sixth woman? And how had she come aboard without his seeing her? He mentally went down the list of crewmen. Three had left wives at home in Massachusetts, several had vowed never to marry, and some admitted sheepishly that their English lady friends had refused their proposals. Jamie snorted. Once Saunders set the example, there must have been a rush among the men to find willing mates. And he'd learned one or two of these ladies had first met the others when they came aboard. They would think nothing of this sixth woman being a stranger among them.

A spy. The thought was so jolting Jamie jumped to his feet and strode across the cabin into the narrow hallway. The second cabin was at the far end of the vessel, and he quickly closed the distance. There he pounded on the heavy wooden door.

"Ladies, make yourselves presentable." He hoped the sternness in his voice would send them hopping, and from the muffled squeals and thumps within, he surmised he'd succeeded. After several minutes, he heard the latch click. As the door swung open, Jamie felt some invisible object slam into his chest.

"Good afternoon, Captain Templeton." Marianne stood before him, an innocent, beatific smile on her flawless face.

"Marianne." The breathless rush of Jamie's voice, the arch of his eyebrows, the widening of his intense brown eyes, sent a surge of satisfaction through Marianne. Her surprise was complete. And long overdue. If she had to stay in this stifling room one more hour—

"Captain, would you be so kind as to escort me to the upper deck?" Marianne glanced over her shoulder at the women she had come to regard as sisters in romance, for they had all shared their love stories to keep up their courage while the ship pitched and rolled in the storm. She then looked back at Jamie, whose expression now bordered on horrified—not what she had hoped for. "I have not seen the sun for ten days. Or is it eleven? Down here, it is difficult to know."

Jamie scowled at her. "What are you doing here?"

His growling tone cut into her. She'd never imagined he would be cross with her.

"Wh-why, I thought—"

"Don't speak." Jamie gripped her arm. "Come with me." He pulled her down the hallway, or whatever these narrow passages were called.

"Ouch." She tugged against him. "Where are you taking me? Are you not pleased to see me? Jamie!" Her last words came out on a sob.

He opened a door and almost shoved her inside. The room—cabin, she corrected herself—was much larger than the other and nicely furnished with a desk, several chairs, and a bed, or berth, built into the wall.

Marianne settled into a chair, huffing with horrified indignation and trying desperately not to cry. "Well, Captain Templeton, it seems I have made a serious mistake. Obviously, all your gentle protestations of love for me were nothing short of a lie."

"Don't," he growled again. "Do not for one moment think that this is about my love for you." He ran a hand through his hair, loosening many strands from his queue, a gesture she had heretofore found charming. Now it seemed the gesture of a man enraged. Enraged at *her*. Papa had never treated Mama thus.

"Jamie." She spoke softly, as Mama did when trying to soothe Papa's ruffled feathers. But unlike her mother, Marianne could not stop her tears. "I love you. I—I thought you loved me. Why should we be separated by foolish social strictures?"

Jamie bent forward, his hands gripping the arms of her chair, his nose inches from hers. "You have no idea what you've done." He straightened and crossed his arms. "Yes, I love you." His tone did not confirm his words. "But you don't belong here, and I can't return you. We are ten days out, and I can't afford to lose time."

She laughed, but it sounded more like a squeak in her ears. "But I do not wish to return." A bitter thought occurred to her. "If you despise me for following you, then take me to my brother Frederick. How difficult can that be? You are sailing to East Florida anyway."

Jamie skewered her with a look. "We're not going directly to East Florida."

"But…wh-where are we going?" She stared down, clasping her hands as more thoughts collected, revealing a horrifying idea. Quince's disrespect. Emma's subtle remarks, disguised as humor, regarding His Majesty. The way the other women aboard the ship avoided certain topics. Marianne lifted her gaze to the man she loved. "Jamie, where are we going?" She was not certain she really wanted to know the answer.

"Boston." The word exploded from his lips.

"But Boston is occupied by the rebelling colonists and—"

As he lifted his chin and narrowed his eyes, she understood at last. Jamie was not the man he claimed to be. He was a rebel, one of those who hoped to drive the British from American shores. But why would he have befriended Papa? What had been his purpose?

Shattering reality struck her heart and mind. He was a spy. And no doubt he had been spying on Papa from the moment he walked into Bennington House last March. Or perhaps it began last year, at the very same time she was falling in love with him.

Indeed, by running away to be with Jamie Templeton, Marianne had made a horrible, irreparable mistake. The realization stole her breath, and she thought she might suffocate. The room became a swirling eddy, pulling her downward. She gasped for air, barely aware of the captain bending over her until he touched her arm.

"Marianne."

The concern in his voice cut through her struggle,

and she pulled in air at last. "No. Do not touch me." Bitter anguish tore through her, and she burst out in sobs she could not control.

Chapter Twenty-Six

He was a beast. No other word would suit him. And Jamie cringed to see the fear in Marianne's face as, right before his eyes, she realized she had run from the safety of her father's house into the custody of her father's enemy. Yet, after she regained her breath, only to succumb to violent weeping, he clenched his jaw, tightened his arms across his chest and stared out through the porthole to keep from taking her into his arms. Why had she not accepted the fact that they couldn't be together? Foolish, wonderful girl. To think he'd once doubted the depth of her love.

He'd never before frightened a woman, and it grieved him deeply to cause this particular lady such pain. He was a Christian above all else, dedicated to serving his Lord even before the Patriot cause. That included treating women with respect and honor. He'd let no harm come to Marianne, but he must stay as far away from her as possible on this vessel.

He shouldn't have told her where they were going. That had revealed everything. Now, if they were accosted by a British vessel, she'd have the tools to give them away. And even if he kept her below deck where she could not alert them, his usefulness to the Glorious Cause had been destroyed forever. He could never return to England, for Bennington would doubtless have him drawn and quartered. Marianne's actions had put an end to his spying. If he were alone, he would laugh out loud. God had granted his wish not to spy anymore.

How had she come aboard? Who helped her? How had the man on watch at the time failed to see she was not like the other women, despite her plain clothing?

As her sobs subsided, he ventured to look in her direction, steeling himself against the temptation to comfort her. There she sat, dabbing her lovely face with a linen handkerchief, staring unfocused at the bulkhead. Her cheeks had grown puffy, and her eyes still leaked copious tears, but her lips formed a firm line. Before she fully gained her emotional footing, he must uncover her accomplice in her mad scheme.

"Whom did you bribe to help you come aboard? My watchman?" Jamie had been too full of grief his first night on board to recall who'd performed that duty, a sure sign he'd slipped in his ability to rule his own ship. "One of the other women?"

She glared at him with chin lifted. Too late. He saw in her sapphire eyes he was now her enemy, and a familiar raw ache settled in his chest. But he must ferret out the information. Who among his crew could be persuaded to betray him this way? Would they also reveal the store of muskets in the hold if a British naval officer came aboard? At least Marianne didn't know about that. Or did she?

"Jamie." Aaron pounded on the door. "Jamie, may I come in?" The urgency in his voice only mildly alarmed

Jamie. Aaron was a passenger. If the ship were about to be accosted, Saunders or the second mate would alert him. But Aaron's interruption might disarm Marianne into revealing her accomplice.

No. Aaron *was* her accomplice. There could be no other explanation.

Jamie yanked open the door. *"You."* Guilt wrote itself across Aaron's face, and only the grace of God restrained Jamie from slamming his fist into his friend's jaw. Emma peered around him, her pale blue eyes blinking. "What were you thinking, man?" He shoved past the two of them, suddenly needing to breathe some fresh air.

Ascending to the main deck, he first saw Brody, one of the newly married crewmen, standing at the gunwale. Brody grinned and touched his hat in an informal salute. A growl rumbled in Jamie's throat, and he strode across the deck and up the steps to the quarterdeck. There Crane, another new groom, stood at the helm. At Jamie's appearance, he also saluted. "How do, Cap'n?"

Not trusting himself to speak, Jamie ordered him away with a jerk of his thumb and gripped the wheel himself. Crane left, scratching his head, probably wondering over the captain's ill temper. But suspicion crept into Jamie's thoughts. Had they all known about Marianne? Clearly, Demetrius had discovered it, although he didn't seem to know her identity. But what of the others? Had their wives said nothing to them?

"Saunders," Jamie bellowed into the wind. In seconds, his first mate stood in front of him, calm curiosity in his eyes.

"Aye, sir." Saunders touched his hat, as Brody had, in

an informal salute, which until today had shown sufficient respect to satisfy Jamie. "Is everything all right?"

"No, everything is not all right." Jamie stared at the distant horizon. "Did you know that we had an extra passenger, a woman, on board?"

Saunders drew back and scratched his bearded chin. "Why, no, sir. Just Mrs. Quince, my Molly, and the other three ladies, our wedded wives." He tilted his head. "Are ye sayin' we got a stowaway?"

Jamie narrowed his eyes and glared at him. He'd always trusted this man...until now. Now Jamie didn't know whom to trust. "So you didn't know about—" He stopped, realizing his near mistake. If the crew learned of Marianne's title, he couldn't predict what their responses might be. "Mr. Quince brought along one of his wife's friends, though I've yet to determine why." Indeed, Aaron had lumped Marianne's entire family into one basket, despising them all. Why would he help her run away?

"He did?" Saunders shook his head. "Sorry, Cap'n Jamie. I should've been payin' more attention when he and his bride come aboard that night. Too much confusion with that extra shipment of wool and all, but that's no excuse."

Jamie believed him. "Very well." If Saunders didn't know about Marianne, few other members of the crew would, either. But how had the other wives kept the secret of their extra companion from their husbands? A fresh wind swept over him, and he inhaled deeply. Then a picture of Marianne came unbidden to his mind. She'd been confined to the cabin below deck for the entire voyage. "The lady might appreciate—"

"Sail, ho," cried the watchman in the crow's nest high above the deck. "Flyin' the Union Jack, Cap'n."

Handing the wheel to Saunders, Jamie retrieved his telescope from his belt and extended it to view the oncoming vessel. A British forty-gun man-of-war was bearing down on them, flying over the waters like a pelican about to devour a fish.

Taking the helm again, Jamie frowned at Saunders. "Pass the word among the crew. They know what to do. Mind what we've practiced."

"Aye, sir." Saunders started to leave, but turned back. "And don't ye be worryin' about the wives, Jamie. They all know what we're about."

His words jolted Jamie. The women knew their husbands were secret revolutionaries, yet they'd kept their own secret about Marianne. Now he truly had no idea of whom to trust.

This had been a bad plan from the beginning, leaving his crew to gad about London for these several months. How could he expect healthy, reputable men not to seek the company of decent ladies? And once they married, how could they keep from revealing their true loyalties to their wives? Yet the ship couldn't have sailed back to America without repairs, which had taken far too long, leaving plenty of time for mischief and mischance. He should be thankful God had protected them all from something far more dangerous than marriages.

Lord, help us. Keep these English sailors from finding our cargo. His instinctive prayer reminded him God had permitted the storm that damaged the mast, and the hull had been long overdue for a careening, something not available in East Florida. No good thing could have come from sailing without those repairs. A certain peace settled over and within him. God had let *all* of these things happen. He would see them through.

The only thing Jamie couldn't reconcile with the Lord was the presence of a certain little aristocrat aboard his ship. And as the man-of-war came alongside, he realized that he'd not sent anyone to imprison her so she couldn't give them away.

Finding her way back to the ladies' cabin, Marianne sensed Quince and Emma close behind her. Were they following to support her or to make certain she did nothing wrong? But what harm could she do to anyone aboard this ship? In the cabin, the other four women eyed her with more than a little interest.

"Well?" Molly, the matronly woman somewhere near Mama in age, gave her a merry smile. "Did you get your man settled down?" She threw back her head and laughed. "My, I thought I'd split a seam seein' the cap'n so put out with you. Tell us, dearie…why, what are these tears?" She raised her arms and Marianne flew into her embrace, weeping against her shoulder for several moments.

"Oh, bother." Marianne lifted her head and blew her nose on her wet handkerchief. "I thought I had finished crying."

"Here, now." Molly handed her a dry cloth. "What's the matter with the cap'n? Wasn't he glad to see you?" She propped her hands on her waist in indignation.

Shaking her head, Marianne continued to sniff. What could she say to these dear women? All they knew about her was her first name and that she had fled her disapproving father to follow Jamie. So far, Quince and Emma had kept her identity secret. In fact, Quince treated her far better as plain Marianne than he ever had when she was Lady Marianne. What a strange twist of events. Now these new friends loved her, while the man she loved turned his back on her. While the man she loved turned out to be a traitor to her father and his king.

A familiar crewman—Nancy's husband—bustled down the passage. "All right, ladies," Brody said. "This is it. This is what we told you about. Do you all remember what to do?"

"That we do, Mr. Brody." Molly, who by reason of her age and strong personality had become the ladies' resident matron, motioned them to come close. She gave Marianne a long look, then turned to Quince. "Sir, does Miss Moberly know what to do?"

Quince wiped a hand across his mouth. "*Miss* Moberly, may I speak with you for a moment?" He tilted his head toward the companionway.

Marianne's thoughts scrambled in a thousand different directions. "What's happened? Are we in danger?" She followed him and Emma to a quiet corner not far from the cabin.

Quince gripped her upper arms gently and seized her gaze with dark, earnest eyes. "Lady Marianne, Mr. Brody's alert means we've been accosted by a British naval vessel."

She gasped. Had Papa sent someone to save her?

As if reading her thoughts, Quince gripped her more tightly. "You must stay with the ladies in the cabin and not make a sound." A pinch of fear crossed his face. "You do realize, of course, that if you give us away, we'll all hang—Jamie included, this very day—and this ship will be commandeered."

Marianne swayed, but this time not from the ship's motion. The lives of these traitors were in her hands. *Dear Lord, what shall I do?*

"I am taking Emma to our cabin. As passengers, we do not expect to be troubled by the British." Quince shook her gently. "Must we bind and muffle you and lock you in our closet?"

"No." The word came out without a thought, but in truth, she had no idea what she would do if the British sailors came below and questioned her.

Chapter Twenty-Seven

Jamie had learned from Lamech Folger, his uncle, mentor and East Florida partner, that full and friendly cooperation was the only way to appease these officious British captains. As the uniformed, thirtyish man climbed over the gunwale, Jamie smiled and tipped his broad-brimmed hat. "Welcome aboard, Captain. Jamie Templeton, at your service."

Flanked by several armed officers and perhaps fifteen sailors, the red-haired man eyed Jamie up and down. "I am Captain Reading of the HMS *Pride.* I see you are flying the Union Jack and Lord Bennington's flag." He glanced toward the top of the mainmast. "However, in these uncertain times, such symbols might be a ploy. You will understand that it is my responsibility to make certain no arms or contraband are aboard your vessel."

"Yes, sir, I do." Jamie thought the man looked reasonable enough, but one officer behind him wore a sneer, and the sailors, armed with cudgels, glared around the ship. A twinge of nausea struck Jamie, and he prayed their captain would not decide to press members of the *Fair Winds'* crew into service. "You will find a large volume of goods in our hold, sir. We sail to East Florida, where my business partner, Lord Bennington, expects to make a tidy profit among the Loyalists who are fleeing all that nonsense in the northern colonies." Should he offer this man his choice of the goods as a bribe?

The captain's left eyebrow flickered briefly. "We will search your vessel, sir, with your permission."

Jamie covered his anger with a coughing chuckle. This treatment was one of the many reasons for the Revolution, this unreasonable searching of ships. "Of course. I would expect nothing less from His Majesty's navy." He gave a quick little nod to confirm his words. "This is how you keep us all safe. May I show you around?"

Reading's eyes narrowed. "No, thank you, sir. My men know what to do."

Despite his growing rage, Jamie managed another smile. "Very well, sir. I am your servant."

Reading motioned to his men, and his three officers took several sailors each to search various parts of the ship, including below deck. The captain then glanced around the main deck. "We have lost several of our crew to unfortunate accidents, and require replacements. You may ask for volunteers or select them yourself. If you choose not to cooperate, I will make my own selections."

Raw fear cut into Jamie's chest. He would die for any of his men, but who else would die if he resisted this demand? And what of the ladies' safety? "Sir, I have a letter from Lord Bennington, also signed by Captain Thomas Moberly, of the HMS *Dauntless.* These should exempt my crew from impressments." Now he would learn just how powerful his former patron was.

After a brief, startled blink, Reading snorted. "You

have notable protectors, Captain Templeton. How shall I know the signatures are not forgeries?"

Jamie faked a lighthearted shrug. "I don't know, sir. But if you'll permit my first mate to fetch my papers..." He beckoned to Saunders, who always kept his head during these boardings.

"Very well." Reading gave a curt nod.

Saunders scampered below deck and within minutes returned with a brown leather satchel. Striding close to the British captain, he gave him a gap-toothed grin. "Here ye go, sir."

Leaning away with lips curled, the captain took the satchel. "That will be all." He set it on a nearby crate and untied the strings, drawing out the life-saving documents. His eyebrows arched as he read through them. "Impressive, indeed. Yes, I recognize Lord Bennington's seal." He frowned as he kept reading. "So Bennington's son has been made a captain. A good man, Thomas Moberly. But I see nothing here exempting your crew from impressments."

His heart hammering almost out of his chest, Jamie considered his options. The men had practiced what to do in case of pirate attacks, but they would have little defense against a forty-gun ship with sailors who were trained for warfare. Yet every person on this sloop had been entrusted to his care, a fact that gave him no other choice. He leveled a solemn gaze upon the British captain. "Captain Reading, I am not prepared to part with any of my crew."

Marianne was pleased to see Molly come to the cabin and take charge. After covering the single porthole, the five ladies huddled silently together in the locked, darkened room. Above them and in the companion-way beyond the door, heavy footsteps thumped against the decks, while an occasional clunk of wood against wood sounded through the walls. Marianne felt Nancy tremble beside her, and drew the slender young girl into her arms. "Shh. It will be all right." Despite Jamie's—Captain Templeton's—betrayal, she knew him to be a competent captain. And of course the British captain would be reasonable and no doubt send them on their way once he had seen Papa's letter.

For the briefest moment, Marianne considered whether she should break out of this cabin and con-fess everything to her countryman. But Quince's words weighed heavy upon her heart. While Captain Temple-ton and even Quince might deserve to hang, she could not reconcile seeing these ladies' husbands likewise punished. An image of their captain strung up on a gib-bet flitted into her mind and cut deep into her. *Lord, forgive me, but I love him still.* Yet he was a traitor to all she held dear, and every word he had spoken to her had been a lie.

Sudden pounding on the door startled her, and be-side her Nancy jumped. "Open up, or we'll break down the door."

More trembling and several quiet sobs shook the women around Marianne.

"Mind yourselves, ladies," Molly whispered. "Re-member what we're to do."

Marianne could hear footsteps shuffle across the dark room. A click of the bolt, another click of the latch, and Molly swung the door open.

A snarling sailor stuck a lantern inside, and his shad-owed face took on a grotesque sneer. "Well, well, what have we here?" Behind him, two other sailors stuck their heads around the doorjamb, leering into the dark and making crude comments.

Molly tried to hold her place and block them from entering, but they shoved her aside.

"I'll take this one." The first sailor grabbed for Nancy, yanking her up from the cot. The other men laughed.

A bolt of rage and protectiveness flashed through Marianne. "How dare you?" She stood and dug her fingernails into the man's bare hand. "Let her go."

He yelped and then drew back his hand to strike Marianne.

"Stop!" An officer holding another lantern entered the low doorway.

The first sailor cursed and stepped back. "Aye, sir." His wolflike growl sent a shudder down Marianne's spine.

"What is this?" The officer's face glowered in the shadowed cabin. "Who are you women?"

"Sir," Molly said, "we are Christian ladies accompanying our husbands to East Florida."

Like the first sailor, the officer sneered. "Ladies, indeed."

"Yes, ladies, indeed." Marianne pushed in front of Molly. "I am *Lady* Marianne Moberly, daughter of Lord Bennington, under whose flag this ship sails." She heard the gasps around her and knew these gentlewomen would never regard her in the same way again. Yet she would still be their friend. Whatever lie she must tell, Lord forgive her, she would save them from these sailors, even if it also meant saving that scoundrel, Jamie Templeton.

The officer raised a questioning eyebrow and his mouth hung open for an instant. Marianne lifted her chin and gave him an imperious glare. He lowered his lantern and bent forward in a deep bow. "My lady, may I have the privilege of escorting you to the upper deck?"

Air. The thought of it almost undid Marianne. But she managed to maintain her hauteur. "You may, my good sir, but only if these ladies are permitted to accompany me. I will not have my friends left to the *care* of your sailors."

The man had the grace to look abashed. "Yes, my lady."

He offered his arm, and she set her hand upon it, praying for wisdom to say the right thing to his superior. Praying for the strength not to look at her erstwhile love, now her nemesis. Was there some way she could alert the British captain that Templeton was a spy and might be carrying secrets to the rebelling colonists in Boston? Nothing came to mind, but she felt certain the Lord would show her exactly what to do.

Coming out into the daylight for the first time in over a week, Marianne winced and blinked, shading her eyes with both hands while the ocean breeze caressed her face and filled her lungs with salty air. She felt a tap on her shoulder and looked back to see Molly, her eyes filled with fear and hope, holding forth a much-mended black parasol.

"Thank you, Molly." Marianne accepted the gift, offered perhaps to gain her favor in protecting Molly's husband from being impressed. Marianne chided herself for such a suspicious thought. But the revelations of these past few hours had utterly destroyed her starry-eyed foolishness. She raised the parasol and found relief from the sun's glare.

Surveying the scene, she noticed the officer who had escorted her on deck had moved toward his captain, a man of medium height who looked familiar. Beyond them, she saw the *Fair Winds* crew standing in a straight line, while several British sailors perused them as if searching for the right horse to buy. Or the right slave. The anger and fear in the Americans' faces sent a troubled pang through her heart. *So this is the reality of impressments.* Marianne shuddered to think what it would be like to be torn from one's friends and forced into an enemy's service.

"Lady Marianne." The captain strode toward her, a wide smile on his freckled face. "What a surprise to find you sailing—"

"Under my father's flag?" She did not return his smile or offer her hand. "Good day, Captain Reading. It has been some time since my brother introduced us when you both received your commissions as lieutenants." She lifted her chin and sniffed. "I shall write to him and describe this meeting."

"Ah, yes, well." Reading stiffened. "We are simply doing our duty to king and country, my lady."

"Indeed. And when does that duty include stealing my father's servants right off of his business partner's ship?" The words came out unplanned, but now she could not give Templeton away without betraying the entire crew. "Do you not realize that this ship carries official mail to the governor of East Florida? Through an act of Parliament, that duty exempts its crew from impressments." If she had not overheard Thomas discussing it with Papa, she never would have known of the law.

Reading tilted his head in a patronizing nod. "My lady, although your esteemed father is this captain's patron, the ship is still an American vessel, not a British mail packet. The law does not apply in this case."

Marianne answered his look with a glare while she considered his words. She would not lose her battle with this intractable man.

The British sailors now dragged away two men, one of whom must be married to Sally, for Marianne heard the girl sobbing behind her. The violence of the sailors toward the hapless men, one of whom was a sweet-faced boy she had seen in the hallway outside the ladies' cabin, seemed entirely unwarranted in light of the two men's cooperation. Perhaps they sought to sacrifice themselves for their fellows. As a British sailor lifted his club to strike, Sally wailed.

"Stop, this instant!" Marianne marched across the deck. "How dare you? Release these men immediately, or you will regret it all your days."

The sailors obeyed, but one had the audacity to leer at her before looking toward his captain. Marianne turned back to Captain Reading. "In the name of King George and Lord Bennington—" she modulated her voice into a lower register and used a cold, hard tone, as Papa did when giving orders *"—release them."*

The shock that swept across the men's faces, both British and American, amused her. While of course she possessed no authority over these men, they had no idea how much or little influence she might actually wield with their superiors. As for Captain Templeton, he puckered a smile and winked away the glint in his eyes. His slight nod, like many that had secretly conveyed his feelings for her these past months, sent a tingle through her traitorous body.

"Captain Reading." Marianne sauntered back toward him, thrown slightly off balance when a swell lifted the ship, but quickly regaining her footing. Another approving nod came from Captain Templeton, but she did not acknowledge it. "If you hope to advance any further in your naval career, I suggest you do not make me unhappy. It may take months, it may take years, but my father, the Admiralty and His Majesty's Privy Council will hear of your treatment of the men who have been assigned the duty to protect me."

Captain Reading clenched his jaw and glared at her for what seemed an eternity. At last, he shrugged and waved his men away from their captives, then swept off his bicorne and bent toward her in an exaggerated bow. "Your servant, my lady." He spun around and barked orders at his crew to leave.

The British sailors clambered into their small boats, but Marianne would not let herself breathe until the last man had returned to His Majesty's man-of-war.

Chapter Twenty-Eight

Marianne stood at the railing with the five other ladies and Mr. Quince to watch the HMS *Pride* tack away, leaving the entire crew of the *Fair Winds* unharmed. When the other vessel was some distance away, even as the crew members hoisted the sails to catch the wind and carry their ship in the opposite direction, everyone cheered. All Marianne felt was desolation.

The other women now eyed her with an odd mix of expressions. Nancy gazed at her as if she were a saint, no doubt because Marianne had stopped the sailor who'd tried to assault her. Sally kissed Marianne's hand and thanked her for saving her husband from impressment. Eleanor glared, her lips curling in disapproval, but Marianne could not guess why, for the woman had always been pleasant to her before. Molly's posture devolved into that of a servant. Only Emma treated her no differently.

How could Marianne continue to share that cramped cabin with women who either worshipped or despised her?

"Lady Marianne." The all too familiar voice spoke behind her. "May I have a word with you?"

She turned to see Captain Templeton standing tall and proud. No, not proud. Intense. His dark brown eyes held her gaze, and her insides began to flutter. She would not do this. She would never again succumb to his charming ways. Pushing past him, she walked toward the steps leading below, even though she dreaded returning to the airless cabin.

He gripped her arm. "May I speak with you?" It was more of a command than a question.

"Let me go."

"Jamie, let her go." Quince stood nearby with Emma, who sent Marianne a quivering smile.

"Stow it, Aaron." Templeton's handsome, well-tanned face creased with annoyance. "You have yet to answer to me for her being here. Don't try to interfere now."

Quince bit his lip and shrugged. "Don't do something you'll regret." He put an arm around Emma and moved away.

The intensity in Templeton's eyes increased. "I must thank you, my lady, for saving my crew from impressment. That, above all, makes your presence aboard my ship nothing short of a blessing." He loosened his grip and winced. "Forgive me. I would not hurt you for the world."

"But you would deceive me…deceive my father, my brothers—" She stopped, recalling the undeniable improvements in Robert's character, little Georgie being saved from drowning, the lightened moods in family gatherings because of this man's humor. Gulping down sudden tears, she leaned away from him, aware of the shuttered glances sent their way by the other women and the crew. "You are a liar and a brigand, a traitor and a spy."

He had the audacity to laugh. "I do believe you've put an end to that latter occupation."

She yanked her arm from his grasp...and felt the loss of his touch. Still, she would not look at him but stared off across the wide, desolate sea at the retreating HMS *Pride*. "Ha. If I could have told Captain Reading the truth about you without ruining these innocent women's lives, I gladly would have watched you hang from your own yardarm." No, that would have destroyed her...and Emma, too. For undoubtedly Quince was also a spy.

"But you did *not* give me away." The mirth in his voice drew her sharp look. "To show my gratitude, you may have my cabin, so you'll be more comfortable for the rest of the voyage. I'll sleep in the crew's quarters, and you'll have access to my library and other amenities."

She drew in a deep breath, grateful for the fresh sea air, and glanced beyond him, where the other ladies watched this little drama. No doubt they would be pleased to have a bit more space in their cabin, but it grated on her sensibilities to accept anything from this man. Yet her thoughts continued to contradict her sentiment. How could she deny that, traitor or not, he had done far more for her family than they had done for him?

"I thank you, Captain Templeton. I accept your offer. And you can be assured you will be paid for my passage when we reach my brother Frederick's home." She could not stop her voice from quavering. "Whenever that might be."

Jamie watched Marianne—*Lady* Marianne, for that was the way he must think of her now and forever—

walk gracefully across the rolling deck toward the ladder, her proud carriage stirring a rush of emotions within him. When she'd accosted that pompous British captain, all of Jamie's anger toward her had dissolved, and he'd seen God's grace clearly enacted. Profound relief flooded him as he considered the miracle that had just unfolded. He wouldn't try to imagine how many good people aboard this ship might have died without her interference, for he knew not one of his crewmen would have suffered his fellows to be impressed. Jamie himself would have joined the fray without a second thought for the consequences.

And now he must also forgive Quince for his part in Lady Marianne's flight. Of course the romantic rascal had intended to secure Jamie's happiness by sneaking her aboard the ship. Instead, now that she realized he'd been spying on her father, she'd never forgive him, and the final obstacle to a future together for them had been set in place. Because of it, Jamie felt an aching loneliness he doubted would ever go away.

Shaking off the tendrils of gloom threatening to entwine around his heart, he thanked the Lord he still could manage to do something of value for the Glorious Cause. If they could catch the right winds to help them sail against the Gulf Stream, they might reach Boston in another six or seven weeks. There he would report his findings to General Washington and receive his orders for taking the Revolution to East Florida. In the meantime, he must treat Lady Marianne with utmost care. Should they encounter another British man-of-war, he would need her continued goodwill toward the other ladies to once again avert tragedy.

Until such time, he would give her the run of the

ship, for she had endured many days of confinement below deck, a fact that stung him when he thought of all she'd given up for love of him, only to face a terrible reality. He would never throw it in her face that he'd warned her, that he'd refused to court her, and only in his weakest moments had surrendered to his longing to hold her in his arms and kiss her. One thing now was certain. Because she'd stowed away, he couldn't escape her presence, and the rest of this voyage would shred his already tattered soul.

He'd not felt the discomfort of a crewman's hammock for seven years, and over the next few nights, he discovered how much he'd grown since his eighteenth birthday. Either his feet or his head must hang out one end or the other, and his shoulders had grown much broader, so he felt folded in half by the canvas sling. Further, the snores of his sleeping crewmen kept him awake and cross. Never mind the smells of sweat and bilge water. He considered taking the helm at night, but a captain should be up and about in the daylight, so he must make do with whatever sleep he could get.

Over a week had passed since the incident with the *Pride,* and Jamie permitted himself some small pleasure in watching Lady Marianne walk about the deck each day. The ragged black parasol wasn't appropriate for a lady who'd always had the best of everything, yet she seemed to take no notice. Jamie offered to bring out one of the fashionable new parasols from the cargo hold. But she snubbed him outright, refusing to answer him or accept the gift, even when the sun's reflection on the sea colored her cheeks with a pink blush and scattered faint freckles across the bridge of her pretty porcelain nose. Surely now she must realize how much she would have sacrificed in becoming his wife. Even if he'd not been a spy and, in her eyes, a traitor, no doubt by now the foolishness of her undertaking would still have been impressed upon her.

Molly and the others ladies hovered around her. Except Eleanor, who kept her distance, though Jamie could not guess why. And his freedom-loving crew members seemed all too willing to give her the homage due to a queen. Even Quince fell under Lady Marianne's spell and permitted Emma to attend to her former mistress's needs. Jamie would have laughed, except that no one but he seemed to realize how their fawning over this lady aristocrat contradicted their dearly held belief in freedom. While this couldn't cause too much trouble as long as they were at sea, he began to wonder if she held the power to sway some of them away from the Revolution. But what nonsense that was, after all he and his crew had been through together. Too little sleep—and a broken heart—were distorting his thinking.

Marianne tried to read the books from Captain Templeton's library, but found her mind drifting like flotsam swaying hither and thither on the ocean waves. She could not imagine what drew men to the sea. If required to spend her days sailing back and forth across the ocean, she would die of boredom. But then, to be fair, the other women, none of whom had ever sailed before, seemed to enjoy themselves without reservation once their mal de mer ceased—thanks to her ginger tea. While Marianne could not comprehend what they saw in their uncultured American husbands, she could not help but feel a few pangs of jealousy over their marital happiness, something she would never enjoy.

And then there was the strange attraction these English women had for the rebellion in the colonies, a truly contradictory behavior. Once Marianne's identity was revealed, they showed her every courtesy her rank demanded, which placed upon her the task, indeed, the responsibility, of reclaiming their loyalty to His Majesty and England. Once the ladies were won, she would help them win over their husbands. But how to go about it? What would Mama do?

Why, she would give a ball.

During the day, Marianne heard the steady metered songs of the men as they went about their work. In the late evenings, the music of a fiddle, fife, flute and drum wafted from somewhere on the ship. While the unknown musicians did not possess exceptional talent, she felt certain they could manage some country dances, a hornpipe, perhaps even a minuet on the rolling deck of the ship. Of course, there must be a supper, too. She would consult with Demetrius about the extent of his food stores when he brought her dinner this very evening.

Despite the renewed sense of purpose these plans gave her, she continued to weep herself to sleep each night, for her heart ached at the realization she had never truly known Captain James Templeton. She had loved an ideal, a noble knight who did not exist, and found the real man, however charming, to be nothing but a deceitful scoundrel no better than Robert's disgusting former friend, Tobias Pincer.

But she was her father's daughter, and she would beat this scoundrel at his own game. She would spy on him and his crew and find out how to undercut his every move.

Chapter Twenty-Nine

"**D**emetrius says he will add some special spices to the salted beef and make oat cakes with raisins." Seated at the captain's desk, Marianne enjoyed the delight in Molly's eyes at this pronouncement. The woman held the esteem of the other ladies, and Marianne wanted to make her an ally in her plans. "We will have *four* removes, even a fish course." Mama would be shocked by fewer than seven removes, with twelve being her preference, but Marianne must make do with what was available. "With peas, pudding and cider, it should make a fine supper. Demetrius has some table linens, and I have given him permission to open the crate of Wedgwood china my mama shipped for my brother's wedding gift. Demetrius and his son will serve as footmen. He says they even will wear white gloves. Can you imagine that? We will set a fine board here in my cabin."

"Oh, my lady, how grand." Molly breathed out the words on a sigh. "The other ladies and I will dig out our finest dresses from the packing barrels and freshen them in the breeze." A frown flitted across her face. "I wish we could do something to help you."

Marianne expected this offer. "Why, you can decorate this cabin and the entire ship. Hmm." She glanced around the room with its stark furnishings. Other than a dozen or so books, two lanterns, and crossed swords mounted on the wall, not one decorative figurine or picture graced the chamber. Captain Templeton had removed his sea chest and other personal items, but his lingering woodsy scent stirred her senses.

She quickly changed the direction of her thoughts. "I would like to have flowers for the table. Do you suppose you could fashion some from bits of fabric? I understand there is a large shipment of lace, silk, cotton and other such material in the ship's hold, all bound for a mercantile shop in East Florida. We can sprinkle the artificial blossoms with perfume." When she reached the colony, she would pay the merchant for the fabric. "If there is any bunting to be had, we'll drape it around the deck."

"Aye, my lady." Molly nodded with enthusiasm. "We're all handy with a needle." Another frown touched her brow. "Do you think the unmarried men will be cross not being invited to our grand supper? My Mr. Saunders says it's not good to have a grumbling crew."

Another concern Marianne had prepared for. "To prevent that, we shall send portions to each of them. And perhaps, if your husbands agree to let you dance with those other gentlemen, they will anticipate the festivities with the same enthusiasm as the rest of us." Marianne tapped her chin thoughtfully. "I shall dance with them myself. That should take care of everything."

"Indeed it should." Molly clasped her hands to her chest as if trying to contain her glee, a response that assured Marianne her efforts would not go unrewarded.

When she sent the older woman to apprise the captain of her desire for a ball and supper, his positive response surprised her. But then, why would he deny his crew both the anticipation of a grand event and its fruition? His compliance, along with Marianne's new freedom to wander the ship at will, gave her all the means she required to begin winning back the crew's loyalty to the king. Each time a pleasant memory of the captain intruded into her thoughts, she forced herself to remember God's true purpose in permitting her ill-advised flight from her home.

"Jamie, you're missing all the fun." Aaron climbed the ladder and ambled across the quarterdeck. "I'd take the wheel, but we'd end up in Bermuda...or back in England."

"We'll head south soon enough, God willing." Jamie squinted into the afternoon sun as he watched the empty horizon. On the main deck, Flint and the other musicians played their lively tunes, while the rest of the crew took turns dancing with the six ladies. Jamie chuckled. He was having difficulty not tapping his feet in time with their music—or laughing at the dancers. His merrymaking men, who could keep their footing in a storm or climb the sheets without misstep, all had need of Mr. Pellam's services. But Jamie's former dance master would be appalled to see Lady Marianne smile so beguilingly and take the roughened hand of a sailor who that very afternoon had scrubbed the deck on which they now danced.

"Seriously, Jamie." Aaron clapped him on the shoulder. "Find someone else to take the wheel, and dance awhile. No doubt a certain young lady would be pleased to be your partner."

"Haven't you noticed?" Jamie gave him a wry grin. "Lady Marianne no longer speaks to me. Maybe it's my pride, but I'll not try again. The men shouldn't see their captain treated with disrespect." Yet he wondered how he could avoid talking to her. And, in fact, longed to do so.

"They seem a bit smitten with her, don't they?" Aaron leaned against a secured barrel and gripped a line above his head for balance. "All that will be over when we reach Boston."

Jamie sent him a sidelong glance. "What makes you think so?" He'd worried about leaving his crew loose in London, where their loyalties might be swayed, but no other plan had presented itself. And now even Saunders and his Molly had abandoned talk of the Revolution in their adoration of Lady Marianne.

"Oh, come now." Aaron punched Jamie's arm. "These are good fellows, true to the Cause."

Jamie grunted. "I've always thought so. But when you think of what we're facing, what we each must give up to win this revolution, maybe they'd prefer to settle down someplace with their brides until it's all finished. I doubt any one of them would turn down land on a Caribbean island." He gripped and turned the wheel as a large swell rolled beneath the ship.

On the main deck, the revelers laughed as they struggled to keep their balance, even Lady Marianne. His lost love continued to surprise Jamie. She'd found her sea legs all too well.

"Whoa!" Aaron's arms flailed about as he tried to stay upright. Jamie caught his shoulder and righted him.

"Thank you, my friend. Can't wait to get back on land. Whose idea was it for me to come with you on this mission, anyway?" His hearty laugh rang out in contradiction to his complaint. "Say, I'm going to drag someone up here to take your place. My Emma would be pleased to dance with you." He staggered across the rolling deck and down the ladder before Jamie could stop him.

Not that he wanted to. By the time Simpson had joined him on the quarterdeck, Jamie felt the bite of mischief. If he could not have Lady Marianne for a wife, or even for a friend, he could put aside his pride and show her his goodwill, maybe reminding her of better times. In fact, he would first go below and don one of his new jackets bought on her brother's advice.

Marianne had no choice. She must place her hand in Captain Templeton's as they moved along the length of the dance line on the way to meet their own partners again. She did not look at him, even when he lightly squeezed her fingers. Nor even when he put his hand on her waist to swing back in the opposite direction—although a thrill shot up her spine at his touch.

"Did Mr. Pellam not tell you, Captain?" she asked above the music. "You are not to grab a lady's waist, but merely touch it."

His dark brown eyes twinkled with mischief, an expression she had grown to love and now must hate, as he bent close to her ear. "Forgive me. You seemed about to fall."

A pleasant chill swept down her neck, but she attributed it to the light wind blowing over the deck. "Have you not noticed, sir? I have very little trouble regaining my footing when adversity or disappointment strikes."

"I *have* noticed, my lady." His grip loosened, but his smirk remained. No doubt the rascal took pride in the strength of his arms and his impressive dancing skill, but she would not give him the satisfaction of her compliments on his grace. Or on his handsome blue silk jacket and tan breeches. Or his shaving balm, a heady bergamot fragrance that brought her some relief from the smells of his unwashed crew. He bent close again. "I've also noticed you've beguiled my men."

She shuddered away another chill and gave him a prim nod. "Indeed I have, and you would do well not to forget it."

His laugh grated on her nerves, and she longed to slap his handsome, self-assured face. Yes, she bore the blame for being here now, but he'd never loved her. Of that she was certain. Those two times he'd kissed her— *no,* she must not think of such things. Lost in a bittersweet memory, she missed a step, only to be rescued by Jamie's strong arms. *Captain Templeton's* strong arms. Goodness, who had invited him to this dance? They swung around the circle, and he returned her to her partner—a Mr. Samples, whose dancing left much to be desired—while reclaiming Emma as his own partner. Her maid, her *former* maid, had the nerve to give Marianne a teasing smile. Had the whole world gone mad? What a cruel joke had been played on her by this man.

As the dance ended, she now faced a worse dilemma. When she and Molly designed the seating for the married couples, Molly had presumed the captain would take the head of the table. Marianne dared not forbid it. And now she, as hostess, must take this odious man's arm as they proceeded to supper in his own cabin. No. She simply could not do it.

"Captain Templeton, sir." Molly looped her arm in the captain's, a gesture Marianne found a bit common, although she knew the warmhearted older woman meant nothing by it. "Will you and Lady Marianne lead us down to supper?"

The captain had the good grace to appear flustered when he looked at Marianne. Then a familiar teasing grin touched his lips as he patted Molly's hand and disengaged from her. "I would be delighted, Miss Molly." He bowed and offered Marianne his arm. "My lady."

Molly's hopeful smile forestalled any protest. Marianne did not curtsy, but touched the captain's arm, albeit lightly that she might not feel its muscular strength through the silk sleeve.

He guided her down the ladder, through the long companionway toward the ship's back—the stern, she reminded herself. In the cabin Demetrius and his son, Stavros, a boy of about ten years, waited beside the beautifully laid table, wearing the semblance of livery Marianne had suggested: brown breeches, white shirts with blue sashes angled across their chests, and white gloves. They had laid planks between the captain's desk and a small table, arranged benches and chairs to accommodate the twelve guests, and covered the boards with a heavy ivory tablecloth, clean but a bit worn in several spots. The Wedgwood china looked exquisite, and even the tin cutlery had a sheen to it. A large bouquet of hand-sewn flowers formed an exquisite, multicolored centerpiece. The lavender perfume Marianne had given Emma for a wedding gift had been splashed upon the artificial blooms and now filled the cabin with a scent to vie with the savory fish course. As crowded as the cabin was, Marianne felt gratified to sit at the foot of the table while Captain Templeton took his place at the head—for she was as far from him as possible.

At Marianne's nod, Demetrius and Stavros began serving, beginning with her and the captain, moving on to the first mate, and so on in descending rank. Not expecting this rough lot to exhibit proper manners, she had prepared the ladies to lead their husbands. To her surprise, Captain Templeton appeared to have done the same with his men, for they followed his example, spooning their soup without slurping and using their linen napkins often. Marianne stifled an urge to compliment the captain. After all, such good manners were not extraordinary. Everyone should eat properly. But when he explained to Simpson that he must not speak across the table, but rather to the persons seated on either side of him, Marianne could hardly contain a smile of approval. Captain Templeton might be a traitorous scoundrel, but he was also a gentleman.

Outside the porthole, an orange-and-red sunset streaked the sky, while inside the cabin lanterns swung on hooks and cast deepening shadows around the room. Demetrius carried away the salted beef and left the cabin to fetch the final remove.

In the companionway, the sudden thump of rapid footsteps neared the cabin. Marianne turned to see a sailor dash in the door, his eyes wide.

"Cap'n Jamie, sir, a British frigate is closing fast on us from the north."

Chapter Thirty

While the ladies gasped and the men groaned, the captain's cheerful countenance dissolved into caution. "You must forgive us, ladies." He stood and maneuvered around the table and out of the cabin, with his men in his wake.

"Lord, help us." Nancy wrung her napkin.

"Shh." Molly patted her hand. "It'll be all right."

"Blimey," Sally huffed. "I'm not staying down here just to have those ruffians threaten us again." She hurried out.

After quick apologies, Nancy and Molly followed her.

"We'll be in our cabin." Quince took Emma's hand to lead her out, and Marianne ached to see the concern in their faces.

Only Eleanor remained in her chair, lazily chewing on a biscuit.

Seated near the door, Marianne tried to stifle her rising panic. *Lord, is this the time? Show me the way to contact this captain and turn Jamie—Captain Templeton—over to him.* The prayer sat like lead on her heart, but she rose from her chair and gazed across the remnants of her fine feast. How inconvenient of this frigate to happen along just when everyone was having such a pleasant time.

Before she could move away from the table, Eleanor stood and, in two long steps, reached the door and barred it. "Where d'you think you're going?"

Marianne drew in a sharp breath. "What? Why, I am going with the others to—"

"No, you aren't going anywhere." Eleanor fisted her hands at her waist. "Just sit yourself down, missy."

Terror flooded Marianne as she regarded the shorter woman of perhaps four and twenty years, whose muscular arms were visible through her gauze sleeves. Never in her life had Marianne experienced such a threat. She had no idea what this woman might do.

"What do you mean, Eleanor?" She emitted a shaky laugh. "I merely want to be with the other ladies on deck. What if the British sailors come below, as they did before, and no one is here to protect us?"

"What if?" Eleanor snorted, a most unladylike sound. "Won't be no different from what the *Quality* men do to my sort when they get the notion."

Nausea rose up in Marianne's throat. "I cannot imagine what you mean." But she could. She had come upon Tobias Pincer kissing an unwilling scullery maid belowstairs in Bennington House. Without her intrusion, the girl might have suffered far more than an unwanted kiss. Her tearful gratitude had assured Marianne that the Lord had sent her downstairs to a hallway she rarely entered. Even rumors of her eldest brother…but she would not think of that.

Again Eleanor snorted. "Your sort never does imagine it." She leaned toward Marianne, eyes narrowed. "Because you *choose* not to see."

Marianne swallowed hard. What would this woman do to her? "But I can see you now, and I would like to see the other ship, and wouldn't you like to see your husband and be reassured that all is well? In fact, I must go upstairs and ensure that none of our crew are kidnapped...impressed, as I did before." She felt so breathless, she thought she might faint.

"Ha!" Eleanor did not smile. "Everybody else is all gooey-eyed at your title, *Lady Marianne,* but I see what you're about. You got caught unawares the first time, but I don't believe for a minute you'll help the cap'n again." She leaned back against the door and crossed her arms. "You think nobody can see you hate him? You stowed away and followed him, but he rejected you." Now she laughed, a dreadful cackling sound for one so young. "You'd make us all suffer to settle that score." She reached out and shoved Marianne's shoulder. "Set down, girl, before I set you down."

Marianne dropped back into her chair and gripped its arms. If she braced herself, she could kick Eleanor away and escape. But her legs felt limp, and no stroke of courage coursed through her to strengthen them. She had never struck another person and could not imagine doing so. *Lord, help me. What shall I do?* What had Eleanor said? What had some "Quality" man done to her to make every aristocrat her enemy?

"Well, then, Eleanor, if we are not going up on deck, come sit with me." Her voice shook, but she forced a smile. "Let us talk to pass the time."

Eleanor laughed, again a mirthless, unpleasant sound. "Right. We'll talk." She pulled a heavy chair in front of the door and sat. "Tea parties and balls. Fashions and French coiffures." She spat out her words, but her eyes filled with sadness.

Only halfway mindful of the muted sounds of men shouting above them, Marianne forced her attention to Eleanor and nodded as if listening to one of her dear little orphans at St. Ann's. "If that is what you would like to discuss. But perhaps first you will help me."

"Help you? Ha. Not likely."

"No, I do not mean do something for me. I mean help me understand what you are saying. What is it that my *sort* chooses not to see?"

Eleanor's jaw dropped. Then her eyes narrowed. "What do you care?"

Marianne considered her question. "I suppose it is because you and I were becoming friends before you knew who I am. Do you remember during the storm how we all encouraged each other, sharing our ginger tea, singing hymns and telling funny stories? I think those many long hours of suffering together made me realize that women are all alike, no matter what our birth rank might be."

A cautious smile appeared, but sadness still filled Eleanor's eyes. "Aye, we did laugh."

"But now you must tell me…" Warmth spread through Marianne's chest, a sincere affection for this woman. Of all the ladies, including brave Molly, Eleanor seemed to possess the stoutest heart. Marianne could imagine her fighting off anyone who tried to snatch her husband from the ship. "Why have you come to hate me?"

Eleanor shook her head. "Not you by name, just by class, though to be fair, you never put on airs with us."

She traced a finger along her chair arm. "Awright, then, I'll tell you." She inhaled a deep breath. "I was born in a village in Sussex outside Lord de Winter's manor." Her lips curled in distaste. "When I was fourteen, I went into service in his lordship's house. He had a son just two years older than me...."

With growing chagrin and nausea, Marianne listened to her story. Having met Lord de Winter's heir her first season in society and endured his unwanted notice, she had no doubt Eleanor's story was true.

"And then they cast me out." Eleanor gazed toward the porthole. "No money. No references. And my wee babe..." Her voice cracked, and she sniffed. "He lies buried outside the churchyard because his mother was not wed."

An icy chill swept up Marianne's arms, and a soft sob escaped her. She tried to recall if any housemaid had been dismissed from her parents' service when her brothers were of that age, but she had been too young to notice such things. Compassion filled her, and she reached out to grasp the other woman's hands. "Oh, Eleanor, I am so sorry. And so very sad for you...and your dear son. I do believe every word you said."

Eleanor gave her a crooked grin. "You're a good sort, after all, Lady Marianne." She grimaced. "I'm sorry for scaring you. If you want to go on deck—"

Marianne laughed softly. "No, there's no need. If someone comes for us, we shall see to it then." She could not fathom the change now occurring inside her, but knew as surely as she breathed that God had ordained for her to hear this woman's story. Never before had she fully comprehended the cruelty and hypocrisy of many people in the society in which she had been reared. Perhaps her parents and Grace Kendall were the only sincere Christians Marianne knew.

"Guess they never boarded us." Eleanor went to the porthole and glanced out. "I never heard a sound of 'em coming below, and I don't see the frigate."

Marianne gulped back a sob at this news, and a strange sense of reprieve filled her. She touched her cheek and found it damp. Were these tears of sympathy for Eleanor? Or of relief that she had not been required to speak to the naval captain? For as surely as Eleanor had kept her from leaving this cabin, Marianne knew the Lord had prevented her from exposing the *Fair Winds'* captain. Perhaps that made her a traitor, too. Perhaps she now must choose between betraying her country and betraying her heart. For despite his lies, despite the conviction that she would never marry such a scoundrel, she would love Jamie Templeton until the day she died.

The British frigate sailed within twenty-five yards of the *Fair Winds* and dropped its sails. On its quarterdeck, the captain lifted his bicorne hat and saluted Jamie. "Ahoy, Captain Templeton."

"Ahoy, Captain Boyd." Jamie returned the salute as he sent up a prayer of thanks. They had first encountered HMS *Margaret* last February on their way to England, and had earned the captain's trust because of their connection to Bennington *and* because of the crate of oranges Jamie had given him. Jamie prayed the captain would still be as well disposed toward them.

"What's your heading, sir?" Boyd cupped his hands to help his voice carry.

"East Florida. Will you come with us?" Jamie infused his voice with good humor. "There'll be another orange harvest in a few months." A reminder of his gift couldn't hurt.

"We'd do well to have 'em to stave off the scurvy, sir." Boyd turned to speak briefly with a sailor. "We spy ladies on your ship, Templeton."

"Aye, sir." Jamie must cut off any wayward thoughts in that regard. "Some of my crew married in London, and their wives are eager to help us colonize East Florida."

"Ah, very good. Building His Majesty's empire."

"May I send you a crate of claret, sir?" Although Jamie didn't expect this captain to try to take any of the *Fair Winds* crew, a gift should ensure it.

"I say, that would be most kind." The dark-haired man gave him a slight bow. "We've done without for a long time."

At Jamie's order, Saunders and two other sailors brought up the wine and lowered a boat to carry it to the *Margaret*. During the interval, Boyd called out a warning to Jamie to steer wide of the northern colonies, adding that the conflict had already given rise to American pirates who would gladly seize the merchant vessel. That news was not unexpected, although Jamie regarded those pirates as privateers.

When Saunders returned, he handed Jamie an exquisitely carved tomahawk pipe.

"A very fine gift." Jamie held it high. "I thank you, Captain Boyd."

"Took it from an obstinate Indian fellow in Nova Scotia. That's where we've been since March, when those confounded rebels drove us out of Boston. Bad show, that. We're headed back to Plymouth for more weaponry and troops. Then we'll teach those rebels their place."

Jamie swallowed a retort, even as a familiar thought nagged at him. How could he go to war with good men like this one? "I'll heed your warning about the pirates, sir."

The ships hoisted sails once again and moved in opposite directions. While lifting a prayer of thanks for the uneventful encounter, Jamie also sought the Lord's wisdom about the privateers, who should be putting their efforts toward the war, not harassing American vessels. For now, Jamie must sail under the Union Jack and Lord Bennington's flag when encountering British ships. But hidden in a safe place under the floor of his cabin was the Grand Union flag, a design General Washington had approved early that year. Jamie had obtained one before sailing to England, but wondered if privateers would respect the Continental flag. Or would he at last have to fight his way past well-armed ships seeking to keep him from his destination?

Chapter Thirty-One

"A ship at sea is a very small world." Marianne walked arm in arm with Molly around the *Fair Winds'* deck. Above them, puffy white clouds reminded her of the pastries Papa's chef always made, a far better fare than the weevily hardtack she now ate. "How do these men manage to spend their lives at sea without going mad with boredom?"

Molly chuckled. "Why, 'tis a good thing they do manage it. How else would people and things get from shore to shore across the wide ocean?" She gave Marianne a worried glance. "Meaning no disrespect, my lady."

"Tut, tut, Molly. Are we not friends? You may say anything to me." In the past six weeks since Marianne's ball and supper, she had grown closer to all the women. Like Eleanor, each one had a story of hardship and heartbreak. And, just as she had done by foolishly stowing away aboard this ship, they had risked their lives for a future filled with hope beside the men they loved. At least in East Florida, none of them would face the dangers of the war. Marianne had no doubt her brother

Frederick would help them all find occupations in St. Johns Towne, where he served as magistrate and managed Papa's plantation.

"You're a true Christian, Lady Marianne." Molly squeezed her arm, a familiar gesture Marianne no longer found inappropriate.

"And you, as well, Molly." She lifted her face to the breeze and inhaled a deep, refreshing breath. Then gasped. "Look. A seagull. Two, three." She released Molly and hurried to the ship's railing to study the horizon. "Does that mean we are nearing land?"

Molly came up beside her and gave her a teasing grin. "Why not ask the captain?"

Marianne wrinkled her nose. "I would rather…" No, she would not speak ill of a man everyone else on board respected. "…not."

Others on deck noticed the large white-winged birds, as well, pointing and smiling or laughing. That was proof enough to her that the gulls were harbingers of good things to come. She had no need to speak to Captain Templeton, whom she always managed to avoid despite the small world of the ship.

To be fair, he too had kept his distance, only occasionally retrieving charts or books from the cabin he had charitably surrendered to her. At his knock on the door, she would make herself presentable, then slip past him into the narrow companionway, returning only when he left, leaving his familiar manly scent behind… along with too many bittersweet memories.

The ritual of staying apart was tedious but necessary. For sometimes, when she watched him man the wheel or engage in friendly banter with his crew or ably lead the ship through a storm, her heart threatened to betray her as she recalled the merry times they had spent with Robert and Grace…or when she recalled his tender kisses. And sometimes, she would turn to find him staring at her across the deck, a sorrowful frown on his sun-browned face, an expression he quickly hid with an impudent grin and an overdone bow. She would avert her gaze even as her heart leapt. Clearly, traitor or not, he suffered as she did. Clearly, he did love her as she loved him. Yet they were and must always remain mortal enemies.

Several days later, long after sunset, Eleanor came to Marianne's cabin. "Come on deck, Lady Marianne. There's lights in the distance. Boston, my lady. *Boston.*" The happy glow on her face dimmed. "Forgive me, ma'am. I know this isn't what you want."

Seated at the captain's desk, where she had been reading by lantern light, Marianne bent her head to hide sudden tears. "No, it is not what I want, but we shall all be in East Florida soon enough after the captain concludes his business here." Whatever that might be.

"But…" A frown darted across Eleanor's face. "My lady, did you not know? We ladies aren't going to East Florida. We're staying here in Boston to help with the Cause."

Marianne opened her mouth, but no words would come. Indeed, what would she say? More treachery. Why had she ever thought she could sway these women or, even more impossible, their husbands? From the beginning, these Englishwomen planned to join the rebellion. And why would they not, after their tragedies and disappointments suffered in the land of their birth? Yet what hope did they have in these colonies, where the mad uprising would soon be crushed by His Majesty's navy and army?

"Go watch the lights, Eleanor. Go look to your new home." Marianne ached to touch land once again. But she would not set one foot in this disloyal colony. In that small way, she could demonstrate her own loyalty to her king and her country, no matter what the other women did.

After a fitful night of sleep, she came on deck to find them moored at the docks. Someone mentioned that these were the very wharves where the infamous Boston Tea Party had taken place back in '73. While the other women laughed, no doubt giddy because they would soon disembark, Marianne tried to swallow her growing grief. Now she would be alone, for she and Emma would be the only ladies left on board, and Emma spent all her time with Quince.

Someone pointed above to the mainmast, where the Union Jack and Papa's flag had been removed, replaced by a red-and-white-striped banner with a blue field in one corner behind red and white crosses.

"'Tis the Continental flag, ladies," Mr. Saunders gleefully announced. "The flag of the Grand Union of the thirteen colonies."

A cheer went up from the others, while Marianne released a weary sigh and returned to her cabin. Sorrow upon sorrow would overcome these good people soon enough. Let them enjoy their ill-founded moments of joy. All she wanted was to take refuge from the gaiety in sleep.

A light tap sounded on the door before she could lie down. She opened it to find Captain Templeton dressed in one of his finer coats, a gentle smile gracing his lips. Her heart jumped to her throat.

"I thought you might want to go ashore, my lady." Was that hope in his eyes?

"I thank you, but no." She looked away, unable to still her trembling brought on by his nearness.

He caught her chin and sought her gaze. "It would do you well, *Lady* Marianne."

She stepped back, breaking his touch...and wishing for it again. "I care not for your concerns for my health. I will walk the deck for exercise, but I will not set foot on these traitorous shores." Her tone lacked conviction, but she could not change it.

Captain Templeton nodded, his gaze still kind. "I go to visit friends. The lady is my cousin and the sister of Frederick's wife. Would you like to meet her?"

Marianne's heart skipped. Soon she would meet Rachel. Soon she must face Frederick, who had urged her to renounce her feelings for Jamie. Now she understood why. Did this mean her brother also had chosen the rebel cause? Nausea threatened to overtake her. She swallowed hard.

"You may convey my..." If she said "good wishes," it would imply approval of their disloyalty. "...my kind sentiments our kinship warrants. Perhaps we shall meet one day under better circumstances."

Disappointment clouded his dark eyes. Young as he was, sun and wind had weathered his complexion, making him appear older than when they had sailed from Southampton just over two months ago. His dark blond hair was now bleached golden by the sun.

"Very well. As you wish." His expression now blank, like that of a footman, he backed out of the cabin, pulling the door closed behind him…depriving her of his strong presence.

Marianne rushed to grasp the latch, to chase after him. But her hand stilled on the curved brass. She crumpled to her knees on the hard wooden deck and wept. "Lord, help me. Oh, please help me to stop loving that man."

"Half of the muskets are to be unloaded here." Charles Weldon lounged back in an upholstered chair in his home above his mercantile shop. "The rest must be delivered to Colonel William Moultrie in Savannah for the Georgia militia. He's made one foray into East Florida but was turned back at Sunbury. These muskets might be just what they need for the next attempt."

"Very good." Jamie took a drink of the first real coffee he'd had in over a month. "How goes the war?"

"Washington's in New York and expects to engage the British any day. In late June, our Patriots repulsed a British sea attack in Charleston Harbor. We're building our navy and have plenty of men willing to join, but we need ships faster than we can construct them."

"Too bad we can't use the Nantucket shipyards." Jamie's *Fair Winds* had been built there.

Charles grimaced. "The islanders' neutrality prevents it. When the British gave the whalers the choice between English service or being sunk, most chose to survive. With no whaling income, the island is pretty much closed down, and the people suffer. The Quaker leadership insists on remaining neutral, although some younger men want to fight."

Jamie sat up, his chest clutching. "And Dinah?" If

his younger sister was in danger of starvation, he must sail to the island and rescue her.

Charles stared down at his hands. "I wish I could give you a good report."

Jamie's caution grew to alarm. "What's she doing?" In truth, he barely knew Dinah, for their parents' deaths had forced their separation in childhood. Yet their rare meetings had instilled in him a great love for her, and family loyalty demanded that he help her if he could.

"That's just it." Charles shrugged. "We have no idea. We do know she does not favor the Revolution...nor is she anywhere to be found on Nantucket Island."

"Dear Lord, protect her." Jamie put his head in his hands. "It's no surprise that the Quaker elders influenced her attitude toward the war, but where on earth would the child be if not there?"

"She's not a child anymore, Jamie." Charles clasped his shoulder. "She's a strong, feisty and opinionated young woman. She'll be all right. You already have enough to do." He stood and walked across the room, retrieving a colorful cloth from a trunk to hand to Jamie. "Look. We have a new flag. Susanna and Eliza have made several, and I'll be happy to give you one."

His heart pounding, Jamie unfolded the flag, a white woolen-and-linen pennant with red stripes and a blue field sporting a circle of thirteen white stars. "I like this even more than the Continental flag. Thank you. I'll fly it with pride."

"Good man." Charles's broad smile eased into a frown. "We've lost many good men, Jamie. And the fighting has only begun." He sat down and stared at his hands. "Granny Brown's younger son died."

Jamie swallowed a groan. No more than sixteen

years old, Wilton Brown had been eager to fight for independence. "We all knew many would die for the Cause. I remember hearing about Patrick Henry's declaration to the Virginia House of Burgesses, 'give me liberty, or give me death,' and how we all cheered in agreement. If we don't mean it, we should send up a white flag, beg forgiveness and let King George continue to grind us under his heels."

Charles chuckled. "That'll not happen. You haven't heard the outcome of the Continental Congress, have you?"

Jamie eyed his kinsman with an artificial glare. "No, I've not heard. Out with it, man, before I forget you're married to my cousin, and pound it out of you."

"Whoa, old boy." Laughing, Charles lifted his hands palms out in a gesture of surrender. "There's a reason some of us fund the Revolution while others fight it. John Hancock and I prefer to put our money behind our warriors." He rose again and retrieved a large folded paper from his desk. "Here, take a look at this. You'll see what we're willing to commit to the Cause. Nothing less than our lives, our fortunes and our sacred honor."

The power of his words sent a shiver down Jamie's spine. "So they did it." He unfolded the printed broadside and silently read the words. *When in the course of human events it becomes necessary for one people to dissolve the political bands which have connected them with another...* He read the entire page until he came to the last line, reading aloud the words Charles had just spoken. "'...and our sacred honor.'" His throat closed, and he could see the fervor in Charles's face, too. "Praise be to God for what He has brought to pass."

He studied the document again. "These names listed at the bottom—they all signed it?"

"Yes. The Virginian Thomas Jefferson composed the declaration, and by the end of July most of the delegates signed it in Philadelphia, others signing later. The *Pennsylvania Evening Post* printed it on July 6, followed by other newspapers. I have no doubt there's a copy in every Patriot home in every colony." He chuckled. "No, no longer colonies. We are now, as this document says, free and independent states. Some have suggested we call ourselves the United States of America."

"Ah, praise God," Jamie repeated. "For He will surely bless us with success." He gently refolded the paper. "Has Frederick Moberly seen this?"

Charles shook his head. "I doubt it. We don't have much communication with East Florida because of the British navy, and overland contacts are difficult. Will you take one to him?" He retrieved two folded newspapers from his desk. "And I have one for you, as well. Eliza has memorized every word and is teaching them to her sister and brother."

Along with his satisfaction over receiving the document, an unexpected pang struck Jamie's chest. His cousin's children, Eliza, Abigail and Charles, reminded him of Lady Marianne's nieces and nephew, children whom he'd grown fond of during their brief acquaintance. Little Georgie's adoration after his rescue from the pond made Jamie think he'd had some good influence on the young aristocrat.

Charles reached over and nudged his shoulder. "I said, will you have some pie?"

He grunted. "Sorry. I was lost in my thoughts."

"Not happy ones, if that moping face tells me anything." Charles narrowed his eyes. "What happened to you over there?"

Jamie gazed around the cozy parlor, so simple in its furnishing compared to the grand homes where he'd whiled away his months in England. Instead of larger-than-life paintings in ornately carved and gilded frames, these walls held Susanna's small sketches in simple frames. Instead of heavy velvet drapes, these windows were bare. And the well-worn furniture had not been re-covered in some time, no doubt because Charles was putting his small profits into the war. But this cozy abode was not ruled by an autocratic father, just an honest Christian merchant who was risking it all that his children might be free from a king's tyranny. That made it a far better home than all the fine manor houses in the world. And yet...

"You may recall when I was here last year that I'd met a young lady in England." Jamie swallowed as an unexpected ache filled his chest.

"Don't you dare say another word." Susanna appeared in the doorway with a tray of apple pie and a silver coffee server. She set it on the low table in front of the settee and shoved a blond curl beneath her crisp white cap. "Not until I serve your pie and can sit down to hear your story." Her dark eyes sparkled. "Now that Rachel has married, I've wondered how long it would be until some female made a landlubber out of you." She handed Jamie a slice of pie on a pewter plate. "Now, tell me all about this lady."

Jamie eyed his cousin, as dear to him as a sister, for her father had raised him from childhood. "I wish I could give you a happy report." Instead, he told them of his decision to break off with Lady Marianne because of the Revolution, their subsequent sad yet idyllic summer of companionship, her foolishness in stowing away aboard his ship, and finally, her horror upon discovering his true loyalties.

"James Templeton." Susanna placed her fists at her waist. "Do you mean to tell me you left that poor lady someplace instead of bringing her to our home?" She glared at him, his "elder sister" once again, as in their childhood. "What have you done with her?"

Even Charles eyed him with concern.

"Done with her?" Indignation rose within him. "The woman ravages my very soul, and you want to know what I've done with her?" He crossed his arms against this outrage. "She refuses to come ashore. Says we're traitors and wants nothing to do with us." He returned Susanna's glare. "I gave her my cabin and the best food Demetrius could prepare." Susanna continued to stare, further raising his ire. He bent toward her and narrowed his eyes. "I slept in a moldy hammock in the crew's smelly quarters."

"Well, then." Susanna glanced at Charles. "There's nothing to be done but for me to visit Lady Marianne right away. Husband, will you come with me?"

Charles waved away the idea. "No, my dear, I will leave that to you. Jamie and I have more important things to attend to." At his lift of an eyebrow, Jamie knew he referred to the muskets.

Susanna marched from the room, but her crossness did not truly offend Jamie. Knowing his dear cousin, he felt certain she would extend some kindness to Lady Marianne, who no doubt needed more than a little benevolence right now. Yet even the assurance of Susanna's generosity stabbed at his heart. He should be the one to minister to the woman he loved more than life, but she refused his every attempt.

He poured thick cream on his apple pie and dug in. Despite Demetrius's best efforts, Jamie had not eaten anything this tasty in over two months. Perhaps as the war continued, he would have few such delicacies to enjoy.

"Susanna," he called, "be sure to take her some of this pie."

The loud clatter of pots and dishes gave a more informative response than words. Jamie and Charles chuckled. Then Jamie sobered as the pie turned to dust in his mouth.

"The unfortunate result of this complication is that I must now send a report to General Washington to explain why I can never return to Lord Bennington."

Chapter Thirty-Two

Marianne fanned herself in the stifling heat of the cabin. She knew a breeze swept over Boston Harbor, one that would cool her on this early September evening. But she would not go up to the main deck, would not put herself in the position of being leered at by sailors or workmen on the wharves. How strange it seemed, after her life in a great manor house, to prefer the misery of this tiny cabin, which sometimes served as a refuge and other times a prison. One small comfort came from the bottom of the single satchel she had brought from home, her forgotten leather-bound journal in whose pages she poured out her heart, using Captain Templeton's quill pens and ink. He had denied her nothing and surely would not mind her using them. But the many words she recorded became muddled on the page as her tears caused the ink to run, just as her thoughts were muddled over this whole affair.

To her great sorrow, just this morning Emma had come to say goodbye. Marianne's little lady's maid, rescued by Mama from the orphanage to a better life than she would have had in any other occupation in England, would now be the mistress of her own home. When Emma announced that Aaron Quince owned a farm in the hills of west Massachusetts, Marianne found herself filled with a curious joy on her former servant's behalf, even as she despaired over her loss. Yet she feared Emma's happiness would be destroyed if Mr. Quince joined the rebellion.

What was she thinking? Of course he had joined the rebellion. He had come as Jamie Templeton's valet to spy for their cause. Marianne could not imagine what useful information her father's servants could have told him. Or whether or not they would say anything if given the chance. But she had no doubt that Quince had searched the house in the family's absence—probably with Emma's help. Marianne felt wicked for thinking such a thing, but after Jamie's—Captain Templeton's—betrayal, whom in this world could she trust?

A soft scratch at the door startled her, and her quill slid across the page, leaving a jagged black line. She rolled her blotter over the ink, closed the journal and slid it into a drawer.

"Wh-who is it?" She cleared her throat, which was raspy from little use and many tears.

"Lady Marianne." A woman's voice, but not familiar. "May I come in?"

Caution accompanied her across the wooden floor. She hesitated, then slid the bolt and pulled open the door. The unmistakable aroma of roast beef and apple pie nearly knocked her over. Her mouth began to water, and her knees grew weak. She gulped. "Yes?"

"Good day, my lady." The dark-eyed woman of about thirty years wore a broad-brimmed straw hat over a white cap, and a plain blue muslin gown. "I brought you something to eat." She lifted a large brown basket covered with a white cloth embroidered with tiny blue flowers.

"Please, come in." Jamie had sent food. Oh, how his tender care shattered her heart. Marianne had not even realized her own hunger. Stepping aside, she waved the diminutive woman in.

Her plain countenance, made pretty by her merry smile, was like Molly's, the sort to inspire goodwill. "Thank you, my lady." As if Marianne were doing *her* a favor.

"And I thank you, Mrs....?"

"Mrs. Charles Weldon. But you must call me Susanna."

"Ah." Frederick's sister-in-law. "And you may call me—"

"Why, Lady Marianne, of course." Susanna bustled about, laying a large linen cloth over the flat desk, then placing on it an exquisite white, bone china plate with a delicate blue pattern to match the basket cloth. She brought out several small, covered tureens and proceeded to ladle out roast beef, gravy, carrots, peas, yams, preserves, apple pie, cream and fresh buttered bread—and not a weevil to be seen.

Marianne almost fell into her chair. "Susanna, I am grateful." She could barely compose herself enough to maintain her manners as she cut into the tender beef. Without the linen napkin Susanna had draped across her lap, she feared she might have drooled like a baby. "This is the very best roast beef I have ever eaten."

Susanna smiled. "Thank you, my lady." She remained standing, just as the maids, butlers and footmen did at home. But this was no servant. She was Marianne's relative by marriage.

"Please call me Marianne." She took a sip of the delicious coffee Susanna had poured. "And please sit down." She indicated the chair across the cabin.

"Thank you." Susanna dragged the heavy chair across the wooden floor and sat with folded hands. "My, you've had quite an adventure, haven't you?"

At her gentle, maternal tone, Marianne gulped down her bite, took another sip of coffee…and burst into tears.

"Don't you want to take her to Nova Scotia, Cap'n?" Saunders stood beside Jamie at the helm while the crew shoved off from the Boston wharf and hoisted the sails. "Them British'll make sure she gets back home safe and sound."

Jamie turned the wheel to catch the wind. "That was my first thought. But our mission to Charleston is urgent, and she'll be better off with her brother in East Florida."

"I s'pose you're right." Saunders stepped to the railing and shouted to the men on the main deck. "Make ready for the change of flags as soon as we reach the mouth of the harbor." When he came back, he wore a worried frown. "D'you think she'll give us any trouble if we're stopped again?"

That was a question Jamie had yet to resolve. Susanna had refused to discuss her visit with Lady Marianne, saying it was women's talk, nothing to do with loyalties or the Revolution. "We can trust your Molly to make sure Lady Marianne stays below deck. Once we deliver her to Frederick Moberly, she will be his responsibility." The idea sat heavy on Jamie's heart.

In one way, he treasured her presence on the ship, for it would be the last time he spent in her company—if one could call it company, the way they avoided each other. Still, just watching her amble around the main deck gave him an odd sort of joy. She took to sailing well, and he knew she'd helped the other women on the passage from Southampton. Her beauty had not diminished in spite of the rugged voyage, nor had her spirits flagged. True, he'd seen traces of tears on her porcelain face from time to time, but she always spoke words of cheer to the crew, and he often saw her laugh with Molly for some unknown reason. More women's talk, he supposed.

As they sailed south, his only attempt to communicate with her beyond polite greetings was to leave on his desk one of the newspapers Charles had given him. With little hope of a response, he prayed the Lord would move her to read it and to understand the Cause he was willing to die for.

Smitten with curiosity, Marianne nudged the folded, yellowed newspaper with one finger. Had it been a sealed document, she would have opened it straightaway, assuming Captain Templeton had left it by mistake. But here it sat, so he must want her to read it. She would not, of course. Papa had frowned upon her reading newspapers, saying they contained only gossip not fit for a young lady to know. She must assume American newspapers would be even worse.

Wearied by being back at sea, she cheered herself with thoughts of seeing Frederick, even though she dreaded learning the truth about his loyalties. If Rachel was as pleasant, well-spoken and kind as her sister, Marianne would love her. In addition to feeding her,

Susanna had insisted upon washing and mending Marianne's small wardrobe, and even had aired her bedding.

Of course Marianne would love her new niece or nephew, who had been expected this past July. An ironic laugh escaped her. She would have to write to Mama and Papa about their new grandchild, Mama's first. But perhaps the missive would not be delivered if the colonists' war continued and covered the seas.

An unnerving suspicion occurred to her. Now that Jamie could no longer spy on Papa, would he use his ship for the rebellion? The thought terrified her. Why, any British warship could easily sink this lightly armed vessel. But then, from what Thomas had said last June, no place was safe for anyone during a war.

Irritation swept through her. Why must there be a war? Why must these colonists speak against the king? Why could they not pay their taxes, as Papa did on the sale of produce from his plantation? She would demand an answer from Frederick.

As white-capped waves swept past the porthole, she paced the small, hot cabin. Her much-used fan had broken at last, so she snatched up the folded newspaper to cool herself. Its limp pages fell open and drifted down to the floor to reveal in large letters at the top Declaration of Independence.

Intrigued, she picked it up and began to read. After the first few lines, she felt the need to sit. As her eyes swept down the page, her mind began to comprehend. Her heart began to believe. This was not the work of common ruffians, but of well-spoken and thoughtful souls who had been brought to the end of their reasoning powers and now must take decisive action, just as she had done over two months ago. Like these colonists, she had sought a peaceful means of obtaining what she believed to be God's will—a tragic error on her part. But the authors of this paper listed honest complaints, many of which she knew to be valid.

Had she not seen her countrymen try to steal sailors from this very ship? Had she not heard from Susanna a tale of misuse by British soldiers, who had quartered in her home, ate her children's food and harassed Susanna and Rachel? How could such things be endured? Even at home, news of the Stamp Act and other taxes had generated sympathy for the colonists. And some members of Parliament, such as her father's former friend Lord Highbury, advocated exactly what this paper now demanded: that the united colonies should be permitted to become their own nation. Indeed, not permitted, for they had gone beyond seeking approval for their actions. They declared before all the governments of the world that they were henceforth free and independent states, and absolved themselves of all allegiance to the Crown—a staggering pronouncement.

At the last line of the document, Marianne felt a tremor sweep through her, for in it she read the character of Captain James Templeton. Like the men who wrote this, he had pledged his all to support their revolution, even at the risk of his life and fortune. And his honor? Could a spy claim that his honor was sacred? Before she could complete the thought, the biblical story of the Hebrew men sent to spy on Jericho came to mind. If God could bless their efforts and not call it sin, how could she condemn Jamie for doing whatever was required to help his country? In fact, was she any better than a spy, to have sneaked around her father all her life to manipulate him?

Marianne brushed away the tears and perspiration covering her cheeks and forehead. She must go to him now and tell him that at last she understood, at last she believed his cause was just. She entertained no delusions his revolution would succeed, for His Majesty's armies would easily defeat the colonists. But win or lose, rise or fall, she would stay by his side—if he would have her.

She folded the newspaper with care and held it close, like a precious treasure. Sliding the bolt and opening the door, she pulled a blast of heat into the cabin, along with the dreadful but familiar smells of bilge water and rancid air. A handkerchief held to her nose and mouth, she hurried along the companionway to the ladder, eager to breathe the fresh sea air. Eager to see Jamie and declare her understanding of his motives.

As she climbed the steps, angry shouts met her ears. Once on deck, she saw a frigate bobbing alongside not twenty yards away. In the center of the *Fair Winds'* main deck stood a uniformed officer and a group of armed British sailors. Two of the men aimed their muskets directly at Jamie's chest.

Chapter Thirty-Three

Our lives, our fortunes and our sacred honor. So be it, Lord. Jamie stared back at the British captain, whose sneer had almost earned him a fist planted on his equine nose.

"I have need of all my men, sir." Jamie scrambled for calm—not an easy task with two muskets pointed at his chest—and sent up another prayer that this man would listen to reason. "We are bound for Loyalist East Florida, and the unruly seas around the Carolina shoals require every sailor."

"I care nothing for your problems, Captain. We are at war, and my needs exceed any that a merchant vessel might have, even a *Loyalist* merchant vessel." His tone shouted his suspicions. "We will search every corner of this vessel and—"

"Really, Captain, this is entirely too much."

Lady Marianne's unmistakable voice almost felled Jamie. Now everything truly was lost. Would his crew remember what to do? Would they be the brave lads he expected them to be? One thing he knew. If God granted him life, he would do all in his power to save Lady Marianne during the coming melee.

She marched toward them in her inimitable way, and he saw the incriminating newspaper clutched in one hand. The sailors who aimed their muskets at him eyed her. At this diversion, he should try to seize their guns. But one man remembered his duty and looked back at Jamie.

"Here now, don't you move." The youth pasted on a fierce look, enough to show he meant business.

"And who might you be, miss?" The captain stared at Lady Marianne, running his eyes up and down, and Jamie vowed to make him pay for the disrespect he showed her.

"I am Lady Marianne Moberly." She lifted her chin and glared at him. "This ship sails under the British flag and my father's banner, and I am more than sick of you nautical ninnies who continually delay my arrival in St. Augustine."

Jamie thought he might fall over from relief, but quickly pulled in a bracing breath.

The captain narrowed his eyes. "How do I know—"

"How dare you?" Marianne's lovely cheeks grew bright pink, and her eyes blazed. "I will report you. What is your name, Captain? Do you have any idea who my father is? Lord Bennington, a member of His Majesty's Privy Council, that's who. I will not suffer one man to be removed from this ship." She moved close to the British officer, putting her face near his and jutting out her jaw. Jamie had been on the receiving end of that scowl and had felt it sharply, but would the captain be equally intimidated? Whether yea or nay, Jamie cheered her courage. Once again his ladylove showed her mettle, although he could not guess why.

"I...well, madam..." The captain looked at his men, at Jamie—who gave him a lopsided grin—and finally at the paper clutched to Lady Marianne's chest. "May I ask, madam, what you are reading?" A sly smile touched his lips.

She looked down as if she'd never seen the paper before. "This?" Her blue eyes blinked, and Jamie could see her mind spin. "Why, an American newspaper, of course. I am taking it to my brother in East Florida. He is Mr. Frederick Moberly, son of Lord Bennington, *and* His Majesty's magistrate."

That's my girl. The bold truth. That should confound him. Jamie winked away a fond look. He had no idea why she was helping him yet again, but prayed she would not back down.

"I see," said the captain. "And why not a London newspaper?"

"How *dare* you question me, you officious idiot." Now real rage covered her face. "My father will hear of this. The Admiralty will hear of your insults to a British lady."

The man stepped back, palms out as if to ward off her attack. "Madam, please. Have you no idea that we are at war?"

She followed him, and he nearly tripped in his retreat. "*If* you would like to continue fighting in this war and not spend it on a prison hulk, I suggest you be on your way." Placing one fist at her waist, she shook the newspaper toward Jamie. "Captain Templeton, why did you not show this man my father's letter?"

Suddenly pale around the edges of his tanned skin,

the captain also looked at Jamie. "You have a letter from Lord Bennington? Why did you not say so?"

Jamie could not get the *Fair Winds* away from the frigate fast enough. He grabbed the sheets himself, along with his crew, to hoist sails. He'd heard a man could die of apoplexy and thought he might have come close to it within the past two hours since the other ship had accosted them.

Lady Marianne stood at the bow, her long raven curls blowing loose in the brisk breeze. Once the ship had caught the wind and he'd set their southerly heading, Jamie approached her, but with caution. Just because she had confronted the British captain to prevent an impressment, Jamie could not assume she had changed her loyalties.

"My lady." He leaned one elbow against the gunwale at a respectful distance from her, trying to appear in-different, yet guarding his heart against another rebuff.

The shy smile she gave him shattered his defenses. "Have you finished all your captain duties?"

He puckered away a foolish grin. "W-well, um, there are always duties for the captain...." He waved one hand aimlessly toward the deck, the mast, the sails.

"I meant do you have time for a chat?" She glanced at the newspaper she clutched against her.

"Oh. You wish to talk with me?" Now, after all these countless weeks of snubbing him?

She looked upward and shook her head. "Yes, Jamie, I wish to talk with you." Her voice sounded like a sooth-ing song. Her azure eyes caught the sky and sparkled like sapphires.

A flood of love and joy surged through him, and he

turned away to gather his emotions, gripping the gunwale and bowing his head. For the first time in well over a year, hope for a future with Marianne exploded in his chest.

She touched his arm, and he jumped. And she jumped. And they both laughed.

She glanced away briefly, then settled her gaze on him. "I do not know what the future holds, Jamie. I do not even know if you will have me. But I love you with all my heart, and I want to spend the rest of my life, whether it be long or short, with you."

Her sweet, shy smile infused him with strength. He touched her cheek, and she pressed it into his palm. He slid his other arm around her and pulled her close, bending to brush a tender kiss across her lips. "Marianne."

In response, she melted against him. Somewhere in the distance, he heard men cheering, though he could not imagine why. For his happiness sang like music on the ocean winds, a symphony to his soul.

"I can understand why you wish to renounce your English loyalties." Marianne sat across the desk from Jamie as they ate their supper. "It is not just the matters discussed so convincingly in the Declaration. When I think of all the times we had to pretend when we were in Papa's presence, it makes me very sad. He claimed to want me happy, but would have denied me my only true source of joy simply because of an accident of birth. Yet for my countrymen…and my father, there can be no other way to structure society."

Jamie reached out to squeeze her hand. "You cannot know how close I came to asking for your hand after…" He shrugged and took a bite of meat.

"After you saved Georgie." Marianne adored his modesty. "I was so angry you did not."

"Will you forgive me…for everything?" His dark eyes shone with love.

Marianne gave him a smug smile. "I am endeavoring to do so." She looked beyond him to Molly, who stood ready to serve their next course. "You know, Molly, we could all eat together, you and Mr. Saunders, the captain and I."

"You're very kind, Lady Marianne. Perhaps next time."

"We shall do that." Marianne sipped her coffee, a tasty brew. "But, dear, you must not call me *Lady* Marianne any longer. Soon I shall be Mrs. Templeton, and just plain Marianne to my friends."

Molly's eyes twinkled. "Aye, my lady, but being English, 'twill be a hard habit for me to break."

"But you are American now, are you not?"

"Aye, my lady." Molly chuckled, then tilted her head toward Jamie and wiggled an eyebrow, as if to say Marianne should be talking with him.

Marianne did as the older woman suggested. She gave Jamie a quivering smile. "I suppose I shall be an American, too."

He gazed at her, concern creasing his forehead. "Will it be that difficult?"

She set down her fork and smoothed her napkin in her lap. "A lifetime of loving one's country cannot be undone in a few days…or by reading a single document, no matter how well reasoned and written. Please understand that I cannot truly renounce my homeland, at least not yet. The war will not last forever, and then…"

She could not speak of her doubts about the Revolution's success.

"You think we'll fail."

Tears sprung to her eyes. "I fear it."

He again reached out to her, and the warm touch of his hand on hers sent a pleasant chill up her arm. "Well, then, if it does..." His voice held a startling merriment. "We'll just have to sail to Mexico or California or China to escape the Crown's retribution."

Molly's eyes widened, and Marianne gaped. They both laughed.

"You have thought this through, have you?" Marianne gazed at the man she loved beyond reason.

"I've counted the cost as best I could, but I'll leave the future to the Almighty. And my deepest instinct says that He'll bless our newborn country. Our...*my* duty is to do my part to ensure it." He gently squeezed her fingers.

Marianne returned an affirming grip on his hand. "And my duty is to stand by you. Wherever you may go, I ask only that you let me go with you."

His eyes twinkling, Jamie glanced over his shoulder. "Molly, would you give us one minute?"

Molly beamed. "Just one minute, Captain." She curtsied and left the cabin, closing the door behind her.

Jamie tugged Marianne up from her chair and held her in a gentle embrace. "Dear one, are you sure you can do this? Are you sure you can leave everything behind for me?"

Her heart ached that he needed to ask, but after their difficulties, she understood why. "Yes, I can do this."

"Because—" he went on as if she had not spoken

"—when you choose to do that, you are choosing the Revolution, too."

She sighed her agreement. "Yes, I understand."

"And it means we are at war with your family, including Robert. Including Thomas."

Marianne looked at Jamie's cravat, a white silk neckpiece of Robert's choosing, and sorrow touched the edges of her soul. "I know."

"You've counted the cost?"

Her eyes blurred, but she nodded. "I have counted the cost."

He brushed away her tears and bent to kiss her, and she stood on tiptoes to give as much as she received. Kissing Jamie Templeton was a very fine diversion, indeed, one she could—and *would*—engage in as often as possible.

"Captain. Lady Marianne." Molly knocked on the door, then opened it. "Your minute has passed."

They moved back from each other just a few inches and laughed.

"Molly…" Jamie set a quick kiss on Marianne's nose. "You're an excellent chaperone."

"Yes, she is." Marianne leaned against his broad chest, feeling his strength. And wishing, just a bit wickedly, that Molly were not quite so diligent in her duties.

Chapter Thirty-Four

"Kezia Marie." Marianne held her three-month-old niece and cooed softly. "Your mama's blond hair and your papa's blue eyes. And all the sweetness of your grandmamma." She swayed back and forth, gazing at the tiny, perfect round face. "Rachel, how did you choose her name?"

Rachel watched from her chair, a maternal glow on her own face. While she resembled her pleasant-featured sister Susanna, this little lady was a true beauty, and motherhood seemed to enhance her loveliness. "My mother's name was Kezia, a Bible name. Many girls in Nantucket are named for the daughters of Job. And of course, Marie is for your own mother. Frederick said it would sound silly to call her Kezia Maria, so we change the final *a* to an *e*." Her fair forehead crinkled into a frown of concern. "I pray Lady Bennington won't mind."

Marianne laughed. "She will not mind in the least, but oh, how I wish Mama could be here to hold her first grandchild. She was quite thrilled to learn you were expecting."

"Yes." Rachel's smooth forehead crinkled again. "Frederick does not often speak of it, but I know it breaks his heart to live so far from his parents. Well, his mother, at least." Her face grew scarlet. "Oh, dear. Forgive me. I know your father has always doted on you… I mean, well, my goodness, I do not seem able to say this right at all."

Marianne kissed her precious niece. "Never mind. I know how Papa has always favored me over my brothers." Her voice caught. "All that has ended now."

"Will you write to him?" Rachel lifted her arms to receive her baby, then opened her dressing gown to feed the fussing infant.

Marianne's own arms suddenly felt empty, and she hugged herself. "Oh, yes. I must tell Papa that I stowed away, that Jamie did not kidnap me." She walked to the second-story window and gazed toward the indigo fields, where numerous black slaves tilled the green plants. One day soon, she must question Frederick about keeping slaves. "But Jamie says he will not dare to go back."

"No, I suppose it wouldn't be wise." Rachel smiled down at her daughter, humming softly. She had a sweet alto voice, and Marianne looked forward to singing duets with her. "Nor can Frederick return. While he has not told your father—or anyone here in St. Johns Towne—of his decision to support the American Revolution, he knows it would be too difficult to hide from Lord Bennington."

"Yes, our father always finds a way of disconcerting his sons. My brothers are all good men, but Papa has never made it easy on any of them. I am surprised but grateful that Frederick has found the courage to go this far on his own, something I pray for our three brothers." Pulling up the fan on her wrist, Marianne waved it before her face. The scrimshaw fan was a gift, carved by Rachel's father, dear Mr. Folger. Marianne had instantly fallen in love with the old whaler who had raised Jamie so well. "My, did it take you long to grow accustomed to this heat?"

"I can't really say I have." Rachel lifted Kezia to her shoulder and patted her back. "I grew up in Massachusetts, and we can have very warm summers there, but the heat is nothing like East Florida's. However, our many trees provide relief, and cool water comes from deep within the earth to fill our cisterns and revive us." She gave Marianne a sympathetic smile. "I'm sorry we can't make you more comfortable."

"I do not mean to complain." Marianne chided herself for revealing her discomfort. "I would endure far worse to be with Jamie."

"Yes, I understand." Rachel kissed Kezia's forehead. "Betty," she called toward the bedroom door.

The maid soon appeared. "Yes, Mrs. Moberly."

"Please change Kezia and see that she naps." Rachel gently lifted her baby, and the maid cradled her in her arms. "We'll be back in a few hours."

"Yes, ma'am." Betty took the infant away.

"Now." Rachel rose and walked to her wardrobe. "If you'll help me into my gown, we can join the men."

Marianne's pulse raced. She had patiently waited for Rachel to complete her maternal duties. Now their attention could be focused on the wedding. Her soon-to-be sister quickly dressed, and they held hands and descended the staircase.

The rest of the family awaited them in the drawing room. Mr. and Mrs. Folger, handsome *older* newlyweds, who were Rachel's father and Marianne's cousin Lydia, sat hand in hand on the settee. Mr. Saunders and his Molly, along with their friend Mr. Patch, stood nearby. By the hearth, Jamie and Frederick laughed over some private joke, but both broke off abruptly at the appearance of Marianne and Rachel. Jamie was first across the room, with Frederick right behind, and they each claimed their respective ladies.

"Lady Marianne." Jamie took both of her hands in his, and his dark eyes sparkled with tender affection. "Are you ready to become plain Mrs. Templeton?"

Before she could answer, Frederick nudged his shoulder. "Now, Templeton, remember what I said. She requires much pampering and many compliments, or you will be very sorry. Oh, and do not forget the diversions. She requires parties and balls—"

"Tut, tut." Marianne tapped her brother's arm with her new fan. "You are speaking of the child I used to be. In case you have not noticed…"

"She is a wise and beautiful woman," Jamie finished. "Now, if we can proceed to the church…" The eagerness in his voice sent a thrill through Marianne's heart, fanning her own excitement.

Amid much chatter and gaiety, the company exited the house, with the ladies taking their places in the carriage and the men riding horseback. Marianne laughed to hear Frederick teasing Jamie about having to ride, and she looked forward to seeing Jamie surprising her brother with his newfound ability to manage a horse more than adequately. Just as she herself planned to manage her home, wherever Jamie decided to settle. For within the hour, Lady Marianne Moberly would cease to exist, and the American housewife with the plain title of Mrs. James Templeton had every intention of taking very good care of her tall, brave, handsome husband.

Jamie thought his heart would burst for joy as he stood hand in hand with his bride before gray-haired Reverend Johnson, vicar of St. Johns Towne. In her new rosy-pink gown, hastily sewn by Rachel's capable hands, Marianne was more than beautiful…she was exquisite. As the minister led them in their marriage vows, Jamie looked down into Marianne's fathomless blue eyes and drew in a long breath to steady himself. He was humbled to think that he, an orphan, a former whaler, a merchant of no great wealth, could secure the love of this extraordinary woman. For his sake, she had given up a life of ease and plenty, and he would do all in his power to make it up to her.

And yet along with this priceless treasure God had bestowed upon him came another responsibility. If they were to live their lives in freedom, he must do his part to help the Revolution succeed. Perhaps his connection to Lord Bennington's family would somehow provide the way. Perhaps that connection would be a hindrance. Only time would reveal how things would turn out. But this time, instead of making any assumptions about wealth or class or rank, Jamie would more diligently seek God's will in the matter. And this time he and Marianne would pray together and wait for His answer, just as they must do in regard to his sister. Jamie's appreciation for his bride's tenacity grew when she declared they must not rest until they learned of Dinah's whereabouts.

Mrs. Jamie Templeton. How good that sounded. As Marianne and her newly wedded husband left the quaint

little church, she felt as if she were walking on a cloud
on the way to their wedding supper.

The vicar's young wife, who Marianne learned had
once snubbed Rachel, had almost fallen into a swoon
when introduced to *Lady* Marianne. Mrs. Johnson insisted upon preparing the wedding supper on the lawn
behind the vicarage. For the sake of peace, Marianne
had accepted with the condition that the entire commu-
nity *and* Jamie's crew would be invited.

While village children scampered about, musicians
played and revelers ate from the lavish buffet, Jamie
took Marianne's hand and sought the quiet of the sanc-
tuary to be alone with her.

"My dear, beautiful bride." His eyes had not ceased to
shine this entire day. "Now that we're wed, we must plan
for our future." His intense gaze softened. "You know
of course that I must find a way to serve the Cause."

She gazed at him through sudden tears. "Yes, I know."

"And you're not afraid?"

She laughed softly. "I did not say that." She drew his
strong, callused hands up to her lips. "We do not know
how the war will end. I pray His Majesty will see reason and let the colonies be free to establish their...*our*
own country." She brushed a hand across his tanned,
well-formed cheek. "This I do know. God has brought
us together, and while we both shall live, I ask only
this—that anywhere you go, wherever it is in this world,
you'll let me go with you."

A frown flitted across his noble brow, but he nodded.
"To be apart from you is not to live at all."

She returned a rueful smile. He had not promised
what she asked. But somehow she understood. And
even if he denied her request, she would never stop

loving him. So much lay ahead of them, but owning Jamie Templeton's heart was worth any sacrifice she must make.

What was she thinking? This was her wedding day! Casting off her gloom, she gave him a quick peck on one cheek, then tugged him toward the door. "Come, my darling husband. Our guests are waiting."

He pulled her back into a firm embrace and kissed her until her knees grew weak. "Come, my darling wife. Our *life* is waiting."

* * * * *

SPECIAL EXCERPT FROM

Love Inspired

Could this bad-boy newcomer spell trouble for an Amish spinster...or be the answer to her prayers?

Read on for a sneak preview of
An Unlikely Amish Match,
the next book in Vannetta Chapman's miniseries
Indiana Amish Brides.

The sun was low in the western sky by the time Micah Fisher hitched a ride to the edge of town. The driver let him out at a dirt road that led to several Amish farms. He'd never been to visit his grandparents in Indiana before. They always came to Maine. But he had no trouble finding their place.

As he drew close to the lane that led to the farmhouse, he noticed a young woman standing by the mailbox. A little girl was holding her hand and another was hopping up and down. They were all staring at him.

"Howdy," he said.

The woman only nodded, but the two girls whispered, "Hello."

"Can we help you?" the woman asked. "Are you...lost?"

"*Nein.* At least I don't think I am."

"You must be if you're here. This is the end of the road."

Micah pointed to the farm next door. "Abigail and John Fisher live there?"

"They do."

"Then I'm not lost." He snatched off his baseball cap, rubbed the top of his head and then yanked the cap back on.

Micah stepped forward and held out his hand. "I'm Micah—Micah Fisher. Pleased to meet you."

"You're not *Englisch*?"

"Of course I'm not."

"So you're Amish?" She stared pointedly at his clothing—tennis shoes, blue jeans, T-shirt and baseball cap. Pretty much what he wore every day.

"I'm as Plain and simple as they come."

"I somehow doubt that."

"Since we're going to be neighbors, I suppose I should know your name."

"Neighbors?"

"*Ja.* I've come to live with my *daddi* and *mammi*—at least for a few months. My parents think it will straighten me out." He peered down the lane. "I thought the bishop lived next door."

"He does."

"Oh. You're the bishop's *doschder*?"

"We all are," the little girl with freckles cried. "I'm Sharon and that's Shiloh and that is Susannah."

"Nice to meet you, Sharon and Shiloh and Susannah."

Sharon lost interest and squatted to pick up some of the rocks. Shiloh hid behind her *schweschder*'s skirt, and Susannah scowled at him.

"I knew the bishop lived next door, but no one told me he had such pretty *doschdern*."

Susannah's eyes widened even more, but it was Shiloh who said, "He just called you pretty."

"Actually I called you all pretty."

Shiloh ducked back behind Susannah.

Susannah narrowed her eyes as if she was squinting into the sun, only she wasn't. "Do you talk to every girl you meet that way?"

"Not all of them—no."

Don't miss
An Unlikely Amish Match *by Vannetta Chapman,*
available February 2020 wherever
Love Inspired® *books and ebooks are sold.*

LoveInspired.com

Looking for inspiration in tales
of hope, faith and heartfelt romance?

Check out **Love Inspired**® and
Love Inspired® **Suspense** books!

New books available every month!

CONNECT WITH US AT:

Facebook.com/groups/HarlequinConnection

Facebook.com/HarlequinBooks

Twitter.com/HarlequinBooks

Instagram.com/HarlequinBooks

Pinterest.com/HarlequinBooks

ReaderService.com

Love Inspired®

LIGENRE2018R2

Clang, clang, clang.

The hammering outside her new schoolhouse grew louder. Eva Coblentz moved to the window to locate the source of the clatter. Across the road she saw a man pounding on an ancient-looking piece of machinery with steel wheels and a scoop-like nose on the front end.

When he had the sheet of metal shaped to fit the front of the machine, he stood back to assess his work. He knelt and hammered on the shovel-like nose three more times. Satisfied, he gathered up his tools and started in her direction.

She stepped back from the window. Was he coming to the school? Why? Had he noticed her gawking? Perhaps he only wanted to welcome the new teacher, although his lack of a beard said he wasn't married.

She glanced around the room. Should she meet him by the door? That seemed too eager. Her eyes settled on the large desk at the front of the classroom. She should look as if she was ready for the school year to start. A professional attitude would put off any suggestion that she was interested in meeting single men.

LIEXP0220

Eva hurried to the desk, pulled out the chair and sat down as the outside door opened. The chair tipped over backward, sending her flailing. Her head hit the wall with a painful thud as she slid to the floor. Stunned, she slowly opened her eyes to see the man leaning over the desk.

He had the most beautiful gray eyes she'd ever beheld. They were rimmed with thick, dark lashes in stark contrast to the mop of curly, dark red hair springing out from beneath his straw hat. Tiny sparks of light whirled around him.

"I'm Willis Gingrich. Local blacksmith." He squatted beside her. "Can you tell me your name?"

The warmth and strength of his hand on her skin sent a sizzle of awareness along her nerve endings. "I'm Eva Coblentz. I am the new teacher and I'm fine now."

Don't miss
The Amish Teacher's Dilemma
by USA TODAY *bestselling author Patricia Davids,*
available March 2020 wherever
Love Inspired books and ebooks are sold.

LoveInspired.com

LIEXP0220

LOVE INSPIRED
INSPIRATIONAL ROMANCE

UPLIFTING STORIES OF FAITH, FORGIVENESS AND HOPE.

Join our social communities to conncct with other readers who share your love!

Sign up for the Love Inspired newsletter at **LoveInspired.com** to be the first to find out about upcoming titles, special promotions and exclusive content.

CONNECT WITH US AT:

Facebook.com/LoveInspiredBooks

Twitter.com/LoveInspiredBks

Facebook.com/groups/HarlequinConnection

HARLEQUIN

Heartfelt or suspenseful, inspiring or passionate, Harlequin has your happily-ever-after.

With new books published
every month, you are sure to find the
satisfying escape you know you deserve.

HNEWS2020